OWN G

SANDY JAMIESON was born and still lives in
Glasgow.
He worked in Fife and Glasgow as a Social Worker.
In 1991 he gave up his job as a Social Work Manager to
become a writer.
Since then he has written three novels "Own Goal", "A
Subtle Sadness" and "The Great Escape?".
He has also written "Graeme Souness - The Iron Lady's
Man -Scotland's successful Thatcherite" due to be
published by Mainstream Publishing in Autumn 1997.
He is President of Who Cares? Scotland, the
organisation for young people who are or have been in
care.

OWN GOAL

Sandy Jamieson

RINGWOOD PUBLISHING

First published in Scotland in 1997 by
Ringwood Publishing
258 Kingsacre Road, Glasgow G73 2EW

ISBN 1 901514 00 5

Printed in Scotland by Bell & Bain Ltd, Glasgow.

Although some of the events and people
referred to in this book are real,
all the characters are fictitious.

The author's thanks are due to technical advisers on
matters political, educational, religious, legal, sporting
and about the detail of guns and Cup Final policing,
especially
JA, BC, SG, LH, TH, ML, VM, RMcC.

to Isobel and Shona,
for keeping the flame alive
and
Anne, Sarah, Tim, Felicity and Nicky for providing the
fuel to feed it.

GAME ONE

THE HUNTER

VERSUS

THE HEADMASTER

CHAPTER ONE- SOME GOAL THAT, DANNY BOY

It was Danny Campbell's goal that disturbed the carefully constructed routine into which Frank Hunter had strapped himself and set in train the sequence of events that left three dead and several more wounded. There can have been few goals in football history that have had such a profound effect, even on a nation as obsessed with the sport as Scotland. Like almost every other Scots boy, it had always been Danny's ambition to score at least one goal of major significance but he had imagined that its consequences would be benign; the eternal gratitude of a proud nation as he rifled home the World Cup winner, or at the very least the roar of the Hampden crowd as he won the Scottish Cup with a last minute rocket. Poor Danny would have been mortified at knowing the full consequences of the goal he did manage. He was devastated enough at the immediate effects.

The longer-term consequences proved to be down to Frank Hunter. Frank had discharged himself from Kamesthorn Hospital, 3 months earlier, in November 1989, the night Scotland qualified for the World Cup Finals in Italy. Neither event had made him happy. He felt better than before his admission, not right but definitely better. He created for himself the security of a firm routine. Every morning, Monday to Friday, he would faithfully go to his place of work, the Mitchell Library, and study for his thesis, his book. Its subject was a summation of everything that was wrong with his world, and why in particular the failure of the Action Campaign to save the LDT Factory was a succinct symbol for the collapse of socialism and the death of its relevance. Every lunch-time, emotionally knackered by his study, he would treat himself to a pub lunch and a long walk through the centre of the beautiful city of culture his beloved Glasgow had become.

It had taken him some time to realise that he always took the same basic route, not that it mattered as there was always more to see and appreciate every time. Every version included a stop-off in George Square to chat with his old friend Willie, the iron man with the heart of stone who had helped him save his sanity in the bleak Hogmanay night of 1979 when his depression about the Devolution Referendum fiasco had reached its peak. Willie had offered him that night a disturbing vision of his future, full of

1

dead bodies and lost women strewn across a devastated wasteland dominated by the simpering face of the hated one, Willie's successor in both iron and stone, that bloody woman. But a vision that had nevertheless held out hope that Frank Hunter would achieve his true destiny one day, and rank alongside Willie and the others in George Square as a true hero of Scotland.

Afternoons were spent in further more thoughtful study, evenings were passed in the pub talking to friends and playing the verbal games of which he was so fond. Nights were something else. Joyce and he did not live together, he liked her far too much for that. But they had a real and mutually-giving relationship. He had known her for years, fancied her from the first but then he had been as always completely faithful to Elaine, his ever-loved wife. At the time he left Elaine, Joyce was still living with Brian Kirk, one of his main Trotskyist foes. She had left Brian shortly after the demise of his parliamentary ambitions, a death in which Frank had had some role as one of the principal assassins. She had decided to leave Brian even if he had won, realising by then the true nature of his relationship with her. Her path had not crossed Frank's during the time each spent in an emotional wilderness of their own making and choosing.

Joyce had been horrified to find out, in her last week as a temporary social worker in Kamesthorn, that a new patient Francis Hunter was her old political goader, Frank Hunter, or what was left of him anyway. She had told him that he didn't need a social worker, and that he didn't need to be in Kamesthorn, and they had left that institution around the same time. But the re-establishing of contact, even on that basis, had been enough and slowly the two less than complete persons had begun to fit together snugly to form a more stable whole. Frank had promised himself that he would be totally honest with her, something he had spared Elaine because he had loved her so.

Joyce went to work in the same Social Work Area Office as Danny Campbell, Frank's lifelong friend. Danny had been his best man when he married Elaine, and Frank had returned the favour twice, as well as holding his hand during several other changes of partner. Currently it was Sheila, another social worker with whom both Frank and Joyce got on well enough to hope that this time it might be different. Joyce's one condition on going to the Southside Area Team was that she be allowed to continue her work with the City Centre Prostitutes Group and Drop-in Centre, which had been a long-term interest of hers. Every Tuesday and Thursday night

2

she would go to the Group and return home after midnight. Often on those evenings she would seek out Frank's body, for comfort rather than pleasure, and he, generous man, was happy to donate it on those terms.

They had kept their separate flats, him in Shawlands her in Strathbungo, but would spend nights in each other's beds on a frequent basis. The nights without Joyce, he would revert to his pre-Kamesthorn pattern of videos till 2 or 3 am, two or three hours sleep, then an early rise and serious reading for pleasure. But this time he absorbed what he read and saw.

Wednesday nights and Saturday afternoons remained key ingredients in his medicinal package, when live football exercised its redemptive effect on his troubled soul. He went to all Celtic's games. He loved the company, even if the football was far removed from the magic of his youth and the Stein teams. There were four of them always there. Paddy McGuire, his wee fat Councillor friend from his Young Socialist days. Gerry Robertson, full-time official with the G&M Union, Frank's long-time ally and consumer of young girls, orally. Gerry couldn't cope with them older than 16, or younger. And Peter McColl, the wealthiest of them all, successful lawyer, suave socialist and thwarted socialite, or vice versa. Frank loved their company and shared their love of football and the commitment to socialism. He only occasionally wondered if it was more than coincidence that the other thing the three had in common was a self-destruct streak that made his own tendency seem mild in comparison. Except most people, including the three of them, would have said that they were all far more successful than him and had made more of what were probably lesser talents and abilities. But at least their streak was likely to ensure that none of them would ever be totally successful. Occasionally Danny Campbell or Jack Reilly would join them, if Clyde or Hearts didn't have an appropriate game on. These two were gentler, if no less self-destructive, and Frank loved them even more.

That routine saw Frank through the early months of his return to social normality. Not much of a life, but at least he functioned, no longer totally disabled by the tremendous sadness in his soul. It was Elaine who had liberated him, allowing him to expose himself again to activities of a more positive and risky nature. He had met her on one of his lunchtime walks, towards the end of January, with her son Michael. She had acknowledged him, gone for coffee with him, shared her son with him and revived in him not only a

3

sense of what he had lost, but of what he still had left. Most importantly her clear belief that he was still capable of achieving something, of having a destiny worthy of the name and of his talents, had rekindled in him the belief that that was the case. He had realised how far he had sunk, into the negativity that he had always despised in his countrymen, and that his true nature was as a Yes man. So he had started the slow journey towards positivity again, towards the search for a way to contribute, to play again in the game of life and to play to win.

And so, when Danny Campbell asked him to play football against St Anne's, the no that would have been his automatic response several weeks earlier found itself replaced by a positive answer. At the very least it would be a chance to get some small measure of revenge against McGoldrick, his old Headmaster. He had always ascribed much of the failures of his life to making the wrong choice when presented with one by McGoldrick. He had often had a fantasy that if he could somehow rerun those events and make the different choice, his life would follow a better and happier pattern, freed from the inability to cope with success, with winning, and restored with the ability to control his own fate and destiny in a way that would be consistent with his talents, his abilities and his old dreams. McGoldrick the Headmaster, had always been the recipient of the blame that Frank Hunter sought to find a home for with an address other than his own. Beating his school would at least be a degree of consolation.

That Thursday night in early March had started well for Frank and Danny. Frank hadn't played a proper game of football for months. He had been too active during the Action Campaign and then too knackered during the aftermath. It was partly out of his continuing concern for him that Danny had been so insistent that he play. "It's not really cheating, or bringing in a ringer" he had assured himself as much as Frank, "After all, you're Joyce's man and the rules have always been staff or partners". It was the annual challenge match between St Anne's teachers and Queens Park social workers, a real needle grudge match with no love or respect on either side. It was bound to be a dirty game, not hard or vicious, just big weans who would enjoy kicking lumps out of each other in a friendly way. Frank knew the worst offenders would be the four from each side who regularly played for the same Labour Party Constituency team. Nothing like the opportunity to kick a team mate, far more fun than kicking an unknown enemy. Frank found games from relatively small pools were often fascinating, because

4

of the range of skill and ability paraded, from ex- or current pros to some who wouldn't otherwise get a game for a Brownies team.

The game was played on the school pitch, a fair sized grass pitch some distance from the actual school. Frank found it strange to be back in those dressing rooms for the first time in twenty years. Not much had changed, not even the smell. Davie, the gym teacher, was still there, on his last year before retirement. He was managing the staff team, but he was delighted to see Frank and they compared notes on the good old days and where the rest of that Scottish Schools Cup winning team were now. Memories of that 1970 season came flooding back to Frank, most of them happy ones. He remembered his confrontation with McGoldrick and was slightly surprised to relearn the strength of his hatred for the man was at least as great as ever. He would enjoy winning this game as a minor triumph against that bastard's empire. He had come across the man over the years, mainly through the Glasgow Herald articles he regularly wrote, the occasional TV appearances and through the local politics, but had avoided much face to face contact. He heard about him regularly from Andy, Billy and the other St Anne teachers in the Labour Party and the pub. They didn't like him or agree with him, but somewhat to Frank's disappointment most of them seemed to admire him. The only real criticism they would make was that he appeared to have lost interest in St Anne's and seemed ready to move on. Frank knew about his interest in the Kings Park seat and thought it was possible he could put up a good show. No Tory could win that seat though, under that Prime Minister.

Just being in the dressing room, with a good group of lads, Frank felt the healing power of football surge through him and re-energise him. He wanted to get out there and use his body appropriately again, to exercise some mastery over a ball and therefore over his destiny. He regretted the long lost months and the absence from action. Pulling the red jersey over his head was better therapy than all the pills in Kamesthorn.

He ran onto the pitch with more excitement than he had mustered for anything else in months. He stretched and bent with enthusiasm. He felt he could do well. He knew he would suffer for the gap and all that he had been through, but it was not as if the standard was that high. There were five ex-pros at this particular game. As well as himself, the Social Work team included big Alan McNair, his old pal from the Viccies Second Division days. Alan was now a high heid yin in the Social Work Department, a constant source of amazement and worry to all who knew the ungenerous, uncaring and completely self-centred nature of the man under pressure. Frank always knew that how they played football was a good guide to people's true nature. The third pro on their team was his G&M pal Tommy "Do" Little. Frank was never quite sure whether the nickname was a comment on his languid style of play, or on the pigeon-toed way he walked. Frank preferred the former explanation and would shamelessly paraphrase the Doc by saying that Tommy was a deceptive player, he was lazier than he looked. He had recently retired from playing and with Danny's help, got a job as a group worker with the Department so his involvement in the team was genuine.

The rest of the social work team was drawn from the local Area Office. Four of them were passable amateurs, and the other four including Danny couldn't pass to save themselves or their team. Danny always ensured that he organised the game and picked the team. He also made sure that no more than 11 players were available. Being essentially an honest man, he knew that even if his nerve held to include himself in the starting line-up at the expense of anyone else, his performance in the first 20 minutes would leave him with little alternative if there was an able bodied man on the bench. "We don't need substitutes or any other of that modern poofy nonsense" he would say if anyone tried to challenge him. Fortunately for Danny, the Social Work office in the area employed few enough males for him to have to go outside, or at least be elastic in definition, to scrape an eleven far less the threatening 12 or the dreaded 14.

Danny's main consolation and comfort was his boss Gordon, the Area Manager, who in some ways was an even worse player than Danny. Danny at least knew his football, he was an intelligent spectator. He could analyse a game with the best of them in the pub. He knew what should be done and what could be done. Even with his own game, his head knew what his feet should do. It was just unfortunate for him, and tragic for Scotland, that the gap between his head and his feet was about two minutes. Gordon's problem was different, he didn't have any gap at all. His feet just moved everywhere and anywhere. He was fit, very fit, even at his age he could probably outrun them all, but he just didn't know what to do or why. Frank, as always, had a theory, that there is definitely something called a football intelligence, quite different from normal IQ. Some otherwise very stupid boys had it in abundance and could split a defence with one perceptive pass, or analyse the oppositions strengths and weaknesses in a few glances. Other otherwise- intelligent players couldn't work out in 90 minutes why they were continually caught offside. Gordon, a naturalised Scot from Birmingham had a football IQ of 50, profoundly handicapped, but he was still dead keen. The nearest to a Eysenckian Frank ever came was in his firm belief that the Scottish male population as a whole had a far higher football IQ than English males. The women too, were about 20 points higher than their English counterparts.

The rules were unwritten but clear. The pros played within themselves, didn't show off and didn't put it about. In consequence, some of the less perceptive dumplings didn't realise the true extent of the gap and had their fantasies sustained that there but for cruel fortune they would have been too, heroes all. Frank relished the responsibility of playing for a team that was likely to get a doing. He took more decisions in that 90 minutes than he had done in the previous nine months since the day his mother died. He reorganised Danny's formation, put himself at sweeper, behind big Alan in the centre of the defence and got Tommy working in the middle of the park. Gordon was told to chase anything that moved up front. He put Danny at left back, covered him himself and talked him through it. He helped some of the others to play above themselves and he and Alan held it tight at the back. It was hard graft. The teachers had some good players including two men in their late thirties that had played professional, two current Juniors and five regular amateur players. That meant they had only two passengers, two less to carry than his team.

They kept it blank till half-time, by willpower as much as anything else. It was a torrid affair, both sides seemed to enjoy getting tore into each other, good and proper. The teachers were real ruffians and barbarians. Frank was glad he had no children. The social workers were held back slightly by their constant absorption in notions of care and caring. At one point Gordon clattered clumsily into their goalkeeper and knocked him into the post, banging his head and causing the ball to drop free. Gordon's immediate instinctive reaction was to stop and enquire if he were all right. The 2 seconds delay it would have taken to hammer the free ball across the goal-line was hardly likely to be crucial to his health and well-being, but that was social workers for you, more concerned with feelings than results.

Early in the second half Danny missed a ball that was clearly his and before Frank could recover, it was whipped across and nodded home by Andy Rogers. Frank's heart sank. He didn't know what was worse. The effect on this game or the knowledge that he would have to hear about it in the pub from the scorer every week for the next year. They held on under greater pressure and weathered the teachers' surge of adrenaline. Once it passed, Frank even had the space to come forward for the first time in the game. A surge, a sway, a swivel and there it was on a plate for big Tommy. Rules is rules and he couldn't score himself but he beat the last defender and slipped it in front of Gordon who by chance was running in the right direction. The previous time must have been his ninety-ninth because this time he hit it straight and they were back in the game.

That's how it stayed, with the aid of a few miracles, until five minutes to go when Danny's goal broke the deadlock. The ball had come in high and slow into the edge of the penalty box. Somehow Danny had been in the right place, alone. He timed it to perfection, the culmination of a thousand nights of dreams. With his back to the goal, he had controlled it on his chest, swivelled round and, as the ball dropped, swung his right boot to make contact with the leather. He even remembered not to lean back and to keep his head down. It was the perfect strike. For the first time in his football life, he achieved perfect synchronisation between intention and execution. The ball positively zipped past the startled goalkeeper into the back of the net, Danny had so carefully helped erect before the game.

All 22 players went mad. Danny's team-mates sank to their knees in despair. All that effort to lose to an own goal. The teachers danced with delight, justice had been done. Billy Kirkwood, who was the one nearest to Danny, planked a big kiss on his drained face. Frank, who had been moving towards Danny to console his devastated friend, heard Andy Rogers say to Billy, "Hold on, you'd better save that for the Headies wife". Frank paused and looked straight at Andy with a look that made the question unnecessary and provoked the required clarification, "Aye, the stupid bastard's knocking off Frankie McGoldrick. The pair of them are the School Board Leisure Resources Subcommittee and conduct all their business in a hotel bedroom." Frank left Danny to the less tender mercies of his colleagues as he absorbed this information. He'd heard vague rumours about her over the years but had never believed they could be true. He asked Andy if many people knew. "No, at least the daft bugger has the

sense not to boast about it. Only me and half the team know".
Andy smiled broadly at the significance of that.

The final few minutes passed quickly and they all trooped off
for their shower. Poor Danny was inconsolable, or would have
been if anyone had tried. Initially, over the first two pints in the
Albert Bar, he took the blame on himself and accepted the
slaggings like a good victim. Frank gave him some sympathy but
would not buy his subsequent attempts to share the blame with
others. No, the goalkeeper didn't need to shout, no the centre half
shouldn't have shoved you out of the way, it was your play and you
blew it. He only intervened again when Gordon the goal hero
started on Danny.

Most of the time in the pub he was fairly quiet and ran the
information about Mrs McGoldrick past himself a few hundred
times to see why it excited him so. He could smell blood in his
mouth and it gave his beer a funny but not unpleasant taste. He
had really enjoyed the game, it had done wonders for him but
some instinct far within him told him that the game would be of
secondary importance to the new piece of knowledge he had.

It took only three more hours before that vague feeling
hardened into concrete reality. Joyce came back to his flat after
her group, anxious to find out how he had done and whether her
office's honour had been saved. He told her all about the game and
how much it had meant to him, and about Danny's shame. She had
got quite upset for him and he had been touched at her concern. He
told her about Frankie McGoldrick and Billy Kirkwood and she
immediately said "Oh, that's nothing, wait till you hear this. The
other night, Janis was telling me that she and her mate Julie had
been in an Edinburgh hotel bar, casually watching the news on the
TV set above the bar when Julie had suddenly said, 'Oh my god,
that's one of my punters. Janis had looked more closely, and there
was McGoldrick being interviewed. She hadn't believed it but Julie
had been insistent, although she knew him by another name."

Joyce always told Frank everything about her work, about all
her cases and their problems, all the dilemmas she had to wrestle
with and all the decisions she had to make, her arguments with her
bosses, her plans and her ambitions. He always listened intently,
and with obvious interest and concern. He loved to see her talk
that way. She would close her eyes, to aid her concentration and he
would study the movements on her face as she talked. Most often,
she told him about her Prostitutes Group, what she had achieved
and what she was hoping to do. He had avoided the trap of some of

9

the other men she knew of sexual fascination and a prurient desire to learn about the detail. He had given her good advice about some of the politics involved, and the likely repercussions. Most of all, he had seemed to understand what it did to her, her sexuality and her awareness of herself as a woman. So she had told him all about the women who attended, their children and their dreams, their pimps and their plans. She had never had the slightest hesitation about sharing everything with him.

But as she told him about Janis and Julie and McGoldrick, she realised that she had made a mistake. She knew Frank knew Janis was one of the stalwarts of her group, and had even met her once or twice. There was something about the look that came over him. A cold hard farawayness that froze her innards. She had had a premonition of that when Janis had first told her. She knew Frank was peculiar about McGoldrick. She had heard him rail against him and his politics in several pub discussions. She knew there was an edge to it that seemed more personal than political. So when Janis had told her, and said she hadn't and wouldn't tell anyone else, Joyce had decided to keep the information to herself. But, in response to his tale about Danny's goal and Frankie McGoldrick, and his obvious excitement, it had slipped out before she could control it.

She tried to recover it. She looked hard at him. "Frank, you know you can't use that. It's privileged information. It would be a breach of my trust and professional confidentiality if you told anyone." There was an edge of panic in her voice that alerted him to reassure her and suppress his immediate instincts to press her for more details. He assured her he would tell no-one about it. He meant at least he would not gossip about it.

He knew about Janis from previous discussions. She was a southside girl who had been at St Anne's, so she would know McGoldrick all right. He had met her some of the times he had picked up Joyce from the Group. He could remember roughly what she looked like; small, thin, reddish curly hair, with a liking for short black skirts and white lacy tops. He knew roughly the patch she worked. He realised that there was no point pursuing Joyce. He knew that she was already feeling that she had told him too much, and that she would get agitated if he seemed over-interested. She would not help him meet Janis or find out more about this Julie. But that didn't matter, he had already worked out who could help him and how, and the less Joyce knew about his interest the better. So he reassured her, made a casual comment about the pair of

10

them, the McGoldricks, and moved the conversation onto more interesting matters like Danny's disgrace and his broken heart. Soon she was asleep in his arms, with her own wrapped firmly round him. She thought her crisis was over, but he knew his was still to come.

Awake in his bed, his brain would not rest. He thought it was the most incredible piece of information he had ever heard in his life. Its effect was to generate so much excitement in himself that he compared himself to Archimedes. This was his moment of truth, when something was learned that would affect the way the universe operated. Part of him found it hard to believe that it was true. He knew he probably wouldn't have believed it had it not been for the earlier information about Frankie McGoldrick's extra-curricular activity. But even so the hypocrisy of the man left him astounded. It had just been the previous week that he had made a major speech in Edinburgh on the decline of family morality as the major problem in Scottish Education and society. Frank had seen him interviewed on STV. He realised that was probably the same interview that Janis and Julie must have seen.

Frank had been interested enough in the man's basic argument to look out the papers the next day. The Glasgow Herald had just had a small entry, so Frank had gone to the Magazine Room and waited for the Scotsman to become available. It had devoted half a page to the speech, as well as a leader column supporting the thrust of his argument. Lying in his bed with Joyce asleep beside him he ran through the essence of McGoldrick's argument and re-evaluated it in the light of what he had just learned about his wife and himself. Slowly the notion of what he was going to do with this information formed in the course of his restless night. By the time Frank rose at 5 a.m. his plan was almost complete, the main sections of it were clear in his mind. He knew he was about to play a game, one that he intended to win. This one would give him immense satisfaction. He knew it would lance the boil of indignation and upset from twenty years before. It would repay an old debt with sufficient interest to also allow him to clear off another debt of his own to an organisation that McGoldrick so despised. By allowing him to present someone else with a choice, it would help Frank regain some sense of control over his own destiny. For the first time in a long, long time, he rose with a sense of purpose and anticipation. He had work to do, work that would have an end product.

That morning in the Mitchell, he abandoned his prearranged plan of study and returned to the back copies of the papers containing McGoldrick's speech. He also looked up other references of his work, previous speeches and articles. Rereading the main article, he realised that it was a more subtle and complex thesis than he had appreciated at first reading. Although the essence of the matter was clear. McGoldrick believed in the sanctity of marriage. The sacredness of marriage vows, and the consequent obligations on family members to provide standards for each other, was the foundation rock on which a healthy society was built. It was obvious from his speech that he believed that Catholic schools were superior to non-denominational schools because of the differential attitude to the importance of family and marriage in Catholic and Protestant circles. He made claims for the better levels of discipline and stability in Catholic schools because of those stronger bonds of church and family. But the main thrust of his discourse was political rather than educational or religious. He blamed the Welfare State for eroding the unity of the family and beginning the process of disintegration that had brought Scottish society to its current sorry state. He particularly despised and derided the Scottish Labourite mentality that society owed Scottish people a living. He equated Scotland's rejection of the Prime Minister with the rejection of the older traditional Scottish virtues of thrift, work and duty, in favour of an emotional rather than intellectual or moral embrace of the decadent effects of socialist sedition. The true greed of today was the belief, fostered by that Labour view, that something could be had for nothing, as a right. Under this pernicious philosophy, it did not matter if a man did not work, or support his family, the State would pick up those responsibilities for him.

McGoldrick detested this view. For him, the family unit was the basic one, in Scotland as much as anywhere else. This was the key level, not some mythical creature called Scottish Society. Only by the exercise of proper responsibilities within this unit could true morality flourish. The ready access to divorce and the casual acceptance of distorted family forms like single parents and cohabitation had contributed to the erosion of moral standards and the decline in respect for law and order. He pointed out that Glasgow had the highest rate in Europe for births out of wedlock, and that no less than one in five of the families in the city were headed by a lone parent.

He made a link from the decline in personal morality to the decline in political morality. In a section that particularly worried Frank, McGoldrick cited the attitude to the Poll Tax as an example of this decline. McGoldrick found it a peculiar notion that people could opt out of paying a tax because they did not like it. He resisted his temptation to apply the same logic to the introduction of a Wealth Tax. There was more, much more, especially about the interconnection of the personal and the political in the Scottish context, some of it exceptionally subtle. But the basic sustaining theme was clear. It was the commitment to marriage that provided the foundation for a correct personal morality, and political morality would derive from the sum of personal moralities. Frank knew that it wasn't new. He had been familiar with all of its elements for years, both in his reading and in his interactions. But the man did express it with clarity and succinctness, and with a style that only slightly suffered from his dominie manner.

Frank rejected the arguments without anger. He knew why he rejected them, why he always had, and what structure of response he would put in opposition in open debate. Reading them, it was not the actual arguments that angered him, although certain bits did reinforce a feeling of personal dislike for this arrogant outsider. In a way he found his re-examination that morning gave him a feeling he could only describe as delicious outrage. He knew this was because he was now in possession of the information that the foundation of McGoldrick's structure, the commitment to the values of the family, was so fatally flawed in his own case. It was the man's hypocrisy that angered him rather than his arguments. Frank had always been like that. He could never stand cheats or liars. From his earliest childhood, he had hated people cheating at games, not playing by the rules. He had never really ever forgiven his Uncle Willie for cheating at Monopoly, when Frank was six. Maybe it was not surprising Willie had become a Headmaster.

His mother had talked to him long and often about why people did things like that, but Frank had never been convinced that it was ever acceptable. It's only a game, was never an excuse for Frank. Games should have their own integrity. Life is nothing more than an interconnected series of games. Disrespect for rules was a route to anarchy, and Frank hated anarchy and anarchists, almost as much as Trotskyists. Although at least anarchists were honest about their dishonesty. Football, Frank's main game, was a difficult game at which to cheat but Frank reserved a particular antipathy towards those who succeeded in finding a way, particularly those on his own side who cheated in the worst way by failing to give of their best. He had once attacked Gerry Riordan for giving up and going home when their street team were 6-0 down. Gerry was two years older at an age when that had mattered but the ferocity of Frank's anger at this form of cheating had overcome the physical disadvantages. The rest of the team had got the message and they had ended up only losing 10-7.

Now McGoldrick was cheating, at the most important game of all. He was building a political platform on a lie, his commitment to the importance of family values, while using a prostitute at the same time his wife was being screwed by one of his own teachers. Well, Frank would turn that lie upon him, the hypocritical arsehole, and expose his cheating. He would not do so publicly. He already knew that he just wanted it to be a private matter between the two of them. He had already worked out how he would give McGoldrick a dilemma of choice of a similar kind to the one which Frank had been subjected by him so long ago.

Frank knew his friend Hazel would help him, and not ask too many questions about what he was doing or why. He had met Hazel in Kamesthorn, the best of several things his stay there had given him. She was the only person he had ever met in his life who carried a greater weight of permanent sadness in her soul than him, and with greater cause. Instinctively drawn to each other by their common burden, they had swapped stories in the long Kamesthorn nights. Hers had made him ashamed of the self-indulgent nature of his own. There had been an early marriage, boredom and brain death; then escape to London, and a living on the edge as a hostess and masseuse, but with pride and integrity maintained. Then she had fallen prey, willingly, to the charms of a Glasgow hardman working for one of the London mobs that had employed her. Marriage and motherhood had followed in the short happy spell of her life but all too soon Billy had overreached himself and they had fled to behind a steel door in Govan, behind which he tried to infiltrate the local Drug market and from which he sent her out to work the streets until he did so. She had gone willingly enough, she was his equal partner, but the price she paid with herself had been high. He had paid an even higher price, murdered brutally in front of her for his cheek. She had had a breakdown after that, with her two young children lost into permanent social work care.

She had recovered a little, enough to survive, living alone in a bedsit, working as school cleaner, renouncing sex and drugs, and

14

accepting the loss of her children as the rightful price she should pay for her sins. Her psychiatrist, who knew she was sane, sent her for a holiday to Kamesthorn at the same time Frank had his little break. They had quickly become close, physically on a couple of occasions, but Frank had convinced himself that they had both agreed that their true relationship was as friends, a view confirmed for him if not his mother by his subsequent coupling with Joyce. But she was his friend, he knew that, and he tried hard to be her good one. He was the only one she allowed herself, and she kept her own assumptions to herself.

He called round to see her after he had finished at the Mitchell. He gave her a carryout chicken curry and explained what he needed her to do. She gave him a funny look, but listened attentively. She assured him that it would be a fairly easy task. She told him she would have more likelihood of success if she dressed for the part, and proceeded to look out and put on the best of her old working gear. He found it strangely erotic watching her lay it all out on her bed. She told him she had vowed never to wear it again, but had kept it as some kind of momento of her haunted past. It was obvious even to him that it must have cost her a good few bob. It had an aura of expensive cheapness, a contrast to the normal Glasgow style of cheap material used to imaginative effect to look expensive. Once it was all laid out, she proceeded to change into it in front of him. Given the size of her place, there was no real choice, but he still had a strange sense that she was both testing him and punishing him. She worked from the top down, slipping off her pullover and bra. He watched with an engineer's fascination and a lecher's jaw as she inserted her swinging breasts into the slight piece of black lace and wire. It pushed them up and forward, and kept them there, pointing menacingly at him. She then took off her shoes and socks and pulled down her jeans.

The sad smile she gave him as she slipped out of her knickers and wriggled into a pair of smooth, tiny shiny black briefs burned a layer of shame into his soul. He did not avert his eyes and continued to watch hypnotised as she put on the black suspender belt, then pulled up the smooth black stockings. They were not fishnet but they would still entrap most prey. Then the final touches, the short lustrous black leather skirt that barely covered her bum, and the exquisite black top of soft, sensuous see-through silk. She then covered it partly with a short black leather jacket that he realised must have cost even more than the one he had so generously given her from Katherine Hamnets at Christmas.

When she slipped on the black patent high heels and stood up and looked straight at him, demanding a response, the dangerous nature of what he was doing was suddenly revealed to him. And only partly by the throbbing push of his erect penis against his trousers. He had known she was attractive, he had recognised that from the first. But he was not prepared for the effect of that kind of effort, distorted as it was. He had seen many prostitutes dressed for work. He had been offered business by a good few, and been vaguely tempted by one or two. He knew some were attractive and others had been. But Hazel in front of him was beautiful. Meet her in a disco and Christmas would come early. On the street and she was just another cheap and dirty whore, no she bloody well wasn't. £10 and she could be had, for the next three minutes at least. He didn't know if he was cuddling her or caressing her, but his arms were round her before he could worry if she would feel the state of his penis. He was cuddling her.

He kissed her hair and said he was sorry. He had failed to consider the capacity for pain he was causing her. Self-centred bastard was his view if not hers. If she had put her hand on his willie he might have been lost, but she had dressed that way to do a job of work, and neither of them wanted to confuse the issue. They were both, in their own ways, delicate enough as it was. She disengaged herself and put her makeup on in front of the mirror, deliberately overdoing it. She reorganised her hair and that was her ready to go. He felt smaller going down the close than he had coming up but that was not because he didn't want to be seen with her. He felt very proud of her, it was himself he was ashamed to be seen with. He walked Hazel to his car, then drove down Victoria Road, swung over onto the Kingston Bridge and came off at the City Centre exit, past the Albany Hotel. He knew Janis wasn't in the league that used the inside of that rather than the outside.

The Friday early evening shift was one of the busiest and best of the week, as men finished their week's work, had their pints and contemplated the joyous prospect of a weekend at home. Frank was fairly certain Janis would work it, and knew the general area where she would be found. He drove slowly round the square route where he knew most of the Group had their patch. Along Bothwell Street, down Pitt Street to Anderson Cross Bus Station. Turn left into Cadogan Street, turn right at the multi-storey car park into Blythswood Street then first left into Holm Street. Along past the

16

massage parlours including the one where Joyce's Group now met, up left into West Campbell Street and back along Waterloo Street. He pulled up across from the Admiral Bar. Vaguely he was aware that if anyone saw her get out of his car there was only one conclusion they would draw, but it didn't worry him at all. As he walked into the Admiral to order a pint of Dryboroughs and sit at the small table at the window, Hazel walked off down Pitt St, to look for Janis. She knew what she was doing and the risks involved. New girls were not welcome on the established patch and there could be trouble. But she was an old pro, and knew how to handle herself. She had married a wimp and lived with a pimp. Nothing left could frighten her after what she had seen.

Thirty-five minutes and one extra pint later, she slipped into the Admiral and sat beside him. She asked for a brandy and he bought her a double without being asked. The barman almost said something, such people were not allowed in that pub, but the look on Frank's face discouraged him. Frank knew only slightly what it must have cost her to don that gear and that role again and go down those mean and dirty streets once more. She told him she had had fourteen offers. She had started saying £100, to make the mean bastards lose interest quickly, but one man in a Vauxhall had accepted those terms. Hazel looked Frank full in the face and told him she had been tempted, that was as much as she cleared in a 38 hour week at the school.

She had found Janis without making it obvious she was looking. She had got her talking without arousing her suspicion. She had said she was just back from a spell in Edinburgh, knowing from Frank that Janis had once done likewise. She had found out from her about Julie without alerting her. Julie was apparently a class act, who no longer worked the streets, but operated a telephone contact system by personal recommendation. Hazel had got the number and had already phoned her. Frank was to meet her in the Cocktail Bar of the Hazeldene Hotel in Edinburgh at 6pm the following Saturday. The two hour session would cost him £200. He had two immediate thoughts as Hazel explained the arrangements to him. One was that if he got the kind of satisfaction he was looking for from it, it would be the best £200 investment of his life.

CHAPTER TWO - THE STORIES OF JULIE AND MARGARET

He became an expert on prostitution in the week before his assignation with Julie. He altered his work schedule to help achieve this. He spent most of his time in the sociology and psychology Sections, reading everything he could about the subject. He drew heavily on the source books, articles and other materials that he had seen at Joyce's or heard her mention, particularly ones written by working women. The rest of his work time was spent in the Legal Section, studying whatever was available about the laws and principles of blackmail, extortion, conspiracy, and demanding with menaces. He was determined to be completely legal in whatever he might do, but he knew fine lines required close scrutiny, and much study of the spaces between them.

He also visited his bank and arranged to make a significant withdrawal on the Friday. At last he would begin to make his redundancy money work for him. He could not expect the co-operation of an unknown woman without making it well worth her while in the only language he could be sure she would understand.

His first crisis point passed without pain. Hazel had obviously done her job subtly and well. He had been tense the whole evening on the Tuesday, wondering if Joyce would come back raging and accusing him of betraying her trust by pursuing an interest in Janis or Julie. But the contact with another working girl had not been sufficiently different to induce any alarm in Janis. He had been less tense but still anxious on the Thursday, but the danger passed.

He felt it a good omen that Celtic were playing Hibs in Edinburgh on the Saturday. He explained to Gerry, Paddy and Peter that he had business to attend to in Edinburgh after the match and that he would take his own car. Peter picked the other two up from their rendezvous in the Mulberry at 12:30 and they travelled through by convoy. By 1:30 they were having a feast of pie, beans and chips in Torley's on Leith Walk. They washed it down with two pints of good Guinness. There were parts of Edinburgh it was possible to feel comfortable in. They were all pleasantly content as they strolled over to Easter Road in good time for the kick-off. He enjoyed his trips to the Big Slope, if more for the ghosts than the current residents. Watching the likes of Stanton, Cormack, Stein, Marinello, Cropley, Higgins, Blackley and Brownlie perform again in his head was better entertainment than they were paying to see. He had loved watching that team, the only one to give Stein's Bhoys a run for their money. Getting to playing for the Viccies against the remnants of it in a cup tie in 1974, and scoring the winning goal, would remain one of the highlights of his life, a hint of what might have been. They went to the terracing. They still preferred to stand at games. The atmosphere, the important sense of being one of the tribe was far greater squashed on the terraces. Frank found that when he wasn't watching the Celtic, or Scotland, he would settle for the more leisurely comfort of somewhere to rest his bum, but serious commitment still called for standing to attention.

Celtic played better than they had for some time and won 2-0. Frank's one slight regret was that his old friend Archibald was no longer there. In the bleak and lonely emotional desert of late 1984, he had partially consoled himself for the loss of Elaine by becoming the President of the SAD boys, the Steve Archibald Devotees. There were five full members, Danny for the Clyde days, Andy Rogers the teacher from Aberdeen, Tony Dixon a Spurs supporting social worker. Gerry Robertson, who went to all Scotland's games, home and abroad grabbed that dimension, and Frank, always the European, claimed to be a life-long Barcelona man. The initial years of SAD activity were very rewarding. They went to Barcelona twice, and to Seville, where he should have crowned it all by winning the European Cup for them but typically did not. Peter McColl had come on all three trips although refusing to join the club or wear the pullover. SAD had gone into relative decline when the man had returned home from Barcelona.

There had been a good trip down to England to stay with Derek Duncan and watch their man star for Blackburn Rovers but it had not quite been the same as a Spanish excursion. A little less glamorous than Barcelona. When he had signed for Hibs, the SAD boys met more regularly. It had been the best reason they had ever found for visiting Edinburgh, far better than anything ever on offer at the Festival. But this past year, when perhaps Frank had needed it most, it had turned sour. The great man's peculiar personality had moved him out of action and then on and away. He had only been a substitute at Parkhead, shortly after Frank's return to spectator duty, and by the New Year had played his last game for Hibs. He had recently rekindled hope and injected new life into

SAD by going back to Barcelona and signing for the other team. They had all agreed to take a trip to Barcelona at the end of April for what might be a farewell performance. The end of an era was in sight.

The others were curious about Frank's business in Edinburgh but they were used to getting no explanation from him. He knew that he would need some story, for Joyce, since they were all meeting later for a few pints in the Victoria then going on for a curry in the Manzil. He had worked out he would tell her that he had met a representative of LDT, up in Edinburgh for a conference, to check out a few aspects of his book. It wasn't a total lie, he had met the man a week earlier, in Glasgow and hadn't told Joyce. He arrived at the Hazeldene Hotel early, declining the opportunity for the usual post-match pint and post-mortem. He had phoned earlier in the week and booked a double room for Saturday night. He had used the name Mr Wharton, the one Hazel had given Julie. He signed the register for both Mr and Mrs Wharton and told them, to their total indifference, that he was expecting his wife shortly. He paid in advance since he would be leaving early in the morning and went up to the bedroom with his suitcase, empty other than his change of clothes to a more respectable image, and his tape machine. The room had two comfortable armchairs which he knew was all he would need, but it also had a large double bed and a single one. All tastes catered for. He changed into his best suit and strolled as casually as he could muster down to the Bar with his Guardian carefully folded under his arm. She was obviously a lady with educated and liberal tastes. Tell him to sit on his own reading the Guardian, and she would come to him, had been her instructions. Looking around the bar he realised the correctness of her view that there wouldn't be more than one person there reading the Guardian. He ordered a half-pint of Export, he was in Edinburgh after all, and sipped it gently without enthusiasm. He opened the paper but couldn't settle to any article.

She appeared at 6pm precisely, looking exactly like he would expect other people to expect his wife to look, very smart in a neat blue suit. She was carrying a suitcase that didn't look as if it were empty. "Hello darling, sorry I'm late" she said and planted an affectionate peck on his somewhat startled cheek. He wasn't sure whether to offer her a drink or not, but decided against it. There was drink in the room and he could always phone room-service. He stood up, took the suitcase from her, and led her up the stairs towards his room. He realised his heart was pounding with a rare

20

form of excitement but he also realised it was not sexual but conspiratorial. It was only when she was safely in his room that he was able to properly look at her. She was considerably taller than the average Scottish prostitute, or woman, maybe 5'9" or 5'10", with long slender legs fading away just below her armpits. She had a slim trim body with good curves, and even through her sedate and proper blouse he could see that she had a larger than average bust. Her hair was in a modern style, medium length and permed into a wavy mass that swept up away from her face. Her hair was blonde, obviously dyed so but successfully, which got her extra marks for effort. Left at that, she was attractive, not sensationally so, but obviously a good looking lady. It was her face that made her outstanding. Her most striking feature, it turned her into something else. It was the face of innocence, yearning for experience hinted at but never known. It was not the look of an under-age Glasgow girl, that haunted, hunted, half-formed vacuousness that so turned on Gerry Robertson, but a more international kind of innocence. It was a peculiar and beguiling mixture. No-one looking at the whole package would mistake her for a fourteen year old, but if only the face was looked at it was possible.

Her appearance, and her sophisticated, cultured and English accent removed a major nagging worry that Frank had been carrying since he first heard about McGoldrick and Julie. He just had not been able to see McGoldrick getting involved with any wee Glasgow lassie, any crude Scots girl, anyone who could have been one of his ex-pupils. His disdain for them as a species would have prevented that. Frank had had to develop a vision of McGoldrick doing the business with his eyes shut and his ears closed, which hadn't seemed too feasible. But seeing and hearing Julie removed those doubts. She had the looks, dress and manners of a well-educated English lady, with an accent to match. And a face out of an artist's impression of a teacher's fantasy, the perfect pupil.

He had spent a week worrying how he was going to tell her he wasn't there for sexual purposes, without scaring her off. He started off by giving her the £200 up front, to seal his claim on her time. He had worked out in advance a story that he was writing a book about prostitutes and their clients. His week's study, and his six months listening to Joyce, had equipped him with sufficient material to make that plausible. But it had the major defect that it was not true, and he wasn't very good at telling lies. He made an instant assessment. He usually knew within 20 seconds of meeting somebody whether or not he liked them. He seldom changed his position, and only in the direction of moving to not like someone he had initially liked, because and when they infringed the ridiculous expectations he laid down for people upon whom he was prepared to bestow his affections. His initial assessment of Julie was positive. She had looked him straight in the eye throughout their contact. He decided he would tell her the truth, at least in stages. He told her first that he didn't want to fuck her, or touch her, or have her touch him. She didn't seem too surprised at that.

What did surprise her was that he did not want her to perform for him, or even to dress up. Hazel had reported to him that Julie had enquired of her what role he would wish her to play for him. She was not a prostitute. She didn't turn tricks, or take punters. She gave performances. Live theatre, with audience participation as a major bonus. She had a large range of roles she would play on demand, including a good number of the classics. French Maid, Nurse, Prison Warden, Schoolgirl, Nun, Barmaid, School Teacher, plus almost anything else that could be requested. Hazel, who knew her Frank and had seen him look at Isobel McCann in Kamesthorn, had said that he would be very interested in the Nurse outfit. Frank had been mildly amused at that and glad she hadn't said Nun. Julie later told him that the most popular one in Edinburgh was Lady Judge, in Glasgow it was her Bus Conductress, but that in both cities School Mistress came a close second. He knew that was what would be in her suitcase, a full Nurse's uniform and related gear. It wasn't uncommon for Julie to be told that they only wanted to talk. Many of them wanted to talk about their work, their worries, even their wives. It never bothered her, it cut down the amount of time once the real work began, and she was an expert at moving them through the various stages, although some never got past the oral. She somehow sensed this one was different though. He told her a little about himself, and told her he needed to know a bit about her, for reasons he would explain later. He reassured her that he was not a policeman, tax-man or journalist, not that she had thought he was likely to be any of them, having plenty professional experience of all three.

For reasons that were not entirely clear to her, she felt she could trust him and soon started talking. He had paid and what harm could it do her. He had always known he could have been a social worker, and that he would have been a better one than most of the many he knew. He had that rare ability to draw out from people their life stories, and their real feelings, and to respond in such a way as to get beyond and behind the cover versions everyone used, to the real detail beneath. He had the correct blend of judicious silence, earnest nod, encouraging smile and occasional comment to extract the most effusive response. All his life he had had that talent and that evening he concentrated on exercising it as well as he ever had. He knew from Danny and Joyce all about the writing of Social Background Reports on people for Courts. The story of a life on two pages, including not only past and present, but also their motivation for the offence that brought them to Court, an estimate of their likely future conduct, and a recommendation as to how the court should dispose of them. Dostoevsky in Crime and Punishment took around 300 pages to write a Social Background Report, but any good social worker could contain it to 2 or 3 sides of A4 paper. All sides seemed to accept the belief that a life could be so concisely summarised to the benefit of the Court. Fine art or professional arrogance, Frank loved reading them anyway and always found them fascinating. Danny was very cautious about giving him access to any, particularly after his sneering comments about the first few he read. Did social workers really understand what motivated people, or the tales they would spin for the benefit of the gullible? Frank knew from Paddy that most lawyers considered Social Background Reports as the best possible pleas in mitigation and would happily charge £40 or £50 to read out verbatim for two or three minutes, what had taken some poor social worker 4 or 5 hours of lowly paid graft to assemble. Danny, a Senior Social Worker, had been driven to despair by the failure of most of his social workers to grasp the basic fact that the two most powerful motivating drives in human activity were sex and money, in that order, and yet most Reports were too polite to examine the subject's access to, or the strength of their desires for, either.

Joyce had had less reservations about letting him read all her Reports. She always wrote them at home anyway, in her own time. She welcomed testing her efforts against his knowledge of Glasgow people and how they operated. He had read the ones she had done for the members of her Prostitutes Support Group, they and she preferred her to do them than to leave it to the local social workers. It was no criticism of Joyce that they all tended to read the same. They all seemed to unveil a similar pattern of deprived social background, unstable family circumstances often with the separation of parents, average intelligence but poor educational performance and early school-leaving, unemployment, early unsatisfactory personal and sexual relationships and marriage, unwanted pregnancies but loved children, financial difficulties, a search for salvation, hope or peace in drink or drugs, and a variety of routes into working on the streets, coupled with a desire to stop. Frank found no one answer in either the books he read, or from Joyce, about why there were so many Glasgow women who shared all those characteristics but avoided the final one, of prostitution. Frank had wondered if it was a bit like Glasgow males and football. There were many amateurs of skill, talent and enthusiasm but the breakthrough to professional status was a peculiar mixture of luck, opportunity, circumstance, chance and arbitrariness. And many who made it were no better or worse than many more who didn't. There was certainly no single guaranteeing factor, no physical or mental symptoms which could allow predictive certainty to apply.

It certainly wasn't moral defectiveness either, Frank knew that Hazel was one of the most moral people he had ever met, and that Joyce was full of admiration for the courage and integrity of many of her Group. The one common thread seemed to be significant forms of abuse by men. Sometimes it had been sexual, by a father, stepfather, uncle or family friend, sometimes it had just been physical or emotional but always it was soul-destroying and desperate. Later relationships seemed no more successful, the forms of abuse even more varied but equally deadly. Once betrayed and severely abused by a male, the taking of money for a quick physical return did not seem such an unsatisfactory or unacceptable transaction. At least it had the virtue of honesty and openness. Both sides got what they expected, no more and no less. It seemed to Frank that there were a series of social and personal constraints which once broken never reapplied in the same way again. He found the Reports depressing but at the same time with a positive core. Prostitutes were just people, survivors as best they could against the tribulations of life. They had as many good qualities and strengths as any other random group.

Frank had long been of the firm view that prostitution should be legalised, that it was essentially a private transaction between consenting adults, and for society to persecute and prosecute one side of that transaction was an act of institutionalised hypocrisy and male authoritarianism that defied any logical justification. It was exactly like arguments about Prohibition, it didn't stop the activity, it only allowed evil pimps and criminal organisers to

24

flourish in the shadows. In Scotland, there was also a nasty streak of the Calvinist male attitude to sex as the work of the devil, in female garb. Frank had once got Paddy, his Councillor friend, drunk enough to promise to move a resolution in the District Council to change the bylaws to allow council run brothels to be established, with proper health checks and unionisation of all employees. Paddy had funny ideas about sex and women, being a good Catholic boy who had only ever done it with his wife. Rationally, he agreed with all of Frank's arguments but emotionally he couldn't cope with them and it was the only promise he ever made Frank that he did not keep. His failure to do so caused him considerable pain, and he did what he could in recompense to help create a climate in Glasgow where Massage Parlours and other off-street ventures were tolerated.

It became clear to Frank as Julie told him about herself that she did not fit entirely into the normal pattern, and would not be at home on the streets of Glasgow. She had neither the lack of confidence nor in-built diffidence of the West Coast woman, nor the hard aggressive edge. She had the assurance and confidence that Glasgow people associate with the English. It came as no surprise to him that that was exactly what she turned out to be. Gradually she forget her role as therapist and moved to the transposed position of someone being paid £100 an hour to pour out their heart and soul to an all-seeing, all-knowing silent seer. She told him things she had never acknowledged to anyone else before, even to herself. And he handled it in the right way to keep it coming.

She had been born in Harrogate, 24 years ago, to an Army Officer and his lady wife. She had loved her cold and distant father in the best way his stiffness would allow, until he had loved her back in the worst way his stiffness could inflict. Her mother, whom she had always despised for her ineffectualness, would have died rather than acknowledge that such a thing could have happened so it had remained Julie's little secret. Fortunately he was seldom home and spent months at a time in Germany or Ulster. She always remembered her mother's awful phrase, forewarning of impending pain, "Your father will be joining us again shortly, my dear". She always used those precise words, and Julie later reflected on their potential Freudian significance. She remembered the last time vividly. Before, she had colluded, passively, knowing what he was doing was wrong but unable to work out how to deal with it, how to stop him without losing him, unable to overcome

25

his verbal protestations of how this was an act of love, proof of the specialness of their relationship.

She had had six months to ponder on her position, and what she could do. She had been twelve years old then, old enough to get married in some cultures. She had promised herself not to be alone with him, at all, and had conscripted her mother into support for that position without having to spell out why. But he had been too clever for her. It had been so easy for him to remove her mother. He had arranged for her to attend a Royal Garden Party. No expense was spared, a new outfit, put up for the night in the best of hotels so as not to miss a moment of the big day. Unfortunately he had only been able to obtain, at some cost, one ticket, but that was no problem, he and Julie would be all right for one night on their own. The stupid woman had been so pleased, she ignored all Julie's desperate protestations. She thought he had gone to that time, expense and trouble so that she could meet her Princess. He had arranged it, at some cost, so that he could meet his little princess.

Julie had been determined to resist. She had worked out more clearly for herself what was so wrong about what he did to her. He did love her so he would respect her position. Her active reluctance had made no difference. He had taken her anyway, mouthing protestations of love as he had rammed his erect soldier in and out of her frail protesting body, until it had finally surrendered with a whimper. That time she had not colluded in his aftermath. She vowed out loud to him that he would never ever do that to her again, and that if he ever tried she would tell. Not his wife, but his superior officer. He must have realised that she was of sterner stuff than his wife, because he had spent considerable time warning her of the consequences. A soldier, he wasted no time on fantasies of removal into care that might not absolutely deter. He made it clear that the consequences for her of talking would be more permanent. He would ensure that she would become a casualty of war, a dead person. That was his trade after all, a young girl would present no difficulties. He would use his military power to deliver on his promise. No-one would believe her and then she would be dead. She had silently wished him dead since she knew then that one of them must die. Her father died that night, but the man married to her mother lasted three more months, before the IRA made him a hero and a martyr, and her a killer, when their land-mine blew him into almost as many pieces as she had wished him.

26

Her mother could not cope. Her daughter's lack of grief was only a minor problem. She had a role to play, hero's widow, to which she was more suited and more committed than single mother. The Army was happy to pay to solve the problem for both of them. A scholarship to one of the better Convent residential schools. The four years there until she was expelled, were far happier than the four before, from when he had started showing her how much he loved her. She had learned that happiness was a relative concept, particularly when the relatives were perverse. Even by the Convent School inmates high standards, she was sexually advanced and educated beyond her years. The natural progressions were made, from young boys, to older girls and onto real men. She gave what they wanted and never understood what it was she was not given back in exchange. It was the drugs rather than the sex that got her the exit visa from education. She had been a bright child, intelligent enough to rebel against almost all of what she was taught. She had been described as having an artistic temperament. Acting came naturally to her, a nurtured gift from her father. All her life was role and performance. After leaving school, she searched through a few roles before settling in Hull, where she joined a Youth Theatre Group, and made a living, just, helping painting scenery and making costumes, for which she had a definite talent. She was allowed to play the occasional bit part, and she had known that once age and maturity was added to her undoubted beauty, she was destined to become an actress. It was just a matter of time and luck.

In 1983 she had come with the company to Edinburgh, where they were putting on a production in the Festival Fringe. She had fallen in love, with the city, with the Festival, and with the funny man who came every night to sit in the front row and applaud every one of her four two-line speeches. She had stayed on after her company went back south of the border. She had stayed on after her new friend proved himself as south of the border as the rest. She had allowed herself to become totally dependent on him, for accommodation, finance, company, stimulation and purpose. Then he had betrayed her. In little ways at first but then in a major one. He had hurt her badly and she had vowed never again to let a man close enough to her to inflict that degree of hurt and pain. She told Frank she had kept to that since then and her subsequent relationships with men only reinforced for her what pathetic and unreliable creatures they were. The pain of her loss had made it a long hard winter for her. She had fallen foul of the false promise

27

of white hope, and fighting disillusion, had injected illusion into her deepest veins.

At her lowest point, when death had seemed an attractive option her supplier had offered her cheaper supplies in return for a little night work. It had been remarkably easy, cleaner healthier sex than any she had known on her own terms. Simpler, less complicated and more rewarding. Or so her defences told her, although not totally efficiently, since she began the sad spiral of doing it to get the money for her habit, then indulging the habit more to help her cope with doing it. The Man never put her on the street, he felt she was too high-class an act for that. He just charged her rent for the use of his premises. She put herself on the street for extras, guided by her friend Flora. But she hadn't liked that at all. The total lack of control had not appealed to her.

The night he put Flora in hospital for corrupting her was the night the long climb back had begun. She had done it all herself, mostly. Fortunately there had been a Doctor amongst the clients he had secured for her, and in return for a free supply of her services he had helped her get off the beast and back to a semblance of health. But basically it was her own character and determination that got her off the drugs and off the street, and enabled her to stay off both. Slowly she had climbed up the hierarchy of her chosen profession. She had first of all worked from her little flat, but that had felt like violation, of her space rather than her body. Again she had used a client to help her move on, an Estate Agent with mortgage insurance connections. She had been able to buy a large and respectable flat in a reasonable part of the New Town. It was her golden rule never to use it for business. It was her private inviolate place. From her proud description Frank knew that any Social Background Report would drool over its respectability and tastefully furnished ambience.

She still regarded herself as an actress, but the size of her mortgage did not allow her to indulge her hobby. She had always promised herself that she would take a holiday from her business every Festival, and take on a small legitimate role. But it always turned out to be the most lucrative period of the year for her profession, and it made little economic sense to close for the duration. So she restricted her contact to her real love to the home-based costume-making contracts that provided her cover for her more lucrative professional activities. And she deluded herself that she was still practising the skills of the acting trade, in a way that would come in useful when she made the change. Night after night, she gave performances, and played out roles. She had a full range, each accompanied by a clever and stunning uniform, made by herself, and an interesting range of accessories. Her pattern was always to arrange her performances for hotels, good hotels. She would turn up in normal clothes, respectable outfits, then change on the premises for the performance. She was not an exotic dancer, her performances were not done to music. She created little scenarios and involved the audience in the final production. Her audiences were generally the same size as some of the Fringe crowds she had performed before, one or two or occasionally three. She had a golden rule, a mathematical formula that helped her survive. Two cost each one twice as much as one, three thrice as much. For four or more, it reverted to the basic rate for each, but she touched them, they did not enter her. These group performances were surprisingly popular in certain Edinburgh legal and business circles, and she preferred them often to the more personal individual performances.

Her business operated by word of mouth, a phone number and a contact point. She preferred regulars, but would occasionally take on a new client if they came recommended by another regular or a working girl. She never worked less than four sessions a week, and never more than ten. This gave her in theory, a gross income of over £60,000 a year, which paid her mortgage and allowed her to indulge the expensive tastes which maintained her sanity at a tolerable level. She had never been charged, even during her spell on the street, and did not have a criminal record. She knew a few policemen, but they tended to be of high rank, and friendly. Frank noted that she earned as much as Paddy and Peter McColl, but he had always regarding lawyers as prostituting themselves with less regard for the truth. The other thing she told Frank about was her relationship with Flora, some of the truth of it anyway. It was clear that it was based on the events of the bleakest hours, during that long cold dead winter, when she had been so down and near to the end. Flora had been the first and only person in her life to risk herself in order to help Julie, and ever since then she had been trying to repay the favour. She was currently involved in a race against time in an enterprise to save Flora's life. Julie had a plan, a vision that had sustained her through many a harrowing performance, of a Boarding House in Bridlington where a living could be made, and an opportunity found to retread the boards. She had an option with the owner, which she was near to calling in. It would have to be soon, if Flora was to join her, so she had stepped up her activities which was why she had taken Hazel's referral. She was near to reaching her target and quitting, a few more thousands and it would be over.

That gave Frank his chance. He could put his proposition into some kind of context and keep alive his relationship as some kind of counsellor. He showed her a picture of McGoldrick he had cut out of the paper. Yes, she knew him, he was one of her regulars, a Mr William Ross, a teacher from one of the posher Edinburgh schools, or so she reckoned. Frank explained that he had a personal score to settle with the man, that he didn't want to hurt him, just to reach an agreement with him not to do something. He wanted Julie's assistance in reaching that state. He assured her that it did not involve blackmail, or breaking any laws. He would pay her £1,000 now, on a promise of her co-operation, and a balance of £4,000 when the deed was done. He had intended to haggle, maybe only offer £2,000 or £3,000, but the money didn't really matter to him, and he liked her so he offered the full amount. He also explained to her that if it worked out the way he anticipated, then it was also possible that she could get at least a similar amount from Mr Ross himself. And if things went wrong, then she could keep anything that might be available from the tabloids, although he did not anticipate such an outcome. She said "You must really hate that man. I find that surprising. He always seemed such a sad and harmless man to me, a gentle man, not one likely to have real enemies. What did he do to you that was so terrible?"

Frank started to protest that he didn't hate him, but stopped himself. For all her obvious intelligence, Julie didn't seem like she would have much sympathy for the importance of football in life, and its relationship to politics, pride and self-truth. He assured her again that he would not hurt the man in any way, just wanted him to feel like Frank had once felt, then leave him to it. He told her Mr Ross's real name. He also told her Mr Wharton's. He knew that she might need to know it when Mr Ross contacted her. She asked how he had found out about her and him and he told her that a friend of his, a hotel porter, had seen them together. He had described her, and then Frank had got a friend of his who was a prostitute, to find out where she was and to make an appointment. She didn't seem interested in the detail so he left it at that. She asked if McGoldrick was famous. She said she had never heard of him, but had once seen him on television without hearing him but thought nothing of it.

At last they were ready for the core of it. He showed her his tape-recorder and said that if she was agreeable, he wished to tape the details of her contact with McGoldrick. She looked at him long and hard. She was still recovering from having bared her soul to him rather than her body. It must have taken an exceptional man to get her to do that, and she still wasn't sure of the implications. She looked into his eyes and decided to go with her instincts. She tossed her head back, smiled at him and said "Okay, Frank. I'll trust you. Let's go for it". He smiled back and thanked her, and told her he was grateful to her and he would make sure she didn't regret it. He switched on the machine and started his new game. He showed her again the picture from the paper, naming the paper, date and page number. He asked her if she knew that man and who he was. She replied "Yes, I know him. He is one of my regulars. His name is William Ross and I believe he is a teacher in an Edinburgh school." He asked her how long she had known him. "Since June 1989. He phoned me up, saying he had been recommended to me by one of my other regulars, and could he meet me. I met him for the first time in the Thistle Hotel. I've met him there, or in the Holiday Inn in Glasgow, about once a month ever since then. He always books a suite, living room, bedroom and bathroom". The details continued to come, in clear, crisp and concise terms. She would make an excellent witness. After each session he would give her an envelope. The first had contained the agreed £150, and a note giving the date, time and place of the next assignation. Every subsequent one had contained £200, and a similar note.

Yes, she was an efficient administrator and record-keeper, she had kept the notes, along with a record of every appointment. Yes, the notes were all in his own handwriting. No, he had never paid by cheque, always by cash. Yes, Frank could have a copy of the full list, and the originals of one or two of the notes. It was the same routine every time. Yes, she would describe it for him in detail. She did, and even he was quite unprepared for what came next. He had known from Hazel that she used the name Margaret Beattie with her clients. Hazel had explained to her that she had already told him that her name was Julie so she had used that with him. What he did not realise was that Margaret Beattie's story was even more dramatic than Julie's tale. She dictated it straight into the tape-recorder and he never interrupted her once. He was too busy trying to visualise the transaction as she described it. He concentrated so intensely that by the end, he could have recited it

31

back, word for word, without the assistance of the machine, but he was still glad he had got it on tape.

****

The tall schoolgirl adjusted her tunic to make sure everything was in order, she needed to look as smart as possible for this. She checked the blouse was buttoned all the way up, her seams were straight, and her white shoes shiny. She felt as she always did on these occasions, an empty nervousness in her stomach. She braced herself for what lay ahead and knocked twice, hesitatingly, on the solid oak door.

"Enter", came the imperious command from the other side. Margaret opened the door and walked nervously in. She always felt the same apprehension as she almost crept towards him over the plush carpet. The room looked like an impressive place of study. The large desk dominated it, with work files laid across it in untidy piles. "Oh yes, Beattie, stand there a minute" the Headmaster said curtly, without appearing to raise his eyes from the papers in front of him. The wait was always the worst part. She marvelled at the way his mere presence induced in her guilt feelings that had remained long dormant. Finally he looked up, put his pen carefully to the side and gave Margaret his full attention which disconcerted her more than his inattention. "Right, Beattie, you know why you are here?" There was a rhetorical edge to the question that stifled any reply from her and increased her feelings of fear. It was not physical fear. The pain was never acute, and the bruises never lasted more than a day or two. It was a fear based on the knowledge of his ability to create in her a feeling of guilt, as if he could make her feel responsible for all her own sins, and everyone else's too. He was much superior at that, than any of the nuns she knew. He eyed her up and down, taking in every detail, the short black gym tunic, the plain white blouse with the black bra underneath clearly visible, the black stockings slipped into the shiny white leather shoes.

"Right", how she hated that word as a symbol for all that was to come. "What is this I've been hearing about you, Beattie. Miss Tompkins tells me she has caught you again. That you have been a very naughty girl, once more, despite the severe warning I gave you the last time. She tells me that she found you and that boy Jenkins, behind the bike shed in what she has delicately described as a compromising position. Is that correct?" "Yes, sir" she blurted out on cue. He gazed at her with a look she could almost mistake for genuine sadness. "I need to know exactly what happened. I want you to tell me, and show me everything that happened there". "It was Jenkins, sir. He made me go there with him. He said he would tell everyone he'd screwed me, if I didn't go with him. I didn't want to, sir, honest." "And what happened then". He appeared totally unmoved by her protestations of innocence. "He kissed me, sir. And stuck his tongue inside my mouth." The next bit always surprised her, even though she knew it was coming. He grabbed her awkwardly and kissed her roughly, forcing his tongue into her mouth. It was as if he were choking, rather than her. "Like that?" he asked, after a moment or two. "Yes, sir, just like that" she nodded meekly. "Right then, what did he do next?" "He pulled the top of my tunic down and unbuttoned my blouse." He pulled down the top of her tunic and unbuttoned her blouse. "And then what?" "He slipped his hands round and undid my bra" It usually took him up to three attempts before his cold hands managed the feat, and then he withdrew them completely. "And then?" "He squeezed my breasts, sir." She had used tits at first but he had winced too much at the vulgarity and altered the script to the more proper term "and started to suck my nipples". He inserted his hands and squeezed her tits, gently and slowly, making the nipples rise. He rubbed each one in turn between his thumb and forefinger, then bent his head down and sucked each one. "Like that?" came up, muffled, from around her chest. "Yes, sir, like that" she said patiently. He never sucked for more than a minute or two. It was as if he didn't see any point to the activity. His face would come back up, looking slightly perplexed, like a baby whose rattle didn't make a noise anymore. "Then what?" "He told me to masturbate him" Wank him off was edited out after the first run, to be replaced by the more dignified version. "So I..."

He stopped her at that and changed tack slightly. "Show me what you did" She unbuttoned his trouser belt and pulled down his zip. The face remained imperious and unmoved. With a little difficulty, she extricated his erect penis from his expensive underpants and brought it out to join the cast and play its part. She rubbed her hand up and down his member twice, and stopped. "It was at this point that Miss Tompkins found us, sir". On one early occasion she had gone four strokes and he had ejaculated all over her hand. He had been mortified at that, and the script had been altered to make sure it didn't happen again, although she often felt from its firmness and quiver that he was still close. "All right then,

Margaret, that will do". He readjusted his dress and put away his penis. He turned, to give her the full facial treatment. "You realise that you will have to be punished. I cannot allow this kind of behaviour to be tolerated in my school. If I turn a blind eye to this, they will all being doing it. I am afraid, very much afraid, I am going to have to give you six of the best." He paused to allow the impact of his words to sink in. "Palms or buttocks". She knew the right answer and in her best girlish voice said "Buttocks, please, sir."

He pulled the chair out from behind the desk and placed it beside her. He sat down on it and looked her straight in the thigh. "Bend over, Beattie". She bent over his knees so that her head and chest were on his left side. She was able to support herself with her hands on the floor, with her bum over his knees, and her long legs stretching over his right side down to the floor. He pulled her gym tunic up to her waist and draped it over her back up towards her head. Her suspender belt, stockings and navy-blue school knickers must have been a peculiar combination, but he proceeded as he always did. First he disconnected her right stocking and slid it gently down her leg, past her calf and off over her ankle and foot. Then he did the same with the left one. "These will just get in the way" he said in a matter of fact way, as if asking a boy to take off a pair of gloves. He unhooked the suspender belt, first time, but let it drape over his knees rather than remove it. He then gripped her knickers firmly with both hands and proceeded to pull them down but not off, exposing her bare buttocks.

He then beat her with the palm of his open right hand, hard. It was sore but not unbearable. Stinging rather than acute. She didn't move or make any sound. The agreed deal was six smacks with each hand, but each time he seemed to get carried away and administer more. She could feel his still erect penis throbbing beneath her. Finally he stopped, and slumped forward. That was her cue to cry, to sob gently and give her performance. "You promised you would only do it six times, each hand. That's not fair." "I know, I know" he said in an awful, wretched, strangled voice. "I am sorry. I am very very sorry. I have been a really bad boy. Please forgive me. I have been very wrong, just like you. I must be punished too."

They always did the role reversal in hushed tones, more suitable for a religious rite than an educational wrong. He would take out from under the left shoulder of the long black gown he had worn throughout, a long shiny black belt, split in the middle into two prongs. He would caress it gently before handing it over to her, introducing it to her as "Old Faithful", now over 60 years old. She found it hard to reconcile his obvious care and attachment to this polished piece of finely stitched leather. He once told her, in the nearest he ever came to casual conversation that he had never been in favour of the double split, and triple prong, too excessive, too violent. He had told her that he had not been allowed to use "Old Faithful" in his work for several years now. It was a matter of some regret to him. He had told her that he prided himself on maintaining a high level of discipline in his school, and that corporal punishment had very seldom been necessary, but he firmly believed that it had had a useful role to play. It had had a deterrent effect on the many, and was a necessary corrective for the few. It was a measure of swift justice, appreciated, understood and accepted by the recipient in a way none of the replacements ever were. He took of his gown and helped her on with it. She found that she enjoyed the next part more than she felt she should. "Right, Ross, do you know why you are here?" She was quite proud of the imperious note she could bring to her tone. "Yes, Miss. I have been a bad boy, and I have to be punished." Somehow the voice was that of a six year old, quiet, hesitant and high. It did not belong to the man who had been there earlier. "Yes. So what will it be? Palms or buttocks?" "Buttocks please, Miss." She pulled his trousers down to his knees, then his underpants too. His penis was always flaccid by this time. She wasn't sure whether he always came or not, but there was often semen dripping on his penis and in his underpants.

She cleared the edge and middle of the desk of all his work papers, and put them carefully on the floor. She found out one time she just jumbled them all together, that they were real and not for theatrical effect. He did use the room to work, and that was why he always had to have a fair sized desk. She then got him to grip each edge with one hand. "Bend over, Ross" was the only command required, and he would bend right over with his face prone on the surface and his buttocks gleaming white at her. She then proceeded to hit him twelve times. She had tried to soften the blows but had learned he would only insist, so she gave him good measure and true. There wasn't room on his neat bum for twelve different strokes without covering the same ground more than once, and it was obvious to her that some considerable pain must be involved, but he never made a sound, not ever even a whimper. Whatever satisfaction he got, his penis was always as flaccid after the last blow as at the first. When she finished, he would pull his trousers up, while she slipped off her gown and became a nervous schoolgirl again. "Right, Beattie" the commanding Head would say "That will be all." "Take that envelope with you on the way out" were always the final words, and she would slip back into the bedroom from whence she had come, remove her uniform, pack it away, and put back on her smart and conservative clothes. She always checked the envelope but it always contained £200 in £20 notes and a note saying "Report to me at 6:15 p.m. on Friday 10th or whenever, giving the location and room number of accommodation obviously already booked."

By the time she came back out of the bedroom, without knocking, he would always be back at the desk, working away as if none of it had ever happened. She knew better than to try any casual conversation with him, and just slipped out quietly.

The routine was always the same. He was obviously a man who relied on the security of routine as much as Frank Hunter had learned to do. She would arrive at the room door, he would be working at the desk. He would show her into the bedroom, where she would close the door and transform herself into the schoolgirl. When she was ready, she would knock on the door and off they would go. Once the script had been knocked into a shape satisfactory to him, it was never altered. The only times he ever engaged her in any kind of social intercourse was in the brief period at the start of the evening before entry into roles. Even then his conversations tended to be about belts, and schools.

She had almost enjoyed it initially. He seemed to have more conception than most of her punters that this was a performance business, a piece of living theatre in which they were the cast of two. He seemed to appreciate that her talent was as an actress. That what they were striving to achieve together was to create art in action, the release of tension through the acting out of drama. He was by no means the weirdest of her regulars. Indeed in many ways, despite the beatings, he was amongst the gentlest and most normal. Nor was his little scenario anyway near the most bizarre she got involved in, just the most carefully crafted and the most literate. The school girl uniform was a classic. She already had it, and used it often, long before he added himself to her list of regulars. Some of her others liked it a lot, but none on such a formalised basis. She told Frank how Mr Ross had requested only one change to her original uniform. He had asked her to replace the silky black briefs with a longer pair of old Navy Blue school knickers. Quite a few of her other customers liked being beaten. One thing she had learned from Mr Ross was the belt. She had subsequently bought one of her own, although she couldn't find a Lochgelly. She had been surprised how many of the others enjoyed her introduction of that, volunteered for it, even begged for it, and offered to pay extra for it. He had definitely helped her improve her act, extend her repertoire and enhance the services she provided. She put up her rates, and no-one complained. She had much to be grateful to him for.

With the tape still running Julie confirmed that Mr Ross had never penetrated her, had never attempted to do so. Frank wasn't perturbed by that. Indeed he felt a brief stab of shame at how superior that knowledge made him feel. He knew that what the man did do with her was even more damaging to him politically than a good straightforward fuck would have been.

"He won't lose his job, will he?" she asked Frank. "I really don't want to hurt him in any way." "No, I can assure you about that. I'm not going to take anything from him, his job, his wife, his money. I'm just going to repay a little lesson with interest. He will offer you money though, and you'll have to work out whether or not you want to take it." She agreed to work with Frank and to take his money. He gave her the envelope with 20 £50 notes in it. He was pleased that she didn't open it and check the amount. He had no reservation about giving her the money. He had this strange sensation that he knew her very well and that he could afford to trust her completely. She was already a friend of his. He explained to her what the next stages would be and how she should react.

Frank confirmed for himself that Mr Ross knew how to contact Julie. He had phoned her number to make the first appointment. Frank started his tape again at the next bit. Only once more had Mr. Ross phoned her, requesting a special appointment, for that evening. He had seemed desperate, so she had rearranged things, to fit him in. That night, he seemed to get stuck at the breast sucking stage. He just kept his face pressed close to her breast, with her nipple in his mouth. he stayed there still, quiet, unmoving for what seemed to her forever, script and scenario forgotten or frozen. Julie had eventually felt the need to move the action on, slightly worried at his state. She had taken down his zip and brought out his penis, which was as erect as it usually was at that point in the process. Her action galvanised him back into life, but his heart had definitely not been in it. He had beaten her more

37

vigorously and longer than usual and in turn asked her, almost begged her, to hit him more often herself. Some instinct made her decide not to humour him. She had stopped and tried to make a joke out of it, saying "You've had your whack then, six of each, a deals a deal" and he had reluctantly let it go. He had given her double money that night, and she had felt some sorrow for the obvious torment in his soul.

Frank received two bonuses. He found out that Julie already had a good quality telephone answering machine so he would not have to lend her his or buy her one. She had bought it for herself, for her business, the best on the market. It would have been tax-deductible, if she paid tax. Frank confirmed that it could record incoming calls, even when they were answered, without the caller being aware of that, and that she had a good supply of blank tapes. The other piece of luck was that the next appointment was due the coming Thursday. With her being English he had to confirm that in fact her "next Thursday" was this Thursday, not the following one. Room 212, Holiday Inn, Glasgow at 7:15pm. He would have waited however long, but with the excitement and energy he was feeling, he wanted the matter progressed as soon as possible.

He ran through for her the sequence of events once more. She was quick, he could see she was filling in the blanks for herself. Soon he was satisfied that the next stage could proceed. Their business was over. There was still 30 minutes left of the time he had paid for. She asked him almost as a joke if he wanted his moneys-worth in the time left. He knew, or thought, she was offering him straight sex between consenting adult friends, and thanked her for that. He told her that he had a close girlfriend and that fidelity was important to him, but that he knew that they were going to be friends no matter how things turned out. If it was a test, he seemed to pass, as did the disappointment felt in his willie at the denial of what he knew would have been a very pleasant experience.

Driving back from Edinburgh, Frank felt ecstatic, more alive and aware than he had been for months, if not years. He was getting better, he would be himself again soon. He knew he had the winning of his game in hand. He would subject McGoldrick to the wrong end of a subtle choice, and do the Labour Party a bit of good into the bargain. He began to look forward to the evening, to savouring the taste of triumph as well as Guinness and Madras.

He left his car and walked through the streets, still at peace with the world. He picked up Joyce at her flat and surprised her by

38

the warmth of his welcome. He relayed to her all the information that he had gleaned from his earlier meeting with Tom Paterson from LDT, implying without actually saying that the meeting had been earlier that evening rather than that week. She was looking forward to the evening, the more so since he seemed in such good mood. She liked both Danny and Sheila, and was learning to see the better side of Paddy. Christine she liked, but then everyone did. As well as the three couples, Gerry Robertson and Peter McColl had been invited to join them for at least some of the evening. It was Sheila's birthday and she had chosen a few drinks and then a curry at the Manzil rather than a more formal evening. Frank had given Joyce £20 to buy a present from both of them, and made the right noises when she showed it to him.

They were in the Victoria Bar before 9:30 and he soon caught up with rounds missed. The Guinness was on fine form and he still felt good. They talked about the football and how Celtic were coming back onto a game at the right time for the Cup, although the wishful thinking surpassed the objective assessment. They lamented Archibald's disappearance from Edinburgh, but cheered themselves up at the prospect of the forthcoming SAD trip to Barcelona. Sheila asked an awkward question. Were women allowed to be SAD people? They let Frank answer that one. He was the expert on SAD nuances and rules. Yes, he said, women were allowed into a state of SADness, but only if they met the criteria for membership. They had to display a history of devotion to the great man, and recount in detail four chances he had missed that mattered to them, and two goals he had scored that had affected their lives. Sheila had come too late to being a Clyde sympathiser to remember the early days. She had seen the misses all right, for Aberdeen against her Celtic but couldn't produce the emotional identification with his goals, so was deemed to have failed the test. Joyce was definitely not eligible, she had never even seen the man, for God's sake. Nonetheless, Frank decreed that they could accompany them to Barcelona if they wished, as visiting non-members, the same category Peter McColl always used, since he refused to recognise the status of the Man as a hero. Sheila and Joyce openly toyed with the notion of going along on the trip at the end of April. In a secret meeting in the toilet, Frank and Danny compared notes and agreed they would not mind at all if they chose to come.

CHAPTER THREE - THE BITTER TASTE OF VICTORY

Scunnered was the word Frank Hunter would have used to describe himself that Saturday night in March, as he sat in the Victoria Bar. Strange to understand on the face of it, with four pints of Guinness in his belly, and a Chicken Madras to come. He had a beautiful and friendly lady companion hanging onto his arm and his every word, as if the latter were valuable instead of just rare. He was in the company of some of his oldest and closest friends. His team had won 2-0 away from home that afternoon. He'd been there and enjoyed it. And most of all, after the session with Julie earlier that evening, he knew he had McGoldrick right where he wanted him. He had won a victory over his oldest ghost.

But that was the problem. He realised with a sudden horror what was wrong. That irritation in his soul was the worst feeling he knew, the bitter taste of victory. It contradicted all his basic principles and philosophy, that winning was, if not the most important thing, at least the point of any game. The nasty aftertaste of defeat was something he knew well, as a player and supporter, and as a person. It was a feeling he hated but had learned to live with. The blind, intense anger directed at the opposition, his team-mates but most of all himself. He had disciplined himself over the years to the point where he could now pretend to congratulate the winners and avoid picking fights with his fellow losers. He knew the rage would ruin Saturday nights, and not a few relationships, but it gradually relapsed and by Sunday morning there were the stupid bastards in the papers to tirade against and the world could return to normal with a pint or two at lunch-time.

No, this was something much worse, this sense of the futility of victory. It was the feeling he dreaded most of all things in the world. It threatened the whole point of life itself. Three or four times before he had felt it, each time it had led him to act disastrously. A bead of chilled sweat trickled down his neck, prompted by genuine fear. He suppressed the thought that it was a pity the beer wasn't that cold and concentrated instead on a greater concern, how would he fuck it up this time?

Memories of the first time he was conscious of feeling this disembowelling pain forced their way out, and he abandoned any pretence at socialisation to surrender completely to the pursuit of full recollection. His body stayed there, sitting in the pub, letting the conversation float over him, smiling appropriately, but the rest of him left the company and wandered off in desperate search of the origins of the feeling, in the hope that he could find any clue that would help him to handle it differently this time. He knew he was still far too fragile too cope with another disaster.

It was a journey back twenty years, he made with one sip of his pint, back to the happier days of 1970. Frank had often made that journey before, usually in the picture house of his mind, to watch a film called "The Biggest Mistake of My Life". This time he altered the title slightly to "The Bitter Taste of Victory - The First Savouring" but it was essentially the same grainy old film, with a very familiar plot and predictable punch-line.

Once the credits rolled, Frank, the hero, emerged from the mist. He was school team captain and St Anne's were in the Final of the Scottish Schools Cup. They had some good players. He counted two that had made it with him into the Seniors and two more that should have done but didn't. He had known though, that the Final would be tight and that they needed him in top form to have any chance of beating Clydesdale High who were much more experienced, and rightly fancied to win by the group of senior scouts and other old men that followed these things. He had never looked forward to anything more in his life. And then it had happened, his big mistake.

The day had started well. It was a Monday, with the Final due that Saturday. He had walked to school as usual, pleased with the world and himself, with none of the tension or anger that had been a feature of much of that year so far. He spent most of the journey planning the game in his mind, with the climax, him as captain lifting the cup.

First thing was always Assembly. Old MacDonald had never bothered with such things, and the school was lucky if they congregated together once a month. But it was one of the first things McGoldrick, the new Headmaster, had instituted, part of his 'school as a community' philosophy, a morning assembly for the entire school. Frank was late and slipped into the side of the hall where his mates tended to congregate. The junior pupils sat in the rows and the seniors stood at the back and the sides. The format was seldom varied. A hymn, a prayer, the Headmaster's address, another hymn, another prayer, some announcements and then off to registration.

The Headmaster was in fine form, his thoughts for today being laid out in a precise and ordered manner. Frank was politically aware enough at 16 to know what he was at, the subtle and insidious indoctrination of his conservative values, fed every morning to the assembled masses in the hope that some of it might soak in subliminally to at least a few of them, aided by the added authority of his position as God in this place. It worked with too many for Frank's comfort, as they both knew the long-term value of getting them young. That day's message was about individual responsibility and collective guilt, the importance of the individual having the strength to resist, in the face of group pressure to do what they were not certain was right. He knew this was a coded denunciation of the Engineers' strike that had dominated the media over the weekend. Nasty things, Trade Unions, and many of the pupils who had not yet had their real education would probably agree. Many of the older ones had already reckoned that with a bit of luck they would never even have to join a real Trade Union.

Frank had been considering this as the second hymn began. He never sang as, apart from his religious objections, he was tone deaf. He became vaguely aware that two or three of the boys beside him were playing a stupid game with the song. One was half a word ahead, another was half a word behind and Joe Anderson was deliberately squeaky. They had co-ordinated it well and there was some confusion, as well as a growing number of titters. He yawned, then grinned and added his silent giggle to the chorus, as he realised the impact of their actions. During the following prayer, he was looking around the hall as usual, when his eye caught the Headmaster's. The words kept flowing smoothly but there was no doubt that he was staring straight into Frank's open eyes. Frank stared right back. He wasn't ashamed of his atheism or frightened of this Tory bastard.

Frank only half-listened to the string of announcements, he was already back to his fantasy visions of how wonderful Saturday would be. But he heard the final one. "Will Frank Hunter report to the Headmaster's Office immediately after Assembly." Christ, it wasn't an offence not to pray, surely to God. Maybe the man wanted to offer him tactical advice for Saturday. He'd had such a summons once or twice before. Each time it had resulted in a meeting with Old Faithful. The pain had never bothered him, only a nagging feeling that he should be beyond this by now. He'd gone through the third year with only the occasional belting, but this last year was even worse than before. Nothing trivial though, only a series of sixes, most of them from the Headmaster. It couldn't be that this time, he hadn't done anything.

He knocked firmly on the door twice. "Enter" came the imperious command from the other side. Frank opened the door and walked confidently in. The room was large. It was quite different from any other in the school. The most noticeable thing in it was the carpet. Some of the wee-er first year pupils were rumoured to have disappeared when asked to stand in it. Frank knew it was thicker than the grass at Hampden Park. The massive mahogany desk was positioned so that anyone standing in front of it in the morning, the normal time for executions, was staring into the rising sun. There were portraits of the previous Headmasters on the walls. Frank glowered at the image of old MacDonald. What a bastard he had been. There wasn't a single boy in Frank's year who hadn't been abused by that old shite. He had clearly enjoyed beating children. Even Frank had no doubts but that McGoldrick was a vast improvement. The school was a much happier, more civilised place under his regime. The last year had seen many significant changes, all for the better.

"Right, Hunter, you know why you are here?" It was a rhetorical question although Frank didn't know the answer. "I will not tolerate such anarchistic attempts to undermine the seriousness and importance of Assembly." He realised from the icy steeliness that the man was genuinely upset. "I am going to make an example out of you to show every one in the school just how unacceptable such behaviour is. You will take six of the belt and will stand in front of the Assembly for the rest of the week leading the singing in a proper and dignified manner". As he spoke these words, Frank knew what had happened. The Headmaster had located the direction of the disruption and had seen Frank standing there in the middle. He looked him straight in the face and said, as calmly as he could manage, "It wasn't me, sir. I can't even sing." "Do not argue with me, boy. I know what I saw. Hold out your hands."

For a brief second Frank considered complying with that request, then he took one of these seemingly innocuous decisions that turn out to fuck up your whole life. "No. I didn't do it. You can't punish me for that. It's ludicrous. I never sing at Assembly." It wasn't that he was frightened of the pain. It wasn't even that he couldn't tolerate the injustice of being belted for something he hadn't done. Just the week before, old Thomson had given him two of the belt which he'd taken calmly enough, even though it wasn't

43

him that had thrown the rubber. These things tended to average out. No, this was more personal. McGoldrick had made a mistake and he wasn't going to let him away with it.

McGoldrick looked very hard right at him. "In that case you will be able to tell me exactly who it was that disrupted the hymn." Frank shook his head in a way that left both of them in no doubt that this was not an option. "Very well, I shall continue to assume that it was you. You have a choice, Hunter. Either you accept six of the belt yourself or you tell me who was responsible so that I can punish them. If you fail to do either, you will be suspended from the school, and all school activities, for the rest of the term." Like a punch to the stomach, Frank immediately felt the significance of the second part of the last sentence. No Cup Final appearance for him on Saturday. "That's blackmail." he managed to say, as the anger and indignation overcame other calculations.

"Do not be impertinent, boy. It is not blackmail. It is facing you with the consequences of your actions. Report to my office first thing after Assembly tomorrow and let me know your decision." The interview was terminated.

He wandered down the corridor, almost in a state of shock. Why and how had this happened and what the hell should he do about it? He reckoned McGoldrick had originally thought it had been him leading the singing. However he guessed that the Head Master had realised during the interview that he had been mistaken. Whatever else he thought of him, he knew Frank was both honest and not frightened of a little physical punishment. Why he had taken the opportunity presented to put him in difficulty, was a more complicated matter. They had crossed swords several times, the 34 year old Head, the bright new hope of the Scottish Tory Party, and the 16 year old Secretary of the Southside Labour Party Young Socialists. The Head had forbidden him to publicise the Young Socialists within the school and made him take all posters off notice-boards. Most of the teachers were sympathetic, and had happily colluded in his political activities within the school and his use of school resources, but the Headmaster would have none of it. Then there had been the Tory public meeting where McGoldrick had been on the platform and Frank had asked a question about an aspect of Conservative education policy, knowing that McGoldrick had recently published an article contrary to that policy and almost identical to Labour's position. But that was good, clean fun and well within normal rules of combat.

No, if it was anything personal it had to be the recent school Mock Election, held as a prelude for the real campaign just starting. Frank had used his unusual influence with the older pupils, based on his personality, intellect and Young Socialist position, to get himself nominated as the Tory spokesman. Not that there had been much competition, the legitimate loyalists preferring a low profile. He had got himself billed as Ted Teeth Hunter. He had stuffed a pillow up his jumper and had heaved his shoulders throughout his performance. Grand comedy it was not, but his audience, the entire school, had loved it. He had deliberately kept the piss-taking from going over the top completely. He had played the political comment straight to start with, although the concessions to and praise of the Labour Government increased steadily throughout his initial speech. It was in the questions and closing summary that he had really gone to town. He had planted his Young Socialist pals throughout the audience to stand up and ask serious questions about the strength of Labour's case and the contradictions within the Conservative position. Each time he would nod his head sagely, admit that the questioner was right and maybe he, Ted Teeth, had got it wrong. Then he would laugh nervously and the shoulders would go great guns. The audience caught the pattern and would wait delightedly for each punch-line. There had also been the tasteless and immature question planted with Paddy McGuire about why he had never married, and the limp wristed response. That was the one bit he had regretted in retrospect.

The summation had been his masterpiece. One by one he went through the major policies, admitting he was wrong and Labour was right and concluding that in all honesty he had no choice but to recommend to the audience, indeed beg them, that they vote for the Labour candidate. He had received a massive standing ovation. He knew there was a danger there but he had worked out beforehand that he couldn't lose. If they followed his direction and voted Labour then he had won an important political victory. If they rewarded his performance by voting for him, it would be seen as a personal triumph for him rather than a political victory for the Tories. Either way it would deflect attention away from the emotional appeal of the SNP. He had been clear in his own mind that he would prefer the political victory to the personal one and that was what he got. The margin of the Labour victory had been considerably more than the school bookie had been predicting, with the SNP comfortably beating the Tory vote into third place.

He had known McGoldrick wouldn't be best pleased, but he had hoped he would appreciate the joke. No chance. One glimpse of his cold deadpan face had been enough to let him know that there would be a price to pay. So maybe this choice was it. This was McGoldrick's revenge.

He had several crisis meetings that day. The first one was in the toilets at the morning break with Didi and some of the others in the team. Tommy Gallagher, the team's hard man, was clear about the solution. Whether they wanted to or not, Joe, Archie and the other guilty parties would just have to go to McGoldrick, confess and say that Frank hadn't been involved. Frank knew that wouldn't solve the problem. McGoldrick would not put it past them to falsely confess to let their football star off the hook. Frank would still have to confirm that it was them. Anyway, Archie wasn't a strong or brave boy and would find six of the belt a terrifying prospect. Frank also knew he couldn't lie and say that it was Tommy or any of the other innocents who volunteered to take the blame to solve the problem. Nor would he break the code that said you didn't clype and shop your mates, whatever the consequences. He knew there were only two real choices open to him. To be prepared to take the punishment himself, which would be at least a tacit lie even if he didn't actually say he had done it, or to be suspended and miss the Final. His team-mates saw this as no problem. It was worth six of the belt to be guaranteed the game.

Separately from the pressure of their peers, Archie, Joe and Jack offered to own up if Frank asked them to do it. He appreciated their courage in making this offer but told them to forget it. It was his problem and he'd solve it one way or another without involving them.

The worst meeting had been with Davie in his little room off the gym, explaining to him that he might not make the Final. "The bastard, the absolute bastard. The man's a heid the ba'. Fucking rugby arsehole. He doesn't give a damn whether the School wins the cup or not. It's not part of his priorities at all. In fact it would suit the bastard's purposes better to be seen to risk sacrificing it on a matter of principle. Principle my arse." The tirade went on for a further five minutes or so. Frank had always liked Davie. He didn't seem like a teacher, he was more like a real person. McGoldrick had reprimanded him shortly after arriving at the school and had forbidden him to wear his tracksuit all the time as had been his previous practice. Frank knew that he didn't get paid for the many extra hours he put in training the football team. It was truly a labour of love, a love of football and everyone who played the beautiful game. They had all teased Davie as he had got more and more excited as the season wore on and the team got better and better. St Anne's had never won the cup, never even come close. They had produced many good players but none of them ever gave their best to the school since the teams as a whole were never quite right. Davie wasn't a good coach. It was Frank and Didi who decided how the team would play, but he was a good manager who could draw the right line when it was needed. Davie knew it would be futile, indeed counterproductive, for him to go to see McGoldrick. He wasn't good with words and always felt intimidated in the man's presence. He would probably end up appearing to agree that the Headmaster had no other choice. The only advice he could offer Frank was to do whatever was required to play. "It would make him happy if you missed the game, so don't give the bastard the satisfaction. You have worked very hard to get here. Some players go their whole career without getting a medal of any kind. Don't miss the chance."

As soon as he could Frank got right away from the school and everyone there. He didn't find their comments helpful or comforting. They didn't realise the nature of the problem as he saw it. The demands on his conception of his own integrity. The only person he could think of who could help him was John McLure. John had helped him a lot over the last few years, as his political identity developed. John was one of the old-school Labour Trade Union managers but with more integrity than most, and more interest in ideas. He was extremely well read and introduced Frank to an early diet of all the great political thinkers, and not just the Marxist ones. Old dusty books, brand new ones in their Left Book Club covers, but most of all library books. John must have cost Glasgow Corporation thousands of pounds as he exercised his democratic right to order every book he could possibly conceive of as relevant to read. He would tell Frank where to find them or pass them on to him for digestion and discussion. Hobbes was his favourite, appealing to his pessimistic and darker side, something he early realised he shared with Frank. They were unlikely allies in some ways, but John had taken an interest in Frank and his ideas ever since he had offered to help deliver leaflets in the 1966 General Election. Every year thereafter Frank had assisted John in his role as election agent at the Corporation elections, taking more and more responsibility each year. By 1969 Frank was effectively a sub agent, organising half a ward. Frank had joined the Labour

Party as soon as he could, on the day of his 15th birthday, the 4th of March, 1969.

John had been his guide to the use of resolutions and amendments, points of order and motions of no confidence as the key tools in the struggle for socialism. The loyalty generated had not survived intact the great Bye-Election campaign where Frank and his Young Socialist machine had been recruited by John to assist the Shop-keeper in his fratricidal struggle against the Minister. Although Frank had ended up for his own reasons delivering the votes for the better candidate against the better man, he never fully forgave John his collusion in the vicious tactics organised by Charlie Spence. The Grocer's campaign manager was a ruthless and unprincipled bastard. Like his shop-keeper crony Spence was a capitalist entrepreneur, a typical West of Scotland Catholic Mafia Socialist role-model. The owner of a haulage business, even his lorries had fallen of the back of other lorries. With every wee and big crook on the Southside his pal, he was a dangerous man to make an enemy of, but Frank succeeded despite being on the same side of a desperate fight.

The campaign against the principled Proddie had reached record depths. Ward packing, raising the dead, pints and pies for votes, favour cashing, rumour mongering, pulpit catholic card playing, all the black political skills had been deployed. And while John had not practised the worst examples he had known of them all and not disapproved and that had been enough to alienate the puritan Frank. For ever afterwards he was always his own man and made his own choices, taking nothing on trust from anyone. But he retained a degree of respect for his mentor and they often worked together.

John listened to his story attentively, the end of his glasses stuck in his mouth. He liked Frank. He wished his own children had Frank's political wit and intelligence. A pity about his conscience but he would learn as the defeats came. He was too interested in football, though. If you're going to take politics seriously, there's no time for anything else. "Aye son, I can see ye've got a problem there. As Ah see it, it comes down to whether you're more interested in football or politics. From what you say, he knows the real score, that you didnae do it, so if you put him in the position of punishing you for proclaiming your innocence, you'll have him on the back foot. Exploit that, force him to act wrongly and you'll gain a moral victory over him. On the other hand, if playing that game of football is more important to you, well then you know what to do."

"Aye thanks, that's really helpful, John." The ironic rebuke was wasted. Frank knew John had a very firm view of the relative importance of football and politics. Football was an occasional if enjoyable diversion from the real fight. He would never worry if a Party or union meeting was on the same night as a big game, unless he felt the defectors might affect a vote he wanted to win. Indeed one or two of his major triumphs had involved pushing things through on nights his opponents had got their priorities wrong. He'd been furious the time he caught Frank trying to rearrange a Young Socialists' meeting just because Celtic were playing a European Cup quarter- final. Frank had missed the game but learned his lesson. The first item of business at that meeting had been his resolution to change the meeting night to Tuesdays.

He left John's wee flat in Hutcheson and slowly made his way up Cathcart Road past the Citizens Theatre and the freight yard. He had never known the old Gorbals well. By the time he was old enough to walk the streets most of them had gone. Although his home was in the Gorbals constituency, he didn't live in the Gorbals. But he knew it well enough to know that 95% of everything written about it recently was shite. It was as safe as anywhere else and the people were better than most. Frank had lived all his life in Govanhill, first the wee private flat in Batson St, then the slightly bigger Corporation one on the top floor of the tenement in Seath St. This was the territory of Matt Craig and his wife. Frank was proud of that as a boy. He loved that book, read it time and again, although after the first time he missed out or skipped over all the bits about art to concentrate on the life. He got a special thrill when the real Matt Craig turned up at his Branch meetings. Frank did love the green bits of his dear place, and not just for playing football on. He realised that without consciously planning it, he had turned right off Cathcart Road instead of left for his home and he was now at the gates of the park that was to give the new name to his constituency. He liked to wander through this park on his own, especially at night. It was safe enough for a big boy like him. He liked walking round the pond, then up the hill to the allotments. He sat at the flagpole at the top and gazed north over Glasgow spread out below him. He did love the city, regarded it as an exciting place to stay. He couldn't envisage any other city offering him more. There was Celtic, Rangers (one without the other would be much less fun), Clyde and Partick

49

Thistle. He knew of 16 Cinemas and already, countless pubs. The only thing that irritated was that there was a Tory administration in George Square, but he knew it was doomed, just a matter of time until the natural order was restored. No, he didn't see any reason why he would ever move away.

The only club that had sent a scout to his door so far, was an English one, Notts County. Even though his mother knew their manager, who had played for Celtic, she had been very relieved when Frank had said he wasn't interested. He had no desire to live in England. He had the conceit to assume that there would be other offers, especially after the Final, but even if there weren't, he was pretty sure that he wouldn't give up everything and go down south. He felt part of something here, in a country and a city that were beginning to re-find their confidence. He wanted to go to university with fellow Scots, which ruled out St Andrews and Edinburgh but left two to choose from in Glasgow.

On the way home, he had decided to tell his parents what the score was. He waited until Coronation Street was over, as he knew his mother wouldn't be able to concentrate on anything else after he told her and the Street was her favourite relaxation. She was indignant at his story. "He can't punish you for something you haven't done". He didn't bother to explain to her the naiveté of that remark. He was very well aware that schools were not halls of justice. Day and daily minor and occasionally major injustices were inflicted on pupils, with no right of appeal. It wasn't the justice or otherwise of it that bothered him. It was his own morality and the correctness of his own actions that was his major concern. He hated lies and liars. He tried never to tell lies, whatever the consequences for himself. Only occasionally he conceded they might be necessary to save other people pain. He saw himself as a very moral person, who did what was right. He had already rejected religion and religious values but reckoned he could work out for himself a satisfactory set of moral rules. His mother had a somewhat similar outlook on life, although she used her Church to help her. She had always taught him the importance of the truth. "You do whatever you think is right, Frank. The important thing is to be true to yourself". It was the advice she always gave him, not telling him what to do, but how to do it. His father was more blunt and less help. "Tell him to piss off, then turn up on Saturday ready to play". They both knew he was struggling with some dilemma of his own creation, the exact terms of which they could not grasp, but they didn't know how to offer

50

much comfort or support. They knew him well enough to know he would work it out himself anyway. His father went to bed early and both of them knew he would be gone to work before Frank got up in the morning. All he said was "Goodnight, son". Two speeches in the one night, no wonder he was retiring early. His mother made Frank a cup of tea and tried to talk to him about other things but it was obvious his heart was not in it.

About ten o'clock, he went out for a walk on his own. Deep in his thoughts and calculations, he was unaware of where his route was taking him. It was passing Cathkin Park that made him aware of his surroundings. He felt a cold shiver as he looked back at the home of Third Lanark. Recently deceased. It shouldn't be allowed to happen to football clubs. He knew how upset he had felt and he wasn't even a supporter. For a real Hi-Hi fan it must have been an inconsolable pain when your beloved team doesn't exist any more. How had that bastard Hiddleston got away without being lynched? Frank had only known death close up through his mother's Aunts. He somehow knew the pain of the death of your team must be much worse. Two minutes later, he was outside the national stadium. He had walked the mile or so from his house to Hampden Park in 15 minutes. He gazed up at the stadium, with the North Stand towering over him. He noticed with dismay how shabby it looked, many of the windows were cracked or broken. But even so, there was a magnificence about it that thrilled him. He decided to walk right round it. As he did, some of the great games he had seen there came back to him.

Just the month before, he had been there three times in a fortnight. The best time had been the middle one, the European Cup semi-final against Leeds United. 135,000 at a club game, a European record. Celtic, the best of Scotland against Leeds, the pick if not the pride of England. He didn't like Leeds, cynical, dirty, untrue to their own potential. They had got their just deserts. Big Yogi had done for them, then Murdoch's cracker. Reluctantly he had been forced to admire Bremner. He was straight out of Hobbes, nasty, brutish and short, but he could play a bit and he had character and commitment. He had also been impressed by Lorimer's strength and Eddie Gray's skill. Frank knew his wee brother, had played against him often. He would be a great player too. He wondered if there was anything racially biased about his choice of stars to admire. No, that Giles was some player and he wasn't Scottish. There wasn't one of the English that would get a game for Celtic though. That night had made it official, Celtic

51

were the best team in Britain, soon to be re-crowned best in Europe. The recollection of that boast made him wince, but the pain soon passed. The game had made many Scots, not just Celtic supporters, happy that night. Frank closed his eyes and saw and heard again the crowd that night refusing to leave, demanding the team come out and take their tribute. Finally they had drifted off, happy. Once again, they had put one over on these arrogant English.

That got him thinking about some of the Scotland-England games he had seen. He fondly remembered the first one he had been to, in 1964. Scotland had won 1-0 and the 10 year old boy had gone home deliriously happy, reassured of the superiority of his nation. Unfortunately the one that seemed stuck in his mind was the 1966 game. That had been the opposite, a very depressing experience, not so much because England had won but rather because the manner of their victory had made him realise that it was quite possible that they would win the World Cup. And of course that's exactly what they did, the dirty bastards. Still at 4-3 it had been a great game to watch, and wee Jinky had been pure magic. Absorbed in his memories he came back round to Somerville Drive and the North Stand. He took a last proud look and headed off up Aikenhead Road back home. Like a trip to Mecca, his walk had reinforced his faith, faith in the value and importance of football. He now knew what he would do the next day. He would play in that Cup Final.

****

Realising suddenly he was no longer at Hampden but back at the Victoria Bar, he wondered what he had missed in the way of conversation while he had been in his little reverie. These days, they were used to him just sitting there in a world of his own. Sometimes they tried to bring him out of it and make him participate but other times, like tonight, they just let him take it at his own pace. He was vaguely aware that Gerry Robertson was expounding his latest theory about why devolution would never happen. It was the kind of argument that could normally rouse Frank from the dead, and produce some kind of retort in response. But this time he just let it quietly pass, squeezed his companion's hand to let her know he was still alive, and returned to his memories to explore again from where that awful feeling had first come.

****

"Enter" the voice sounded out firmly answering his tentative knock. He opened the door and slipped in as quietly as he could.

"Oh yes, Hunter. Stand there a minute" he said, indicating to the favourite spot in front of his desk. He continued writing into the note book in front of him for the longest three minutes Frank had known since he made the mistake of agreeing to settle his argument with big Willie Goldie in a boxing ring. Finally McGoldrick looked up, put his pen carefully to the side and gave Frank his full attention. "Right then, Hunter, have we thought any more about it ". The "we" jarred with Frank, this was not a co-operative enterprise. "What is it to be?"

"I'll take the belt, sir" Frank said in as controlled a voice as he could manage. "Admitting our guilt, are we then? " came the response. Frank had been straining to see if he would catch any intonation of disappointment but the tone was flat and controlled. He had known this would be the crunch. He couldn't deny it and succeed but he knew that he would not be able to admit it either. He relied instead on the inertia of dumb acceptance. McGoldrick appeared to think about it for a moment then to decide to settle for that. "Palms or buttocks?". In other situations Frank had found this choice hilarious, a vestige of his English experiences that had no echo in this place. Several boys had had their dose doubled by giggling hysterically when suddenly confronted with this prospect. The only boy foolish enough to experiment with this weird new option had been able to convince the rest of the school to stick to the safe and known. It was rumoured that he had made £1 10s by showing his marks in the toilet at a shilling a time. No-one knew whether or not to believe him that he had had to take his trousers and Y- fronts down, but they weren't curious enough to find out the hard way. "Palms, sir" said Frank. He knew the physical pain would be the easiest bit of the whole business.

McGoldrick was wearing his black gown over his smart suit. He always seemed to wear it before he performed. After his initial weeks, when he had worn it all the time, it had become a less and less frequent part of his normal working attire except when physical punishment was called for, or the School was in formal session. He kept "Old Faithful" under his gown, over his left shoulder. Frank watched him pull the belt out from its resting place. It was a famous belt, this one. It was long and black and very shiny. It was a true Lochgelly, with a wicked split in the middle. MacDonald claimed that he had had it made especially for him when he started in his first school, which would have made it well over 40 years old. It had been a legend in St Anne's ever since MacDonald had become Headmaster in the mid-Forties. Whole generations of Southside Catholic children had felt the pain that only a genuine Lochgelly can inflict, especially when wielded with force by a true believer in the corrective power of leather.

Whatever else could have been said about MacDonald he was not a sexist. Girls received the same measures as boys with only a minimum recognition for their frailty in the reduction of force. It had several times become an issue, the frequency and force with which he used it, but each time the Catholic hierarchy had supported him publicly. Only at the very end did Father Andrew have a quiet word in his ear that he had better tone down a little, or else, or so he had claimed to Frank's mother when she had remonstrated to him about its iniquity. When McGoldrick had arrived in June 1969 to work himself in for the final month alongside MacDonald, the old Headmaster had used a public forum in front of the assembled school to formally hand over his trusted enforcer to his successor. Frank had thought at the time that he could see distinct distaste on the new man's face and had confidently predicted that "Old Faithful" would join MacDonald in a well-earned retirement. It had been a shock and disappointment to him, and most of the younger teachers, when it had reappeared after the summer. To be fair, it was one of the very few parts of the former regime that did reappear. And he used it much less. The new Head had told a relieved school at his first solo assembly that he did not believe that corporal punishment should be necessary very often, but it did have its place in a well ordered school. He did not believe in it for girls at all.

Neither could he use it properly. Word had soon got round that "the new Headie cannae belt for toffee". No-one had told him that of course. And it still hurt. He had this funny habit of running his hands up and down both sides of it, then swishing it through the air with both hands on it. "Right, Hunter, both hands out please." Frank stared at him but could detect no emotion on his face. "This will teach you to disrupt my Assembly". As soon as the words were out he swung the belt back and brought it crashing down on Frank's outstretched hands. As soon as the words were out Frank knew he had made a mistake but that it was too late. Three times the stinging pain shot through his hands. "Right, cross them" and three times the other hand took the initial brunt. There was no doubt that he put more of himself into it this time than usual, but even so it was nothing special in pain terms. "You can go now and do not ever dare to do anything like that again." The issue of Frank leading the singing from the front of Assembly was quietly forgotten about.

The sickness Frank felt as he squeezed his hands between his thighs in the corridor was of the heart and not the body. Frank did not fully realise how until much later, but he knew that somehow McGoldrick had emerged from this episode truer unto himself than he had been.

Joyce came back with him to his flat, after their trip to the Manzil. In the restaurant, he had returned to their company from wherever he had been in the pub, and joined a little in over-Curry conversation, if obviously still subdued and thoughtful. His companions had noticed his abrupt change of mood with some anxiety. They had been very pleased with him earlier, pleased to see him so buoyant about the football, full of excitement and plans for Barcelona. He had looked better, sounded better, than they had seen or heard him for a long time. Then all of a sudden out of nothing, he had gone quiet and pale and slipped away from them. They let him go, they had learned over the recent past that that Frank could not be pushed or cajoled. Gerry had made one attempt to bring him back, with a political argument of the kind that the old Frank would have been unable to resist. Normally he would have been at Gerry's throat for his thesis that Labour's Scottish leadership could have no vested interest in a real Scottish Parliament, and therefore it would never happen, but this night he barely seemed to hear the arguments, far less wish to join in. So they left him to it and to Joyce to give him what comfort she could, holding his arm and his hand, and squeezing life into him whenever she felt a tremor.

When they were at last alone together, Joyce tried to explore the source of his mood. He kissed her and told her he was just a little depressed, that the earlier session with Paterson had awakened for him memories about the LDT Action Committee, his mother and what he had lost. She settled for accepting that as the explanation for his sadness, and took him to his bed and gave him her own special kind of anti-depressant medicine. She turned out to be of the old school, physical immersions and the laying on of hands. He submitted totally to the treatment but she had this curious feeling that somehow she lost him halfway through. She exorcised more than the devils in him, or maybe that was all he consisted of, with them gone there was nothing left. She lay there afterwards cuddling the sad and deserted hulk, kissing him gently and telling him lies, that he would be all right, and that things would get better. She wished to herself that he would get a job, any job, but knew that he would not. Her main hope, her principal strategy, was that once his book was finished, she would be able to persuade him to go back to University. He had the intelligence and the ability, there was absolutely no doubt about that. She felt that he would make a very good social worker, or even a teacher. He had a strong sense of care and compassion, allied to great commitment to people.

He would have cried even more than he did if he had known these were the last thoughts she was thinking as she drifted off to sleep beside him, leaving him to recover from that strange session where he had floated helplessly against the ceiling while a stranger had used his body to make love with Joyce. He knew he could not sleep. His mind was alive, active, restless and unsettled. The revived memories of his first conflict with McGoldrick had upset him more than he had imagined. He had often over the years wished that somehow he could get an opportunity to rerun these events and produce a different outcome. He knew that he was now on the verge of such an opportunity, but the prospect no longer seemed so important.

He knew that one of the keys to his understanding of this lay in the bitter sensation he had felt in the pub and the memories it had re-awoken for him of his feelings that terrible Saturday afternoon. He knew he would have to work through the rest of the events of that long ago summer and try to make some sense of why his euphoria had given way to despair and bitterness.

He lay naked on the top of his bed and tried to work out what it was really all about. He had had six pints of Guinness over the course of the evening, but the last of them had been almost three hours ago. He didn't feel as if he were drunk, nor did he feel depressed as he had done most often recently after a few pints. He did feel frightened. He felt real fear in his stomach, a sense of dread, a premonition of disaster. He knew that the three or four times previously he had suffered the feeling he had been assailed with in the pub, he had done things he forever after regretted and great pain and unhappiness had soon followed. He knew he had coped with that before from positions of some strength. He knew also that that was no longer so. He was weak and vulnerable now. He had done his best, he had really tried to rebuild himself, to pull himself up from the depths of the previous year, and remake a human being from the remnants of the wreck. But he was deeply conscious of the fragility of the structure, of the vulnerability to the slightest storm. And this time there could be no return from another trip below the waves.

Once he was certain that Joyce was asleep, and he was truly alone again, he closed his eyes and resumed his journey back to the original source of the feeling. He knew he was going to play that cup final again. Maybe it would have a different ending this time.

****

So he reluctantly returned to the mental back stalls to watch another version of his favourite horror movie. Basically this film was a day in the life of Frank Hunter, the day of the Scottish Schools Cup Final, an X-certificate special, sometimes entitled "The Worst Day of My Life".

Like all the best horror movies it started off peacefully enough. After his belting by McGoldrick, things had seemed to go well. Frank had kept from everyone his feeling that he had made the wrong choice and soon he managed to convince himself that it had only been a passing sensation. Only John McLure had been disappointed at the choice he had made and even he said he would come and watch, and expect to see them win. The team were pleased that he was back with them, and Davie had hugged him in delight and told him to concentrate on Saturday. "Get a hat-trick and sicken the sod, if he comes that is."

Frank's mother was really looking forward to the game. It seemed like the whole Coyle clan were coming, including relatives from Ireland. All the Uncles were particularly excited. They had fostered Frank's love of football and taken him to games as soon as his mother would let them. They felt a genuine pride that they would see him playing in a real big game. They had watched him play before, for the school but they had doubled the crowd by turning up. This would be different, there would be some atmosphere. His father was less exuberant, but even he had said he would be there. His father wasn't a great fan in that he no longer went to many games, but he knew his football, even if he was a Rangers man. Frank didn't know if his father was proud of his football ability or not. The few times he had watched him in recent years, he had made several critical comments, valid ones, about what Frank hadn't done.

The rest of the week had flown past. The final training session had gone very well, everything seemed to be clicking into place. Frank really felt that they could do it. He and Didi had been to see Clydesdale in their semi-final. They were good, there was no

58

denying that. They had two really sharp players, both in the Scottish Schoolboys squad. That squad was selected early in the season, from the better-known Schools. Davie had submitted four names, including Frank's, but as far as they were aware no-one had even come to look at them until near the end of the season. Well bugger them, winning the Cup would be more important. Although he, Didi and Tommy Gallagher had eventually been picked for the Glasgow Schools squad. Frank and Didi had talked about their tactics at length and had felt their basic game would be well suited, with one or two adaptations to take care of the danger men. They had detected a certain softness in the opposition stars. A couple of exposures early on to Tommy Gallagher tackles and they might well fade away. No, they really had felt a good result was a real possibility.

The night before the Final, Frank and Didi spent the evening immersing themselves in the football history which was so important a part of their intellectual and cultural heritage. They drew strength and vitality from their recent memories of the Stein teams that had given them five-in-a-row and the promise of many more to come. Plus of course the miracle of Lisbon and many nights of glory in Europe. They reminisced about games they had seen, and the great attacking football they had been privileged to hail as their own. A model for how the beautiful game could and should be played.

Didi's real name was Derek Duncan, the nickname a product of Glasgow irony rather than any resemblance to the great Brazilian. He was what is politely known as a ball-winner. He would emerge from crunching tackles with the ball, then give it to Frank to do something constructive with it. He was an intelligent player and had already signed with St Mirren and was set for a successful career as a professional footballer.

They knew the team, they had picked it for Davie on the Wednesday. They played the next day's game several times with Subbuteo players on the bedroom floor. Each time they won more convincingly. Eventually Frank's mother intervened and ordered an end to their preparations.

Frank always smiled each time he saw the re-run of the exchange between them. "You've got a big day tomorrow, both of you. You should try to get a good nights sleep". "Not much chance of that " Derek had replied "unless I can be guaranteed of dreaming about scoring the winning goal". "Well it would be a minor miracle that and no mistake " she had countered "since you haven't scored one all season, but I'll offer up a prayer to St Jude for you if you like."

Awake in his bed Frank dreamed of holding the Cup aloft, a captain victorious. More than that he desperately wanted his first medal. Didi already had five of them, won with his Boys Club team for whom he played on Saturday afternoons. Frank had originally played for a similar Boys Club on Saturdays but had soon fallen out on a matter of truth and principle with the man who ran it and had signed instead for a Sunday team of lower standard, secretly half-pleased to be able to resume spending Saturday afternoons in the Jungle. He was jealous though of his pal's silverware and wanted one of his own. The Scottish Schools Cup one would do nicely.

The morning of the Final his alarm woke him early. He wanted to savour as much of this magical day as possible. He re-immersed himself in football thoughts and memories. Twice in the previous four weeks Frank had attended a Cup Final expecting to see his side win. He had strolled along to nearby Hampden for the Scottish Cup Final confidently expecting to see the third leg of yet another treble concluded, only to be shattered by an Aberdeen victory. Then the one that had really hurt, still did, the trip to the European Cup Final. It was still a festering wound with Frank that his parents had not let him accompany his Uncles to Lisbon in 1967. But this time, three years older, he had prevailed against lesser opposition and had been allowed to fly to Milan with his mother's four brothers and his cousin Peter. There he had watched in stunned disbelief as Celtic were outplayed by a better-prepared Feyenoord team and almost worse, the Celtic supporters had been decisively out-noised by the out-numbered but better-equipped Dutch fans. It was so bad the Celtic fans couldn't even face getting drunk and they had slunk quietly away into the night. It was typical of Frank Hunter's luck to get to go to the wrong game, to miss out on the Lisbon Lions and have to settle instead for the Milan Mice.

The game had been disconcerting evidence that Jock Stein might be human after all. He had under-estimated his opponents. Well Frank Hunter would not make that mistake. Celtic's two Final defeats made Frank more determined to be successful in his own. If that was how badly he felt about defeat when he was only watching, how on earth would he feel when he had been playing. There was no way he was going to collect a hat-trick of Cup Final defeats in the one month. No way.

The second section of the film, the Road to the Cup, was short but significant, not for its action but for the meaning he would later give to its symbolism, him on the same road as his two colleagues before their paths significantly diverged. In it, Frank walked to school, where the team were to gather in the playground. He picked Tommy Gallagher and Didi up on the way and they chatted excitedly but grew quiet as they approached the school. They were the three key players in the team. Frank and Didi were the brains, the ones who determined tactics, who organised how the team would play. Frank had the greater skill but Didi's intelligence was every bit as keen and although Frank was captain they worked as a collective. Tommy provided the muscle, with a football intelligence that more than compensated for a relative lack of ball control. In some ways, they treated Davie the gym teacher as a bit of a joke. Already they had the disdain of the professional for the enthusiastic but talentless amateur. Still, they appreciated all the hard work he had put in, on his own, because of the football fever that infected him. So, though they ignored him as a coach they respected him as their manager, the Boss. Despite their alternative Boys Club careers, and their already signed professional contracts, Tommy and Derek wanted to win this one as much as Frank, almost, and all their talk was centred on how to guarantee it. Clydesdale had a better tradition than St Anne's in this tournament and were favoured to win by the experts who studied these matters. It wasn't that St Anne's, with a large catchment area on Glasgow's southside, had not produced many fine players. Its problem was more the opposite, it regularly produced players who were more committed to more serious matters.

As the walk and the talk progressed, through the subtle use of flash-forwards the audience was allowed to see what the boys only assumed, that all three would go on in their future to become professional footballers. Derek Duncan went on to play for St Mirren, Blackburn Rovers and Everton. He was capped five times for Scotland. In England he won the League and FA Cup and was voted Player of the Year by his peers. He was denied the chance to win the Big One by English hooligans but managed to get his hands on one of the others before the ban came down. Tommy Gallagher played for Hibs for several years before being transferred for a large fee to Aston Villa. He made several other big moves and was recognised for years as the hardest and one of the best central defenders in the game. The Director indulgently included a TV clip of Frank Hunter scoring one of the candidates for a goal of the season competition, against Hibs in a Scottish Cup tie, but otherwise gave the audience no clues about his football future. There were two other players in the St Anne's team whom the three heroes reckoned had sufficient ability to make it into the senior ranks with them but it was revealed that with a typical Scottish combination of poor luck and gross character defect they were to be denied the career their basic abilities may have been said to deserve, or at least make feasible.

Once the whole team was assembled, they boarded the Executive Coach specially hired for the occasion and after a short detour via a posh southside hotel for lunch they made their way across the city to Firhill Park, home of Partick Thistle. They all felt a special rush of pride as they approached the Players Entrance, reduced slightly when none of the small boys hanging about asked for their autographs.

Tommy Gallagher offered his to the smallest boy there but the offer was rejected. "You'll be sorry about that one day " Tommy had said with some accuracy. Tommy was the modern kind of ball-player. You moved near him and he kicked you in the goolies. He was one tough bastard. Several times when Frank had been getting a hard time from defenders who marked him out, literally, as St Anne's creative force, Tommy had intervened to ensure that he got a little more space. Frank was never sure whether he completely approved of where Tommy drew his own moral line, but he certainly knew that he'd rather play with him than agin him. And if there was trouble after a game, as there sometimes was, Tommy was worth three of most oppositions. He had created a major stir the previous month by being sent off in a game for the school team for a strong but late tackle, ten minutes after getting booked for a particularly hard one, to earn a Schools Association ban for three games. McGoldrick had thought it worthy enough of consideration to devote all of his comments at the Monday School Assembly to standards of behaviour and what was expected of people who represent St Anne's. McGoldrick had nearly banned him completely and only Davie's inspired borrowing of the concept of double jeopardy from a lawyer friend had allowed Tommy to resume playing for the school after his ban expired.

In the dressing room Father Andrew wished them luck in that firm way of his and insisted in leading them in a moment of quiet prayer. It was more welcome than most, at least the quiet was helpful. McGoldrick did pop in for a moment. He was obviously ill at ease. The team did not contain any of the older, more academic, pupils with whom he was familiar and most them had only met him with "Old Faithful" in hand. He avoided any contact, even of the eye, with Frank even though he was the captain, and they could all sense the relief, theirs as well as his, when he left them with a "Good luck, chaps." The use of the word amazed them. Didi broke the tension with his comment "Isn't that something cowboys wear when peeing on a cactus?" and then the door was locked and they got down to serious business.

Frank the reluctant spectator never tired of the next bit, the comedic relief, a welcome break which still always managed a sentimental tug at his feelings.

Davie's team talks had become minor classics of their kind. Once he had realised that he had strayed into over-reliance on cliché and that they weren't listening anymore, he had deliberately adopted a self-parodying approach that was witty enough to catch their attention at least for a moment or two. He could do a fair Shankly imitation that they particularly liked. "Now just eh remember lads, football's not a matter eh of life and death, eh, it's much more important eh than that." They all loved that one. He used it for this speech and reminded them that many good players went their whole careers without ever reaching a Cup Final and here they were in one at 15 or 16 years of age. He concluded with their favourite ending, again borrowed from Shankly in the gruff accent "Ah just eh want you all to go oot ther eh an enjoy yersels eh but don't bloody bother coming back if you lose." They spontaneously broke into applause when he had finished. They all knew and appreciated the time and effort Davie had put in over the years and that this was a bigger moment for him even than it was for them. In their usual slagging way they insisted that he lead them out as if it were Wembley, and in his usual diffident way he was very pleased.

Then to the central core of the film, the game itself. No matter how many times he watched it, and it must have been hundreds, all the details were always exactly the same. No even slight variation was ever allowed, it was unalterable, immutable, horror petrified.

It was a good feeling to run out the Tunnel to applause. Frank looked up to where his parents should be, and there they were. The Coyles seemed to take up a whole row. He waved to them and smiled shyly. There must have been about two thousand people in the ground, mostly from the two schools. Frank lost the toss and found himself given the choice of ends, which is what he would have taken if he had won, so he reckoned that was a good omen for starters. He felt this meant that the opposition were over-excited and going to start off like maniacs, so he quickly spread the word to keep it cool and tight at the back from the off. Sure enough, straight from the kick-off Clydesdale surged forward in great waves. The pressure was relentless for the first ten minutes and big Pat McDermott in goal had to leap smartly to cut out one or two dangerous crosses. Gradually however the pressure was weathered and St Anne's began to get more of the ball. They stroked it around well in a calm and thoughtful manner, taking their time and waiting for the right opportunity to step up a gear.

It came in the 23rd minute. Tommy Gallagher clattered through their centre-forward who was fannying about just inside the St Anne's half. He emerged with the ball at his feet and the opponent lying behind him moaning. He knocked it forward to Didi in space on the half way line. As he did so, Frank started running diagonally towards the left hand corner of the penalty box. He didn't even have to shout, they'd done this a thousand times together in parks, playgrounds and streets. The ball arrived at him just outside the box. Knowing exactly how, when and where it would come gave him that edge over the defender and he was round him before the wrong-footed opponent could move in on him. He took three strides forward then cracked the ball with his right foot. It was a perfect shot, right towards the bottom-left hand corner of the net, but somehow their keeper got his hand to it and pushed it out. Joe McCafferty the St Anne's centre-forward was the quickest to react and hooked the ball high into the empty net.

Then came the only sex scene in the film.

The rush of adrenaline in Frank was massive. He jumped high into the air and even before he landed he was heading towards Joe at full pelt. Ugly big bastard or not, he was going to kiss him. Frank always felt sorry for people who could not understand why footballers celebrate goals by embracing each other. It was nothing to do with money, or status or importance. From Maracana to Hampden Park, from Glasgow Green to Queens Park, from World Cup Final to street kick-about, good goals were met by kisses and if people had never experienced the special surge of joy that comes from a well-executed strike, then Frank felt sorry for them.

The goal seemed to knock the heart out of Clydesdale. They were a bit like Celtic in Milan, nothing went right for them and they knew somehow it wasn't going to be their day. Des Riordan added another for St Anne's after a lovely move involving six of their team, including an excellent and decisive through-pass from Frank. By half-time they were totally in control and the second half looked like it would be a doddle. Frank waved to his parents as he trotted off and gave them a broad grin. Davie was ecstatic in the dressing room. "It's in the bag, boys, just keep it going the way you have been and the cup is yours". Frank sat there on the flat wooden bench and felt truly happy. The Cup was his to hoist, and he could already feel the cold metal medal in his warm grubby paw. He didn't join in the excited chatter but his thoughts were pleasant ones and he had no premonition of the disaster to come.

The second half continued in the same pattern as the first had ended, all St Anne's with another goal looking likely each time they attacked. After ten minutes they got a third when Gerry O'Leary, their fullback, overlapped on the left and crossed the ball low and hard into the penalty area. It bounced about for a moment or two before breaking to Didi who thumped it home from 10 yards. Frank knew his mother must have prayed to St Jude after all. He owed her one after the success she had made of her marriage. There was no way Clydesdale could come back now. Victory was his.

Then came the bit that Frank could never bear to watch, the section the viewing of which always brought him close to tears. Real tears, wet ones, which would run down the outside of his face. He knew this section as The Road to Ruin, incorporating the Long Short Walk.

Frank found his concentration wandering. He went over in his mind the events of earlier on in the week and how near he had come to not playing in this game. "Come on, Frank, that should have been your ball. Fucking gie yerself a shake, big man." The sharp edge to Tommy's rebuke brought him back temporarily to the game, but within a few minutes he was back in a wee world of his own, oblivious to the action around him other than in a remote robotic way. He kept hearing voices from the last few days. "You have to ask yourself what is more important to you, politics or football"; "the most important thing is to be true to yourself"; "admitting our guilt, are we then?"; "Damn."

He suddenly felt completely drained and empty as if someone had switched off the power supply to this robot he had become. A truly terrible sense of futility and pointlessness descended upon him. It tore at his gut and chest, it made his head reel. "This is not right, I shouldn't be here.", he muttered to himself. He felt really dizzy and wanted to sit down. The play continued round about him. It is far easier for an intelligent player to stay out of a game than it is for an stupid player to get into it. Just get into the wrong position at the right time and the game would go on without you. At the first opportunity of a hard tackle he went down and stayed down, feigning injury. Davie came on with his magic sponge and rubbed his leg. "You OK, Frank? You seem to have gone quiet for a bit. Do you want to come off. The game's won.". He swithered for a moment but opted, as all his life, against the easy answer. Frank shook his head "No, I'll be all right, it's just a bit of a knock." He got up and ran downfield, trying to shake off the terrifying feeling but it was no good.

Then it happened, he just knew right to the core of his being that he didn't want to continue anymore, that he had to submit to the logic of the taste corroding his soul. That sour taste meant he could not swallow from the cup of victory life now offered him. He had just grasped the significance and implications of this, when the referee gave him his opportunity. Frank clattered into their Right Half after the ball had gone, harder than he needed to, a foul but not a particularly dirty or malicious tackle. The whistle blew instantly and the shrill voice cried out "Foul, Clydesdale" in a magisterial tone.

"Don't be so fucking stupid". He knew as soon as the words came out that what was about to happen was what he wanted to happen. The pompous little runt had made it very clear in the Dressing Room before the game that he would not tolerate any dissent and that foul language was instant dismissal. "What did you say, young man ?" he asked, his face quivering with indignant rage. "I said 'don't be so fucking stupid'. That was never a foul." He looked straight into his eyes. Would the little bugger's nerve hold. "Right. You're off. Now. Go" Frank drew himself together and trotted off trying to look as if he was upset. His team-mates certainly were, Didi cuddled him and Gerry put his arm round his shoulder and lead him off. Tommy muttered that he was a stupid bastard. He was quite right. Frank hated indiscipline himself, all his career as a player he thought it was utterly stupid and unforgivable to get booked or ordered off for mouthing. They're not going to change their minds and abuse certainly wouldn't achieve that. He'd never been sent off before but he had been booked several times. Anyone who was a hard tackler was always going to cross some referee's line about mis-timed, late or deliberate. The law of averages alone would guarantee that. But he

66

had never before been, nor was he ever again, punished for dissent. This case was different, it wasn't indiscipline, it was insanity.

As he got to the touchline, Davie grabbed him and hugged him tightly. "Sorry, big man," he whispered, "but at least the game is over and the cup is ours. Get dressed and come back out and join me." Frank forced himself to look up to where his parents were as he went up the tunnel. He saw them all in that brief moment of frozen time. His distraught mother; his silent father; his Gran yelling abuse at the ref., surrounded by her noisy family; Father Andrew shaking his head; McGoldrick furious at the disgrace; the array of Scouts scoring his name out of their books. It was only years later that he found out, from a friend of his at Parkhead, the true cost and consequence of his action. Celtic had already watched him on a couple of occasions and sent not only their Chief Scout but their Assistant Manager to the Final. They had been very impressed with his first-half showing, but when he got himself sent-off, the thumb had been turned down. "That's not the kind of temperament we are looking for." He often thought that sentence could serve as his epitaph. Most other clubs represented there had reacted in the same way, and he eventually only received one offer, not a very good one at that.

Alone in the empty dressing room Frank didn't need to pretend to be upset. The enormity and stupidity of what he had done seemed to overwhelm him. He broke down in uncontrollable tears, sobbing furiously for what seemed an eternity. Slowly the intensity of the pain subsided a little. He took his shower cold as a punishment on himself, letting the freezing water numb as much as possible. He towelled himself inadequately and dressed quickly. He couldn't face the prospect of joining Davie on the bench. He just wanted to crawl away and avoid anyone he knew. The sense of shame burned deep into him. The only consolation he felt was that he knew the team would win. Even with only ten men there was no way Tommy, Didi, Gerry and company would lose a three goal lead, especially in the last ten minutes. He knew he wouldn't get to lift the Cup, he reckoned he probably wouldn't even get his medal, it would most likely be withheld because of his poor conduct but he didn't want to hang about to be told that.

He found the way out from the dressing room to the Front Entrance. It was unlocked so he let himself out into Firhill St. He had the pound note his father had given him that morning so he could have afforded to get a taxi to the southside but that wouldn't have seemed right. He was still too shocked and upset to consider rationally whether or not he was walking away from responsibilities he should stay and face. Flight seemed the only available course for him. The only consequence he could grasp and wrestle with was a worry about whether or not his mother would go to the post-match reception, and how she would feel if he was not there. His father had already indicated that he would not be going.

The final Road segment was more difficult to name, if easier to watch. It was the Road back to his past, his roots, in search of the explanation why the Hunter in him could behave so.

He walked down Maryhill Road for about half a mile then jumped on a bus to the city centre. From there he walked over the suspension bridge. He stopped halfway across and tried to get some peace from looking at the river. He didn't consider jumping in, which he felt was maybe a positive sign. He walked up Gorbals St. unsure where he was going. He knew he wasn't ready to go home yet. He didn't have a girl-friend to turn to, there had been a few girls, a few sexual gropes and more, but nothing that had meant anything to him. Girls were definitely way down his list behind football, politics and drink. He knew he needed, or rather, wanted comfort with censure, so it wasn't too difficult for him to work out where to go. To the woman he would want to marry if she had been born 60 years later. The one who knew both how good he could be, but also all about the genetic inheritance he carried that threatened to destroy all his promise.

Amongst other things, Mary Ewing was his family historian, his one guide to the darker side of his background, the Hunter legacy. She had been a lifelong friend of his granny Jessie. Mary taught him all he ever knew about his Orange grandfather Willie Hunter, and the family reasons why his father Dave was such a silent man. And let him know the real history of his class and the true nature of the political struggles in which she had been an active participant all her life.

Mary Ewing was pleased to see him when he turned up on the doorstep of her flat in Westmoreland Street. She knew the game was on that day and her first assumption from a look at his face was that they must have lost but she quickly realised it was more serious than that. The poor lad was in some state but she couldn't work out exactly why he seemed so upset. She knew her football and she knew her people; being sent off, when your team has won, or after it has lost, didn't do any harm. In most ways it was a plus

68

if anything. No, there was more to it than that but he wasn't talking. It didn't matter, she would give him what she could.

She had known Frank all his life. She wasn't his Auntie and had never played the game of pretending that she was, but she had been of more use to him than that. It still saddened her heart when she thought of how poor Jessie had been denied the joy that her only grandchild should have given her. Christ, her life had been bleak enough, married to that bastard Willie Hunter and all her troubles trying to keep her son Dave close. What a losing battle that had been. Frank's birth should have been a bonus, a wonderful source of some comfort and consolation, but it had not worked out that way. Well at least the boy's mother, Shona, had tried to involve her but the odds were too great against her. Willie, in the only acknowledgement that he ever made that he had a grandchild, had forbidden Jessie ever to see "that wee fenian bastard" and with three early, furtive exceptions she had stuck to that for the rest of her miserable life. Mary had done what she could as a source of information and that had helped Jessie a little until cancer had liberated her before Frank was three years old.

He was a great boy too, very bright and very sensitive, obviously all his positive genes came from the female lines. He liked talking to her and, more unusual, listening to her. She knew she was his only link to a closed part of his heritage, his Thompson blood, his father's mother's side of his history. He was always greedy for what she could give him. He was astute enough to see the faults and brave enough to grasp them. He soaked up everything she could tell him about his grandfather, the orange politics, the fenian-bashing, the strike-breaking, the fervent Protestant anti-socialism. He was also very interested in her other tales of pre-war Glasgow politics. She had been quite a fighter in her time and he used to listen attentively to all her tales of rent strikes and wives camps and all the other activities that had once seemed so important to her.

She felt sure he would become a politician one day, a Labour one and that should send a shiver through Willie Hunter's grave. She hoped the bastard caught pneumonia, if you could in hell. She looked down at the 16-year old boy sitting with his head on her lap crying. Well that was at least something, neither of the other two Hunter men had ever felt, far less displayed, any emotion. There might be a slight hope for this one. She stroked his head gently with her old fingers twisted and bent. "You're a funny boy, Frank son, almost as funny as your faither."

69

Frank had heard her make remarks like that before. He'd always tried to ignore or dismiss them but he knew deep down what she was on about and it depressed him even more. He always felt great pain in what she revealed about that side of his family background. There was none of the love, warmth and comfort that was strongly present on both the Coyle and Rogan sides. No wonder his father was the way he was but please God let him be different.

Her flat was very bare and sparsely furnished. Mary had never been one for creature comforts and now she had no money anyway. She kept it clean but she wouldn't take help or charity from anyone so it was pretty basic. This was the reward for a lifetime of struggle to help other people, not much of an incentive, thought Frank. She did not have a telephone but somehow, without appearing to leave the flat, she got a message to Shona when it was time to come and collect her boy.

Frank's other grand-mother, Jean Coyle, had one major rule in life; if there wasn't an obscure reason for a family party, invent one. She had seen the Cup Final as an obvious excuse for a gathering of the Rogan and Coyle clans, and had made all the arrangements to have it in Seath Street. She had been aware that the guest of honour might have other obligations with the team, but he would join them when he could, they'd have it anyway. By the time he had walked home with his mother, the party was in full swing. He always found these gatherings a welcome antidote to the cold ghosts on the Hunter Thompson side. Warm, happy, friendly, noisy. The love and affection were tangible. Everyone talked at once, but always seemed to listen, too. On the way over, he had been a bit apprehensive about the welcome he would get, but he needn't have bothered. He didn't get a hero's reception but they didn't regard it as a disaster either, that was left to him.

His Uncles slagged him vigorously, but he found he could cope. From their point of view, it was unfortunate rather than desperate, after all the team won, so what harm was done. It just gave them something to hammer the stupid bastard over the head with, to stop him getting too big-headed. It might have been different if they had been losing or drawing, but then he knew what they didn't, that in those circumstances he wouldn't have done it. The love and warmth of his family, his Gran, his four Uncles and their wives, his cousins, and the other relatives, restored some reality and life to his shattered soul. By the end of the evening, he was even able to grin thinly as the last ones out the door warned his mother "Have a red card handy when you tell him he's got to go to bed. He'll probably swear at you in language you've never heard before." His father didn't really speak to him all evening, but then what was new in that. The only comment he made about the game seemed more in advice than anger, "Stupid bastard, that was quite unnecessary. You'd better learn a bit of discipline, quick, son". He knew his father didn't like these gatherings of his mother's family.

There was one unexpected bonus for Frank. McGoldrick had intervened with the officials at the end of the match to say that he felt the medal should be withheld from him because of his disgraceful conduct and because he had let down the standards expected of representatives of St Anne's. That had been their own inclination anyway. In the confusion and excitement of the presentation of the Cup and medals the last man up had been Stevie McGrath, the substitute whom kind Davie had put onto the park for the last two minutes. Stevie had seen the extra box sitting on the table and before anyone realised exactly what he was doing had said "I'll take that and give it to our spare man." By the time it dawned on them whom he meant he was well away and had passed it on to someone else. There was a half-hearted attempt to retrieve it but it had vanished. Didi brought it round to Frank later that evening and so he had gone to sleep with it clenched firmly in his fist after all and he would have gladly been expelled or worse rather than ever give it up.

McGoldrick had had a further petty revenge. At Assembly in front of the whole school there had been a long moral lecture in which Frank's behaviour had been used as an example of the selfish indiscipline that was wrong with the modern world and he had been barred from representing the school, indefinitely. It had been of no import. The football season was over with the Final, most of the squad had left school within weeks and although Frank stayed on for a final year, the professional club for which he signed in the summer arranged for him to play with a juvenile team every Saturday.

The formal film finished with that touching scene of the young boy slipping off to sleep with his medal tightly clutched in his little fist but there was a further section omitted from the released version, a special Director's Cut, that Frank Hunter generally needed to watch every time he played his little game, and in the interests of full understanding would have to force himself to watch again.

71

Through that night and the next few days, Frank slowly regained some composure and control. OK, he told himself, it's bad but the world hasn't ended. They had won the Cup. He knew that the rest of the team would be well aware that he'd played a crucial role in that victory. That was important to him. His teammates knew how close a line it was, a late tackle here, a loose word there, it could have been any of them, and his contribution had still been one of the more important ones. Most people close to him thought he was so upset because he had been sent off. Only he knew he had been upset because he had wanted to get himself sent off. He had never ever in his life told anyone else, even Elaine, that he had done it deliberately. He tried to analyse what had happened, how he had felt and how he had handled it. He knew the key to it was the bitter, empty feeling he had experienced when he had achieved victory and everything he thought he wanted. It was only later, much later, that he was able to make much sense of it at all. He was never the same person again after that afternoon. He had lost his innocent belief in the value of victory and his faith in his ability to rationally control his own destiny. He developed a fear of success that haunted him forever after.

As the final credits rolled across the dawning of realisation that he was different from other people, he realised he was soaking wet, a combination of sweat on his back and chest and tears on his face and neck. The sadist in the projection room did not immediately ease his suffering because although the main feature was over, onto the screen rolled enticing trailers for the other disaster movies of his life. Work, Football, Relationships, they were all covered and documented.

****

The one respite he allowed himself from the pursuit of his thoughts and memories was a rerun of the argument he had not had with Gerry. He ran his friend's argument past himself and shared with himself the reply he had denied Gerry. Some part of him had been listening more than he had realised because he was able to repeat to himself Gerry's words later, much later, that night. He felt less alone as Gerry's words revisited his head. "It's a dangerous and misleading argument to use, in favour of the likelihood of a Scottish Parliament, about the quality of the Scottish Labour MPs in and on the fringes of, the Shadow Cabinet. Just look at who they are, even look at what they are called and you'll see what I mean. Can you get a more typical English name than John Smith? Is there a more common English surname than Brown? Take Cook, or our friend Robertson, or Wilson. All English names to the core. These people have no Scottish identity or soul. They have allied themselves to the British cause because that is where they want to be. Smith put the Devolution Bill through Parliament, like the good lawyer he is, without believing for a moment in the rightness of the case he was arguing. Have you heard him utter one word in support of that case since then, far less lead the campaign? No, you haven't, because he wants to be Prime Minister and supporting Scotland's cause would harm his. The same with Brown, he wants to be Chancellor in Number 11, before moving into Number 10. He doesn't want to be diverted back to Edinburgh. Cook has come from far over the other side to make some of the right noises, but the closer he gets to the smell of Cabinet power, the more likely will his new found ardour be to diminish. Robertson still talks of Scotland as a region, for God's sake. He and Wilson, both nationalists as boys, have a convert's pathological hatred and fear of the potential of their own people.

Their quality, as you would call it, Frank, I have another word for it, actually makes it less rather than more likely that there will be any meaningful form of Scottish Devolution from Labour, especially once the inevitable price-tab of reduced Scottish representation at Westminster becomes clear." Lying there in his bed, listening to his friend in his head, Frank smiled his first smile for several long sad hours. Gerry, you're right and you're wrong, but why can't you draw the correct conclusions from your own argument. But for once it was not politics that interested him most, but some football match from long ago, and he returned again to the replays in his mind.

****

That afternoon so brutally captured on film had set a pattern that had pursued him throughout his life. Several other times in his life he had encountered that same awful feeling, and each time its effect on him had been disastrous, for the Frank Hunter that he had wanted to be, for the Frank Hunter he might have been. There had been the sunny day in June 1973, at the end of his first year at Glasgow University, when he had read the boards in University Avenue and discovered that he was in the top two of his classes in both his main subjects, Politics and History. The warm glow of success had turned sourly bitter in his mouth and even before he had reached Gibson Street and a cleansing curry, he had known that his University career was over, and he would deliberately chose to return to the labouring jobs from which his father and grandfather had come but from which his education should have enabled him to escape.

And worse, much worse than that, most devastating and destructive of all his self-mutilations, had been that awful early morning in July 1984 when he had awoken early after a truly wonderful 6th Wedding Anniversary day which had culminated in he and his lovely wife Elaine making satisfying love before falling asleep together in the perfect cuddle. He had walked up to his hilltop in Queens Park, looked out over his city, savoured the success of his marriage, and had known from the bitterness of the taste that it was over. Not much of the real Frank Hunter had survived that particular savouring.

The remnants had gone on their own sad journey downhill, far into an internal slough of despond, slowly at first, uneventfully, until in the early summer of 1989 the rope broke and the fall was full and free. He had lost not only his job at LDT but also his campaign to save the factory, and his last lingering belief in the value of collective action and commitment. The day after the closure, with wondrous timing, his mother had died in her boyfriend's bed and Frank had at last succumbed to the subtle sadness that had always threatened to overwhelm him. He had retreated into a silent world of his own, in which his long dead dad would have felt at home. He never ventured out his flat, never sought human company or conversation, was content to be alone with his video tapes, his books and his satellite football games. Desperate to be better, he spent two weeks in Kamesthorn Hospital, the southside loony-bin. Eventually he was saved, sort of, by a Pole who scored four goals in the one game and still lost and a wee Glaswegian Psychiatrist who let him win at verbal tennis in order not to lose him. He had emerged a wiser and no sadder man, with a relationship with the Hospital social worker Joyce that offered some hope, and a friendship with a fellow patient Hazel that offered more but looked like less.

There were other times, less traumatic but still painful and destructive, when he had reacted by refusing to get into the winning position at all. At least that was the excuse he later gave himself, that he had deliberately chosen not to achieve success that might have been his, rather than risk his own response to such success. That was truest in politics where he never achieved the results that his political awareness and organisational skills might have been expected, certainly by others, to bring him. Occasionally he sought another victim, blaming his response to the peculiar failure of his side's "victory" in the 1979 Referendum campaign. A true Yes man, he never really recovered from the failure of his people to grasp their opportunity to shape their own destiny. He helped his friend Paddy McGuire become a successful Councillor but always declined similar opportunities for himself and his failure to move forward became a backward journey. Likewise he declined all the efforts of Gerry Robertson and others to transform his considerable lay Trade Union activities into full-time salaried employment.

His football career followed a different pattern. After making the breakthrough into the first team at the Viccies, a mediocre Second Division club, he had a couple of moderately successful seasons before suffering a crippling knee injury from which he never really recovered, in any of the possible senses. Thus had his major dream turned to nothing and he never found the motivation to implement the other fantasies of his youth, or even to analyse too closely why he failed to do so and whether it was, as claimed, out of fear of the consequences of success, or something baser. This was his normal judgement on what had been the pattern of his life, occasional complete success quickly followed by the appearance of the bitter taste and a disastrous response, or a more prevalent failure to achieve the success which might have been his.

****

By the end of his long return through the pain and shame of those events of that sad Saturday afternoon so long ago, and the disasters which had later repeated it, Frank found he was crying uncontrollably. Real outward tears, too, wet ones that ran down his face and ran into the pillow where he buried his head. He wept for the loss of his innocence, and for the loss of his belief that he could control his destiny by the application of reason and logic. He wept for the little boy who could never more happily dream of being a winner, and he wept a few more tears for the man that little boy had become. Through all the thoughts and memories, and the tears and the fears he did manage to come to one conclusion. He knew that the feelings he had had earlier that evening in the pub when he realised he had effectively won his

75

latest battle with McGoldrick were similar to the empty sense of pointlessness he had felt that afternoon long ago. Twice more in his life, he had felt that extreme bitter taste of victory and twice more it had screwed him up in a major way. Now he had felt it again this very night. But this time there would be a different outcome.

He had always given into that feeling of futility before, and walked away from winning positions. This time he would not walk away. This time he would play the game to its conclusion and find out how he could cope with complete victory. He would take his pictures, then he would make his phonecall to McGoldrick. Maybe the replay of his contest would give him the opportunity to remove the kink from his life. Maybe he could achieve a victory that would exorcise his soul, and allow him to build something of value out of the remains of his life. Out of the anguish of that long night he began to rediscover the possibilities of hope, the first stirrings of optimism, less heady than the initial euphoria of the previous evening but maybe a sounder base for the rebuilding of his life. He spent much time over the next few days and nights, especially the nights, revisiting his past, re-examining his roots trying to make some sense of who he was and how he had got to where he was, but he never deviated from the main product of his night of pain, a determination that this time he would finish the game, as a winner. He would have to. He could not cope with further disaster. This time he would exult in the joyous taste of victory.

CHAPTER FIVE - A SATISFIED MAN

"Satisfied" was the word Robin McGoldrick would have used to describe himself that Saturday night in March, as he sat in the Ubiquitous Chip Restaurant. Which was strange to understand on the face of it, since he was there with a wife he had not slept with, far less made love to, for many months. He did not like this restaurant with its phoney atmosphere and expensive pretensions. The food was unsubtle and overdone, and the company they were with made the food seem congenial. Their one saving grace was that their self-absorption and conceit were such that he would get away without having to contribute to the conversation to any great extent.

Satisfied was nevertheless the correct description. The meeting that afternoon with the office-bearers of the Constituency Association had gone very well, and the last remaining minor obstacles had been removed. The nomination was effectively his, although the official process and formal announcement would take several weeks. Even the premature indication in the Tom Shield's Diary in the "Herald" had improved his position rather than the reverse, which was just as well since it had been he who had organised its release. He knew he was on the verge of successfully implementing his master-plan, and in several important ways, the timing was even better than he could have hoped for when the plan first took shape and form some ten years before. He knew exactly what he wanted and why. He was well aware that he had gone as far as he could at St Anne's and that he could no longer sustain the curve of diminishing returns at its plateau peak. He knew that it had been on the verge of drifting down for the last few years. It had been hard work at first, being the new headmaster in a mediocre School, but once he had turned it round it became much easier.

He smiled to himself at the irony of the fact that the word that seemed to him most appropriate to describe the last few years was "doddle". Maybe he was becoming corrupted after all. He knew better than anyone that a well-ordered school runs itself. The combination of the new technology he had introduced and the old Depute he had appointed, ensured that the school ran smoothly. The Depute was a man totally devoid of that quality so dangerous in a Depute, imagination, but full of the safer virtues of energy, efficiency and loyalty. This satisfactory state of affairs had allowed him to spend more and more of his time outwith St Anne's. He doubted if he had spent one five day week there in the last five years. He filled his time with conferences, generally with himself as one of the main speakers; working parties; and divisional, regional and national remits. On top of that there was the education work he did for the Catholic Hierarchy which a tolerant Department recognised as official duties. He was very conscious of the perverse irony, the less time he spent doing the job he was paid to perform, the higher his professional credibility became.

In addition, he had spent an increasing amount of time over the past few years on his Chester Street duties for the Conservative Party. He had been able to do a surprising amount of this in work time, "assisting the Scottish Office and the S.E.D.", but other parts had required the sacrifice of his own time. He knew it had been time well spent. He had achieved more than he had ever envisaged as possible. Almost single-handed, he had sold the notions of School Boards and Opting Out to the relevant Scottish politicians and then provided the intellectual base and the policy and implementation proposals that had formed the core of the White Papers and subsequent Bills and Acts. When he had first mooted the proposals, he had been uniformly told that even if their basis were to be accepted as desirable, which was unlikely, then they could still never be implemented against the combined forces of all the serried ranks of the Scottish Education and political establishments, including and especially the Civil Servants. They had had a little luck on their side, certainly, including, with hindsight, the massacre of the Scottish Tories in 1987 and the inept leadership of the E.I.S. and the other teaching Unions. But the combination of his intellectual prowess and Young Michael's political skills, acumen and guts had enabled them to achieve the unthinkable. School Boards were now an operating reality and the Opting Out legislation was now on the Statute Book.

Even he had thought at best it would have taken another Parliament to achieve so much. The tactical stupidity and naivety of the Teachers Unions had amazed even him. The civil servants had been taken care of by Michael, and the old Educational establishment had demonstrated its brain death by its inability to respond in any significant way. The Labour Party had huffed and puffed in a remarkably pompous style but they had not grasped the magnitude of the revolution he was promoting and had had no coherent intellectual vision to offer in its place other than more of the same old recipe that had so clearly failed in the past. He took tremendous satisfaction from this achievement. He knew he had transformed the whole basis of the Scottish education system. He regarded this as a not insignificant contribution. He had also taken considerable personal satisfaction from the positive acceptance of his reforms by his own Regional Council which might have been expected to be negative and resistant. Again he knew that much of the credit for this lay in his own contribution. But that in itself was a reminder of why it was time to move on. It was one thing being the radical voice of educational reform and good standards within the context of a conservative and inefficient administration at both political and officer level; it would be quite a different matter under the new regime of the Tallyman and his crew, efficient, community orientated and intellectually disciplined as they were threatening to be.

He knew too that the timing would never be better for him to move into the political arena as a Member of Parliament. The 1987 massacre had left the Scottish Tories bereft of talent. The nadir had been reached though and the next election should see the turn of the anti-Tory tide. He knew the potential opportunities for an intelligent Scots Tory M.P. were immense. He would be guaranteed a Minister's post. He secretly believed that his prospects were even better than that. He was not handicapped by being inescapably Scottish. He had a national, that is British, reputation as an educationalist. He was aware, painfully aware, that the last few Conservative Governments had not been educationally innovative enough for the Prime Minister and that there would be considerable political mileage in having a high profile in this area. Alone in his bed at night his unarticulated but nevertheless clear fantasy involved no less than the Secretary for State for Education's seat at the Cabinet table. After all, some of the last few had appeared unable even to spell, far less formulate appropriate and radical new educational policy. When the time came for that, in the fourth term, he would be well placed to offer something valuable, if he were in the House. He was aware this was all premised on two assumptions but he had rigorously done his homework on each.

He had worked it out very carefully and thoroughly. The Conservative Party could not lose the next election. The electoral arithmetic was unassailable. Labour leads in opinion polls not withstanding, the swings required for the Tories to lose control had never happened before and would not happen this time. He was grateful to a recent detailed article in the Daily Telegraph for confirming much of the work he had already done for himself with his computer and political textbooks. The Telegraph scenario had been a Tory majority of at least 30 seats. His own, on slightly tighter and less charitable assumptions, had placed the absolute bottom line at an overall majority of 18 seats. He also knew that this would not mean much in the way of assisting in his aspirations if he were not to be one of that majority. He was something of an expert in Scottish political history, which had been neglected by both demoralised Tories and hideously complacent Socialists. He knew the Scottish tradition involved swings and movements different from the national pattern. He was one of the few people active in current political life who knew all the details of every post-war election in Scotland and what they had meant. He was well aware of the now almost inconceivable fact that in 1955 the Tory Party had got an absolute majority of the votes cast in Scotland and that in 1959 the Scottish pattern was different from the national one as it had been at almost every recent Election. It would be different too in 1991 or 1992. Three seats were still at risk, ironically including Michael's and George's. So much for the rewards of success. Overall, though, 1987 would be seen to be the lowest point and the next election would bring more success. There were half a dozen possible winnable seats and he had been approached about four of them. There only ever was one that he would consider, where several factors taken together meant that he, more than any other potential candidate, would have a realistic chance of success.

This was Kings Park, the very one he had tied up that afternoon. It was basically the same constituency, with minor and now beneficial boundary changes, that had belonged to the Tories for the whole post-war period until that unforgettable night in 1979 when Scotland had again asserted its differences and, against a backcloth of sweeping Tory gains nationally, "our next Secretary of State for Scotland" had unfortunately lost his seat. Robin had been ambivalent about that. He had not liked the man, whom he regarded as a crude and vulgar populist boor. Robin had been active in neighbouring seats and had not played too high a profile in the campaign, although he had appeared on several public platforms with him. It would have been handy to have such close links with the Secretary of State but in practice it had probably suited him better to have him go south and more congenial replacements found. Robin had assisted in the unsuccessful campaigns of 1983 and 1987 where the seat had turned into one apparently safe for the Labour Party. Robin knew this to be an illusion and that any Conservative candidate would come closer the next time. Recent developments in the agreement of the District Council to private building development, the demolition of many of the houses in the worst two areas, and the explosion in the sale of Council Houses had altered the demographic balance substantially. Robin knew that he had two major advantages that would tip the balance in his favour and perhaps see him into Westminster if he were to be the Conservative candidate. One was that he had a high public profile in the area, having had by now two whole generations of southside children through his school. He was now educating the children of his first intakes. He had run the school as a resource for the whole community and had developed positive links and a high credibility with an amazing range of groups and interests. He had a visibility and a credibility that was rare in one identified as a Tory in Glasgow.

The other more important factor was the religious one. Kings Park included the largest Catholic reservation in the West of Scotland, both working and middle classes in large numbers. It was not just that Robin was Catholic. That would have helped but it would not have been decisive on its own. What would be crucial would be his links with the Catholic Church organisation. From His Grace, the Archbishop, through Father Andrew, who pulled all the strings, down to every single parish priest, Robin knew them all personally. His expectation was that their respect and admiration for him was such that some of them would instruct their flocks of their duty to depart from their normal habits, desert Labour and deliver their support and their vote to him. Even Father Andrew would be ambivalent, he was worried about the renewed pressure in the City Labour Party over educational segregation and relied on Robin's guidance for the protection that opting-out might offer their schools. Not all of the flocks would come of course, but the muddying of the waters and the cutting of the umbilical chord to Labour, he winced with genuine pain at his own unpleasing mixing of metaphor, would be sufficient to ensure that enough would do so to guarantee him victory. The fact that the existing MP was a Protestant, and one honest enough to have publicly committed himself recently to the need to end segregated schooling and as in favour of abortion on demand, were just extra bonuses. Robin did not have any ethical difficulty with this, the system had benefited the Labour Party so often in the past, it was only fair that for once it would work the other way.

Robin as a Catholic Tory, was well aware of the irony that it was the decline in influence of the Church of Scotland that had been so damaging to his Party, and the maintenance of the collective faith and loyalty of his religion that had been so beneficial to the Labour Party in Scotland. It would amuse him to blur those lines in favour of what he saw as a more rational alignment. He knew that the work he had put into studying modern polling techniques would be an assistance in his campaign. His wife, Francesca, would also be an asset. She already had a high profile in the area due to her charitable and Church work. She would enjoy the prospect of being a candidate's wife, although she would enjoy being a Government Minister's wife even more. He knew all the theory and conventional wisdom about how little impact individual candidates, or campaigns, had in General Elections but he had convinced himself that the combination of all the factors present here made it entirely possible that he would be successful. Once elected, he knew he would be seen as an MP of the highest calibre. No, 54 was not too old to start a new career. He would also have the most powerful and influential friends within the Government and Party. He was definitely "one of us" but he combined that with a visible and undeniable commitment to the welfare of the community through the provision of the best possible standards of education. He brought an intellectual coherence and integrity to concepts that in the hands of others sounded dangerous and dogmatic slogans. Educational vouchers, school boards, opting out provisions, community use of facilities, the re-introduction of adults, the role of market forces, the benefits of compulsory testing of children and appraisal of teachers - he could describe the place and positive educational role of these and many more both in a Scottish and an English context. He had seriously considered his other option, to stand for an English seat. One or two feelers had been put out in this direction but they had come to nothing. He knew one element in this was a discrimination against him because of his Scottishness, an irony he knew others would appreciate more than he.

He had a secondary aspect to his plan, one that he knew Francesca considered both more likely and more desirable than his own and was very much her preferred option. He was well aware that further development of the irrational but widespread regional hatred of the Prime Minister and thus of her Party could threaten the envisaged backward swing of his pro-Tory pendulum north of the so-called border. On his blacker days which seemed to be more frequent, he could even envisage a scenario where they lost more seats and gained none, not even his despite all the factors in his favour. But although depressing that did not make him suicidal. He saw the silver lining that kind of disaster could offer to him. He knew that even being an unsuccessful candidate could carry with it rewards, if he came close against a Scottish context of further Tory losses and overall national victory. There would need to be the creation of Scottish Tory Peers with the ability to run the Scottish Office. Lord and Lady McGoldrick of Thom, she had already chosen the title after their favourite Loch and walk. His plan B, her favoured option, would have its definite compensations and was not without its appeal to him. It would remove some of the more unattractive and irritating aspects of democratic involvement. But although he would happily accept the other scenario, winning Kings Park was still his first preference, it was the logical culmination of his work of the last twenty years.

A very full twenty years it had been too. He remembered the apprehension with which he had first arrived in Glasgow, although it had been as nothing compared to Francesca's fear. Nothing in his life until then had adequately prepared him for this city. People who met him for the first time, certainly almost all Scots people, generally took him to be English. He had a fine Standard English accent which he had taken great care to ensure had not been corrupted by exposure to the ugly abuse of the language so prevalent in Glasgow. But in fact, he had been born in Scotland, to an English father with a Scottish name, and a Scottish mother with an English name. The family home had been in one of those parts of Edinburgh that is for all important purposes not in Scotland. At the age of five, a confused and devastated little boy had been sent away from his mother to a residential preparatory school in the Oxfordshire countryside. He had already lost his father to the war two years before, and never really found him again. His father had been something in Intelligence although it never involved leaving London. After the war, he had resumed his very successful career as the Managing Director of an Edinburgh based company, specialising in high finance and had seemed content to have Edinburgh as his base for the rest of his career. His mother had been born in Edinburgh, into a very successful legal family and within the limits created by her Catholicism had become one of the premier hostesses and leading ladies of the city. She had been much too busy to have any more children after him, and arranged for the family doctor to testify to the strong medical reasons why it would be so positively dangerous to have any more. Contraception was scarcely an issue as she hardly saw her husband from 1939 to 1945, and after that the habit had been lost. Robin knew she had been glad to get rid of him to residential school as soon as possible. She had described him once as difficult, clinging, moaning child. She had had a war to organise and he just got in the way. Even briefing the Nanny took too much time.

He could never adequately describe the horrors of that first school. He never found anybody who seemed to be interested enough to listen. It was not that there was physical pain. Most pupils were physically abused, some on a very regular basis, but Robin went through his life never contravening rules and the brutality was directed elsewhere. There had been one significant exception to that rule that had scarred Robin both physically and much more seriously, mentally. Mad Brother O'Mally who regularly thrashed seven year old boys until in his own eloquent phrase "the blood runs down their legs" had been in a particularly vile mood. Robin was terrified of him and had developed his early notions of the Devil around O'Mally's black form. He had always managed to stay out his way and had from his earliest time there memorised in Latin the catechisms and other works that the brute would demand recitation of, in a gruesome game of double punishment or salvation through knowledge. That night there was no escape possible through academic competence. The beast demanded blood, gallons of it, and all present would contribute, irrespective of worth or guilt.

Someone or no-one had stolen money from O'Mally. A ten shilling note had been there five minutes ago and now it was gone. He gave the assembled group five minutes for the guilty party to own up, or the entire group would get severely punished. It was obvious he was considerably drunk. It was clear to the boys, at least the older and wiser ones, that he had in fact, intentionally or otherwise, invented the offence. There was nobody to confess, nobody to blame, nobody to divert the wrath towards. Robin often wondered if he would have told if he had known. He thought it probable given the intense fear that paralysed him, the physical pain that seared through his stomach at the prospect of the unknown terror to come. Robin had never ever been hit before, by anyone for anything. He was fifth in line. The screams of the first four did little to diminish his terror. It seemed to have taken them to warm the Brother up and by Robin's turn he was in his best rhythm. He could not speak and all the protestations of innocence were stillborn. He could scarcely undo his trousers for the shaking of his hands and he had thought for a gruesome and terrifying moment that the man was going to do it for him. He managed them off and pulled them down to his ankles along with his underpants. Trembling all over he leant over the chair as instructed and closed his eyes tightly. He had seen the cane in the man's hand, it looked very thick and gnarled. The first blow was excruciating, the pain flooded his brain and forced the tears out his eyes and the sounds out his mouth. The second one was worse, he somehow knew he was going to die. The third stroke hit the first weal and he started to fade away. He never felt the fourth one.

He came round in the sick bay with the headmaster, Brother Joseph, mopping his forehead with a damp cloth. There was no woman in the school, not ever, not even a stern Matron or a slovenly cleaning lady. The Brothers did it all. His backside was already bandaged, but it was sticky with the blood that continued to flow. He vomited before he could speak, then took over the wiping of his own face. Brother Joseph was sympathetic but firm. Discipline had to be maintained otherwise there would be anarchy, but this was unfortunate and perhaps a little excessive. No apology came but even at that age Robin was clever enough to decode the message. His parents need never know and the headmaster's gratitude would include keeping a bright boy like him well rewarded for his discretion and well away from Brother O'Mally. Like he would all his life, Robin had accepted the system's terms and flourished within them.

He had enjoyed his temporary status as hero with the other boys and had even overcome his reclusive instincts to allow a general examination of his quite impressive scars. Brother O'Mally had been temporarily removed from direct contact with boys, which had increased his other abuse, of the bottle. Three weeks later, in a thunder storm, he had fallen down stairs and broken his neck, which had confirmed Robin's beliefs in the power of prayer and the benevolence of the Lord. The whole experience, the only time at either of his schools that he was physically disciplined, left a considerable mark with Robin. He could not accept the philosophy that the price for ensuring the guilty never go free is that sometimes the innocent must be punished as well. He was horrified to find on arrival at St Anne's that it was standard practice to punish whole classes in the name of this theory, or other distorted notions of collective guilt. He had put a stop to that practice although he had no dispute with the efficacy of corporal punishment, in appropriate cases.

He had always managed to hide his feelings sufficiently enough to avoid appearing pathetic and thus become the subject of the terrible bullying that went on between pupils. He was never a popular boy but both there and at St Phillip's, his public school, he managed to avoid becoming the subject of other people's spite. His heart had wept for those who had not been so lucky but he knew that to befriend them was to invite similar treatment. It was the emotional pain that he remembered, whenever he was unlucky enough to think about it. Pain that alternated with vast emptiness. He found his only solace and company in literature. By the age of eight, he had virtually memorised all of Hardy, Scott and Thackeray. He did not like Dickens but read him all anyway. He observed first hand the benefits of doing well academically and found it came naturally to him to succeed without rubbing others noses in it. He looked forward obsessively to the end of terms and a return home, but soon found out that these did not offer experiences of a warmer nature. There was no-one at that first school who had offered anything to him emotionally. There was no female presence, nor young teachers. His ability was recognised and had certain rewards but they did not include any kind of relationship. He felt himself to be the loneliest boy in the world and learned to rely on his own company for whatever satisfactions he could extract from life. Every book he read became a lifelong friend and it later became an obsession with him to regain possession of those he had read in childhood but had been unable to keep. Money had never been a problem, his mother was generous that way. His father had paid him several fleeting visits to the School, unannounced but very welcome. Robin always wondered afterwards why he never told the truth to his father about how unhappy he was, probably because he knew the man had more important things on his mind. He both idealised and idolised his father, and did not blame him for his predicament at all. He was proud of the pride his father seemed to take in his academic progress and his literary awareness.

Somehow the six years eventually passed and then it was on to St Phillip's, the premier Catholic public school which his father had so fondly attended. This was a much more civilised and bearable experience, but Robin knew at one level that the harm had been done. The only joke Robin ever made about his time at St Josiah's was whenever anyone at St Phillip's mentioned the old Jesuit adage "Give me the child at 7 and I will give you the man" Robin replied that the Brothers' motto was "Give me the child at 5 and we will give you the half man". He knew how much bitter truth there was in that for him. St Phillip's had been much better. There were people there that had genuinely felt some care and concern for the intense and intelligent young man he had become. One teacher in particular, Smethwick, had taken a considerable and genuine interest in him and his devotion to literature. He had ensured Robin had a ready stream of references to pursue, not only in English, Greek and Latin but also in several modern languages as well. Together they would discuss Mann, Canetti, Borges, Boll and the rest well into many a winter's evening. He had even made one or two special friends among the other boys. His intellect and capacity for clear self-expression meant that eventually he became one of the more prominent intellectual leaders in a school that had placed more importance on this than some of the other aspects of residential school life. There had been discipline but no abuse, fagging but nothing to offend a sensitive soul with his instincts for survival. He had developed one major crush, on a beautiful young poet named Wilbur Thompson, who at the age of 19 devastated not just Robin but the whole school and a wider literary community by hanging himself shortly after the publication of his first collection. Robin's most treasured possession had always been the sad sonnet Wilbur had dedicated to him, hand-written on school note-paper. He had always intended to write the definitive biography, and include the unpublished sonnet in it. Maybe he still would one day. He certainly knew more about the circumstances of the suicide than had ever yet been published. What a sadness that had been, what a tragic loss, but he had understood the logic and the motivation.

There had even been contact with women at St Phillip's. A housemother who had been particularly kind to him, a nurse who had made gentle jokes about him. Teachers' wives who had taken a genuine interest in their husbands' brightest pupil. Girls were a different matter. Other than his cousins in Edinburgh, Robin had never been alone with a girl until he went to Oxford. They might as well have been a foreign species, something the nature of which was loosely divined from books, something of which he was intensely afraid.

Contact with home had been better from St Phillip's. For one thing, his father was usually there. His mother took delight in telling her friends of his academic prowess. Unlike most Catholic mothers, she never even hinted that it would be fine if he wanted to be a priest. She was delighted that he was a good Catholic but she wanted the family line to continue. It was almost as if she had come to terms with whatever guilt she might have felt about him by investing emotionally in his future family and life rather than in his present. She had hoped that he would become a lawyer, but an educationalist, her son would never be a mere teacher, was still eminently respectable in her terms. Both parents assumed that he would go to Oxford and demonstrated great satisfaction when his place was assured. He never lacked for the comforts money can bring a young man. He never developed any friends in Edinburgh, even the one or two from St Phillip's that lived locally were not his type, being physical rather than cerebral. Things had improved however, when slightly to his surprise he had been invited to spend part of his second summer with his friend Michael Powell and his family. Thereafter, there was seldom a holiday went past without either him joining one family or another, or one of his friends would come to his. Edinburgh under those circumstances was a delight with an endless collection of galleries, theatres and bookshops to explore. The Festival became the focal point of every year, and often his mother would ensure that famous people, authors, musicians or performers either stayed with them or at least came for tea. She, of course, was one of the organisers, had been on the original Festival planning group and an indispensable member throughout its existence.

The other group of people who regularly came to tea were the Catholic Hierarchy. From Cardinal through Archbishop to sundry Bishops and rising Priests, Kathleen McGoldrick knew them all and had an intense personal relationship with at least the good-looking or powerful ones. It was only later that Robin learned why his father never appeared to mind her fairly shameless behaviour, and he then kept introducing Francesca to Glasgow's ecclesiastical answer to Paul Newman and others but without similar success. Robin had not realised until much later the irony of the position of the Catholic Church in Scotland, with its mass of membership being its Irish stock in the West but its lay aristocracy being its high Anglican strain in the East. It amused him slightly that he was about the only lay member he ever met who straddled both sides of that immense social divide. Not that he ever had any doubts about to which side he belonged. In that respect at least, he was always his mother's son. The major enduring effect of his St Josiah's experience, which the more positive St Phillip's one had served to reinforce, was to give him the only passionate commitment of his life. He developed early on a deep-rooted desire to influence the quality of education provided to children, so that none would have to suffer as he had done these dark dark years. He swithered in the strength of his desire, only between whether it was more important to reform residential education from within or to improve the state sector so that the private lost its attraction. The glittering alternative career possibilities opened up by his exceptional academic success at first St Phillip's, then Oxford were never able to divert him from this aim. He did not despise the academic life and often had fantasies about ending up back at Oxford but he always maintained an enthusiasm to demonstrate his notions at a practical as well as academic level. Once his mentors realised that he would not be dissuaded, that his commitment was genuine, he was helped with entry to the most suitable starting and learning points. He had six different jobs within the first eleven years after leaving Oxford. He rose quickly through the ranks, in both the private and public sectors, from teacher, principal teacher, head of department, Assistant Head, Depute Head, all the time producing policy papers of a high quality that received critical professional acclaim.

Then early in 1969 the message had come from his mother that Father Andrew wanted to see him. He was surprised when he realised that Father Andrew was coming to England, to his School and that it could not wait until one of his infrequent trips home. He awaited his visit with interest. Father Andrew did not waste time on social calls. He was an interesting man. Chameleon like, he could be perfectly at home in social settings like Robin's mother's dining room, holding his own over the finest brandy with the leading artists of the day. Yet Robin knew that his true métier was in the backrooms of Glasgow where he acted as the Pope's plenipotentiary in the real world, making and breaking deals and careers and facing the hard decisions of power. He ran the Corporation Education Department from a co-opted seat on the Committee and the Catholic Labour Mafia that normally ran the city never turned a corner without his say-so. He ran the Catholic Care society and services from behind a front man. He had scorned the normal routes of advancement in the organisation but even in Rome his exceptional power and influence were acknowledged and was often given special and interesting remits. Yes, whatever he had to come 400 miles to say had to be worth hearing.

It was an offer to Robin to come north to Glasgow to become the Headmaster of St Anne's Secondary School, one of the largest schools in Britain. It had a tough catchment area on the south side of Glasgow, stretching from Gorbals at one end to Castlemilk on the other. It had had a good reputation once but had run down considerably over the last twenty years under a reactionary old-fashioned and draconian head. In Father Andrew's words "It needs bringing into the twentieth century before it's too late. There is considerable scope for new ideas and new methods. You would be given a blank cheque to write your own script." He certainly knew how to hit Robin's soft spot. Robin had worried about the political aspects. He had made no secret in his public writing that he was a committed Conservative, deeply opposed to what he saw as the imposition of socialist dogmas onto the education system. Father Andrew told him not to worry about that. For once, Glasgow Corporation was currently under Tory control, and Father Andrew had no doubt that they would be delighted to break the hegemony of Labour appointments to Heads posts. More importantly, there would be no opposition from the Labour politicians who were bound to regain control soon. Father Andrew decided who were to be the Heads of Catholic schools and their religious convictions were more important than their political ones. Robin had smiled wryly at this as he knew the strength of Father Andrew's commitment to the Labour cause. "No, the job is yours if you want it. You will be the youngest Headmaster in Glasgow but I'm confident that you would quickly be recognised as the best. Think of the challenge and the opportunity, there are exciting times ahead and you could be in the vanguard of them."

He had found it an irresistible offer, a major headship several years ahead of schedule, a poor base to build from and considerable potential to implement all his ideas and plans. The question of coming back to Scotland had raised for him the issue of his nationality and identity. He would have had no qualms at all about Edinburgh but Glasgow was different. They did not even speak English there. He had only been to Glasgow twice in his life before he was offered the job, and he had not liked it as a city. There was an energy and a noise about it that actually frightened him. There was a total lack of refinement that had appalled him. He had been taken aback by the fact that people in the street had actually verbally challenged him, and expected him to engage in reply. It had been friendly enough but he had felt it could easily have turned nasty, and anyway his mind did not operate in that kind of tight sharpness. He would come in some state of fear, not to a foreign country but definitely to a foreign city. He did not consider himself as Scottish, never had but neither did he consider himself as English. He belonged to that rare breed, the Briton. The language of the Briton was English, as was the culture and history. He could never see the excitement involved in contests between teams representing the individual countries of the United Kingdom. He felt no partisanship whatsoever. While at Oxford, he had been selected to represent an England Youth Bridge team. It had never occurred to him to decline on the grounds that he was born in Scotland. Likewise, it never occurred to him to decline subsequent selection for the Scottish national team on the grounds that he had already played for England.

If he had been slightly frightened at the prospect of coming to Glasgow, Francesca had been frankly terrified. She had only reluctantly accepted it on the basis of the tremendous benefit to him and the fact that, as Father Andrew had pointed out, it would make her the youngest and most attractive Headmaster's wife in Christendom. Robin had assured her it would only be another temporary move and after an experience like that, he would have the pick of plum and prestigious jobs in more salubrious areas. They had both been instantly reassured by Pollokshields where with help from their parents they bought a large mansion only two miles from the school but in a different world from most of its catchment area. It had been surprisingly easy to insulate themselves from the Glasgow of their early images, to the extent that it even existed. They both found very quickly that they actually enjoyed living in Glasgow. It literally was a dear green place. They never ceased to boast to their old friends about the number of parks in the city. They were actually surrounded by them where they lived. Maxwell Park, Queens Park, Pollok Park, Bellahouston Park, they were all within a few minutes walk of the house. Pollok Park especially was a delight, with Pollok House and the Gardens. They had enjoyed many a fine stroll through that Park. Then the delight had been made more exquisite, when the Burrell Gallery opened in that same Park. Every Sunday they were able to walk briskly from their house to this free treasure trove of delicacies, then home again through that park and two others, all in under an hour of actual walking time.

Robin's mother had ensured their passage into the appropriate artistic sets and they both, but especially Francesca, had found roles for themselves in the management and advisory committees of the kind of organisations that were important to them. Francesca soon had become so enmeshed in what she regarded as acceptable society and role, that he knew staying longer would not be the issue he had at first feared it might. With the right money, status or connections, Glasgow in the 1970s was a remarkably civilised place to live, and amazingly, it became considerably more so during the 1980s, with the ultimate climax of 1990 when the rest of the civilised world finally acknowledged Glasgow's place there as of right with its recent crowning as European City of Culture. They were both proud of the contribution they had been able to make over these twenty years, they were not just grateful recipients. They had made a conscious effort to contribute what skills and time they could. Patrons of Scottish Opera, Friends of the Citizens Theatre, Members of the Scottish National Orchestra, Directors of the Glasgow Film Theatre, Committee members of this and that, supporters of everything else worthwhile, even the Mayfest after initial abstention on grounds of political dubiety, everything in fact but 7:84 and Wildcat.

They never had cause to see the wild side of Glasgow. They never went anywhere other than by car or taxi and the unique joys and experiences of the Glasgow public transport systems were denied to them. They lost the chance to overhear the conversations on the number 5 bus to Castlemilk although it passed near their door. They never entered real Glasgow pubs, preferring instead to do their little social drinking in posh restaurants and country clubs, so they were denied a decent argument. They never ventured into the city centre, or indeed any part of the city, late at night so they never saw the boisterous heart of the city beating irregularly. They never ate fried food so the need to stand in a fish'n'chip queue and hear the mysteries of the world explained never manifested itself. The really sad thing was that they never had any sense of loss, only one of relief that the monsters of their imagination stayed safely in their cages and reservations. Robin gained considerable academic and political mileage from his bravery in associating himself with the terrible problems of Glasgow in general and the Gorbals in particular. His basic honesty and integrity meant he gained even more credibility by downplaying the myths and defending the basic decency of the children and adults to whom he was exposed. Contact with the southside of Glasgow had rounded out his political education but the net effect had been to confirm in him a contempt for the ignorance and inefficiency of municipal socialism.

His tenure in St Anne's had been a great success from the beginning. He had spent the month of June 1969 watching his predecessor make his departure. Then he had sacrificed his summer holidays that year to plan his new empire in detail. He had returned in August and over the next seven years worked very hard to transform St Anne's into the best, most modern school in Glasgow. He had then had to work much less hard over the next thirteen years to keep it in the forefront. He had opened it up to the community in the most radical and innovative ways, which had formed the model for the new Region to follow. He had reintroduced adult pupils into his classrooms while others had panicked at the very notion. He had introduced parental involvement in the running of the school, a direct forerunner of School Boards, and he had profitably used his own experiences and lessons to define and clarify his thinking on the issue. The final legislative product, to his regret, was a pale shadow of his own St Anne's Board. He had introduced all manner of new technology for staff and pupils as well as administrators. He had opened up the extensive school educational and recreational facilities to evening and weekend use in a way that seemed very radical for the time but which had only been common sense to him. As a by-product he had made his two janitors into millionaires, but that was typical of the trade-union dominated lunacy of the Labour administration's rules. One of them had actually, with overtime, earned more than him in three out of the last four years, if you did not count his earnings from his books, articles and conference fees.

Father Andrew had been right, he had had no difficulty from the Labour politicians, first on the Corporation, then on the Regional Council. Indeed they had been more sympathetic to what he was trying to achieve than the grey and wooden men in Bath Street. He despised the regional education hierarchy; petty unimaginative men with no redeeming features. With no convictions there could be no courage. He had had one or two allies, surprising ones given his politics. Arthur Neilson, the strongly Labour head of a similar school on the north of the river had emulated many of his reforms and pioneered a few of his own that Robin had been swift to copy. The Tallyman, although a rising Labour star gave him consistent support from first Division then Region, but in the main it had been a constant struggle against a negative and obstructive administration terrified of the new, the strange the unknown, the controversial and the different. He had been sounded out about a job at Regional HQ at the time of regionalisation in 1974/75 but he had quite wisely decided against it. He knew he would have more power, more influence, more freedom, more time and more money as the head of one of the biggest Secondary Schools. If they had offered him the Director's job, it might have been different, but that was all stitched up politically in 1974 and only the second tier posts were available, and he did not want anything to do with them. He was openly contemptuous of the Director, the man with no name. Robin often wondered ruefully how on earth it was possible to be the Director of one of the largest Education Authorities in Europe, by far the largest in Scotland, and have absolutely no public profile. Maybe it was not necessary or desirable to go as far as the big man in Social Work did, but Robin knew that if he had had the job, his name would have been very prominently known by everyone in Strathclyde. He also knew that anonymity was probably the least of the Director's faults. Robin had always known that the politics of the Region meant that he could never hope to attain the position of Director but that had ceased to bother him many years ago, when his more ambitious scheme started to formulate.

One aspect of life in Glasgow had been easier than he had feared. He had worried about the aggressiveness of the natives, even the professional ones. He had seen it as the Glasgow character to challenge and fight. He knew that he hated conflict and that he could not cope directly with anger and abuse. In practice, open conflict had been remarkably easy to avoid. The hierarchy above, as well as not being Glaswegian, were no threat or challenge to him. They were in awe of his intellect and his reputation and he was given an easy ride. The school could have been different but he insulated himself behind a succession of hard but loyal deputes. He made the decisions and organised the changes, they then communicated them and handled the protests. He ensured he was only available as the appeal of last resort on a very formalised and therefore safe level dealing with people's rational arguments rather than the much more threatening emotional response. Even in his political activities, he managed to avoid conflict and aggression. He would supply the intellect and leave it to others to provide the muscle. He surprised himself by the extent he was able to hide his weaknesses and prosper despite his defects. He lived in literal fear of being exposed, of being taken on and apart by aggressive people as talented as himself but more direct and happier with the positive use of conflict. But it never happened. His insulation systems worked. He knew too, that his reputation for hard work was undeserved and that he was essentially a lazy man. He worked long and productive hours, but it was always on his terms, and to his ends. He was in full control, a situation conducive to laziness.

He had early grasped the importance of publicity and the value of the written word. From his arrival in Glasgow, he had produced a string of articles, papers and books about his own experiences and the wider educational and social implications of what was happening and not happening in the education world. He was a very elegant writer, with beautiful construction of sentences and paragraphs. A well-crafted paper was the most satisfying piece of work imaginable to him and he took considerable pride in the growth and development of his published oeuvre. He was aware that he was a much better writer than speaker. His major speeches tended to be written as papers, then read out. An intensely shy and painfully private man he hated performing in public. He knew that he did not have the personality to be a demagogue, but he had disciplined himself to learn a few presentational tricks and techniques that had slowly boosted his entertainment value. He was popular on the conference circuit in both educational and political circles. He had been pleasantly surprised how financially lucrative this could be.

He had resisted the lure of Academia, although he had hooked himself into the international lecture circuit it generated. Last year alone, he had been to conferences in Norway, Sardinia, Amsterdam, Canada, New Zealand and the United States. He still had fond memories of his recent trip to Brazil. At all of them, he had delivered major papers. He seldom travelled just to listen to others. There was considerable international interest in the Scottish education system and his political position gave him an unusual edge. He found it mildly ironic that he, a committed supporter of this Government, could be much more trenchantly and radically critical of the existing system than the socialist lackeys of the old Scottish Labour regimes that had created and maintained the present messes. The events of the past few years, post 1987, had been particularly energising, creating a political climate in Scotland where radical change was positively sought, particularly in education. He took great delight that the radical proposals that were around came from the Right and that the so called progressive left were intellectually bankrupt.

He was a peculiar contradictory mixture of free market ideas and a commitment to public education. He strongly believed that public education had to be, and was, capable of offering a product equal to that in private education, but for this to be the case, the structure and framework within which it was provided had to be radically altered. He read extensively on educational research throughout the world. A simple professional duty neglected by so many of the complacent Scottish elite he despised. This knowledge infused his thinking and his writing, and in turn increased his influence. In 1988 he had been seconded for a month to Wellington, where he had helped establish a system of School Boards akin to the St Anne's model. It was another of the ironies he collected that it was a New Zealand Labour Government that had legislated for a stronger and more truly democratic model, while his own Government had made concessions to the enemy which left his and their creations vulnerable to the teaching mafias. It was still a hope of his that they could be further strengthened, although he played down to Michael the effects on that Labour Government of the reforms they had instituted.

He remembered fondly the famous television interview that had helped to establish his public reputation in Scotland. It was several years ago when he had been introducing some of his measures in St Anne's giving parents a genuine role in the school. The young smart-ass interviewing him had not done his homework very well, but he had picked up that Robin's own two daughters, after attending State primary schools were now receiving private education at boarding schools in England. The aggressive lead-in had been predictable "How can you claim such benefits for the state system, and ask parents to make such a commitment to it, while at the same time sending your own children to private school?"

Well, in the Glasgow phrase he hated, it had been like stealing sweeties from a wean. He had demolished the man entirely. To their credit, and his surprise and gratitude, S.T.V. had shown the interview in full although it had not been a live recording. The high point of his tirade, and the one that seemed to have most impressed the majority of Scots who measure a man's importance by the salary he can command, was when he had taken out of his pocket a letter which he had said contained an offer from a prominent English Public School to become their Headmaster at a salary more than twice what he was currently getting from Strathclyde. He had waved this letter energetically in the interviewer's face while patiently but firmly explaining that he was refusing the offer precisely because he had such a personal commitment to the provision of state education, an education that was capable of being as fine as anything offered by the private sector. The position of his own daughters was one of the sacrifices he had had to make because of this commitment to the state sector. He had such a high profile locally, as a somewhat controversial Headmaster, that it would not be fair to his own children to expose them to the consequences of that profile by insisting on educating them within that same system. He knew himself that his logic was quite defective and that a better interviewer, with a cooler head and a sharper brain, would have given him a much harder time. Fortunately the letter waving had been very effective and the interviewer had been very obviously impressed with his response. Most of the papers the next day had picked up his performance in flattering terms and the Glasgow Herald leader had gone on about how good it was to hear such a spirited and convincing defence of public education and how lucky Glasgow was to have such a man in its ranks.

The letter had actually been a reminder from his Insurance Company that his house contents policy was now overdue. He did not feel guilty about that at all. He knew it was all a game, and anyway there had been several offers, at higher salaries if not quite double. Afterall he did have a high national reputation as both a headmaster and an educationalist. Also it was very true that the loss of his daughters was a great personal sacrifice for him. He felt a deep sense of private loss and sorrow there. There was no educational or social reason why they could not have gone to a neighbouring school. Even his own would have been no great hardship for them, he was convinced of that. It had been his devil's bargain with his wife, part of the terms on which she had agreed to come to Glasgow. She had agreed that they would attend primary school in their new neighbourhood, particularly after she had visited the very smart and socially acceptable little primary school in Pollokshields with its carefully crafted catchment area. But once they were 12 years old they had to attend her old school, a smart residential Catholic school for girls in Essex. It had seemed an acceptable deal at the time, after all Hannah had only been three years old and for all he had known, they could have been back in the south of England long before the delivery date was due. And he was a man who kept his word, who respected his bargains whatever the personal cost, whether they were with God, himself, his staff, his pupils or as most often, with his wife.

He was well aware that overall he had benefited considerably from the many bargains he had made and kept with his wife. If it had not been for her active co-operation he knew that he would probably never have been able to marry. The absence of a wife would have been a major, if not fatal, handicap for an aspiring Headmaster and Tory politician. She had always carried out both wife roles with exceptional ability and great enthusiasm and he knew the considerable debt he owed her on each front. At Oxford there had been several women interested in him, but they had all terrified him and he had successfully avoided all but the most platonic of relationships. He had devoted himself to his studies, his books and his political and artistic interests. He had been active in several relevant societies and clubs and had had a fair range of male friends, but women he kept himself a safe distance from, whenever possible. The jobs he took after Oxford offered little threatening contact with eligible women, although the wives of one or two of his older teaching colleagues had confirmed his fears and reinforced his terror by appearing to be trying to seduce him. He found their advances easy to resist, and none seemed determined to persist.

Then Francesca came into his life. He had just started at Mertons as the new Principal English teacher. He had become very close, professionally, to the Headmaster and had moved into a Staff House next door to him. His wife had taken a more maternal interest in the new arrival than some of her colleagues and he was frequently in their house for meals, long chats and serious games of bridge. The Headmaster, who was one of the top educationalists in the land and the real reason Robin went to Merton, was if anything even more impressed by his bridge abilities than his educational ones and wanted to make the most of the opportunities this presented. When their 17 year old daughter arrived home from her summer stint abroad after finishing her school career, she was almost destined to fall hopelessly in love with this romantic figure, so good-looking, so kind and considerate, so thoughtful and gentle, so obviously intelligent and sensitive. He was the first man she had ever seen her father acknowledge as an equal. She was delighted to find it was not hopeless. He shared her interest in music, in art and literature, in books and films. He was so much better read and educated. Over the next few months he broadened her horizons in many directions and they spent a considerable time alone together or as a foursome with her parents. The night he and she beat her parents at bridge then went for a candlelit dinner for two down by the river was the happiest night of her short and untroubled life.

When he proposed, she had no hesitation in accepting. She assumed the passion would come after consummation, everything in its proper order and place. Her parents regarded him as an exceptionally good partner for her. They were a little worried about her relative youth but at least it meant that she would not get into trouble. It was agreed that they would get married in the summer of 1962, he would be 26 and she would be 18 years old. Robin regarded himself as being very lucky. He half-realised that he could only ever have wooed and won a child, any woman would have exposed his weaknesses at least to himself and he or they would have backed off. And the older he became the less likely a child would have been as a realistic possibility. He had sensed that Francesca was his first and last chance. She was beautiful but that was only a bonus. At 17, she looked like a sophisticated woman in her mid-twenties. At 46 she looked like a sophisticated woman in her mid-thirties. Looking back he found it hard to place the crossover point. He was later able to contrast this with the Glasgow phenomenon where most girls look much younger than their age until about the age of twenty-five, and then much older than their age from about the age of thirty. It was her personality that had attracted him. She was intelligent and intellectual, but decidedly unacademic. She could have gone to Oxford but had not the slightest desire to do so. She considered herself very fortunate to enter her chosen career, as wife of an important man, without having to serve a lengthy apprenticeship or extended preparation, other than her whole life to date.

They had spent their honeymoon in Florence, having agreed that Venice was too smelly. The art galleries and museums had been wonderful, breathtaking, an experience to be savoured and repeated time and again. The climax of the holiday was a trip to Milan to attend the Opera. They had finished drained and exhausted, hanging onto each other for strength and support. The food was a success, generally leaving them satisfied but anxious for more. They experimented with new vintages, trying a variety of different wines to find the ones that would give most satisfaction and pleasure. The only disappointment was the sex. Robin had never made any kind of love to a woman before the trip. Francesca had never gone beyond a breathless grope and a fevered light petting. He knew nothing of the mechanics of foreplay or the secrets of a woman's private anatomy. He had even read the wrong kind of literature to be of any practical use. Fortunately she was excited enough any way that his initial entry did not cause her any great pain or difficulty. He ejaculated ninety seconds after entering her, and gave a silent shudder before withdrawing. Perhaps if they had spoken about it immediately it might have been different, but a pattern was set where sex became a silent experience, never to be talked about before, during or afterwards. The next few times were slightly better as he broke the two and three minute barriers, but then it hit a plateau. The other excitements of the holiday were enough to sustain them through their respective disappointments at the poor quality of the physical interaction.

Thereafter sex became a matter of perfunctory couplings on a decreasing basis until it just disappeared altogether. That took many years to achieve and happened very gradually rather than by conscious decision of one or other. The final point of no return had been in 1982 when Francesca contracted mumps. She had been very distressed and feverish and he had moved out of their bedroom into the spare room, to give her space and peace. Neither ever discussed the matter but both just accepted that he would stay there and never move back. They still shared a double bed on holidays and whenever she accompanied him on his trips abroad, but sexual intercourse was replaced completely by social intercourse. Very occasionally, in the middle of empty Glasgow nights, she would slip into his room and his bed, sometimes just for comfort, less often to force him to have sex.

He had never once given her an orgasm, even when his knowledge and technique had improved. She had been very disappointed at first, but had kept hoping that matters would improve over time. She was eventually forced to the unpalatable conclusion that it was getting worse rather than better and never would improve. It was not the lack of orgasm. She had lived with that herself for many years, and took her own responsibility for her satisfaction. It was his failure to use physical lovemaking as an expression of the affection and care she knew he felt for her. His attachment to opera was passionate, his feeling for his books was passionate, his response to good music was passionate, his commitment to the theatre was passionate but all his relationships with people, even her, were rational and logical.

She shared his passion for the arts but eventually had to extend it to the artists. She could not live her life devoid of the physical

100

expression of some of her strongest feelings. She took her marriage and her marriage vows very seriously and the concept of adultery was alien to her. She truly loved him and wanted to cherish him rather than hurt or humiliate him. But the pain and the passion had built up inside her and one wet Glasgow evening the body could stand no less and she had made love all evening to an obliging Scottish violinist who knew what and where her clitoris was and how to play the sweetest mouth music on it. Years of accumulated passion and desire expended themselves on this bemused and grateful musician. She had gone home that night unsure whether or not she would or should tell him. He had noticed nothing and she thought discretion would be sensible and that no harm had been done. Once the dam was burst, the land could never be totally dry again and she found herself repeating the activity on a regular basis. She had evolved several elaborate rules that she tended to keep to, with only the occasional lapse. She would select, she was attractive enough to be able to do the selecting with some guarantee of success, only younger men. Men not known personally to her husband or at least not friends or colleagues of his. She never picked married men, or vulnerable, sensitive ones. She had to be able to rely on their discretion and on the likelihood that they would be happy to enjoy the experience and move on at her timing. She was a good judge of character and fortunately for her, her charitable and cultural activities brought her into regular enough contact with sufficient suitable young men to satisfy her needs. She never had more than one on the go at a time, and often would go months without indulging. She never brought them to the house or met them anywhere for assignations other than hotel rooms in establishments outside Glasgow. She never paid for the room the first time, but thereafter was conscientious about paying her share.

It was two years into this pattern before Robin confronted her with his suspicions, although he had guessed for a miserable month before raising it. She had been remarkably frank with him and told him what she had been doing, with whom, for how long and under what rules. In a funny way the fact that it had been going on for two years had reassured him, since it demonstrated that discretion could be maintained. He had always assumed that her infidelity would be unacceptable to him and would lead to the inevitable end of the marriage, but she turned out to be a better reader of him than he was. He could not find it in him to leave her or ask her to leave. He was too fond of her for that, and knew he needed her too much, on a variety of levels. He did like her, she was his best and almost only friend and they had many shared happy aspects of life together. They did enjoy the same experiences, the same range of interests, hobbies and occupations. They loved the holidays they took together every year, carefully chosen and planned to allow them to develop or pursue certain aspects of these interests. He had allowed her to become a joint owner and collector of his books which were by now one of the finest and most valuable private collections in the city. In return she had shared with him the classical record collection she had inherited from her father's father, which was a source of constant pleasure as they scoured little shops throughout Scotland seeking to add to it. They went together whenever possible to every opera, concert, ballet and stage production that played in Glasgow, which amounted almost to a full-time activity in itself. She supported him fully in his school, his educational and his political activities, not as the little woman but as a shrewd and intelligent assistant.

Much to his surprise he had had the maturity and strength to rank all that over his feelings of betrayal. She would have put it in slightly different terms but it had always been her assessment that they would survive his discovery of her infidelities. It was just a question of the price she would have to pay. Robin learned to live with it as a painful part of their life together. It was not sexual jealousy that caused the pain, or even social jealousy for she continued to spend much enjoyable time with and devoted to him. There was even a strong element of relief that the pressure on him to be physical had been removed. He had long ago accepted that he appeared to have a very low or non-existent sex drive but had felt obliged to continue for her sake. It was not fear that she would leave him, because he knew that was not the kind of relationship she was having, or the kind of thing she would do. The pain and misery was caused by his profound and constant fear of the embarrassment and social consequences which would be caused by her indiscretions becoming public, of it becoming something he would have to deal with with other people. He had realised he could cope with her doing anything, with anybody, as long as it was kept a secret. That was the most important bargain he ever made with her. He would tolerate her infidelities as long as she was totally discreet. He did not even want to know, as long as no-one else did either. Once, when he had discovered she had had a liaison with one of his staff who had moved onto another school, he had become the most emotional and animated she had ever known him to be and had told her in uncompromising terms that if her indiscretions cost him his job or harmed his career then he would kill her. That was a promise he made to her, and he always kept his promises. She had reassured him that the successful development of his career and his political ambitions was as important to her as it was to him, and that she would never do anything to jeopardise it. She meant it too and he knew she did.

He had been particularly hurt that the ex-colleague had been the School E.I.S. shop-steward. He had wondered in a concerned way how genuine the man's motivation had been towards her rather than against him. Fortunately, he had been sensible enough to be totally discreet. Robin could not understand how any teacher could be stupid enough to get involved with a Headmaster's wife. Surely no sexual excitement could be worth the risk of jeopardising your career. He was aware that Francesca had considerable involvement with his staff group, particularly since the development of his School Board and its associated offshoots with which she had become intimately involved. However he was relatively confident that she had never become involved with any of his current staff. She seemed more interested in young artists of one kind or another. She would take a special interest in their career, give them appropriate support and encouragement, then she would give them something more. He would sometimes guess who it currently was, and she was always willing to tell him the truth if he wanted to know, but he generally preferred to remain in blissless ignorance. She had not told him who the current one was, or whether there even was one, but he guessed from her pattern of evening commitments that there was someone currently selected for the honour of servicing her needs.

He never retaliated in kind, though not for lack of opportunity. Although most Glasgow men would have described him as a lang streak o' misery, with a doleful face fit only for funerals, women of all kinds seemed to find him a good-looking and attractive man. He was perceived as intelligent, kind, sensitive, thoughtful, considerate, handsome and powerful. Robin was seldom aware of the extent of this, and when he was, he did not appreciate it, or capitalise on it. Whole successions of women attempted to make their interest plain. Teachers, mothers, wives, Tory Party ladies and not just Young Conservatives, conference attendees, all tried to attract him. In an ironic cycle which he had not the social skill to break, his very disinterest and lack of response made him even more attractive. A constant stream attempted to break through the resistance with determined efforts at seduction but all were doomed to failure. It was not so much his commitment to fidelity, although he believed in that concept strongly, it was more a total fear of intimacy and a total disinterest in sex. Beautiful women did not attract him unless they could talk about education or politics or the arts, or play bridge to championship standard. If they met those criteria, whether they were beautiful or not, he would allow a measure of detached social intercourse without intimacy, but always lurking behind was his fear of their motivation and a concern to protect himself from violation.

Her mother had arranged for Francesca to pursue effective contraceptive methods in time for their honeymoon. Robin had been against any contraceptive measures, although it was one area where his religious views were not absolute. But, even at 18, Francesca had been clear in her own mind that she was too young for motherhood and that she wanted to enjoy married life for some time first. Her making the arrangements kept both their consciences clear. After about a year and a half, she had agreed that she was now ready and Dawn was born in late 1964. Hannah followed in 1966 and then Francesca had indicated firmly that enough was enough and that that was her contribution to the Catholic population problem completed. This removal of procreation as a possible outcome had further reduced Robin's commitment to regular sexual relations.

Francesca had been a good mother. He had sometimes adversely noticed her similarity in many respects to his own mother but in this regard, she was much superior. Despite the other similarities, almost all of them irritating, he never regretted marrying her and was always very grateful to her for saving him from a lonely life on his own. The arrival of his daughters had had a considerable effect on Robin. For the only time in his life he gave himself, if reservedly, to other human beings. He adored his baby daughters and lavished affection upon them before they were able to respond. He was very busy, professionally over the period when Dawn turned from a baby into a real person, and missed out on much of this. He was able to be more involved with Hannah, and no matter how he tried to be balanced, he had to admit to himself that he was more positive about one daughter than the other. Whatever the cause and effect, this pattern maintained itself throughout their childhood. Dawn became a child who often irritated him and reminded him of his own mother in her self-centredness and her control of her own priorities. Hannah became the focal point of his emotional giving, limited as it was, and he knew he loved her dearly although he never told her so.

He was happy with the relationship he had with them while they were at the local primary school. He would discuss with them in detail their school day and took a genuine interest in all aspects of their education. Holidays were a particular delight, the one time when the four of them were a functioning family group with no distractions. They always had two weeks away with the girls, then he and Francesca had two weeks on their own while the children went to grandparents. Both girls seemed to find him an awesome and distant figure, but he valued what he received from them and gave them what he could. He had tried to re-negotiate his agreement with Francesca as Dawn came near the age to start at boarding school. Francesca was adamant, however, and he had had to honour his bargain. He acknowledged that her determination was not negative or motivated by a desire to get rid of them. She genuinely loved her daughters and had a much warmer and more open relationship with both of them than he had. She had been remarkably happy herself at St Brigid's and wanted her daughters to have the same positive experiences. She did not want them to be brought up totally as Scottish girls, certainly not as Glaswegians, and she was well aware that exposure to St Brigid's would leave them much more rounded and developed socially.

It was not such a tragedy at first when Dawn left. It had given him more time to concentrate on his relationship with Hannah. That had been a good period but all too soon it was time for her to go too, and so the happiest period of his life ended, the only time he ever had a warm giving relationship with anyone was over, and by 1978, he and Francesca were alone together again. Even the holidays were no longer the same. The period away had been too long and the gap between father and daughters grew too large for a painfully shy and reserved man to easily close. By the time he had made tentative efforts to re-establish contact, they were off again, something made worse by their annoying habit of bringing friends with them, or even worse of spending large parts of their holiday with the families of school friends, in England. Their relationship with their mother did not seem to suffer. She took delight in visiting them at St Brigid's, something he was always too busy to do. During term times, she would talk to them for hours on the telephone, to his intense irritation. He had never learned how to use the telephone as an instrument for social communication and had a purely functional view as to its use.

Left alone again, he and Francesca had worked out a satisfactory enough social life. She was attractive company, physically and socially. She always maintained herself very well. She spent much of his money on expensive clothes but he never grudged her this investment. She was a witty conversationalist, much more so than he, and enjoyed entertaining the kind of people he needed to invite. They regularly held small dinner parties to which people from the little Glasgow village worlds of the Arts, Education, Politics and Religion were always glad to be invited. They were regularly invited back to similar soirees, and to many others in which they would never dream of reciprocating an invitation to their hosts. They had an interesting circle of friends and acquaintances. They also had social obligations to spend time with people who were much less interesting, which became increasingly irksome to him but which he knew was an inevitable part of his political ambitions. Francesca handled that so much better than he did.

This evening had been a good example. She had controlled the conversation, drawing him in only when necessary and appropriate and generally allowing him to be alone in his thoughts and recollections for most of the evening. The only time he had been genuinely interested enough to get involved in the conversation had been when it was mentioned that some of the new Glasgow writers had a habit of coming into the restaurant. So much, he sneered, for their proletarian identification. He explained to the company how much he despised Collie and the other Glasgow writers who claimed to be the authentic voice of the Scottish working classes. He expounded his view that their work was almost unreadable, with its unnatural, highly artificial pidgin English. He explained how it was profoundly patronising and a glorification of the corrupt. Robin much preferred the correct and measured tones of such as Raymond Church, who had become a close personal friend over the past few years. Raymond had demonstrated that it was possible for a Scottish writer to use the English language properly without compromising his message or his Scottishness. It was maybe all a matter of loyalties after all. The autographed copy of Raymond's book with the personal and political message of hope to him was one of Robin's most treasured possessions.

Robin had entered the great linguistics debate and had contributed several pieces of written work to both local and national publications. He had argued consistently and vociferously against making any concessions to Lallans, whatever that might be. He believed strongly that there was no such thing as a Scots tongue or language, and that Gaelic was a historical relic of no relevance to 95% of Scots. The so-called Scots language, such as it was, was in the main just an inferior form of English. He was very aware that this was not just true of language but of many other areas of Scottish life. He found the arrogance and complacency of the "Whaes like us" brigade an insult to intelligence. The irony was that deep down very few Scots really believed it and most had an almost in-built inferiority in the face of all things and people English. It was just that they liked to pretend to hide it behind a hollow sham of assumed superiority. He felt that the better way to overcome this, was to help Scottish people talk their own language, English, better, rather than to attempt to keep alive and venerate some of the corruptions and abuses that disabled so many of his pupils.

Robin was obsessive about good grammar and the proper use of language. A split infinitive would cause him literal pain. He had never enjoyed the normal staff-room game of retelling classroom howlers. He found them distressing and upsetting. He was convinced that Glasgow people did not talk any language other than English, but it saddened him to his core how badly and corruptly they used and abused this beautiful language. It was an important part of his creed that Scottish people were not ethnically different from English people. With an English father and Scottish mother, he had taken a deep interest in this subject and researched it extensively. He had found that there was no basis to the myth that the Scots were a race of Celts. Most Scots and English were from exactly the same racial origins and backgrounds and the continued mixing over centuries had further diluted whatever differences there might have been. There was no such thing as a Scots race separate from other British stock. The only Scots who were exceptions to this were Irish. Truly we were all British now, what a pity he was one of the few to recognise this.

His philosophy of, and views on, language and nationality were very popular in Tory circles, locally and nationally. He was one of the more articulate defenders of the Union, four countries united by common language, history and culture. He argued cogently and publicly against the folly of his party making any concessions to

Scottish values and culture. He was well aware of the political potential of Scottish nationalism and how vulnerable the commitment to the Union had become in the face of Labour vacillation. It was especially important that the Tories in Scotland did not panic and undermine the essential nature of the Union in a way that would create irreversible damage. He knew the next decade would be crucial and that vigilance needed to be maintained to avoid the perils of emotional Scottishness leading to political and then economic and social disaster.

He used his own particular area of special expertise to highlight his point. He argued that one of the so-called Scottish strengths, the finest education system in the world, was in reality a myth, and in fact a source of weakness. He was able to demonstrate with incontrovertible evidence, that Scottish educational standards were significantly inferior to English ones at all levels of education, in terms of any valid comparative measure of results or outcomes. What was required was not more Scottishness, more Scottish control and independent development but less, a move into the mainstream developments of English education with its greater emphasis on quality and standards. There was considerable scope for improvement and radical reappraisal, but that would never be provided by handing over the system to the permanent control of the dead hand of Scottish socialist complacency which had created the inferior status in the first place.

These were the views and attitudes that meant he was definitely "one of us" despite a slight dampness in certain areas. He had a radical and uncompromising belief in the value of the individual and the family against the overprotective interference of the bureaucratic machinery of local and central government. He despaired of the extent of the grip that socialist collectivism had in this part of the United Kingdom. The fact that it was brain-dead made it harder to tolerate. The only intelligent political debate north of the border was being conducted by members of his own party, everyone else was pursuing their own navel in contemplation of the number of angels that could sit in an assembly that should never and would never exist. There would have to be a reward for that one day. He looked forward with satisfaction to having a more public platform from which to argue his point of view, and to more effective influence to carry through the major changes which were required.

CHAPTER SIX - THE NEW CHOICE

Robin McGoldrick put down his Daily Telegraph with a slight sigh. If it had not been for the appointment with Hunter, he would have a full hour to himself. He had not been very pleased at the time to have to take the telephone call from Frank Hunter. But for Mrs Little and her gentle reminder about his mother, he might have persisted in his view that he was too busy to speak to him. Shona Hunter had been a fine woman and had done much good work for the Church, so he had taken the call. Hunter had been obviously anxious to come to speak to him about a personal matter. Hunter had stressed he wished to see him in the Headmaster's own office but would give no clue as to the reason why. Robin had finally, rather grudgingly given him a 15 minute slot the following day. Since then it had dawned on him what it must be about. The school had a vacancy for a janitor, that had not yet been advertised. Hunter must have been tipped off about it by one of his Union cronies and was trying to get in first. He vaguely remembered saying something to Hunter at his mother's funeral about if he could do anything to help, just to let him know. Why was it that the Scots tended to take these social politenesses more seriously than other people? Well, if Hunter thought someone with his political and trades union background had the slightest chance of obtaining a post in Robin's school, then he was about to be sorely disappointed. Still, he might quite enjoy explaining that fact of life to Hunter, personally.

He knew well who Hunter was. He remembered the insolent arrogance of his political activities within the school, activities which had the active collusion of some of the staff, activities to which he had had to put a stop. He remembered with distaste the farce Hunter had made of his first Mock Election in the school, and how he had had to assert more control subsequently to avoid any repetition. He remembered Hunter's loutish behaviour in general, and the particularly disgraceful performance in the Schools Cup Final. As captain he should have been particularly conscious of his role as representative of the school, but he had been unconcerned about that and had let St Anne's down badly. Robin had learned from that and involved himself in the selection of all such posts. It was not enough to leave it to the best player, or performer. There was not a direct relationship between talent and responsibility, indeed if anything Robin's view was that the relationship was more often inverse.

He had never seen Hunter as one of the brighter pupils and had not been disappointed when he left school before his final year and went to work as a labourer in a factory. Robin had learned subsequently that Hunter had gone onto University but he had not been surprised when he could not handle the pressures there and had left after his first year to seek refuge in manual labour. He had known of Hunter's continued involvement in the Labour Party on the southside but had had little direct contact with him through that, other than at election times. He had been aware that Hunter had pursued his obsession against Catholic schools within the Labour Party, but Father Andrew had kept him informed about the failure of that campaign. Still, that made him dangerous, if only for the influence he might have on his much more powerful friend, McGuire.

He was vaguely aware that Hunter had pursued a career as a professional footballer for a time, but that he had not quite been good enough and had drifted into the Juniors and early retirement. Some of that cup-winning team, Duncan and Gallagher in particular, had gone on to real success and given the school some cause for pride, but Hunter had not been one of them. Robin had been disappointed, indeed in truth almost horrified, when that attractive and lovely young girl, Elaine Duncan, had married Hunter. He had known then that she was a qualified teacher, and he was a labourer. It always depressed him the fascination otherwise intelligent Scotswomen had for thugs and ruffians. Fairly predictably, it had ended in tears, and he knew that she was now much more appropriately settled with another teacher, with young children of the second marriage. She had a beautiful face that girl, beautiful. As far as Robin knew Hunter was still single and unemployed. He had been aware, of course, of his role in the futile attempt to resist the operation of market forces in the LDT business. That had been a last sad vestige of the Scottish Labour Movement's complete lack of insight or imagination, which had quite predictably ended in total failure. Well, as far as he was concerned, Hunter could stay unemployed, he would certainly not get the opportunity to import trades union activity and consciousness into the tightly run ship of St Anne's.

Robin had had more direct contact with Shona Hunter. In a funny way, she had had certain similarities with his mother, they were certainly two of the few Catholic lay women he knew who refused to accept the confines the church usually laid down for women. Despite the handicap of a Protestant husband, a peculiar man by all account and another trades unionist, and later, after his death, vague rumours of a liaison with a married man, she had become very influential in her own right. Father Andrew had obviously liked her very much, and they had been allies on many issues. She had been a civilised socialist, not like her aggressive son and his crude, fat lawyer friend, and Robin had been able to work very happily with the two of them, on the whole range of social, educational and welfare interests of the Church. He had been genuinely saddened by news of her sudden death, and had had no hesitation about attending her funeral. That had been the last occasion on which he had seen her son. He recalled Father Andrew telling him recently that Hunter had taken his mother's death very badly, and had had what was in effect a nervous breakdown and had to be admitted to mental hospital. He felt a sudden pang of fear. He would have to be very careful how he handled him, he might still be unstable and capable of violence.

Robin was still feeling very pleased with himself, the forthcoming interview with Hunter was only a minor irritant in a wonderful perspective. He knew that he had made two important public speeches in recent weeks. The first one, in Edinburgh, on the role of the family in modern life had been particularly successful, and Robin had been very pleased with it. It had been a concise exposition of his viewpoint. It had been a trenchant attack on the Scottish diseases, and it had argued that only by returning to more traditional Tory values could real progress be expected. He had been particularly pleased that he had managed to turn the greed argument around on its head. He was sick of the hypocritical claptrap about the Greedy Society and the attempts of the socialist Scottish Media and establishment to identify the Prime Minister and the Conservative Government with greed and evil. He had very clearly laid out the fallacies in that argument, and gone on to show that it was the Labour Party and its philosophy that was based on greed, with its expectations that people were owed something for nothing. Political debate in Scotland needed to become less emotional and more realistic. Robin felt that he had made a major contribution to restoring the moral basis and superiority of conservatism in Scotland, and reinforcing morale within the Party. He was particularly pleased that his platform had not been a partisan political one, and that serious coverage had been given to his message. The speech had received good publicity. He had been interviewed on television and had even appeared on the evening news on S.T.V. Most of the papers had given the speech good coverage and the Scotsman had even run a leader on it. His friend Raymond Church had picked up the theme in his column and had been typically generous in his praise of Robin.

Then just four days ago, on the Friday, he had spoken in Glasgow to the Association of Headteachers about educational matters. The speech had been well received by his peers, and it had also received wider and favourable publicity. He was definitely quietly pleased. Things were building up to a good crescendo for the Selection Conference and announcement of his adoption as prospective candidate. He had no doubt but that he would be successful. The meeting two Saturdays before with the Constituency Executive had left him in no doubt about the outcome. He was calm about the current political climate. There was still a long way to go before an Election would be called, and he well knew the unprecedented electoral arithmetic required for a Labour victory.

The thought of his Glasgow speech brought to mind another matter that was a cause of some ambivalence to him. He had been both deeply disappointed and greatly relieved when Margaret had told him on the Thursday night that she would not be able to make the next appointment he had given her, or any other one. She had said she was moving back to England within the next couple of weeks. At least it was the end of an episode in his life and probably just as well with him about to enter the political arena publicly. The risks were just too great. He knew he would make no attempt to replace her. He was very aware that he could never be so lucky again. She had been the perfect partner for him. And that was the source of his regret. The need she met for him, or helped him meet for himself, was a real one, a valid part of what and who he was. He had been horrified at first with the realisation of that, but had long since come to accept and enjoy it. From now on that need would have to remain unmet, along with the other. But at least he would have his memories, and a political career to absorb his attentions. Dear Margaret, he would miss her, but not the panic and fear that always accompanied his use of her. Yes, maybe it was good that it should end now, with the announcement coming up. Her move to England carried some reassurance of discretion and safety.

He sipped the tea Mrs Little had brought into him. He had managed to train her to make a proper cup of good quality, Earl Grey or Lapsang Souchong. It had taken several years but now she seemed to know his moods, and when each should be used. Over his tea he allowed himself to think non-work thoughts. It had been many weeks since he and Francesca had spent a quiet night at home together, and that night would be no exception. He would be glad in a way when this festival of culture was over and they could reduce the dose to two or three nights per week, rather than twice nightly as it currently was, or was beginning to seem. But even as he thought the thought, he rejected it. There were so many delights still to come. In particular, he was looking forward to the Big Man. For once he felt he understood a Glasgow term. He had his tickets secure. As one of the organising Committee he would even be guaranteed to meet him in person. He had been polishing up his conversation, determined to be able fluently to converse with the man in his own language. Francesca who put in much less work than him was irritatingly expert, she sounded like an Italian, he knew he merely sounded like an educated Englishman. No doubt he would prefer to converse with her anyway, but at least Robin would get to meet him. The months of painstaking grind on the various organising forums were now paying rich dividends. Apart from anything else, they both now seemed to get free tickets to almost every event, often two each.

****

Frank Hunter decided to walk to school. He had never done anything else as a pupil and he wanted to recapture as much of the atmosphere of the past as possible. He knew exactly how he was going to play this next part of the game. He figured he would have the advantages of surprise and the first blow this round, but he knew equally well that it was a Two Act play he was creating, and that he was keeping the better script for the second half. He reckoned after his session with Julie the previous Saturday, and the photographs he had taken on the Thursday, that he now had a noose around McGoldrick's neck. He knew he needed only two little bits more to well and truly tighten it, and he was confident he would have them soon, if he played this first session right.

He thought back over the last few days. He had enjoyed last Thursday. There was only one main entrance to the Hotel. If he had got McGoldrick's psychology correct, there was no way the man would use any other entrance. He would stride up the main steps. It was just a matter of waiting and capturing the moment. The whole business had given Frank a sense of being involved in a military operation. He had enjoyed the precision planning, the detail of organisation required, and the peculiar excitement the whole process generated in himself. It was a form of adrenaline he had never known before. He had purchased a new camera, a Canon 255. He had consulted the keenest photographer he knew, his friend Alan McNair, without revealing the detail of what he wanted or why. Alan's office was up in India Street, only a minute or two's walk from the Hotel he knew McGoldrick and Julie would be using. He had timed it well. He met Alan at his office, and walked him down to the lunch table he had booked for them both at the Ho Wong, past the front doors of the Hotel on Argyle Street. The talk had been about cameras and what kind Alan would advise Frank to buy. Passing the Hotel entrance, Frank had casually asked what kind of lens the security police used for people coming and going, or demonstrating outside. It was the Hotel the Prime Minister had used on a couple of recent fleeting visits. He had then asked him, as an apparent after-thought, what kind private detectives would use for bursting into peoples bedrooms, and other such forms of indoor use. Alan had been amused at the notion and had been happy to give him very specific and detailed technical information about which equipment could best be used for each purpose.

After an enjoyable lunch talking about football, he had dropped Alan back off at India Street and continued on alone up to Williamson and Wolfe's at Charing Cross. The staff there were exceptionally helpful to him, allowing him to take cameras outside and aim them, and answering all his questions patiently and constructively. Alan had not been far off the mark in his advice, and Frank left the shop with the recommended goods, fairly sure of how to operate them. Only £672 and he had ownership of the superb Canon 255, with an extra Canon 557 Zoom lens for his external shots, and a dedicated flash unit for inside well-lit hotels. The staff had not understood his reluctance to consider adding a tripod to his list of purchases. The money didn't bother him, rather the reverse in fact, he was glad of a chance to spend. His redundancy money, and especially his inheritance from his mother, lay about his shoulders like dead mutton. His decision never to work again had almost been nullified in its significance and made obscene instead of noble, by the circumstances which meant that he could conceivably survive for years, if not for ever, without having to do so. He wanted rid of as much as possible, to hasten the day when his decision would lead to the kind of decisive crisis he had originally envisaged.

He had had a practice run at another Hotel nearby, the Albany, and from his parked car in Pitt Street had produced fascinating shots of the various comers and goers. He wondered what stories lay behind the pictures he developed himself in his makeshift dark room cupboard. Maybe they were even more interesting than McGoldrick's one. The women going in on their own fascinated him. He wondered how many of them were selling their body. Or would for the right price or in the wrong circumstances. He reckoned most of those he snapped that early Wednesday evening either were, or were capable of doing so. He knew enough about the game by then to understand something of the hierarchy that operated. He knew the Hotel workers were near the top, above the massage parlour girls, with the street walkers bottom of the league. Escort agency status, or even the elite solo superstars. None of them appeared as attractive to him as Julie had been, even in her conservative gear.

He had known from Julie's note exactly which suite would be used on the Thursday. So on the Wednesday afternoon he had strolled into the Holiday Inn with his camera. He had dressed as appropriately as he could, which had been rather difficult given his wardrobe. Thank god for America. No-one had challenged his progress and he had soon found the door. He knew that proof that they had both been in the same Hotel was interesting but hardly conclusive. He needed a closer tie, to the same room. He studied the direction the door opened from and the angles from various parts of the hall. He could not afford the slightest danger of alerting McGoldrick, and causing him to flee from Julie. Ideally he wanted Julie at the door, going in, and McGoldrick at the door and coming out. He figured it must have been easier in the days when people actually signed hotel registers. A quick snapshot of that would link McGoldrick to the room. He knew he would not need such detail for his purposes. A picture of Julie outside the door, and going in would do for him. Coming out would be a bonus, but probably was too risky. He had taken one of the closed door, for starters.

The real operation on the Thursday had gone with a precision that had pleased the engineer in him. McGoldrick had arrived at 6:14pm. He had parked his Rover in the Hotel carpark. A picture of him getting out his car was a bonus for Frank, sitting in his own car, carefully parked in the best spot from very early that day to secure the appropriate position from which to photograph the main entrance to the Hotel. At 6:16p.m. McGoldrick had entered the Hotel, carrying a suitcase in his right hand and a briefcase in his left one. It had been perfect for Frank, as he had had to put down the suitcase to open the door. Frank had taken four photographs altogether. They had developed well. McGoldrick had been caught frozen, obviously about to enter the Hotel to stay, at least for an overnight. Julie had been less nerve-wracking for him. She arrived by taxi, exactly on cue, at 7:13pm. He snapped her going in, with her smart little blue leather suitcase. He had then followed her into the lobby and up the stairs to the second floor. She had waited in the hall until he had nodded that he was in position, then she had knocked on the door. He had got a good clear picture of her outside the door, a more blurred one of her knocking on it, and a reasonable one of her disappearing in the open door. He had not been able to get the slightest trace of McGoldrick at the door. He had earlier toyed with the notion of dressing up as a waiter and knocking on the door, surreptitiously snapping McGoldrick as he answered. But he knew the risks attached to such a venture far outweighed any benefit even if it went exactly to plan, so he stuck to the safe and the minimum. He did not need McGoldrick at the door. He had gone back down and sat in his car. Despite an effort not to, he could not help himself visualising what might be going on in room 212 while he sat in his car waiting. It seemed more appealing than the book he had brought.

He took a picture of her coming out the Hotel at 8:35 p.m. She had been five minutes out in her prediction. He had whistled her over, and driven her off to the Balbir in Elderslie Street, where he had booked a table for two for 9 o'clock. He had enjoyed the meal, and especially the company. She had looked good, in her sensible blue suit. To convey managerial competence, she had explained to him. She had been both subdued and exhilarated. She had found the experience of doing the business with him as normal, a proper test of her acting talents. She had described it to him as a normal session, following almost exactly the lines she had sketched out for him in graphic detail the previous Saturday, with the addition of the bit Frank had told her to add. Frank had been slightly disappointed that such recent exposure to McGoldrick and his perverse behaviour had not removed or reduced her obvious sympathy for him. She spoke again of him as an attractive person, gentle for all the violence and somehow a lost and sensitive soul. It had been Frank's understanding and expectation that prostitutes had a universal contempt for all their clients. He found her reaction to McGoldrick a bit disconcerting.

They both enjoyed the meal. They shared vegetable pakora and somosa, and took half of each others main courses, a Lamb Pasanda and a Chicken Masala, with fried rice and a Nan Bread. It had been a long time since either had dined alone with a member of the opposite sex without the spectre of imminent sexual activity of a contractual nature of one kind or another. Eventually he had had to remind himself, and her, that in fact they did have a contractual arrangement to fulfil. Towards the end of the meal, he had insisted on rehearsing with her several times what the next stage for her would be likely to be, and what her exact script should be. He confirmed that all the necessary technology was in place, and in definite working order. He gave her two copies of the correct make of blank tape. She had quickly grasped the essentials, then explored with him some of the potential nuances and how she might play them. She had sought a further assurance from him that Mr Ross would not be devoured in the web they were weaving for him. By unspoken agreement, they had spun out their meal and their evening to the last possible moment, and then he had driven her to Queen Street Station and put her in the first class compartment of the last train to Edinburgh Waverley, from where she would take a taxi home. As he had watched the train pull away, and walked out the draughty and deserted station to his car, he had realised that he had really enjoyed the evening, and her company, and that the feelings he felt were ones of genuine affection and friendship.

Back home in his flat, he had with some difficulty, deliberately disciplined himself not to immediately develop the film he had used, in case Joyce should come round. She had come, not long after he had got back. He had been consumed with a strong desire to fornicate, and fortunately, Joyce's experiences of earlier that evening had not been of the more depressing kind that often put her off the notion. He had asked himself if any of his extra stiffness, any of his fevered thrusting, was directed to his business partner rather than his lady love. But while she might have contributed to his mood, his fantasies and his feelings were directed towards Joyce and he was not guilty in the least degree of any act of infidelity, even of the mental variety. He was aware that it would have been perverse to deny himself the opportunity to

117

fuck Julie, because of fidelity to Joyce, and then fuck Joyce while fantasising about Julie, but people often were perverse, and many would even consider such actions logically and morally consistent. Well, he was not perverse whatever else he was. And he had not cheated Joyce. He did love her and it had been her to whom he had made love that evening. She had been pleased at his ardour, he knew that she had been worried over the previous few months, that his mental state had eroded his passion and desire and left him a more passive participant than she felt he had been in his past, and than she wished him to be.

He had developed the film the following morning, as soon as Joyce had gone out to work. She didn't take time off for her Tuesday and Thursday night efforts, nor did she claim overtime. It was a form of protest, to do the work she felt most important on her own terms. Frank had tried to at least make her take the money, for the principle but on that they talked a different language. The pictures were good enough for his needs. As soon as he had satisfied himself about that, he had moved onto the next stage and phoned the school, asking for the Headmaster's office. He knew from Julie's theory, that McGoldrick would not be there, he would be at some conference or another. Plan F had worked. He had recognised the voice right away as Mrs Little. She had been the Headmaster's Secretary since his time at St Anne's. Frank knew that she had always liked him. She had been friendly with his mother, and had been at the funeral. She had placed her hand on his arm and given him a silent but helpful pat. He had reckoned that he could afford to enlist her support. He knew the power of the diary holder in important men's lives so he had told her what he required. He needed half an hour with McGoldrick, as soon as possible, on a personal matter. It must be in his office. She had checked his diary and gave him the best advice. Phone again on Monday morning at 9:25am. on the button, and aim for an appointment for Tuesday morning at 11:30. She would do what she could to ensure that McGoldrick took the call, gave him the time and accepted the appointment. Other than that his only free times that week were Thursday afternoon and Friday morning. Frank had then checked with Julie and ensured that she would make herself available from 11:30 on Tuesday for the rest of the day, and that she would be free on the Thursday.

He had phoned on the Monday morning at exactly the time advised by Mrs Little and was put through to her. He had held on for what had seemed too long, but then he was put through to

118

McGoldrick himself. He had felt the coldness, stiffness and distance in the voice but ignored it and played his craven role to order. Frank had been suitably apologetic and servile, vague but somehow still insistent, and had emerged with his appointment for the Tuesday. He had been very relieved. He knew that in one way that had been the major hurdle, and it was now behind him. His clockwork model was going exactly to plan. He did not go to the pub that night, but conducted his interview with McGoldrick 216 times. He had emerged with the correct outcome on 178 of them. A betting man like himself could live with that kind of ratio, but the engineer wanted more, so early on the Tuesday morning he had practised it again and again.

He had dressed with care that morning. He knew he wanted to convey an impression of downness, shabbiness, defeatism and inefficiency. He had put on old brown cords, dilapidated old gutties, a frayed brown shirt that had never seen better days and the dirtier of his two anoraks. He had tried several ties but they all had smartened him up too much, so he left the top button undone. No-one was likely to mistake that man for a winner.

As he walked to school again, he returned from his thoughts of the recent past and accelerated off into more distant times. He found it vaguely alarming the ways the years slipped off him the nearer he got to St Anne's. It was almost regression, except that it was upward, to a peak. Frank realised with some sadness that he had been more in control of himself and his destiny at 16 than he had been at any subsequent point in his life. He felt a degree of that control, and that excitement, return to him. He realised just how much of the responsibility for all the things that had happened and that hadn't happened to him in later life he had attributed to that turning point in 1970. Motivating him now was an unspoken, unformed thought that perhaps if he reran those events with him in control, he could turn his life around yet, and make something valuable out of it.

He walked through the main gates, half-expecting to be given 100 lines or two of the belt for not being there by 8:55. There was a quietness about the place, that did not accord with his memories and their noises. There was not a pupil to be seen or heard. He felt an eerieness in his innards. He was delighted to find that the reception area had barely changed. He stopped in the large hall before the four rolls of honour, Head Boy, Head Girl, Dux and Sports. He sought comfort and continuity in reading the familiar names, though they were too far back up the lists for real comfort.

119

Still, the ones he knew were glorified for all eternity. What rules of nature decreed that Head Boys had to be such pricks, that Duxes had to be so stupid? The St Anne's of his time had produced several outstanding leaders, and some very clever people, but none of them featured in that golden scroll on the fine black wood. He checked his watch. 11:28, he would be punctual, no problem about that. He wandered down the hall and into Mrs Little's large outer office. There were one or two signs of change and progress, including a word-processor and a large computer. "Hello, Frank, how nice to see you again." The welcome was warm and sincere, so was her smile, and some of his nervousness diminished. "Take a seat for a few minutes, and I'll check if Mr McGoldrick is ready for you." Waiting, he felt again the apprehension he had always felt, on the occasions he had been waiting to see the Headmaster, whether McGoldrick or MacDonald. It wasn't fear, but it wasn't pleasant either. A few minutes later, Mrs Little indicated that he should knock and go in.

He knocked twice on the heavy oak door, fighting to compose himself and also remembering that he wanted to look nervous. "Enter" the assured command came, wafting across the years. He grasped the handle, opened it and walked in. The room was not much changed. He had expected it to seem smaller, but the reverse was true. The carpet was different, but it was almost as deep and soft as he had remembered its predecessor. The desk was changed, for one bigger, bolder, with more leather. There were in fact now two of them, one smaller one with its own machine where the author could write his own papers and articles. There were no filing cabinets now, which maybe contributed to the sense of increased space. Old MacDonald was still there, in exactly the same place. Frank was surprised to realise that he had hoped he would have gone by now. The real one was dead of course, buried in a South Uist cemetery since 1977. He still looked the same though, an evil old bastard. Frank spat in his eye for old times sake, while preparing to do the same to his successor. McGoldrick was still employing the same old trick. The routine was the same and the only concession to Frank's changed status was that this time he was given a chair to sweat in rather than a space, while McGoldrick pretended to finish off his piece of work. He had his gown on, which Frank found both interesting and ominous given its previous connotations.

Frank would have preferred to jump straight in but his prediction that the man would feel obliged to make some

120

concession to civility and mention his poor dead mother proved accurate. Still, the pleasantries passed without an excess of unpleasantness and then it was time. "Well, Hunter, you wanted to see me?" The art of intonation was still alive. Frank knew he was being treated like an older pupil rather than a 36 year old Poll Tax payer but then McGoldrick probably, and wrongly, reckoned Frank would not be paying his. He let it pass anyway, indeed he welcomed it. It was a positive indication of the frame of mind McGoldrick was bringing to the interview. Frank knew that the more McGoldrick underestimated him, the better. "Yes" He had vowed not to call him sir, but made his tone submissive all the same. "Thank you for giving me the time. I would like to say I don't think you will regret it, but I don't think I can. I read your speech last week in Edinburgh on the importance of family values and the maintenance of proper standards." McGoldrick involuntarily tightened his stomach in dismay. The thought raced through his mind that he was going to be attacked, politically, or even worse, physically. This madman wasn't likely to be about to compliment him on that speech. Robin was not a brave man, in that sense. He always hated direct conflict and argument. He did not like dissension, even when he knew he was right.

To his surprise he heard Hunter start to say that he agreed with at least one part of what he had said. "That it was important that public and elected representatives reflect these values to the highest possible extent, and offer an example to their electorate. That is a fair summary of what you said, was it not?" "Yes, in part, but I'm surprised that you welcomed the message of what I was saying." Frank could tell from his tone of patronising contempt that not only did McGoldrick think that all members of the Labour Party were stupid, he thought that Frank was a particularly unintelligent example of the species. Good. Frank ignored McGoldrick's thrust and exposed the hook "Do you still stand by those sentiments?" "Yes, of course I do, but what is the relevance of this? What has it to do with you?" "In that case, I must ask you to give me your assurance that you will reconsider your plans to become a Conservative Party candidate at the General Election." He paused for exactly the right length of time in the stunned silence that followed his remark, then pushed the bait onto the hook. "Last weekend I had a long conversation with an Edinburgh prostitute, Margaret Beattie, about the nature of your relationship with her. In the light of what she said to me, it is obvious that by your own standards of that speech, you are not a suitable person to be an elected representative. I am expecting her to give me a written statement confirming that relationship. If you reconsider quietly, that will be the end of the matter, as far as I am concerned. I give you my word on that. If you do not give an assurance that you will reconsider, then I might feel compelled to share her statement with the Sun or another paper and then you would find it impossible to proceed as a candidate anyway. So you can do it the easy way, or the hard way, but either way, you have a choice to make."

Frank had been studying McGoldrick closely as he spoke. The effect of his words was truly dramatic. The colour went from the man. He was pale at the best of times, but it was as if Frank's words drilled a little hole in his neck and let the little remaining colour drain away. Fear flitted over his face for the second time. The first time, at Frank's initial words, Frank knew was fear that he would leap over the desk and land one on him. The second time was a different, more haunting kind of fear, the fear of life and the pain it can bring, a fear of the future and all it contained. Frank stopped, and waited for the words to come. Better even than he had ever dreamed, out they came. A strangled gasp, then, weakly, "That is blackmail" "No", Frank interrupted, "that is not blackmail, that is facing you with the consequences of your actions."

He had waited twenty years to say those words, and savoured the taste as they rolled out his lips and wrapped themselves around McGoldrick's neck. He knew he needed to conclude the interview quickly, get out and leave McGoldrick to do what he would. There was one bit he needed to add, to safeguard himself. "I'm not interested in anything for myself. I just want to help you live up to the ideals in your speech. I'll be back again, on Friday at 10:30. You can tell me your decision then." He terminated the interview and was gone out the door, before his shaken foe realised what was happening.

As Hunter closed the door behind him, Robin McGoldrick could not avoid the images of doors closing that invaded his head. His head hurt, so he rested it in his hands, and wept. He felt a faint sense of disbelief but also knew it to be true. He was ruined. He had a mental image of Francesca. In an instant he summonsed up for himself her reaction. Public support and private contempt. The web he had woven round her to keep them bound together was held tight on both sides by his moral superiority and her weakness. He knew that if these threads were severed he would be lost, and she would be lost and he would be left with nothing. She might not leave him, but he would lose something more important to him than her presence.

He knew he did not have the right kind of character to cope with the public knowledge of his activities. He would rather die than face his colleagues, his peers, his public, knowing that they knew that about him and were laughing at him, sniggering behind his back. No, he could not live with that kind of publicity. He must prevent that happening, at any cost. How had Hunter found out? He thought of Margaret, with her sad, soft, innocent face. He had always felt from the moment he had first seen her, that he could trust her, that he would be able to rely on her discretion. He had always realised how near he was never to starting this whole wretched business. If it had been any other woman who had turned up that first time, in the Thistle Hotel, he knew he would not have been able to proceed with it. But she had been such a lady, so well-dressed and presentable. And she had spoken so well, that had been very important to him. The first guttural tongue or tone, the first piece of verbal crudity or language mangling, and it would all have been over, unstarted. Instead, she had treated the matter intelligently, responded to his notions seriously, and worked very hard on making them viable.

Even so, I must have been mad, he thought for the thousandth time, why did I do it? He had often asked himself that question. He could still remember, even sitting there in his office with his head in his hands, the peculiar feeling of excitement, a stirring in his groin he had long thought extinct, as Bill McFarlane had droned on, in one of the coffee breaks at a Chester Street meeting, about this marvellous turn his Chamber of Commerce had put on at one of its recent nights. Nothing as crude as a stripper, he had stressed, but a genuine performer, the Belle of St Ninians. He had described her in some detail, the fishnet stockings, the bare thigh-tops, the sexy bra, and the amazing things she had done with a hockey stick. If that had been all, he might have been disgusted rather than interested, but McFarlane had enthused on about one extra dimension, the angelic innocence of her face. An unpoetic man, he had nevertheless been sufficiently inspired by the vision he had seen, to wax lyrical enough to release some hidden part of Robin.

The image had haunted him through several days and nights, and much to his surprise he had found himself phoning McFarlane. He had said there was a male colleague of his leaving for a new job, a bit of a lad, and he thought it might be quite an

123

appropriate notion for his leaving do, how could he get in touch with her. McFarlane had been very amused. Robin could still hear him saying, "I wouldn't have thought it was quite your scene, McGoldrick, old chap. Bit of a dark horse aren't we?" But he had given him a number where Miss Beattie could be contacted. Robin had almost expired of embarrassment, shame and fear at a subsequent Committee meeting, when McFarlane had boomed out to all and sundry over coffee, "What did you make of that stripper lass then, eh, Robin, Eh?" He had had to compose himself as best he could, and lie that he had just passed the number on, and, of course, had not even gone to the do himself, but he had heard that it had been very well appreciated. He had thought he had got away with it at the time, but Robin realised with some despair that now McFarlane at least would remember, if there were any publicity, and so would the others there when reminded, including one or two that would be delighted to see him humbled. There would be a queue to confirm the facts.

He had got through to Margaret in three calls, one to the number McFarlane gave him, which was some kind of clearing house, and from there to another number at which he was given what he later assumed to be Margaret's own number. He had made the arrangement to meet her in the Thistle Hotel. He had already booked the suite before he phoned her. He had tended to do that, over the past few years. Whenever he had a paper to give, or an important early morning meeting in Edinburgh, he would book into a suite the night before, to give himself the opportunity to prepare properly. Occasionally even when his conference was in Glasgow he would do the same. He hated giving speeches. He knew it was important to do so well, and he knew the importance of good preparation in ensuring a good performance. But they were long empty evenings, which reinforced his aloneness and stirred distant memories for him. He often found himself reading Wilbur's poems, and wishing life had worked out differently. He would wish he had more courage, and would castigate himself for his weaknesses of thought and deed. He had not really believed it would be possible for him to do what he did. He never once considered what he was embarking on as using a prostitute. He would never do such a thing, never. Even so he was very conscious that only Margaret could have enabled him to proceed. She had been so alert, so sensitive, so sympathetic, so understanding. He was aware that she had looked more like a mature Young Conservative in her smart suits than anything else. He was dimly aware of an unspoken half-fantasy that he had never dared articulate, that something about her reminded him vaguely of the Prime Minister.

He was certain, he did not believe, that she could be in any way responsible for whatever had happened with Hunter. Hunter had described her as a prostitute. Robin knew that was not a word Margaret would use about herself, she was not a prostitute. He ran through what had happened and tried as calmly as he could, to work out what Hunter could know, and what he could prove. He had obviously misjudged Hunter, he was no pathetic victim, but a brutal and vicious thug. How could he have found out? He must have seen something the previous Thursday, at the Holiday Inn, or been tipped off by someone else, a porter or a waiter. They might be in his bloody union. Robin had always known that bringing Margaret to Glasgow was an extra risk. But they had never been together outside his suites. If that were the case, then all Hunter could have was Margaret's word, and he had obviously not yet got that in writing. Suddenly the fog in his head cleared a little. He must get hold of Margaret and ask her, beg her, not to sacrifice him. He wondered what inducement Hunter could possibly have offered her. After all he was unemployed. He had heard that LDT had made generous redundancy settlements, but that wouldn't last long, particularly if Hunter was in the pub every night, as rumoured.

With awful suspicion, he wondered whether he might have access to someone else's resources. Given Hunter's demand, could it really be possible that the Labour Party was funding him? No, surely not, he could not believe that even they would stoop to that level. No, Hunter must be acting on his own. He had just left Robin's office. If Robin could get to Margaret before Hunter did, then he might still be able to salvage something from this mess. Hunter had talked about the weekend, but he could not afford to waste any time. He knew that whatever else, Hunter did have some perverted kind of integrity. Robin did not believe that he was after any financial reward for himself, so there was no point in trying to deal with him. No, it seemed to be political with Hunter, not financial, and personal too, although for the life of him, Robin could not see why.

Already he felt better, much better. All was not yet lost. He paced up and down the room several times, locked in intense thought. He must be logical about this, avoid panic. He was more intelligent than Hunter, there must be ways of making that advantage tell. He knew that going to the police was out of the question. Once they knew about Margaret, he would be very vulnerable to it leaking out, at least into the rumour mill. No, that would make matters worse. Anyway, he was not sure he was the victim of any crime. Hunter was not after anything for himself. No, the key to his salvation lay with Margaret, and the securing of her silence. Without her there could be nothing to harm him.

He made sure the door was securely shut, and gave Mrs Little strict instructions to ensure that he was not disturbed. He sat down again, and composed himself and the message he was going to give Margaret. Then he dialled the Edinburgh number for her. Please be in, he prayed with an intensity long absent from his evening devotions, and by God's grace or fortunate chance, she was. He recognised her cultured voice even through her cautious and neutral Hello and repetition of the number. "Hello, Margaret. It is Ross here, William Ross." He paused slightly, "I need to talk to you urgently, can we possibly meet, as soon as possible." "Slow down, Mr Ross, take your time. Tell me what the problem is." She sounded calm, soothing and friendly, so any reservation was overcome. "Has anyone approached you recently, about me?" "Oh, God, I thought it might be that. Has he been bothering you, too? A scruffy looking fellow?" "Yes, He visited me this morning. How did he get in touch with you?" "He phoned me up on Saturday and arranged to meet me on Sunday. He actually said he had been recommended by someone I knew, a Mr McGoldrick. The name didn't mean anything at the time, but as you know, I'm trying to do as much business as possible before I leave, so I took the chance. I thought nothing of it at the time, but all he wanted to do was to talk about you. He had a picture of you from some newspaper, with a caption which said that was your name. That's right, isn't it? Not that it's any of my business."

"Yes, Yes. That is me. What did he want? What did you say to him?" "I was very careful not to tell him anything he did not already know. He seemed to know for certain somehow that we had shared a room on Thursday night at the Holiday Inn, so I didn't deny it." "Did you tell him anything else? Or give him anything in writing?" "No, certainly not. Don't be silly. I didn't tell him about any of the other times, or about what we do. He didn't seem interested in the details. All he kept going on about was whether or not I would give him a written statement that we were together in a bedroom in the Holiday Inn. He said he would meet me again next Sunday, and give me £2,500 in cash, if I would sign a statement to that effect. Look Mr Ross, I'll be honest with you. I don't want to hurt you in any way. You've always been very good to me. But, as I told you on Thursday, I'm going back to England in the next couple of weeks, and the thought of that kind of money did have some appeal, so I said I would think about it." "Look, Margaret, it is very important to me that our relationship stays a secret. I'll give you twice what he has offered you, if you promise not to speak to him again, or to anyone else"

She paused briefly to look again at the sheets of script that Frank had given her. It had all gone to plan so far, but he had stressed to her that this next part was the crucial one. "No, really, You don't have to do that. I've been very unhappy, thinking about it since Sunday, and I am not going to give him a written statement. I don't want to hurt you, or any other of my regulars, it wouldn't be right. And anyway, I doubt very much if he has it. He didn't look the type to have that much money available to him." "No. I insist. I shall give you the money, and help you make a new start. I want to do that. As long as you do not see that man again." "Well, it's up to you., but you don't have to do so. I'm leaving Edinburgh anyway and you needn't give me anything. If you do, it would just be a farewell gift, with no strings attached. You do understand that?" "Yes, yes, that is fine. I understand. But I would be happier knowing that you have enough to give you a clean break. I would not be able to see you again properly, it would be far too risky for me, but I must meet you in the next few days and tidy this business up." She knew from what Frank had told her, that Thursday afternoon was the best time for the rendezvous, so she suggested the time and place he had written down for her, the Sir Walter Scott Bar which Frank had carefully selected because of its one entrance and its proximity to the cafe across the way. "Yes, that will be fine. I'll meet you there then, and I'll have the money with me."

He came off the phone a much relieved man. He had pulled the situation back from the brink of disaster. He would see Margaret on the Thursday, in Edinburgh, give her the money and impress on her the absolute necessity for complete discretion. And that would be that, an episode in his life closed. He would have a nice surprise for Hunter when he returned on the Friday morning. He would warn him that any attempt to harass her would result in the police being brought in. Already he knew he would need to decide before then whether or not he should offer Hunter that job as

Assistant Janitor. It might be the least dangerous of the alternative options, to have himself in a position of authority over him.

Once he savoured his release, he phoned the manager of his Building Society and explained his requirements. "£5,500 in cash for Thursday morning, certainly sir, no problem at all, sir. You do realise, sir, that there is a slight penalty for cash withdrawals over a certain amount at that kind of notice. I quite understand. See you on Thursday then, Mr McGoldrick."

He had decided to take out the extra £500. He would buy Margaret a small present, maybe some piece of jewellery. She was doing something for him, and he wanted to reinforce the personal nature of their understanding. The total sum was no problem. He put all his conference fees, his speech fees, his royalties, his payments for his newspaper and magazine articles, and his radio and television appearance money into a separate Building Society High Interest Account, that was in his name alone. Francesca would never need to know. Maybe he should buy her a small present also, he had neglected her in that way recently. Yes, he had handled things very well, but it had been one hell of a fright, he would not want to risk repeating that experience. He would never expose himself again to the slightest possibility of such a danger.

CHAPTER SEVEN - SIR WALTER SCOTT

Frank Hunter never felt as comfortable in Edinburgh pubs as he did in Glasgow ones. At least the city centre ones. They seemed to him temples designed for purposes other than the consumption of alcohol, more machines for the separation of tourists from their money. There were one or two exceptions though, and he had downed a good few pints in his time in some of the more tolerable ones. He had come through to Edinburgh on the 11am train. He had tried to read the "Independent" he had bought at John Menzies, but had spent most of the journey considering what he was doing and why. He knew it was very important that he was not seen anywhere near Julie at the time she was meeting McGoldrick. He didn't reckon the man would have the bottle, or the sense, to go to the police, but he could not be absolutely certain about that, nor that he would not have enlisted the assistance of more worldly friends who might protect him from himself. He knew that there was a risk in him being involved in this part at all. It would be much safer just to let Julie collect the money and tape the conversation. He knew from his detailed study of the telephone conversation tape that she was good, very good. She could stick to the essence of the script, but be flexible and intelligent enough to handle his input and guide the exchange back to the required destinations. But he wanted more than that. He wanted the image of the two of them together. Undeniable proof of involvement, or something else.

The old phrase, the camera never lies, came back into his head. He knew it wasn't true. Images could easily be created to misrepresent. Reality could be manufactured out of diversity. Nothing need be what it seemed. Strangers passing in the day could be portrayed as intimates, a photo-sculpture created by a master craftsman, proving everything and nothing. I saw it in the papers, I saw it on the television, therefore it must be true. You can't fool me, I know what I saw. The man who believes the evidence of his own eyes is a gullible fool. But that was his audience. There could be no photos of them in bed or in flagrante, because they had never been in either. He mentally reran his video of McGoldrick's little play, as he found himself doing more often than was comfortable for him. An exhibit in the collection for the

Year of Culture, but under what category. A love story, an exploding circus, or an educational morality tale. The dominie theory of politics. Pull one and they all fall down. It had worried him how erotic he had found Julie's tale of their performance. What bits appealed to him? Was it the skelping of McGoldrick's bum, or a desire to have his own beaten? He liked women's bums, but denied any desire to beat them, or enter them. He wondered what the script really meant for McGoldrick. What secret traumas were released or re-enacted for his soul in these sessions? What thoughts was he left with after them? Even a practical thought nagged him. How could he bear to sit down afterwards, or did he do it only to ensure that he gave his speeches and papers on his feet?

He had decided to start in the Cafe Royale, the public bar. It was shabby enough to pass for a Glasgow pub. He settled down at a small table with his pint of McEwans 80/-. He knew it would be another two hours before McGoldrick appeared at the entrance to the Sir Walter Scott, and an hour and a half before he had booked the window table at Giustis, but he wanted to be absolutely ready, and take no risks. He knew Julie would already be in Scotts, either at, or waiting for the table in the far corner. The time passed slowly. He had known he would not have a high concentration level, so he had brought a light book, one of the Glasgow detective novels. He took it out his bag and left the bag with the camera, the lenses and his paper, under the table. He knew he had to be very careful to resist the temptation to join them. He had one more pint, which he nursed for almost an hour, then bought a third with no intention of drinking it. He would be back for a similar one, but only once he had done his David Bailey impersonation.

He left the pub exactly on his schedule, walked round the corner and into the long narrow street where both the restaurant and pub vied with a hundred similar for a bottomless pool of transient trade. He had looked behind to see if he were being followed, more for dramatic interest than out of any expectation, and sure enough, he wasn't being. He paused in the middle of the road, and looked into the restaurant. It was impossible to tell if his table were empty, far less occupied by a snapper. It would work. Unless McGoldrick came across the road and stared right in the window he would be safe. He had booked the table, the specific table, by phone. In the name of Mr Ring and this time he remembered why in time to remember who he was. They hadn't seemed surprised that he had insisted on that particular table. It was quiet enough to suggest that it had maybe been an unnecessary precaution, but so much the better. He kept his coat and scarf on. He had worked out that it would be better to rest the camera on the table from the start rather than bring it out later. He noticed with pleasure that they had definitely cleaned the tinted window, inside and out, since his last visit. No-one in the restaurant then had seemed to find it peculiar that the solitary diner occasionally lifted his camera and snapped the passing fauna. There were certainly more peculiar sights on the outside than the inside. The slight purple tinge on the glass had not adversely affected the quality of his pictures. He had been particularly pleased at the young sweethearts who had come out the Sir Walter Scott, but one American lady strolling down the street had been a real cracker. He had kept the best picture of her, and built a slight fantasy around it.

He ordered a light meal, and settled down for his prey. He wondered if McGoldrick would appreciate the political significance of the choice of venue. He would be bound to be a Scott man, no doubt about that. Frank hated Sir Walter and all that he stood for, the false romantic Scottish patriotism but the real pragmatic endorsement of the Union and all its advantages, the high Toryism and the hatred and fear of anything radical. Frank had had several arguments with Jack Reilly, who credited Scott with naming his team, about whether Scott was primarily a Scot or a Briton. Jack, a romantic soul, saw only the pre-Culloden heroics and ignored the later essence of marriage into the benefits of Empire. Frank had had better discussions with Willie in George Square, who had grasped the essential core of his Conservatism and Unionism. Still, Frank had had to concede to Jack that no man who wrote that "And life is itself but a game at football" could be totally without redeeming feature. He wondered if McGoldrick had ever read the Lay of the Last Minstrel and what he made of that philosophy. Maybe Shankly had.

Julie checked her watch yet again. A quarter to two. She ran over it one more time. Frank had insisted that she get to the pub early, and secure the table in the corner, shut off by an alcove on one side and a curtain frame on the other. She had already worked out exactly where she would place him, and the best location for her bag, where her recorder was primed for action. She took out and read the typed script pages one last time. She would not be able to consult them during the action this time but she was a professional, it would be no problem for her. She had a wee fantasy that it would be like doing a television play after having done a radio one. She had been touched by Frank's obvious determination to help her avoid the slightest possibility of any vulnerability to a charge of extortion, or conspiracy. He had warned her that it was possible that McGoldrick would be wired for sound himself, and that she would have to be particularly judicious in her choice of words. He had described it to her like a human chess match. She was uncertain how she would feel about him once they were together. She knew now his real name was McGoldrick, but she still thought of him as Mr Ross. She had no sympathy for most of her regulars, contempt would be nearer the mark, but there was a quiet and desperate vulnerability about Mr Ross that had touched something in her.

Frank had insisted that she ran all her feelings about it past him, and talked about all the moral arguments about what she was doing. He had stressed to her that she must regard the question of any money from McGoldrick as a bonus, fine if she could get it on the right terms, but to settle for his guaranteed £4,000 rather than run any risk at all. She wondered a little about him at that. She would welcome the money, she would need every penny if she was going to get Flora out in time, and give them a real chance. Still, it wouldn't help Flora if she was in jail. Frank had warned her that McGoldrick had very influential friends, he had stressed the influential, and that if he chose to go to them for help, either before or after, then both she and Frank could be in very serious trouble. He had made it clear that unless they were very careful, and maybe even then, they could conceivably both end up in prison, or be destroyed. The Scottish Establishment protects its own, he had told her. It worried her slightly that Frank did not seem to consider he had a future anyway, but she had definite plans. She was young enough to believe that her dreams could still be attained. So yes, she had agreed, to herself, that she would be very careful. She would only take the extra money if it went according to script, but she had her own sense that Frank's analysis was right. The man did not seem like a fighter to her. He was not the kind to roll up his sleeves and fight back. He was a man who would find the gutter too distasteful.

She was pleased she had won her point about the order of events. Frank had wanted her to greet him at the door, and escort him in. He had been worried that a controlled joint exit might be more difficult to manage than an unavoidable togetherness at the beginning. He had talked of a nice picture on arrival, her putting

132

her hand out to him, ushering him in perhaps, in a shepherdess manner. She had argued that it was too risky. It would make her too conspicuous in the pub, up and down to the door, looking for him, waiting for him, rising and retreating. Even though it wasn't Glasgow there was still the danger of comments about up and down more often than a whore's knickers. She had assured him, eventually, that she would be able to manage the exit in a manner designed to meet his needs. She had her own unshared vision, a realistic one to her, of some kind of embrace, or even a kiss, as they parted, forever. The couple at the table next to her left. That was an added bonus. 2p.m. on the pub clock came with its usual noise. She did not worry that her meticulously punctual Mr Ross did not come with its whirr and clang. She had checked thoroughly. The pub clock was five and a half minutes fast, a legacy from more rigid licensing laws. The crystals on her watch just turned to nought as he walked in the door, pathetic really she should afford something better.

It was a dark pub, emptying by that hour, and it took a moment or two for him to locate her. She imagined a faint look of surprise on the barman's face. She had dressed at her most conservative, and no-one had misunderstood or attempted to assist her. Once he spotted her, he strode up to the table, with a grin like a strangled cat's forced onto his face. As he slipped into the reserved space she indicated to him, her finger pushed the start button down and eased its way out of her bag as she readjusted its location between them. "Thank you for coming," he said in his normal, formal tone. "I was a little worried that you might not show up." "No. It sounded very important to you on the telephone, so I made sure I was here in good time." He offered her a drink so she asked for her third gin and tonic and watched with interest as he ordered himself a half pint of beer. "Has our mutual friend been back in touch with you?" She shook her head, then realising that wouldn't appear on the tape, told the truth and said, "I haven't seen him again since you were on the phone to me." That seemed to give him some satisfaction. He was silent for a moment, then launched into what she reckoned to be a prepared speech. "I have given the matter a great deal of thought. All he can know is that we were both in the Holiday Inn on the same evening. Without a written statement from you, there is no way he, or anyone else, can make anything of that." Again she told the truth, whatever that might be, "I have absolutely no intention of giving him any statement in writing. I am quite definite about that. I do not want to hurt you." He seemed to detect a sincerity of tone in these statements, for he physically relaxed a little and poured himself more into his seat, as she poured more of her gin into herself. The beer lay untouched. She used the opportunity to proceed. "I'm going to England next week and I don't suppose I'll ever see him again after that, but even in the unlikely event of him finding out where I'm gone to and following me, I'll give him nothing."

"I am very grateful to you for that attitude." he said in a tone that seemed to her other than gratitude. "It really would cause me extreme difficulties if our scruffy friend were ever to get a statement of that nature from you. It would be much better if you were able to just quietly disappear." The words stifled any sympathy she had been developing for him. Better for whom, you self-centred bastard. It's your problem so I should just disappear. Why don't you disappear instead. But she was an actress, a professional, so she suppressed any feelings of her own and continued with the script. "Yes, within a week I'll be gone, and so will any threat to you." She paused, as she knew the next part would need to come from him. "Look, I would like to make a contribution towards your new start. To give you a help over the transition period." It never occurred to him at any stage in the affair to wonder about her financial position. He knew from Francesca's familiarity with expensive labels that the outfits she wore outwith her performances must have cost her a great deal of money, but he never considered if that was an argument for her having less rather than more. He had never considered what she might earn in a week, if his was a typical contribution, or what her expenses might be.

She knew the next bit was crucial. "You don't have to do that, you know. It won't make the slightest difference to my response to your friend." She was quite proud of the verity of that second part, her own ad-lib. "It's entirely up to you. I have no expectation, and I'm making no demand" That was back to Frank's script. She noticed that once again he responded with a double positive. "Yes, Yes, I appreciate that, I do," - she vaguely wondered if that made a negative - "but I genuinely would like to help you. A token of my appreciation and a contribution towards a new life." He handed her a large brown envelope he had extracted from inside his folded coat. "I think you will find that more than compensates you for anything that our scruffy friend might have been able to give you." She recognised the slight sneer in his tone and realised that he was choosing his own words almost as carefully as she was. She paused in her acceptance of the envelope to add the stress. "This is not necessary, you know. You do not have to give me anything at all." She felt a surge of triumph. She knew the main danger was now passed. He had not used any of the phrases Frank had predicted he might if the interview were a set-up on his part to trap her into an extortion or conspiracy charge. So she had no need for the careful, cunningly crafted responses he had worked out so fastidiously over the past few weeks. This wasn't the clash of competing intellects and wills Frank had hinted at, but a walkover. "I want you to have it, I insist."

She realised Frank had been right. The tape was there, whirring silently away, as much for her protection as his entrapment. But having secured the former, she needed to move onto the latter objective a bit more. "We did have some good times together" she said in as fawning a manner as she felt he could swallow, "I'm going to miss our little rendezvous.". Frank had wanted sessions but she knew her man and her French plurals better. "So am I, my dear, so am I," he murmured in a tone she was certain was genuinely wistful. "So am I. I will always remember you fondly. I wish I had had the time to get to know you better." It wasn't time that was the problem, son, it was you, she told herself, which made it easier to add "You are the nicest of all my regulars. You've always treated me like a perfect gentleman should treat a lady, even when he's paid for the pleasure.". He gave her a startled look, but she realised with relief that he was looking for irony or resentment, not a shovel or a pit. "It is particularly important to me that our relationship should remain our secret." She had been about to say to herself that she had yet to meet a punter who didn't believe that, when she remembered Richard. He paid for her because that was the only way he could get her, but he wasn't ashamed of their relationship, rather the reverse. He took what she considered a perverse pride in taking her to public places. Sometimes, only sometimes, like right then, she thought she might be better off marrying him, like he so much wanted her to do, but the feeling passed quickly even as she returned to Mr Ross and his unfinished soliloquy on the benefits and virtues of complete discretion.

She again gave him the required reassurances, her word to him, binding as she always regarded, for the rest of his life. She got her reward, an unexpected bonus, when he told her, which he obviously did not need to do but which he obviously seemed to feel he should, that he would not be replacing her with another prostitute. He, the mealy mouthed man, did not use the plain noun she so carefully avoided herself, he used a much more delicate phrase, lady of the night. She did not use or like euphemisms, she generally protected herself by a much more effective device, denial, more satisfactorily effective to the extent that you can believe what you do not tell yourself. However he had put it, it was a definite bonus for her, an admission in his own words, rather than the previous non-disagreement and negative acceptance, that their relationship was one of buyer and seller. She knew Frank would be pleased with the product, she was able to settle for her pleasure at the process. She briefly considered, in terms of fairness, if she should allow him a qualification, a declaration that their relationship had never been consummated, but remembered in time that she was a player not a referee.

She realised that he had something more he wished to say to her. He was telling her that she had been special to him, that he would never be able to replace what they had created together. She thanked him, silently, for the together. The end product had owed something to her. Although his tortured imagination had to take most of the credit, she had given it life and form and substance. He told her he wanted to give her something extra, something personal, in recognition of what she had meant to him. She looked closely at his face, his eyes were averted from hers. He was finding this difficult. He seemed genuinely sentimental and moved, but she had learned to distrust expressions of sentiment. She realised as he spoke that she did not trust this one. "I want you to have this, as well. As a more personal momento." The poor man obviously still had no clue that nothing was more personal than money. He took out of his jacket a small green box and handed it to her. She was used to small gifts, indeed often larger ones, from her regulars but this was somehow different. She opened it in silence. It contained a beautiful butterfly brooch, of gold, silver and diamond. She knew from her first glance that it must have cost him around £300. She knew that it was the kind of jewellery that smart Tory wives in their late thirties would wear on their best suit jackets for dinner. Well she had dressed like them every time he had seen her, going to work. She had once said to him, the only personal thing she had ever said to him, that she sometimes felt like a butterfly. She was impressed that he had remembered. His eyes were watching hers now. "It's beautiful. Thank you very much. It will be a good reminder of you."

136

He offered her another drink but seemed relieved when she declined. They both knew their business was concluded, and the sooner they were on their separate ways the better. His social skills were not geared to smooth exits, so she helped him out, of the situation, the pub and the relationship. She gathered up her coat and bag, taking care to switch off her machine unobtrusively. The last act was to be visual not aural. She knew she would not see him again. But she also knew that the thing about him that was most important to her was already safely in her handbag. It would be no sweet sorrow to let the rest go for good. But she knew she still had one more part of her new role to play. It was obvious to her that Mr Ross had half-thought that he could just leave her at the table, but she went with him and steered him through the one pub door, and into the quiet and narrow street. She paused and stopped him, put her hand on his arm. She knew where Frank would be and chose her angle well to suit his needs. She delivered her farewell address, with her hand still on his arm, then leaned forward to kiss him on the cheek, on the side that would produce the best image. "Good luck, Mr Ross, take care of yourself." "And you, Margaret", a mutual squeeze and to his relief she was gone, leaving him to hurry down towards Princes Street and the steps to the station. She headed west, towards the back entrance of Marks and Spencers. Frank had told her that there was a possibility that she might be followed, and that she should go to several shops before going back home.

Frank was delighted with her performance. It was much more natural and touching than any attempt at the beginning would have been. He took ten pictures, in the less than two minutes between them emerging from the pub and McGoldrick scuttling off down the road. He could tell from her demeanour that it must have gone well. No-one followed them out of the bar. That had been his major worry, that McGoldrick would have involved the police, private detectives or friends, but it looked like his assumption had been correct, the man had been confident that he could sort it out on his own. Well, let him enjoy his moment of triumph. Frank forced himself to have one more coffee, then paid his bill and went back to the Cafe Royale. It owed him a pint after all. He had three hours to spare before he was due to meet up with Julie, in Bennets. So he had planned how he would spend it. A leisurely pint, a walk along Princes Street, with particular time in John Menzies and W.H. Smiths. A stroll up Lothian Road, left at the Usher Hall and right into Football Crazy. No trip to Edinburgh was complete without a browse there. Then a walk up the Meadows, and across to Bennets. He wouldn't mind a quiet pint on his own before Julie joined him.

He carried out his plan with the same precision he was applying to all his activities these days. He was particularly pleased with a purchase he made in Football Crazy, a Celtic away European programme that he had been looking for for years. It was an unmistakable omen that his luck had changed. Yes, he thought over his pint, things are working out well at last. I'm glad I decided to continue to play the game. I am going to enjoy the taste of this victory. He lifted the pint up to his ear. Quiet, it was bloody silent. He savoured its taste and did his inventory.

Julie arrived on time, just as the last few satisfying gulps slipped down his throat. He bought her a gin and tonic and himself another pint. 70/- it was, and cheap at the price. He listened with growing pleasure as she described to him the progress of her encounter with McGoldrick. It was his assessment that McGoldrick had not been working to an agenda, or at least not one designed to hang them, rather one to save himself. He had got the man's character right, that gave him great satisfaction. Julie had booked a table for 7p.m. at the Shamiana, only two minutes walk away from Bennets. She was deliberately attacking his prejudice that only Glasgow could provide good curries, and was confident that he would find Shamianas as satisfying as Balbirs had been the previous Thursday. In the pub, she gave him several things. The tape from her telephone answering machine. She had played it to him several times over the phone but now she delivered it over to him. She gave him the tape from her recorder of her afternoon chat with Mr Ross. She had already played it back to herself and found it to be of good quality, both in tone and content. She gave him three notes in McGoldrick's handwriting, instructing her to report to the Headmaster's office, including the one for the Holiday Inn tryst. She gave him a list of dates, times and places of all their meetings. To keep her right in her conversation with Mr Ross, he did not ask her for, and she did not give him, a written or signed statement. In return for all this he gave her her second plain brown envelope of the day, this one containing £4,000. He had chosen it carefully, 10 £100 notes, 20 £50 notes and 100 £20 notes. He had agreed with her that she should deposit McGoldrick's money into her account but not his. Against his better judgement he made a remark to her that that was not bad at all, £9,000 for one day's work, or £10,000 for a fortnight's. Not bad at all, whichever way you look at it. She didn't reply directly but told him about the brooch, although she did not show it to him.

She knew she did not have a bad conscience about what she had done. She knew she was in a business, but a more complicated business than the girls who only offered straight quick sexual relief, a fuck, a wank, a gobble, not much dream material there, just relief. She operated in the much more dangerous territory, the realisation of fantasies, putting the come into making dreams come true. She remembered the only thing her father's mother seemed to have left her, the warning that people should be careful about asking for what they wanted, they might get it. A fair number of her regulars didn't want sex, or at least not sexual intercourse. Mr Ross wasn't that weird or unusual in that respect. She knew that what she had given him was very important to him. It seemed to her only fair that he should have rewarded her appropriately for the experience. She had not considered it as blackmail, or extortion. She had used their relationship to get additional benefits for herself, but that had been his suggestion not hers. Of course she had had the kind of fantasy in the past that crosses the minds of most girls who know with whom they are doing business, but she had always managed to avoid the temptation, even in the small and petty ways that would be so easy. She did not regard herself as having succumbed in this case.

She had been well-rewarded for her assistance to Frank. He had kept his promise to her, but she had kept hers to him, and given him exactly what he wanted. She also knew that whatever Frank was after, it was not money. She knew as much as she wanted to about the nature of the conflict between Frank and Mr Ross, or McGoldrick or whatever his name was. That was their business. She believed his claim that he did not want to expose McGoldrick, only to get his own back by stopping him doing something. As always she had done her own analysis of the likely possibilities and covered herself as best she could. She had lost a client, but it would have taken her four years to get that much from him. The two lots of money would help considerably to get Flora away before she died. And she had gained a friend. She felt sure about that. She had been surprised in the hotel when she had offered to sleep with him anyway, although she knew it had something to do with the power of the confessional. She had been even more surprised when he had declined. She knew he found her attractive. She had enjoyed working with him. It had been the first normal non-sexual relationship of trust she had had with a man for years, maybe ever if she were honest. He had treated her as intelligent, and been appreciative of her contribution to his enterprise. He had been genuine in his desire to protect her from adverse consequences. He had been genuinely interested in her plans for the future. They hadn't spent that much time together. The first Saturday, the Thursday evening. The whole Sunday, that had been a good day, and evening. Almost a normal day, and perfect with it. Several long telephone conversations. But it had felt like much longer. Prime time, she now knew what that concept meant.

They had settled for conversational intimacy, the hardest kind. He had told her about Elaine. About Mary Ewing and Mary-Ann Ewing, the grand-daughter he had proxy-fucked for a fabulous fortnight. He had not told her Joyce's real name or occupation. She had mentioned in one of their first conversations that she was friendly with a girl from Glasgow, who was involved with a Prostitutes Support Group, and that there was a social worker there who was very good. He hadn't wanted to run any risk of anything getting back to Joyce so he had said his girl-friend was a teacher. But apart from that he had talked a lot about her, and how important she was to him. He had also talked a great deal about Hazel and she reckoned from his implication that that was how he knew what he knew and how he had found her. It had saddened her to hear him talk about Elaine. What a stupid bastard he was, but nice with it. He had talked to her more personally than any other man. What she didn't know but somehow guessed, was that his few short conversations with her were also more than he had ever given anyone else either that way, although he claimed to be trying hard with his teacher. She had exposed herself so thoroughly and so surprisingly to him on that first occasion, that there had seemed no point in holding anything back later. So she hadn't. She would like the friendship to continue. He had said he did too, and that he would certainly at least phone her regularly in England.

After the business was concluded, they continued to talk and converse. They had walked from Bennets round to the Shamiana. It had seemed natural to hold her hand, casually. She looked good, too good to be out with a scruff like him, but there they were. They both enjoyed the meal. Frank found it more delicate than the delights he was used to in Glasgow, but he had to acknowledge that maybe civilisation had finally reached the Eaglesham of the East after all. He liked his dinner companion, liked her very much.

140

Another time, another circumstance, he kept saying to himself. Although he kept getting flashes and glimpses of the sad and confused wee girl huddling underneath, in the main he was very impressed with her calm, rational and intelligent exterior and her determination to control her own destiny. He knew that she lived with a woman, and that the relationship was a close and emotional one. He had learned from Joyce, and from Joan and Katy, that most of his original views about lesbianism were, well, wrong was the best word. Life was more complicated than that, and some women at least found it possible to be bisexual without destroying their identity or creating a new one. Eventually and reluctantly, she put him on the last train to Glasgow. As it began to move he leaned out the door window and they were both conscious of some irony as she kissed him on the cheek. They both promised they would keep in touch and neither believed it would be the last time they would ever see each other again. He watched from the window as the train pulled away. She waved to him and he wondered.

He wasn't unhappy that night that Joyce didn't come round to his flat after her group. He still had homework to do for his meeting with the Headmaster the next morning, and pictures to develop. When he went to his bed, he was content and looking forward to the next day, two old friends that he had not slept with for many a long year.

Francesca McGoldrick was not really enjoying her Thursday evening of Polish symphony music at the City Hall. She was too polite to show her boredom but her disinterest gave her a welcome opportunity to have a rest. Robin was enjoying himself, but given the excited mood he had been in all evening he would have been likely to enjoy anything, even Bolivian she thought with that tight little smile that always took ten years off her face. It was the first time for almost two months that the two of them had gone alone to something which they had not either been involved in organising, or were combining with some form of focused socialising. For the first time that year she wondered if even she were flagging, if she had plumbed at last the depth of her ability to enjoy and appreciate an unending range of music, dance, drama, art and film. She was pleased that Robin was enjoying himself, even if his discrimination was below its usual high standard. She wondered what had caused the recent sudden changes in his mood. For months he had seemed on a high plane of contentment, which had suited her, leaving her free to pursue her own personal and artistic agendas without having to administer too often to his needs. She knew the advancing of his political ambitions, and the events of the Year of Culture had made him happier than she could remember, certainly since Hannah had gone off to school. He had seemed to her to be sublimely happy, or at least well-satisfied. 1990 was going to be a memorable year, no doubt of that.

Then two days ago, he had suddenly been extremely agitated. She had learned to be very sensitive to his moods. He normally disguised them very well from everyone else but she was always aware of every quiver and every waver, every nuance and shiver. It had not required her special skills to realise he had been very upset on Tuesday. He had paced around the house flitting from room to room and activity to activity, not allowing his neat bum to rest in any one place. He had given up his ticket to the Ballet Supremski, although he had been looking forward to it for weeks. He had told her that he was not feeling too well, and he had insisted she go, and give his ticket to James. Wednesday too, he had been unsettled, anxious, uneasy, unable to concentrate, although he had tried. Fortunately the play had been a light one, requiring no powers of concentration to appreciate. At the party afterwards he had been even less there than usual and she had had to take him home earlier than she would normally have wished. But tonight was so different. Whatever worry it was had passed, and left him euphoric, laying positive praise upon the mildly talented. There was a glow about him that evening, a radiance almost, as if the light bulb in his head had been replaced with one of higher wattage.

She positioned her body in the seat to give the appearance of concentration, then settled to enjoy her own thoughts. She was glad she had finally reconciled herself to staying in Glasgow. She remembered it had taken a long time. For most of the seventies and the early eighties, she had held the view that Robin had stayed too long and should move on. She had been eager that he take the offers of Headmastership of some of the more prestigious Public Schools that he had been offered, or the Professorship in the Midlands. She had urged him to seriously consider the offers from America, particularly the California one, or at least make the move back to Oxford. All these to her had made more sense for him than remaining exiled in the barren wilderness of Glasgow. After about 1976 she knew it was not the challenge of St Anne's that was keeping him. He had assured her in general terms that he had known what he was doing, and what he would do, and that she should be patient. She knew 1979 had been the crucial year, and the nearest she had come to seeing him consider moving on, and taking her back to England. They had both voted No in the Referendum and then Yes for the Prime Minister. She knew that if either decision had gone the other way, they would have left and returned to a more civilised climate.

But Robin had been intrigued by the possibilities created by that particular conjunction, particularly the opportunity to assist a minority Government in a hostile land. He had enjoyed himself immensely particularly over the last few years since his obnoxious little friend had become so influential. Francesca shivered slightly as she thought of him. She disliked him and most of Robin's other closest political colleagues. Arrogant, commercial creeps, she found them, with their talk of public relations and images. Most of them totally lacked Robin's appreciation of history and culture, tradition and the arts. Raymond Church was different, of course, but politically he wasn't one of those new Tories with whom Robin associated. They were quite different from her father's generation of Conservatives, men for whom compassion, care and concern were meaningful political concepts. She knew her father would despise them even more than she did. She also knew she could not afford to show the slightest hint of her real feelings. It was the one political thing about which she and Robin disagreed. He liked the people and the politics, she just liked the politics.

She knew Robin's strategy of course, he had discussed it often with her over the past few months. She would be very pleased if it were successful. She knew he was terminally bored with St Anne's now and that only his political activities, and his national and international conferencing were keeping him occupied and amused during working hours. He had shared with her fully his plans for Kings Park, and involved her in impressing the local Constituency Association officials, many of whom she had already known. They were a more palatable form of Conservative for her tastes, and she had taken genuine pleasure in furthering his cause with them. She knew he was a certainty to be selected. The meeting a couple of Saturdays ago had more or less confirmed the inevitability of that outcome. She knew what would be expected of her as a Tory candidate's wife. She enjoyed that role, and knew that she would enjoy the role of a Tory MP's wife even more. It was a role she was born to play, she had long ago developed all the skills required. She knew that if he were elected as a Scottish MP with a fourth government under the Tories, then he would be bound to be seen as Ministerial material, at least at Scottish Office level, given the paucity of competition. She knew her husband, and how his mind operated, and knew his aspirations would go even higher than that. He liked to succeed at whatever he turned to, and politics would be no exception. He delivered too, education, bridge, he was always the best.

She knew she was less of a dreamer than he was. She was a stronger believer in pragmatic development, in taking one step at a time. She looked at him sitting beside her, hunched shoulders, leaning forward, hands clasped together, eyes closed,. concentrating on the music. She felt a strong tenderness towards him, and at the same time a slight shudder of concern. She knew his dream land was built on one fundamental premise, and that she had considerable reservations about its correctness. She did not regard Kings Park as an eminently winnable seat. She knew the strength of the irrational hatred of the Prime Minister in this hostile city, and the widespread unpopularity of the Tory Party. He had explained all his theories to her, all the factors and elements that he had convinced himself pieced together would allow him to win. She knew they were all true to some extent, would all help and that he would do a far better job than anyone else could possibly do. She even had one potential scenario to add that he had utterly rejected as heresy but which would help him, that the Prime Minister would be jettisoned by the Tory Party and replaced by someone, anyone, more acceptable to Scots. Francesca had often wondered about the depth and strength of Robin's feeling for the Prime Minister, in its own way it was as irrational as the intense hatred that was the more common response in this city. She had a more balanced admiration, she still felt the Prime Minister could carry England again if not Scotland.

Looking at the back of his scrawny neck she realised two things she had often thought over the past few months but never actually verbalised to herself. I still love this man. She had never really doubted that but for a while had stopped reminding herself. The other more worrying admission was a clear conclusion that she did not think Kings Park was winnable, not even by him. She shuddered as she considered what failure might do to him. He had never ever failed to get any job he had applied for, or to achieve any goal he had set himself. She worried about the impact on him of that happening in something in which he had invested so much hope and energy. She had tried to prepare him. She had accepted the positives of his analysis but had tried gently to point out the negatives, but for once he had been unwilling to give her reservations any credence. The most he conceded was that if things got so bad for the Tories at the next Election that even he could not win, then the Scots Tory MPs would be wiped out, including his friend, and the severe constitutional crisis would require the creation of several Scottish peers to help run the Scottish Office. She had liked that notion more than he. Lady McGoldrick of Thom definitely had a nice ring about it. At least he had conceived of the possibility of failure, and had seen the potentialities that even that could bring him, but she wished that he, as she did, saw it as the more likely if not the more desirable outcome.

She had been made painfully aware that Robin had been more concerned about her own potential negative impact on his plans, than about the obstacles she had identified. She had deciphered from the elaborate codes he had used that he was very concerned about the possible effect of her social activities on his political prospects. He had put it so delicately and circuitously that even she had had difficulty initially in decoding his message. He really was quite mealy-mouthed. She smiled at her use of the term. She knew she had a more positive attitude than Robin to the adoption of the best of Scots words, and incorporated many into her own vocabulary. She had the ability denied to Robin, not that he saw it as an asset, to adapt her language according to her company, and the sense not to see guid auld words as corruption. However when she had helped him establish what he was trying to say, she understood that his basic fear was that it would be very detrimental to his political ambitions for her to be seen as anything other than devoutly monogamous. She had a genuine sympathy for him and his anxieties, although a small secret inner part of her resented that his concern was political rather than personal. She knew for an absolute certainty that she did not want to harm him or his prospects in any way. That would be a total denial of everything her life was geared to be about. But she also feared her libido was now too liberated to ever stuff back into its container. Her lamp had been rubbed too often for that.

She despaired, for the millionth time, of his sexlessness. Like her, he had become more attractive, the older he had become. Unlike her, his graph was not threatening daily to dip, as the ravages of age and wrinkle began to wreak havoc on her hitherto smooth skin. Her neck had been the first betrayer. She fingered her silk cravat ruefully. She had had to alter her style and wardrobe to compensate for the fact that she could no longer swan it. Not him. Even at 54, he was lean and gorgeous, in a slightly vulnerable wide-eyed way that she knew women of all ages found irresistibly attractive. She knew that his social gaucheness was such that he would never be able to sustain any relationship, but she knew that casual sex and short flings were there for his taking if he ever so chose. She had watched with increasingly detached amusement over the years as a variety of women, of all ages and types, including some claiming to be friends of hers, had attempted to interest him in their wares. She knew there must have been many more attempts of which she was totally unaware. She was absolutely certain that he had never been ensnared, and that he had not only resisted all attempts, but had set several 'running backwards' records and compiled millions of miles in total, most in a state of barely controlled panic. She remembered with some shame the early days of her own fall from grace when she had fervently wished he would fall too, to lessen her crippling guilt and make them more equal again. But that feeling had passed, as she had learned to live with it, herself and him, and now she knew she would be hurt and resentful if he bestowed the physical attention he denied her on any other woman.

His interest in her body was minimal these days. Occasionally in the dead heart of live nights when she was afire with restless fever, she would slip into his room and his bed and cuddle him. Sometimes she would slide her hand round onto his penis and gently instil some blood into that anaemic creature. Mostly he would pretend to stay asleep even while and after coming over her working hand. Very occasionally, and not yet this year of culture, he would acknowledge her presence and return her actions, a few gropes of her chest, a quick rub of her privates, a hurried insertion, a few wriggles, a moan and he was come and gone again. She sometimes accompanied him to conferences or lectures just so she could spend a night or two in bed with him. He was definitely more passionate, a relative concept admittedly, in warmer climes. Once two years ago at a conference in Greece where he had been the main speaker, they had made love twice in five days. She often wished he would take one of the jobs in California they kept offering him. She looked at him again, sitting there erect, getting his jollies on good music, and wondered again what connection was missing.

She knew he was not a man more comfortable in the company of other men. He found male company threatening, he was disturbed by the potential for hostility and aggression, particularly that lurking in all Scots males. She doubted if he had ever been in a Glasgow pub, but she knew that would be close to his vision of hell, aggressive little runts talking loudly about football in a language he couldn't grasp. She knew too that he did not seek out the company of young boys, even refined ones. No, she knew then, as she always had known, that if she had any rival at all for his affections and suppressed longings, it was from a ghost, a memory and a concept, and not from a human form of either sex. She loved him. She cursed him often for his asexuality, but she loved him dearly for everything else that he was. She knew too that he loved and adored her, and needed her far more even than she needed him. She fingered the brooch on her blouse and smiled ruefully at her initial thoughts on receiving it. She had known at first glance that it must have cost him about £200. It was the first such present he had bought her for several months, and she had had a fleeting thought that it must be the product of a guilty conscience. She had remembered his agitation of earlier in the week and his subsequent elation. That was consistent with the behaviour of a man in love, or at least in an affair, but she had instantly dismissed the thought. No, whatever his moods were about it was not because he was emotionally involved with another woman. The brooch was silver, shaped like a ewe. She had wondered about that. At least it wasn't bovine, but was there any message there about mutton and lamb? Not really his style of communication. Having eliminated his conscience she returned to her own, which removed the smile from her face.

She had told herself for months that his parliamentary candidacy would have to be some kind of watershed for herself. It had been coming anyway. She become more conscious of her dignity. She knew that was not the right word, but she could not find a more correct one. She knew she was losing the battle with her flesh, so she had resolved to end the war. She put her hand on her stomach and felt the yield. Before she could stop herself she moved on to the next test and lifted up her right breast with the same hand. She measured the sag as she let it go, and sighed sadly. She did this little routine more and more these days, since she had first failed the pencil test. She knew she was still slim and trim. 5'2" and 7 stone, 13 pounds, well proportioned with it. But keeping it that way was becoming harder and harder work. She had a dread of ageing, of becoming the kind of elderly matron that young men sneer at surreptitiously before servicing for reasons of a non-sexual nature. She knew she still looked younger than her age, by a good few years. She dressed to consolidate that impression. She knew that more and more she was relying on the packaging to carry the day. At least she could afford expensive clothes, the best. She had an ability to look good in clothes less attractive women would never have the confidence to wear. She did not dress conservatively. She was always modern, ahead of the game, not outrageous but never cautious. She liked outfits where she could roll up the sleeves, look relaxed but not casual. She had decided early on that pink was her colour and pursued the theme, with excellent choice of balance and offset.

She always wore expensive earrings, visible ones but never vulgar ones. Her collection was one of her prides. Billy had called her the Bet Lynch of Pollokshields. She could take a compliment well, and a joke. She used other jewellery effectively, simple but expensive. She tended to decorate her wrists and neck, at least until that Judas skin had let her down and she had had to change to high necks or expensive light scarves or cravats. Her hair had a red tinge to it, which she accentuated but kept natural. Her greatest fear was that the tinge would go, to be replaced by grey, but so far it had held without help. She wore it shorter these days, and spent an absolute fortune keeping it natural, but it was an ally. She had always had good legs, but with a smart posterior was often able to wear trousers, jump suits and a range of other leg coverings other than expensive skirts. One pretty damn smart attractive lady was not only her own assessment. Her face was not her fortune, but it gave evidence that she had one. Most of the time it was superior, with an aura of control and composure, but she knew, and not just because she kept being told, that she had a wondrous smile that opened her up, and allowed sunshine to illuminate not only herself but any company. Billy had not been the first to tell her that she looked English solemn, and a Glaswegian when she smiled. At first, she had gone back to the mirror in dismay but eventually decided that it was a coincidence rather than a problem. She was pleased with the way she moved too. Feline, more panther than cat, lean and sleek, too dangerous and lethal for most, but capable of purring for the elect. But she knew, admitted to herself that night, that her face was requiring more and more assistance, time and expenditure, to retain its smooth vigour. The panther could not be held in captivity much longer.

She had reconciled herself to that easier than she had earlier imagined. She knew that she could face the prospect of growing older gracefully more easily if she were to be an MP's or a Government Minister's wife rather than a Headmaster's one. So she had made a New Year's resolution that she had faithfully sworn to herself inside the City Chambers at midnight. 1990 could have been for her the Year of Culture thrash with a vengeance. An almost unlimited supply of able young artists passing through for very short periods. She soon had physical evidence that she could have started the year with a bang. Rudolf Whittier had rubbed his trousered penis up against her front in the hall of the party they had gone onto after the Civic Reception in George Square. He had offered with less than his rumoured sophistication to insert it inside her. The generosity of young men these days. She had surprised herself slightly by keeping her resolution and declining, even as she had clocked the extraordinary length of his sensitive fingers. No artists this year was her abstemious resolution. Culture to be taken every which way but intra-vaginally. She had known that the alternative, or the failure of her resolution, could have been a string of short performances which cumulatively could have compromised everything else she wanted. She had not promised

149

total abstinence then but had started to make the right preparatory inner rationalisations as to why she soon must.

Then Billy Kirkwood had happened. Despite herself she could not restrain the slight smile that forced itself out of her at the mention of his name. He was a cocky little bugger, that one. She had had no intention of any kind of relationship with him, but he had been so persistent, so insistent, and so confident. They had ended up alone one evening, as the only two on the Leisure and Recreation Sub-Committee to turn up. She had grudgingly agreed to conduct the business over a drink and had driven him in her car. She had realised that whatever her conscious position, her car had taken her to one of the hotels where she knew they could discretely get a room if they wanted. He had wanted to, and promised her complete discretion. He would not risk his job and his career by letting anyone know. It had been almost three months since she had ended her last little arrangement. The holiday period had had a physical emptiness that Robin had not filled, and she felt in need of a good bunk-up. So against most of her better judgement she found herself in passionate embrace with Billy. She had once more or less promised Robin, after he had been so mortified about her brief relationship with Jimmy Raybone, that she would never again have a relationship with anyone from his school or work. She had fully intended to honour that promise. But for once she had not been totally in control of the selection and the ground-rules. It was partly his fault for giving her so little in return for her artistic sacrifices, not that she had told him about her resolution.

She had regretted breaking her promise but she had not regretted Billy, not at first at least. Whatever he had given, it certainly wasn't cerebral. He had a hardness of body and personality, but no great intellect. She had realised he was the first Glaswegian she had had any kind of relationship with, and he had confirmed most of her prejudices. He was smaller than her average artist, but far harder, not fitter or more athletic sexually, just harder. He had good patter, at least when sober, that strong Glasgow wit, dry, unsentimental, almost cruel with a self-lacerating edge. But his topics of conversation were so limited; to football, in which she had absolutely no interest; and politics, in which they were so far apart as to make conversation hazardous; and work, which was in constant danger of contravening the unwritten agreement not to talk about his boss or her husband; and sex, where his talk was fairly juvenile. Which matched his technique, not a great lover like some she had known. But. But

150

what he lacked in technique and timing, he more than compensated for in animal ferocity mixed up with some strange form of suppressed tenderness.

Francesca never mastered the understanding of the place of football. Everywhere she went in Glasgow where Scottish men were, even and especially priests and artists, their primary topic of conversation was football. She had lost her potential fantasies about the two most glamorous Catholic idols in the West, the Archbishop and the Conman, when alone at last in a room with both of them and Father Andrew, all the three of them could seem to do was to attempt to analyse the major social problem of the day, the irreversible decline of the Glasgow Celtic. The artists were no more immune, appearing to feel some creative inferiority to unknown geniuses with names like Baxter, Hamilton, Cooke and Connolly. That was one reason she was glad their closest social circle was composed of English émigrés and Edinburgh escapees.

But for all that, she enjoyed listening to Billy, in small doses. It was a series of performances rather than any conversation or dialogue, but he could amuse her, make her laugh and give her some sense of identification and involvement with this strange city from which she had so successfully protected herself for so long. Then he had broken the rules, her rules, and she had watched with growing horror as he had become more and more attached to her and their relationship. She had tried to explain to him, in words of one syllable, that emotional involvement was not allowed, that it was a brief relationship to be savoured and enjoyed for itself but with no deeper meaning. He had been incapable of grasping the concept. As much as he did, he had dismissed it as obscene. He wanted more, needed more, was already giving and receiving more, the poor simple deluded boy. She had known then that she would have to end it anyway, because of that, but the proximity of Robin's selection conference had made that decision more pressing and urgent.

Sitting there, with the Polish music making no impact, she physically winced as she remembered the occasion. It had been almost three weeks ago now, a Friday night. Robin had been away, preparing to give a major speech the following day. Billy had been totally unsuspecting. He had been full of himself, insisting on telling her all the boring details of some stupid football match he had starred in the night before, for St Anne's and her husband's honour. He had won, of course. She had swithered all day about whether she should sleep with him first, a farewell performance. She had often done that in the past, but she knew Billy was different. He did not have the maturity to cope with that, which was why she was having to do what she was doing, so she had resigned herself to telling him over the drink and going home alone and unfulfilled. He had been devastated, even worse than she had feared. In turns hurt, upset, angry, abusive, tearful, pathetic, pleading and then cold. At one point, he had threatened to tell Robin. He had not been blackmailing her, she knew that, just thrashing out wildly, looking for a way to hold on to what he had. She had calmly disabused him of every option but resigned acceptance, and left him fully aware of the need for continued and complete discretion, for his own sake as well as hers. She had finally kissed him gently on the cheek and walked away from an era in her life.

She had always considered herself morally different to, indeed when she was honest, superior to, Sarah and her other friends whom she knew cheated on their husbands. That was her word not theirs. She knew Sarah no longer loved James. The affairs she had with other men were in search of that elusive commodity. But she stayed married, cynically, because it suited her, and because she was frightened of what she would lose. Francesca could not imagine living with a man without love. It did not seem right to her. Francesca had never lost love, or never sought it. She loved Robin and wanted to stay with him. The guilt she felt was at her weakness not her treachery. Well now she was strong again to demonstrate her love unequivocally. They could have a more equal relationship again. She liked Sarah, she was probably her closest friend, but she had never given her the slightest hint of her little arrangements, despite Sarah giving her a full account of her infidelities. She knew she suspected though. Artistic Glasgow was such a little village.

She had done her best to make sure that her daughters were sexually experienced before they married, and knew all about that aspect of their husband before committing themselves. They were both well settled in England, in good marriages and good homes. They were both committed to their careers, Dawn in business, like her other grandfather, and Hannah in television. She knew it would be a while yet before grandchildren came. She understood that. She felt that her own chosen career was just about to start in earnest, and understood why it would take precedence over other things. She felt her recent sacrifice somehow bring her closer to her daughters, to whom she had often tried to explain that being their father's wife was not an unfulfilling role, and one with which she was perfectly at peace. She was ready for her career going into a new and higher phase. She would be a success and make her husband and her daughters proud of her. She knew they were both proud of their father but wished they were able to give him a little more. But even as she thought it again, she knew it was him rather than them. He had not even visited Dawn's new house yet, and his one trip to Hannah's had been a major disappointment to him.

She slipped her hand over the back of Robin's neck. He was still totally absorbed in the music, leaning forward, blissful in his concentration and consummation. She rubbed his neck gently and would have sworn she heard him purr. She would not let him down. There would be no more young men. She would concentrate again on stimulating his sexuality, conveying, somehow, to him that that would be part of her new bargain with him. She would let him know tonight that his worries were over. She and he would avoid the worst indignities of her private fantasies. If she were lucky, power would act as an aphrodisiac on him. She would not hold her breath though. She was not too disappointed. Sex was important to her, she knew that, but equally she knew that status was even more so. She had had that dream or fantasy one night, she was never later sure exactly which, where her extramarital activities had become public knowledge, and had destroyed her husband's career and her marriage. She had realised that it represented the end of everything she had built her life to do.

Ever since then the external sex had been less sweet. And the mental strain, of preparing herself to meet young men as an equal had become more and more telling as the physical defects began to eat into the psychological assets. Well, that was all over now. In a phrase that she knew would begin to mean more to her again, it was now more worth the candle not to.

CHAPTER NINE - THE CHOICE REINFORCED

It was a much happier Robin McGoldrick who awaited Frank Hunter's attendance in his office that Friday morning. He had been in a state of grace continuously since he had left the Sir Walter Scott. He had been surprised how much he had enjoyed the journey back to Glasgow, relaxing in his first-class seat, assessing the state of play. It had been a quiet euphoria at first. He had felt that he had handled a potentially difficult and indeed disastrous situation remarkably well. The euphoria had grown more strident throughout a wonderful evening. He and Francesca had gone out together, just the two of them for the first time in months. The music had been exquisite. He had sat entranced all night, transported into an inner world of pure bliss. He closed his eyes again in his office and recreated in his head some of the finer points. Penderecki was definitely one to follow in the future. Almost as good as the music had been Francesca, and her little present to him. She had appreciated the brooch. He was very glad he had given her something special and personal. She had not appreciated the finer points of the music, which was unusual for her, but she had seemed calm and tranquil nevertheless, pleased to be with him. She had then seduced him when they got back home. He gave a strange smile at the memory. It was a long time since that had happened. He had had a couple of large whiskies when they got back, much more than he usually drank, his special Islay malt. She had played some of their favourite music on the CD player. They had sat together on the black leather couch in silent contentment, then when his second drink was done, she had sexually assaulted him in a gentle but persistent way. That had been acceptable enough but what had really completed his evening was that she had told him that she had no other relationship and would never have one again.

She had not quite used those exact words but he was certain that was what the message had been. She had assured him that she would not run the slightest risk of jeopardising his political future. They were the sweetest words she could have whispered to him. He knew she was dubious about his chances in Kings Park, but she did not have his political insight, nor had she done the depth of analysis and study that he had. He knew that in some ways, she would even prefer his own alternative scenario, the Tories wiped out in Scotland but victorious in England and creating peers to help run the Scottish Office. She did want to be a Lady. Now she was guaranteeing to act like one so as not to risk the prospect. He was so relieved. His major weakness removed, at the same time as he had acted decisively to head off the risk from his own little act of foolishness and indiscretion.

As he reran the events of the last few days, and prepared for the forthcoming interview, he experienced a feeling entirely new to him. All his life he had been a man of letters, one who used words, preferably written but occasionally spoken, to succeed in his chosen aims. There had always been a tremendous satisfaction in that, but he had now found for the first time in his life the special excitement attached to being a man of action. He was delighted with himself and what he had achieved. He had faced a terrible situation and responded to it by his actions in a way which had made it work out satisfactorily. His success opened up new fantasies for him. It reinforced his conviction that he did have the capacity to cope with the harsh world of politics. Nothing awaiting him in that world could carry as much danger and risk as the previous few days had.

He was now fairly confident that the major risk had passed. Compared to him, Hunter was an incompetent amateur, acting on his own without direction or vision. He was still potentially dangerous though. Robin was well aware of that. Although he was no longer in a position to prove his allegations, even making them carried a considerable risk to Robin. He had worked out what he was going to do about that. He would offer him the Janitor's job, but make it clear to him that it was conditional, on his continued good behaviour and loyalty. He would be on probation initially, and the more time passed, long before the two years of industrial tribunal entitlement, the less dangerous any unsubstantiated rumours would be. Margaret would be far away and lost by then.

He still puzzled a little at what was motivating Hunter, what he wanted for himself. Robin did not really believe that he was after money. He did not want Robin's and if he was after money from the tabloids he would surely have gone straight to them. He wondered if the political aspect alone was justifying his actions. He knew Hunter was a Labour fanatic, had been from his earliest days at St Anne's. Not that he had ever got anywhere, unlike that fat friend of his. He had come across Hunter at the hustings through the years, but they had never spoken, not even pleasantries, with the unavoidable exception of his mother's funeral. Maybe Hunter was shrewd enough to share his own analysis about his chances in Kings Park. But he could sense some other motivation than the political, some more personal if twisted aspect of revenge or bitterness. He knew from what Father Andrew had said that the man was mentally ill, had been an in-patient in that awful establishment, Kamesthorn. That would help erode his credibility if it ever came to public slander. But why pick on him?

He searched his memory for their previous contact, for any basis for this incredible persecution. He remembered belting him on several occasions. There had been the Assembly singing disruption. He had a vague peculiar memory of feeling for a brief period that possibly the boy was actually innocent there, but he had eventually accepted responsibility and taken his punishment without complaint. He had a nagging feeling that there was more to it than that, but could not put his finger on it. No, it was most likely his response to Hunter's performance at that Schools Cup Final. He remembered his own insistence that Hunter should not get his medal. He remembered too his public denunciation at the school assembly of the boy and his disgraceful behaviour, and his permanent ban on playing for the School. He remembered Hunter had left school a year early. That's what would be at the root of it. Well, he had brought it on himself, with his thuggery, his complete lack of self-control and self-discipline, his failure to act on his leadership responsibilities. He had disgraced himself and his school, and got what he deserved but apparently he had chosen to blame the responding authority rather than himself. Pathetic really but not untypical of these football types.

Robin still had a slight worry that Hunter might react badly to the defeat of his plan, and might attack him. He had considered bringing the police in, but had concluded that there was even less point than before. He would have to offer his carrot early. He knew the job would give Hunter more income than he was used to getting. Hunter on the payroll and the premises would be a constant reminder to himself that there was danger around, but it might be no bad thing. It would ensure that he would never be tempted to do anything so stupid again.

****

Frank Hunter packed his school bag with some care that morning. He took less care with his clothes. He had no need to try

156

so consciously to look like a loser, as he had done on Tuesday. He could dress as normal, and achieve the same effect. He smiled at the thought. Sartorial elegance was not his scene. But today he would not be a loser. He put two tape-recorders in his bag. The smaller, more compact one would remain there, and tape the whole conversation, for his own and Julie's protection as much as anything else. He still had some fear of ending up prosecuted for his pains. He had a sneaking suspicion that he might have played his hand too successfully, and been counter-productive. If McGoldrick now believed he was perfectly safe, he might have decided he could afford to bring in the police. He, or they, might be taping this interview. Frank knew he would to have to continue to choose his words with care, to avoid any accusation of extortion or conspiracy. The other recorder he would bring out when necessary to demonstrate to McGoldrick what he had on tape. He had already re-recorded both the telephone conversation and the pub conversation onto several different tapes. He had hidden the master copies and other copies, in different places outwith his flat, just in case the police or anyone else broke in looking for them. He was not bringing with him a complete copy of either conversation, only a couple of tapes with edited highlights from each.

The photographs from Giustis had turned out well, the kiss in particular was an excellent one. Clear and natural. It looked nothing like a set-up. Deny that, ya bass. The negatives and copies were also safe. He packed in his bag some snaps from the Holiday Inn, and a couple from Edinburgh. McGoldrick could keep them as souvenirs.

Frank had practised his tactics and his game plan many times. He had a final rehearsal as he walked over the hill and into Govanhill. He wasn't elated but he felt quietly pleased at the way things were going. He was looking forward to successfully concluding this episode, then getting onto something more positive once his ghosts were slain.

He walked into the school less hesitantly this time. He knew exactly what he was going to see, and could concentrate on the other bits. Mrs Little smiled at him again. "Nice to see you again, Frank. Mr McGoldrick is expecting you. I'll just let him know you have arrived." One minute later she was back and told him just to go right in. He chose to knock all the same. Keep the rituals right and the parallels exact. "Enter". He did, switching on his machine in time to catch the sonorous tone. The room was the same as Tuesday, so was the routine. He noticed with pleasure that the

157

cloak was on, as was the game of preoccupation with work. The wait was less painful or stressful this time. Frank felt a strong sense of control.

"Right, Hunter," he finally closed his papers and looked straight at Frank. There was a slight pause, but Frank knew he should let McGoldrick take the initiative, it was safer that way. "You are waiting for some kind of answer from me, I believe." Frank looked straight back, motionless and silent. "It may surprise you to know that I too have spoken to Miss Beattie. She has assured me that she has no intention of speaking to you again, and she most certainly will not be giving you any written statement, no matter what you offer her. I must warn you that if you attempt to bother or harass her, I have her permission to bring in the police." He paused to let that information sink in to his stupid, silent foe. Frank's instinct that more was to come proved correct. "However, I am acutely aware that the information you thought you had about me, is potentially harmful. Even without the slightest proof, such an allegation could conceivably damage my name and reputation. There is nothing to be gained by either of us from such an eventuality." He paused to change gear. "I am a magnanimous man." Frank felt honoured the man assumed he would know what that meant. "I know that you have had your own troubles recently. I was very sorry about your mother. She did much good work in the Church, and the community. I have considerable respect for her memory. I know too that you are unemployed, and," a slight hesitation well- clocked by Frank, "that you have not been in the best of health. Well, I think I can help you. I am willing to offer you an opportunity of resuming employment. I can arrange for you to have a trial period as one of the assistant janitors at this school. There is a consistent level of overtime, with weekend and evening work, this being a community school. As Headmaster, of course I would require your absolute loyalty."

"Very neat," thought Frank, one of several thoughts to sweep into his head. "That would be interesting, me as shop-steward in McGoldrick's school." was another. He knew all the ancillary staff were in the G&M, they had had Glasgow all tied up ever since the old Corporation carve-up days. Frank knew the shop-stewards, the Branch Secretary and the full-time official well. Very briefly he was tempted, but as a vision it passed even before the echo of McGoldrick's words reverberated round the holy chamber. A further uninvited thought was that he would be able to play for St Anne's in the next match and kick lumps out of all those social

158

workers. The final one was that he too would now have to make a choice. But even as he thought it, he knew there was no choice for him to make, this was not a cross-roads leading in any direction he wished to travel.

"Well, what about it. What do you have to say for yourself?" His arrogance, conceit, self-satisfaction and unignorable air of superiority allowed Frank no thought of mercy or stay of execution. He relied on his rehearsed script, the scenario so far meant there was only need for minor modification. "You are mistaken in one small but crucial regard. That I am not in a position to prove the information I have about you and your relationship with Miss Beattie. I have here photographs of both you and Miss Beattie entering the Holiday Inn. Of Miss Beattie outside your room. Of Miss Beattie entering your room. Of Miss Beattie leaving the Hotel." He passed them over the desk. The monitored face showed no reaction. They both knew that these separate photos did not represent any conclusive proof of his claim.

"I also have," his own pause for dramatic effect and to allow him to bring his machine out his bag, "a tape of your telephone conversation with Miss Beattie made immediately after I left your office on Tuesday." He pressed the play button and let fourteen words out. "Look, Margaret, it is very important to me that our relationship stays a secret." Most people have a reaction of disbelief and mild dismay to hearing their voice on a poor quality recorder. McGoldrick's reaction was rather more than mild. He turned white and began to die. Impressed, Frank pressed the stop button, then the eject one. He lifted the tape out and inserted the other one. "I also have a tape of your conversation with Miss Beattie in the Sir Walter Scott." He pressed the play button again and let it spit fifteen more nails into the coffin lid. "I will never again make use of the services of a lady of the night." Stop, eject, tape back into the bag. "I also have a photograph of your touching farewell scene." He slid a copy of the best one across the wide desk. Frank found it fascinating watching the man's face age and decay in front of him. He had a momentary vision of the only equivalent he had ever seen in his life, sitting on a wooden bench in Cordoba watching Iranians. But that had taken two games. This was even more spectacular. From cool, assured, confident, ageless and handsome to old, tired, haggard, beaten and silenced in less than two minutes.

159

"She has betrayed me." he eventually said in a strangled voice to no-one in particular. Frank knew this was his, and her, danger point and stepped in rapidly with his script. "No she did not. Any close examination of those tapes will show that she did not tell any lies. She has not given me any written statement, and has no intention of doing so. Nor did she ever ask for any money from you. Indeed she stressed that you did not need to give her anything. In both conversations you accept that and insist on giving her some as an unconditional gift. She also made it quite clear to both you and me, that she had no desire to harm you. It is beyond her now, and solely between you and me. There is no point in either of us having any more contact with her. I have all the evidence I need, irrespective of anything she may subsequently say or do." The man seemed to let the point go and was silent again, so Frank proceeded. "I know you may well need time to assimilate the information you now know I possess. But it seems to me you do have a choice to make: whether or not to proceed with your plans for a political career now that you know your hypocritical behaviour, which is contrary to your own stated standards, is no longer your own little secret. But that is entirely your choice. I want nothing from you, nor do I wish you to do anything in particular. You do not even need to let me know what you decide to do. I do not think we need to meet again. I will know from the papers which choice you have made. I want nothing from you at all, not a thing." Having said what he had determined to say, Frank stood and left the room as quickly as possible. He even denied himself the pleasure of a backward glance until closing the door. The contest was over. That tired and weeping old man could inflict no more harm on him. The closing door shut on an era, and freed him from his past.

He smiled goodbye at Mrs Little. She said, "I hope we see you again soon, Frank". He replied, following a strong instinctive urge, "By the way, you might well at that, you know. He's," and a nod backward to the room, "just offered me a job as Assistant Jannie, subject to one or two wee details." She seemed so genuinely pleased for him that he felt ashamed of himself and hurried off. He went to the Albert Bar, the nearest of his pubs, for a pint and a ponder.

He enjoyed his ponder even more than his pint. There was a lot to think about and assess. He knew that basically he was well pleased with himself. He had set himself a goal, a target and had attained his aim through a cleverly conducted campaign. He felt he had achieved something important. Done something to a high specification, proved himself capable of conquering. It was a feeling he had not enjoyed for a long time, so he savoured it, and had another pint.

His first task was to check all his actions of the last week against his Gordon tests. Had he passed safely or were Julie and he still at some risk if the broken man went to the police? He had enjoyed his legal study sessions in the Mitchell much more than he had anticipated. He had thought it would be arid stuff, choking on the dusty tomes and dry words, devoid of life and humanity. Instead it had been intellectually exciting and full of great human interest. He realised for the first time some of the thrill to which Paddy and Peter McColl had often alluded. Not the theatrical excitement of the Court, but the stretching of the intellect in the effort to bend the flexible law to the required shape in a manner that would convince rigorous scrutineers. He had learned much about the law of Scotland, and of the kind of risks he and Julie were running. He felt he grasped the basics well, and soon became wise to the subtleties. He had always felt that he could have been as successful as Paddy and Peter, his short period of study did nothing to diminish that fantasy. It was important to him that he respect the law in his dealing with McGoldrick. Not just to avoid the risk of punishment, although that was a factor, especially in his responsibility to Julie. But for himself he also had a moral motive. He wanted his triumph to be fair and square, within the rules, just, with no cheating on his part. He had always been fanatical about the need to respect the rules of the game, any game he played, and this was a game, so he had to keep within the rules, the laws of society.

He had discovered that he was at no risk of his first fear, a charge of blackmail. It was not really a term or concept in Scots Law, certainly not a crime. But his study showed there were two crimes he was at risk of committing, and a third one with regard to

Julie. For a Glasgow man, used since pre-playground days to a daily currency of threats and challenges, it was a surprise to learn of the criminal nature of such activity in itself, even if never backed up. It must be the first crime every Scots boy commits, from well below the age of criminal responsibility. "Ah'me gonna batter you, or get ma big brother/father/mother to batter you." To say the words alone is a criminal act, to say it was a joke is no defence. To carry it through is a different crime, of assault, but the uttering of the words is an offence of threat. The threat need not be of violence to be a crime. He was initially alarmed to discover, from his study of the fate of James Miller in 1862, that threats to injure a man's reputation were as much a crime as threats to his body. He was even more alarmed to find that a man can be charged with threatening somebody with the truth about themselves.

The strange case of Alex Crawford taught him that the truth can be an offensive weapon, if used to threaten. Paddy had helped him make some sense of that initial paradox, with the story of the pure and wonderful crucifix, which was used to batter in a nun's head. The crucifix remained pure, it was the use to which it was put that made the difference. Always was a good Catholic that boy. Given the nature of his own enterprise it had been a sobering discovery that the truth of his instrument of justice was no guarantee against criminality of its use. Poor Marion Macdonald reached out from her resting place in hell and showed him that the threat to expose sexual immorality could still be a criminal offence, no matter the truth of the claim or the extent of the immorality. He loved reading these old cases, with their evocation of ghosts and drama. If that was musty old law he loved it. He felt he came to know James Miller, and Alex Crawford, and especially Marion, as well as he did Matt Craig or Conn Docherty or any of the other mythical heroes of his past. They and their epic flawed deeds deserved a wider audience yet they were lost to sight of all but a few conscientious law students.

The second and even more serious crime of which he soon learned he stood at some risk of committing was the one of extortion. The extra dimension that moved the crime of threat into the more serious plane was the linking of a threat to the seeking to induce a course of action by the threat, either to the advantage of the threatener, or even just to the detriment of the threatened. "Ah'll batter you unless you gie me that playpiece, or unless you stand on that toley." Given his plan, it was no comfort to learn that the crime of extortion exists, once the threat and demand are made, whether or not the demand is met or the threat implemented.

Julie was at risk of a charge of conspiracy, to either of his potential crimes of threat and extortion but also to one of conspiracy to defraud. Her risks were lesser though, and easier to defend against.

At first he had wondered in despair if it would be possible to do what he intended without breaking the rules and exposing himself and her to the risk of those charges. But eventually his hours of study paid off, and he was able to work out the ground-rules and requirements that would keep them both safely within the law, if sailing damn close to the edge. He owed his principal debt to Professor Gordon. His Criminal Law of Scotland was the best and most authoritative of the many books he read. It was also the most enjoyable, and the one that offered him his guidelines for security.

So he sat in the Albert Bar over his second pint and tested their performance against the Professor's guidelines. Julie was the easier of the two to protect. He had learned the key in her case was the magic phrase "No harmful intent." She had made it clear to him that she did not wish McGoldrick harmed, and only co-operated upon receiving that assurance. She had also made it clear to McGoldrick she did not wish to hurt him. There was no evidence of any desire to induce McGoldrick to act to his prejudice. On the fraud side she was precise on both tapes that he need not give her anything, she did not require anything from him, and anything he did give her was entirely at his own desire. He was satisfied that she would be in the clear.

His own case was slightly more complicated. He had learned from his studies that the key to his own salvation lay in making no demand of McGoldrick, even if he could not avoid threatening him. He learned the relevant quote from Gordon off by heart, "It is doubtful whether a threat to expose a man's immoral or improper behaviour would be a crime where the threat was to expose the truth and it was unaccompanied by any demand." Some other sources disputed that, at least theoretically, but none had Gordon's status and authority. So he had been very careful to make no demand of McGoldrick. Pointing out to him he had a choice to make was not the same as making a demand of him, and he had been very careful, very subtle, especially in the taped second interview, not to even express any preference for which choice he should make. No, he was satisfied that he had made no demand of

McGoldrick. More, he had done better than that minimum Gordon had indicated for his safety. It was his view that he had not even made any threat. He replayed the tape of the second interview to confirm that for himself. He had made no explicit threat, never even mentioned what he might do, never even hinted at exposure. Even in the first interview he hadn't actually said he would definitely go to the newspapers. So even Gordon's doubt in his favour was not necessary, he had made no threat far less a demand. He was safe from prosecution, no Procurator-Fiscal in the land would take that case to Court. He was also safe from his own more serious charge of cheating, of breaking the rules of the game. It was a grey area though, and if the system were absolutely determined to get him, and her, then they no doubt would find a way. After all, he had only studied the law for a fortnight, some of them had been at it for all their lives, and their fathers. He still felt quite pleased with his own cleverness, though.

Okay he had kept within the law and won his victory but was he proud of himself, that was the more difficult question he asked himself. Frank knew that one of his problems was that he set himself impossibly high standards. Not just of deed but thought. When younger he had strived to be perfect, but had sadly learned that that ambition was beyond him. He was not a Christian, never had been, but somehow maybe from the influence of his Gran and his mother, he had used Christ as some kind of role model for behaviour. Always be good, in thought as well as deed. Never do harm to anyone else, never think uncharitable thoughts. Never tell lies, to yourself even more than to others. He had always tried to live up to those standards and expectations. He did like and respect other people, long after he learned what bastards many of them could be. There were always explanations and justifications for the wrong that other people did. He always found it much harder to justify and excuse his own wrongdoing, even on its much more restricted scale. But he prided himself that he did not hurt other people. He never engaged in acts of violence. As a footballer, he had been a hard tackler, but never a clogger nor even a professional fouler. He had had some arguments with Tommy Gallagher about football morality where Tommy had not really had a clue what Frank was on about. Tommy would say there was a referee, and a system of punishments for transgressions, Frank would talk about a higher morality. But it wasn't Tommy who had been sent off in a cup final. And Frank had never been in fights, other than protecting himself in melees. He hated and despised the

164

whole hardman myth, hated his grandfather Willie and his vindication through violence. In the Union and the Labour Party over the years, he had done some people down, but it had never been personal, it had always been in pursuit of issues and principles, and he had tried to talk to them as people afterwards. He did not want to be a saint, but he had an almost desperate need to be good.

He had two systems by which he always tried to regulate his own behaviour and by which he judged himself. The first and best test was whether his Gran Jean would be proud of what he was doing, and how he would feel telling her about it. Even after she died, he continued to hang onto this test. Funnily enough, she became even harder to please from her new home in his head and his heart. The other test involved an even sterner critic. He had developed the ability from an early age, to film himself in every situation in his life, and simultaneously to living it, sit in a small projector room in his head and watch the show, assessing the performance of the characters playing Frank Hunter. He seldom gave them pass-marks, and was most often grievously appalled at the ordinariness, the pettiness and the lack of true charity and worth displayed by those little people in the B-movie and inferior soap of his life, especially the so-called star.

Over his second pint, he applied those two tests to the events of the last few weeks and hours. He knew his Gran would not have shed any tears for McGoldrick. She would have thought him a supercilious English Tory git. She would have been appalled at his hypocrisy, his advocacy of the sanctity of the family and his use of a prostitute. She would have agreed that he deserved sorting out. She had never really understood what had happened to Frank in 1970 but she knew McGoldrick had done him wrong. He knew she would approve of what he was doing to McGoldrick now, and that it would seem mild as a form of revenge. He was less convinced himself. He knew with a sudden clarity, at last, the truth that he had been denying to himself for 20 years, that it was his own reaction to the dilemma in 1970 that had been the real problem, not McGoldrick. He had had a choice to make, and had not been true to himself in making it. That was his fault, not that of the poser of the dilemma. But that failure, and its consequences, had festered over the years and he had been delighted at the chance of a rerun. He felt that the choice he had given McGoldrick was not as subtle as the one McGoldrick had given him. He had been given the choice of losing something very important to him, or accepting responsibility for something he had not done. He had given McGoldrick the choice of losing something very important to him, or to risk having publicly to attempt to deny or cope with the responsibility for something he had done. He knew that he had not meant to do McGoldrick harm. It was not the outcome that was the issue, but facing him with the situation of having to consider a choice.

He realised as he sat there in the Albert Bar, quite happy and at peace for the first time in a long time, that he really did not care which choice McGoldrick made. It amused him to think that if McGoldrick had the bottle to make the right choice he would not come to any harm at all. Frank knew, had always known, that he had not the slightest intention of taking his proof to the Sun. He loathed and despised that paper and everything it stood for. Particularly its fervent, blind support for the Prime Minister; but also its hypocrisy; its racialism and jingoism; its blatant disregard for truth and decency. Nor would he go to any other tabloid. He would settle for knowing, and knowing McGoldrick knew he knew. Even if he had thought there was any real chance that McGoldrick could win back Kings Park he wouldn't use that material.

McGoldrick had been exposed as a hypocrite, but Frank had always known that all Tories were hypocrites, it was the inevitable essence of their philosophy. This was just a more blatant example. No, if the man held his nerve and called Frank's bluff, he would be home and free. He would escape with only a warning, and a small fine of course. It amused Frank to think that if McGoldrick knew his enemy well, and was a good judge of Frank's character and nature, he would be all right. But he wasn't, he underestimated and despised Frank, so let the bastard take the consequences of that mis-assessment. Frank knew too, that he had overestimated McGoldrick and his strength of character. That was a weak man he had seen disintegrate in front of his eyes. He doubted very much if he would have the strength of character to go for it. But that would be his choice, his decision and if it had as negative an effect on his life as Frank's choice had had on his, well then that would only be fair. The man wasn't going to win that seat anyway, or any other Scottish one. Let him go back to England and take his chances there. Frank would not pursue him across the border.

No, the outcome had not been the point. The point had been to place McGoldrick in the same position he had placed Frank, of having to search his soul and character in response to a dilemma

166

of choice. The fact that he would probably make the wrong choice, just as Frank had done, was just an added bonus. The main point was to slay the ghosts of the past and release Frank from the burden of his failure, to allow him to face the future unencumbered by a fear of success and start to make what he could of the rest of his life. Frank realised that he would not in fact be disappointed or upset if McGoldrick were to make the other choice. In a funny way, he would actually be pleased. Either way, he was now free. Not only of McGoldrick and his choice, but of the other darker ghost, that had come back to haunt him that Saturday night in the Victoria a few weeks ago, the fear of that bitter taste of victory, the inability to cope with getting what he wanted. For the first time, he had swallowed hard on that taste, overcome that feeling and persevered on to full victory. Never more would that feeling haunt him, and fuck up his life.

That realisation was good medicine for him, so he ordered a third pint, and a steak pie, chips and beans. He realised that his victory over his old Headmaster had cost him over £6,000, and considerable time, effort and ingenuity. It never occurred to him that it had not been worth it. He considered it money well spent. His money embarrassed him. He did not want it. It made his hatred and rejection of the Prime Minister less valid. It threatened his perception and classification of himself as a good working-class Glasgow boy. 36 years old, he was still a boy in Glasgow, no doubt about that, but the rest? That was more complicated, especially the money. He relished the irony that for most of his closest and oldest friends there was no doubt. Paddy, and his fat income, and his big house in Pollokshields. Peter McColl and his big house in Baillieston, and his more money than sense. Elaine, a professional married to another professional in their own house with two cars and two children. All now irredeemably middle-class, by occupation, by housing, by income and by social behaviour. Dinner parties ya bass. Derek Duncan and Tommy Gallagher who had used football rather than education as their escape route, but still ended up in big houses in English middle-class areas, business men to the core. Even Danny, poorest paid of them all as a social worker, still owned his own flat and was classified occupationally as middle-class lower managerial. And Joyce similarly owned her own flat and called herself a professional. Jack Reilly and Vera, from probably the poorest backgrounds of them all, now lived in the big house on the hill, with him a high-status career man and big earner. Even Tommy

Little was going to end up a social work professional. All his mates and drinking pals in the Labour Party, Andy Rogers, Tony Dixon, Billy Kirkwood and the rest, teachers and social workers, lecturers and lawyers the lot. Every single one of the ones he mentioned were from definite working-class backgrounds, but had made the great escape in the past decade or so. Under the Prime Minister and her evil regime. At least they all still voted Labour. Gerry Robertson and he were the only two that defied easy reclassification. A Trade Union official who owned his own flat, and an unemployed labourer who owned his own flat and had well over 100 grand in the bank. He was the only one who had not used education or football to escape, yet he had more money in the bank than any of them, and a house full of every labour saving or pleasure giving device known to man. Automatic washing machine, tumble-dryer, a Hoover that also cleaned windows and made cups of tea, 2 TV sets, a Video-recorder, Satellite TV. The modern face of poverty it definitely wasn't.

It was complicated enough to require another pint. He knew the other side well too. There was Hazel, a school-cleaner with two kids in care and a poky bedsit. There were all the boys he had been at school with, Joe Anderson and Willie Goldie, Archie, Kenny Simpson and big Paul who were now out of work, and didn't have 100 pence in the bank, or much hope in their hearts. There was the next generation who seemed to have it worse, or coped less well with it anyway. Mars Bar Billy, the boy he'd met at Kamesthorn, and his pathetic pals, spaced out on dope, jellies and shit. Then there were the worst ones of all, the ones who weren't out of work, and who would buy him pints because he was. They thought they were winning and he was losing. They were only half-right. He had done it himself, often, before LDT closed. You would see a decent guy, nursing a pint all night and avoiding company in case he got involved in a round he couldn't match. So you would join him for a 'pint on you' on the way out, and say you'd get one back from him another time. Now most folk in his southside pubs who knew him at all, knew he was out of work and would try the same kind of thing with him. He held them off as long as possible with tales of redundancy money but the best of them told him not to waste that in drink and that it wouldn't go far as he thought.

None of them knew about his mother's poisoned legacy to him. Shona Hunter had left school at 14, to work in one of Sludden's Stores as a shop-assistant. Over the years her keen intelligence, her integrity and her initiative had enabled her to progress through the hierarchy to a very key role. For years, all through his childhood, she had been under-paid and under-rewarded but then the two original Sludden Brothers had retired and the sole heir, Peter the nephew, had continued to rely upon her but also treated her right, made her a director, given her shares. Frank had always been proud of his mother but he had been horrified when, three days after she died in his bed, Peter Sludden told him that his mother's total legacy to him would be a six figure sum. Along with his generous redundancy settlement from LDT, it meant the annual interest alone was more than his modest needs. Despite his collecting of ironies, he did not appreciate that the two great disasters of 1989 that had so damaged his health had done so much for his wealth.

He took his unemployment money, on principle, since it was his right, Mary Ewing had taught him well, but like her he would never have claimed off the Social Security. An empty gesture given his ineligibility. He signed on, by post, and got his giro every fortnight, £74:70. He kept it separate and used it as his beer money. He appreciated the irony of that, with its reinforcement of one of the Prime Minister's favourite myths, but what else could he do? He had decided against giving his money away to the poor, in little or large measures, but he invented his own little system of income redistribution which caused him as many problems as it solved. He knew neither he nor his intended recipients were in favour of charity, but they were all betting men, so he broke the habits of a lifetime and began to bet to lose. He tried to be subtle about it, betting not so much on facts he knew to be wrong but on possible outcomes he knew to be unlikely. Nothing heavy, £2 there, a fiver here, the odd tenner, enough to cover a few rounds or an Indian meal. He had worries about whether or not he was being patronising and eventually decided he was, but it was Buster Douglas who made him give it up, after Frank put £5 on him to beat Tyson, at 10-1, with Archie Balfour because Archie was really close to the bone. Archie was an honourable man and insisted on paying him, at a £1 a week and that transaction became a regular reminder to Frank of the folly of interfering with the laws of nature. He settled thereafter for the less risky course of being thought a generous fool.

His money had weighed heavy on him. He had had this strange but real feeling after LDT voted to close that he would never work again, not 'work work' anyway. He knew there would be definite consequences for him of that determination. A reckoning to be

169

had. But his money, especially his mum's money, had not only postponed that but threatened to put it off indefinitely. He could live off the interest alone, and never get near any moment of truth. Himself in that state, and all his friends prospering and flourishing, and he spent most of his time working himself into a frenzy about the injustice and evil of the world under the greedy Prime Minister. He could tell himself all he liked about the other side. As well as what he knew and saw directly, Danny and Joyce kept him well informed through their work about the real effects of the economic miracle on the lives of so many devastated Glasgow families and children. Paddy and Peter McColl told all he wanted to know and more about the other side of the enterprise culture, too, about the crooks and fraudsters that got caught and punished unlike the suited ones that flourished and were lauded as living examples of the Prime Minister's values. He knew all about the cancer of drugs that was sweeping through so many Glasgow communities and destroying so many hopeless young lives. He wouldn't bet on Billy making next Christmas. Nothing made him feel more impotent than that. He had no answer, no alternative solution, other than "shoot the bastards supplying it", but others would just take their place. No, he knew all that, but he kept coming back to the success of so many of his friends and the obscenity of his own position. The old hard but comforting realities had gone for good, and the new world was a more complex place. Yet he still knew right from wrong, and he was right and she was wrong.

His pudding, a dollop of ice-cream alone in a big plate, reminded him of a strange irritation he had felt recently about the failure of his money. Not only could it not seem to provide him with moral security, its possession eroded the value of many of his most prized memories. He had walked into the Brooklyn Cafe, for a tub of the best ice-cream in Glasgow to carry back to his flat. He had noticed it sitting on a shelf. A bottle of their very own Raspberry Sauce. 80p a bottle, no problem, "I'll have one of those please." As a wee boy he had specialised in relying on his impish charm to get an extra shake free. "Hi missus, gies an extra dod for a growing boy, eh." Often worked too, and he would lick the extra off his fingers. So he took his bottle back to the privacy and emptiness of his home and poured it all over his plate. It was sweet, sickly and horrible and ruined his ice-cream. The devastation and disappointment had almost given him a relapse. What would his psychiatrist Wee Ewan make of that. "Well yes, I have been back on the sauce, and it's depressed me, but it's no' the drink, doctor, its the raspberry sauce. Help me, and I promise I'll never touch it again." The condensed milk had been almost as traumatic. The greatest childhood treats he could remember were his mother letting him have one spoonful every time she made tablet, and then scraping the tin, and the time he and Derek stole a small tin from Ronaldson's and made two sandwiches each. So he had taken two tins down from Safeways, and eaten the lot with a big spoon, one depressed afternoon. The experience had deepened his depression and he had never tried again.

He still felt better than he usually did after such conversations with himself. The feeling of satisfaction from his triumph over McGoldrick remained. He knew he wouldn't go to the Mitchell for the afternoon as he had originally planned, but he determined that from Monday, he would get a grip on himself, and work seriously on his book. He had a good feeling that he would be able to concentrate on it properly now, and maybe be able to make some kind of important political statement. It could maybe contribute to the important debates that were going to have to take place in Scotland over the next few years. There would be a certain appropriate irony in using his LDT money to pay to get his book printed. That notion began to appeal to him. Then he would do Mary Ewing's letters. They had been brought back across the Atlantic to him after her death, by her Canadian grand-daughter Mary-Ann. They were wonderful letters, providing a unique social and political dissection of Scotland over the period 1946-1979 and outlining the inevitability of Scotland's people one day asserting enough confidence to grasp their right to take democratic control of their destiny. They deserved a wide audience. Again, if it came to it, if it was the only way, he could use his money to ensure they were published.

These were the thoughts that sustained and warmed Frank Hunter as he walked into Queens Park and up to his favourite seat and his favourite view. He had slain not one but two of his obstructive ghosts, and could now concentrate on retrieving what he could from the mess his life had become. He had re-found that most vital of all commodities, a hope for the future and a dream or two to aim for, he was on a journey again.

CHAPTER ELEVEN - THE CHOICE MADE

Robin McGoldrick never really recovered from the blow Frank Hunter inflicted upon him in their little private school reunion party. The man who had always looked upon himself as a winner, and had always been regarded in that way by others, turned out to be unable to handle being a loser. As Jean Coyle once said to her small grandson Frank after another Celtic defeat in the lean pre-Stein years, the true heroes of life are not the regular easy winners but the losers who learn and grow from the experience. After Hunter left him alone with a speed and suddenness that upset him, he slumped into his chair and cried. He put his forehead on the leather section of his desk, and left it there until the two skins of unequal thickness merged and became as one, with the salt tears aiding the unification process. When he was finally ready for a separation, he cancelled his two afternoon appointments and told Mrs Little over the intercom that he was locking himself in his room to finish a speech, and must not be disturbed under any circumstances.

He made one other phone-call, to Francesca. He told her as flatly as he could that he would be late home, and that he would not be able to go to the Ballet, or to the party after. He told her he had received a phone call about an article to write which he must deliver on Saturday morning. She did not disbelieve him, as she knew he loved that particular ballet and been enthusiastically and genuinely looking forward to it, if not the party, the night before. However there was something in his tone that worried her considerably. She could sense that the euphoria of the previous evening had finally worn off, and had been replaced by something almost as dramatic in the opposite direction. She would really have to talk to him about whatever it was as soon as she could. After the previous evening she felt they were closer than they had been for a long time, and she wanted to build on the good of that.

That Friday evening, while Frank Hunter delighted his friends in the Victoria Bar by talking and laughing and planning like the Frank of old, and started a new and more promising phase of his life, Robin prowled around his empty house like a wolf with worms, rubbing his arse relentlessly on every stopping place and finding satisfaction in none.

He wanted to believe that Hunter was giving him a genuine choice. Undoubtedly there was an aura of cold, hard fanaticism about Hunter which meant that Robin felt he could be certain that Hunter would have no hesitation in exposing him if he were to proceed to become the candidate. But could he believe that there was something about that man which meant Robin could accept that Hunter would not use the information he had about him unless he proceeded to become a Tory Party candidate? Robin attempted to unravel the double negatives and double positives in his own head. He considered the option of bluffing it out, of denying any relationship and trying again to get Margaret to deny it. Some might believe him. At worst, it would be his word against that of a prostitute and a madman. But there was the little matter of the proof. He knew Francesca would know he was lying. He knew that brazening it out was not possible in any case, with his personality. He could not possibly cope with the public encounters inevitable in such a revelation. He could never expose his private face in public, even if it were clean. He would not be able to cope with the sniggers, the nudges, the winks, the grins, the silences and the comments. It would be far worse in Glasgow, too, with that awful openness and brashness. He had learned to rely on moral superiority and distance to survive, without either he would drown.

He knew he was not a good or accomplished liar, to other than himself anyway. He would not be able to deny what he knew to be true, and a public explanation of the real nature of the truth was unthinkable anyway. Maybe it was that inability to deny the truth that meant he was unfitted to be a politician anyway. He knew that politically he would not survive a disclosure, whether hinted or explicit. But he also realised, more damningly, that he would not survive personally or professionally either. His authority as an educationalist would be irreversibly eroded. Every little pupil tittering behind his back, every grubby teacher wallowing in his downfall, audiences coming to see him rather than to listen to his words. No, if it came out, he would lose not only everything he wanted, but also everything he had.

He found most sanctuary in his study. It was his favourite room, scene of his best work, where he wrote his articles and his books, composed his speeches, drafted his policy papers and hammered out his briefing notes. It was a well-organised room, spacious but planned. He had several machines there, a computer cum word-processor, a television and a compact but powerful music system. Plus his books, or at least some of them. His main collection of books, including all his old friends, was in what he and Francesca called the library. But his work books, and his political books, and his extensive range of magazines and periodicals he kept in his study. Because of the work he did there, this was the room of his dreams, and this was the room where he finally settled to work through their dissolution. He knew reading was out of the question so he put on the blackest music he possessed and poured himself another large whisky. He rested his head on his Chesterfield and once more sought solace in leather. He used the whisky to help him analyse his position and consider his options, and to feel sorry for himself as he rued his lot.

Somewhere towards the end of his period of consciousness, through one of the dead skins, a malignant maggot crawled out from the buried memory of a rare moment of passion and leeched itself pestilently into his brain. He had once made a promise to Francesca that he meant at the time but would never have been able to keep, about what he would do to her if her nocturnal proclivities ever cost him his dreams or ambitions. He was a man who believed that he always kept his promises. The logic that he should now apply the same sanction to himself for the same offence began to seem inescapable to his brain in its self-pitying and malfunctioning state.

He knew he was not a strong person. He was not a fighter against adversity, or against others. He was a hard worker, but his work was about conflict with ideas, words, notions and philosophies. It was about restoring or creating order in concepts. In schools he had always relied on others to handle the aggressions and hostilities arising from the imposition of his ideas and concepts. In politics, too, he provided the modern and deadly ammunition but he had always relied on more brutal personalities to make the transitions from concept to reality.

He wished he had a friend, one in the whole world, to whom he could reveal his secret and from whom he could seek succour in their continued acceptance of him for himself. He knew Francesca was his only real friend, and he dreaded her response. He knew that it was him who had created the climate in which she would respond negatively. His stern disapproval of her and her outlet for her needs, his role or lack of it in the meeting of her needs and the creation of her pursuit of alternatives. His injured air of superiority, his condescending acceptance of her flawed nature. All that and the rest flowed from his position of moral superiority.

174

Reveal the flawed nature of that assumption, and the whole edifice would fall.

He could hear the disbelief in her tones. A prostitute, you went to a prostitute. She would not be able to understand or appreciate that he and Margaret were not about sexual gratification, but about some other, deeper, darker need. It would be no defence to explain that he had never had intercourse with her, that would even make it worse. She would despise him for his weakness, but more she would hate him for his hypocrisy. She might be able to forgive him, would be able to forgive the former, but he knew with icy certainty that she would not accept or forgive the latter. Not after the years of treatment he had given her. It would drive a wedge between him and his only friend. The whisky or pain allowed him to evoke the future with vivid clarity. He could see her public face, of the loyal and dutiful wife, supporting and standing beside her husband, defending him against the untruths and injustices of unfair and untrue allegations. But he could also see the private face, and shuddered uncontrollably at the thought of her private coldness and rejection. He realised then how much he truly loved her: how much he depended on her for the only real human contacts in his life, for the only true closeness he ever experienced, for the only real sharing he ever indulged in, and for the only real intimacies he had ever achieved. No, no, no no, he could not risk that, he could not accept that, life after that would be worse than no life at all. The tears soaked not only his face but also his shirt, but it did not matter, as it was already sodden with sweat and fear stains. He knew he should have a shower, and attempt to wash it all away, but he only had enough energy left to turn the record and pour himself another whisky.

He knew many people and knew he had the respect of most of them. Many of them seemed to like his company, far more than he liked theirs. He realised in his roll-call that there was no woman with whom he had anything more than a casual acquaintanceship, none he could consider talking to about anything real. He had always been suspicious of women, and with good cause. He did have some males who were more than colleagues, more than acquaintances, but he knew they were less than friends, at least in the sense he required. There were people he could talk to about education, about politics, about art and literature and music and drama, about society, but not about self. The nearest was probably Raymond. He seized upon the name and thought about the man. He had a gentleness of tone and nature that had seemed unthreatening to Robin. Not like a Scotsman at all, although he was one. His politics were very similar to Robin's own, radically anti-socialist and anti-collectivist, but imbued with a sense of fairness and care as well as efficiency. Together they were the acceptable face of radical conservatism in Scotland. They both avoided the ideological excesses and course brutalities of the St Andrews men, but equally rejected the older loyalties of the gentlemen's brigade. They both saw a future worth building for Britain, and were keen to liberate Scotland from the dead hand and head of failed municipal socialism through closer integration and true union with the rest of the United Kingdom.

Robin knew that Raymond was more fastidious than himself, and wouldn't even talk to the new barbarians, had cautioned him against too close an involvement with their games. But that was the only real difference between them. They talked the same language, using the same language, a celebration of good English uncorrupted by the linguistic perversions all around them. Robin admired Raymond's control of words, more elegant than his own. He had read and admired all the books, the articles were the first things he turned to when the relevant papers appeared. A glimmer of hope suddenly appeared at the recognition of the relevance of that remark. Of course, Raymond was a journalist. He would have contacts in that world. He would know what the likelihoods were, and whether there was any hope. He would also be astute enough to know all about the political dimensions and ramifications, including the Labour Party angle. He even had a friend or two in the Labour Party, unlike Robin. But he knew he would not be able to tell him about Margaret. Raymond was a novelist, he would understand. Robin knew that with his head, but something inner held him back and he knew he would never be able to talk about that, not even with him.

Robin had never mastered the coarseness of male social intercourse, the casualness of self-revelation and the idleness of boast. He had managed to isolate himself from the worst examples, which meant all Glaswegians and most Scotsmen, and had developed some kind of social circle and social skills involving cultured men. But he allowed no man to know the contours of his soul or the shape of his hump. Still, if anyone could help him then Raymond was the one. So he made one half-hearted attempt to extricate himself from his difficulties and enlist the support of another human being. He phoned his friend Raymond at his Tayside home. It took him four attempts to dial the number, but sufficient courage slipped through the final time and contact was established. Robin was not a great lover of irony, and he certainly would not have appreciated the eventual outcome of his request to his friend, if he had ever been able to realise what it actually was.

Francesca knew something was wrong, seriously wrong, but she did not know what and could not get him to talk about it. She had returned home very late on Friday night, to find him asleep on the couch in his study in what she took to be a drunken stupor. She had put a downy over him and left him there. On the Saturday he was in a terrible state. She had hoped at first that it was only a hangover, he was not used to strong drink in excess and suffered terrible headaches. But she had to admit to herself that this was more than that. He opted out of the shopping trip and exhibition they had carefully planned. More seriously, he opted out of the Saturday night they had planned even more carefully, a trip to the theatre followed by the party at the Broomloan's where several of the Constituency Association office-bearers were certain to be. He had told her that she would have to go alone, make his apologies to James and Susan, and his excuses to everyone else. Bad migraines, whatever, make some excuse and do what she can to minimise any damage. He was adamant he could not, would not go, nor did he want her not to go. She knew that he was seriously upset, disturbed even, but he resisted all her attempts to talk about it, and clearly wanted to be on his own. Well, at least she would do the business with the Constituency people. She was actually far better at that than he was, and she would be able to feel she was doing something useful to help him. She thought for a moment he was going to cry, as she explained and reassured him about how conscientious she would be on his behalf.

Robin spent much of Saturday calmly wrestling with what he saw as the two questions the answers to which would determine what he should do. He did this without the benefit of alcohol. Whatever mad fever had possessed him the previous night had subsided enough for colder, more disciplined consideration. The first question, could he rely on Hunter to go to the press if he proceeded with his political ambitions, was relatively easy to answer. It had to be yes, why else would he have gone to all that effort if not to proceed. He also knew that the consequences of that action by Hunter would be absolutely impossible for him to cope with. So the conclusion was clear. His dreams were over. Stillborn. Beyond resuscitation. He would have to withdraw from the selection process. He assumed that Hunter's logic and words would apply to the acceptance of a peerage, as much as a seat, so even that option was gone. He wept again, more internally, and for Francesca as well as himself.

What could he tell the Party, what could he tell her, more able to know when he was lying, what could he tell himself about what was left for him? That line of thought took him onto his second question, the harder one. Could he rely upon Hunter's word that he would not use the information he had about him if he did not pursue a political career? What if the man ever wanted, or needed money. The temptation would always be there to try to sell the story. It would always be of some interest, even if he were not a prominent Tory. He did have a certain eminence in society. He toyed with the notion that the whole thing was not political at all, but an elaborate blackmail plot. Maybe Hunter had been lying about seeing or contacting him again, and the process was just beginning rather than ending. There was something nasty and vindictive about the man. Some personal animosity and venom that defied reason and therefore could not be relied upon. And he was mentally unstable. No, he was not a man whose word could be relied upon. He had tried to deny his responsibility for the Assembly disruption, all to avoid six of the belt. He had married Elaine Duncan in a chapel, and then deserted her. What more of his word would he deny for £20,000, or whatever such a story might be worth?

Nor could Robin depend upon Margaret any more. That was a crueller blow. He realised with some surprise, how much of himself he had invested in his relationship with her. He had believed her concern for him, her stated desire not to hurt or embarrass him. He had genuinely felt that there had been some personal feeling between them, that somehow mattered to her as well as him. What a stupid man he had been. He had been relating to a fantasy woman, not the common whore she had proved herself to be. It had all been lies, very cleverly done right enough, but she had betrayed him, and no doubt would and could do so again, if it was made worth her while. He realised with some horror, that she could damage him even more than Hunter, if she were ever to reveal the true nature of their intercourse. He wept again, this time for the death of his Margaret, the only one who had seen, the only one he had trusted to show, that other strange part of himself. Whenever he envisaged her, whenever he called her up to succour him, he always had her wearing her Conservative clothes, her impressive blue. He knew he did not want to pursue too far exactly who his Margaret was, and what she represented to him, but she was dead now anyway, along with his political dreams.

He knew he would always be vulnerable to one or other of them, Hunter or Miss Beattie, needing or wanting more. He knew he could not live with that degree of insecurity, never knowing if his carefully controlled world was about to be blown apart in a painful and humiliating way. It would be an intolerable strain. He knew he was not a brave man. Not a fighter. He craved peace and security, loathed conflict, chaos and uncertainty. The elimination of stress and uncertainty had always been his major aim in life. From his early school days at St Josiah's he had carefully crafted and structured his world to place certainty and security in the centre. He developed a reliance on books, as words and ideas were more reliable than people. One secret attraction of education to him was the unspoken realisation that it was a safe substitute for a real world of grown-up people. He had gone from school to University and back to school without having to join the other society, of those who have left school. All his life he had avoided those escapees as unpredictable and dangerous, not subject to the controls and disciplines that made his world so secure and safe. The knowledge that a bomb existed which could blast through that protective screen and shatter even his sheltered educational world was too complex and destabilising to contemplate.

So coldly and calmly this time, he re-entered the world accessed through a bottle of malt and once more drank himself into oblivion, something he had never sought to do before. He had cultivated the habit, over late night paper writing, of a small malt or two to aid his concentration. But drinking on his own, never, ever. Now a second night in a row, and this time deliberate. He passed through the levels of release of inhibition, up through the misconception of heightened perception and down into the dangerous depths of poisonous depression. Somewhere just short of oblivion, the arguments and realisations coalesced into perfect harmony, into a definite understanding of the only viable course of action open to him that was both moral, just and true.

To keep him company through his long journey, he read all of Wilbur's poetry, and his letters to Robin. That was the best period, before the descent into deeper depression, when the whisky still had a distinctive taste, almost as much bite as the acerbic and beautiful words. He did not really need to read them, he knew all of the words and sentences by heart. He had always felt himself inferior to the vision offered by Wilbur's words. He had always lived in the shadow cast by the unfavourable comparison of himself to that ideal. Wilbur's gentle chiding words of criticism carried always like a self-reproach. His own personalised hair-shirt. "You are too cautious, Robin, too controlled, too conservative. You need more sense of the romantic. You should discipline yourself to make one romantic gesture a year. Do one dangerous thing every year, Robin, or else your soul will wither and your potential die." Creating his drama with Margaret had been the only time in his life he had followed that heartfelt advice. It had been Wilbur's voice that had helped him re-dial her number after hanging up before an answer. It had been Wilbur's approval that had helped make him keep that first appointment when all his instincts cried out in protest against such an unnatural act. One gesture in his life, and look at the cost.

But then, if you are going to follow someone else's advice, you should evaluate first what it has done for them. That was the debate he was at last coming close to solving. He felt a genuine and warming sense of intellectual excitement. Wilbur's death had been something that had troubled Robin all those years. He had known, privileged and alone, the full extent and fineness of Wilbur's vision, the structure and concept of his dream, and of the harsh ugliness that had appeared to scar and threaten its flowering. Wilbur had explained to him that life was only valuable as a route to dream fulfilment. Once that possibility had been totally removed from him, he had willingly sought release rather than settle for gentle and tame decline. Robin had carried a heavy sense of waste and regret with him ever since. Slowly that evening, he unravelled the threads of those feelings and realised the folly of their construction. Around midnight he was helped to arrive at the logical conclusion. It brought a strong sense of relief, and an inner peace unlike any he had known before, ever. He went to bed, and instant deep sleep, happy. He was going to meet his friend on equal terms.

For once he was not pretending, when Francesca looked into his room and saw him asleep in his own bed. She thought that was definite progress after the previous night, and he would have agreed with her, although she would not have agreed with herself if she had known the product that had produced such peaceful sleep. She thought it was made in Islay, he knew its source was much nearer heaven.

He woke early on the Sunday morning, with the sense of peace still dominant, and no inclination to challenge or review his

180

decision of the previous evening. He went through to Francesca's room and looked at her sleeping peacefully. He would miss her, but she would flourish. She was beautiful, he saw that, and would have no difficulty in getting a man who could happily reconcile both sides of her personality. As he bent down over her, he realised that he had no headache, and no heartache either. He kissed her gently on the forehead, then made her a cup of Lapsang Souchong, which he presented to her on her favourite Chinese tray, along with two slices of crisp toast and thin marmalade, no butter. She was pleased at his calmness and was not too concerned at his refusal to accompany her to morning mass. With the upset of the last two days, he had missed a deadline and needed to get back on course. He had added that he would make his own communication with God later in the day. It was only afterwards that the significance of that remark hit her and she hoped he was right in his analysis. He usually was, she knew, but the position seemed clear and unambiguous. When she was leaving, he kissed her not on the cheek but the forehead and said not goodbye, dear, but goodbye my love.

She felt he was much better, but she left still worried about him, sufficiently worried to resolve to seek help from Father Andrew. She sought him out after the service and enlisted his support. She told him about the wild mood changes, from calm satisfaction on Monday, to agitation on Tuesday and Wednesday, through euphoria on Thursday onto deep despair on Friday, distance on Saturday and calm peace on Sunday. He had exhibited a greater range of emotional activity in those seven days, then in the previous thirty years of their marriage. She knew there was something up, and she hoped Father Andrew, with his pragmatism and worldly sense, could get close enough to help. She knew that for all their political differences, they had a great deal of mutual respect and could work very closely together.

At least since Shona Hunter had died and left him, Francesca was Father Andrew's favourite lady of his flock. Among the under-sixties anyway. He found it amusing how similar she was to the legendary Mrs McGoldrick, and how different. Similar model, but with most of the faults of the original removed, and a few added on of her own. Still, he liked her considerably. She was the best kind of Tory, with a sense of order which incorporated within it care and respect for all. And she was lively. Witty, entertaining, provocative but never raucous, she was close to being his vision of the perfect dinner companion, in a large company. Yet she was so different from Shona, who was always his nominated choice for dinner for two. He had known they had not got on well. Frankie had been too paternalistic for Shona's taste, but they each had developed a healthy regard for the other. Andrew knew she was sensible and shrewd. If she was worried about Robin, there would be cause to so be. He was surprised though. He had known Robin since he was a young man, and had never once seen him out of control. Detached, perhaps, socially uncomfortable definitely, but never exhibiting anything less than a feeling of a man in control of himself and his destiny.

Andrew remembered his first encounter with the shy and awkward young man, when, as the almost as young priest, he had been wheeled out to entertain Robin's mother and guests as the latest example of unpredictable but potent western clergy. Robin had not joined in the general conversation but had sought out Andrew after dinner, and they had had the first of many enjoyable discussions about Taillard de Chardin, and other books that he had read. It had been obvious to Andrew that the young man had a considerable intellect, and he had followed his Oxford career with interest. It had suited Andrew to maintain an association with Mrs McGoldrick's Mafia. He had followed Robin's career as an educationalist with even greater interest. Andrew had always been proud, not a sin in moderation, of his imaginative action in enticing Robin up to run St Anne's. He had exceeded even Andrew's expectations turning the school right round, erasing all traces of that old harridan MacDonald and making the school a model for the whole country. Keeping him had been an unexpected bonus. Andrew had assumed they would lose him after several years but for whatever reasons of his own, he had been willing enough to stay on, and at St Anne's too. Their home had become a very acceptable addition to the list of places where he was both very welcome, and very keen to go. Andrew had been very aware of Francesca's less undiluted delight in remaining in Glasgow, and he had done much to assist in involving her productively in the life of the Church, the community and the artistic establishment.

He and Robin had worked closely together over the years, inculcating the lessons and benefits of St Anne's into the whole Catholic education sector. They had been strong and powerful allies in the many combats with the bureaucratic deadheads and Labour conservatives at Bath St, City Chambers and later India Street, for the benefit of the Proddy schools as well as their own. Recently they had been working very closely together to secure the future of the Hierarchy education sector. They had detailed and revolutionary proposals to take advantage of the opt-out provisions in a way that would enhance the Catholic service and deal a major blow to the local authority system. Robin had convinced a reluctant Andrew that such a solution would not only guarantee the future of Catholic education, but also liberate it from the dead hand of traditional control and allow a better service to be created. As one of the more active fingers in that old hand, Andrew had his reservations, but the alternative scenarios were not very promising, and this one actually offered hope of improvement and increased strength. The major difference left between them was that Robin saw this as the preferred scenario, and Andrew still hoped that it would not be necessary. The few people that had been given access to this vision of the future were quite frightened by it, and Andrew knew that it would require Robin at his best to help him steer it through if it should become necessary. So if there were any problem, he would certainly wish to do what he could to help.

He liked Robin, despite the political differences that had become more pronounced over the last few years, as Robin had enthusiastically embraced the Prime Minister and her evil ways. The irony for Andrew was that he regarded Robin as wet. A soft and sheltered man, out of his environment in a city where conflict was seen as healthy as well as normal. Andrew loved conflict, but he had seen Robin wince at its merest approach. Andrew knew Robin was going to get the Kings Park nomination, and that he would do well. He felt the local Labour Party were being complacent in their lack of concern at the prospect. Andrew knew that many of his flock, as individuals, would follow Robin, vote for him. Andrew would not lead them, or follow them, but he had already determined that he would not strive officiously to prevent them going. Robin was a well-known and well-respected man in the community. He was unlikely to win but he would certainly give them a damn good run for their money. It could get quite interesting, if Robin were to get a job in the Scottish Office dealing with education. That was a thought to savour. He assured Frankie that he would come round on Monday night, and spend time with Robin.

Francesca returned home, straight from her discussion with Father Andrew. She had found that reassuring, he was such a wise and sensible man, and had such an obvious regard for Robin and his strengths. Robin was not there. His car was not in the garage. Maybe he had gone out to get another Sunday paper. Sometimes, particularly when he was restless or working, the Sunday Times was not enough and he would go to get a Telegraph, or occasionally the Observer, to help occupy him. He had not left her a note, so he could not be intending to be away long.

She was worried enough by his continued absence that by five o'clock when the phone rang, she desperately hoped it was him, but it was only Raymond Church. Her worry communicated itself to him and he added to it by sharing his own with her. He did not, then or later, share with her the nature of his communications with her husband, only that they had taken place and they had caused him to be concerned for his friend. When his phone had rung, late on Friday night, Raymond had initially been delighted that his friend had taken the initiative to contact him. Spontaneous contact was not Robin's style. But that delight had soon been dissolved in the weird brew of incoherence that had poured through his ivory mouthpiece. He had soon realised that Robin was, if not drunk, then otherwise disconnected from his normally highly-lucid thought processes. Robin had not shared his dilemma in full, or more than just hinted at the true awfulness of it. It had taken Raymond a long time to extract what he took to be the essence, from under the tangled layers of confused and often meaningless verbiage. He had finally grasped that Robin believed there was some plot afoot, possibly supported by the Labour Party in Scotland at the highest levels, to discredit Robin, to fit him up and to disgrace him, to rule him out as a viable parliamentary candidate. He seemed to be asking, although he never quite actually did, if Raymond could use his journalistic contacts to find out if the Sun or any of the other tabloids had any whiff of this, and whether they had or not, whether it was likely that they would dare feature such a story.

Raymond was a sensitive man, a wise man if not a totally worldly one. He really admired Robin and found his political views outstanding, his ability to translate them into effective policy proposals unrivalled. In Raymond's book, Robin's views and ideas were backed by a concern and humanity far in excess of any of the socialist ideologues whose temple he was pulling down. He had encouraged Robin, sensed his social difficulties, and offered safe haven and moral support. He had been encouraged in return by Robin's obvious regard for his own writings, the fiction and the articles. Raymond shared his love for bridge and wine and music, and regarded the evenings they had spent over the last few years, when he had persuaded Robin to come to his quiet, rural home, almost as close to perfection as social company could provide. The two men had had long walks by the river with Raymond's two dogs, talking politics, usually of the Roman and Greek empires but occasionally of the Iron Lady's. Then after wonderful meals washed down with Raymond's finest French wines, the four of them would play bridge. Robin was better than him, alas, but Francesca was better than Alice, so Raymond had partnered Frankie and the games had always been close.

Some woman, that Frankie. Raymond, more perceptive than many of their Tory acquaintants, had realised that she and Robin were a good balance, with her supplying the outgoing sociability. She would be a definite asset to Robin in his political plans. Robin had discussed his political ambitions with Raymond, at least his immediate ones, and the novelist in him had sensed the whiff of lust that lay beyond the narrower dream. Raymond had been more sympathetic than anyone else to the feasibility of that kind of local Tory candidate being able to conceive of winning a Scottish seat, but had still counselled him against too high an expectation of success. He had reinforced the belief that a good close performance would be rewarded politically, if not by a seat then at least by some form of political advancement.

Raymond could not believe that his friend would be at risk of public scandal. As a novelist, he thought he knew better than most the complexities of human behaviour and motivation. He knew Robin was far too cautious ever to be a bettor or a gambler, or to risk the loss of control associated with any form of drug use. He would turn down a third glass of 1947 claret rather than risk losing a game of bridge where the only stakes were numbers and pride. As for sex, he had an obviously loving, giving wife and an even more-obvious fear of other women. He knew from his discussion of Socratic methods that little boys were not food for fantasy for his friend. Money would be no problem, Robin was careful but not obsessive or ungenerous. Raymond had heard very vague suggestions of stories about Frankie, maybe there was an essence there which could make Robin vulnerable, but Raymond doubted it. He had never met a more intelligent woman so obviously bred to promote her husband's career. But there was obviously something, even if it was as unreal as Robin was trying to convey. He had never known Robin so uncomposed. He had felt a strong sense that his friend was in trouble, and had felt pain for his strangely vulnerable and tormented soul. Raymond had given serious consideration to the thesis that the Labour Party might be involved in some attempt to smear or discredit Robin. He knew stranger things than that happened in Scottish politics. He had been aware of the rumours about his own Party's involvement in the previous downfall of one of their own, but the truth about that had never yet emerged and he did not expect it to do so, or to look that shape.

He had slept on his concerns, then in the morning after a light breakfast had decided to carry out his promise to his friend and conduct a few very discreet enquiries. He had made some phonecalls across his newspaper contacts, including the one man he could bear to talk to at that irredeemably disgusting rag at News International. The uniform response was clear and unambiguous. There was not the slightest hint of a blemish in the man's files, and no-one was even remotely looking for one. His cultured but cynical little friend from Keir Hardie House, unlike Robin he did have civilised relations with a few of the enemy, had laughed at the notion that McGoldrick would be seen as any kind of threat, or that any information about him would be used. "We leave that kind of thing to your wee man's pals." The words had rang louder in his ears than he had anticipated.

He had phoned Robin back early on Saturday evening with the results of his investigations, hoping that his news might reassure him and release him. He had also wanted to arrange to come through to Glasgow to talk to his friend. He wanted to find out what this was all about and to see if he could somehow help. He had known that Robin was not a worldly man and would not have any friends in Glasgow with whom he could open his heart. Robin had seemed worse, more coherent, without the fever, but a great deal flatter, almost horizontal. He had assured Robin that no-one had any story on him, and had accompanied that news with a categorical assurance that even the Sun, who would love any lurid dirt on him, would not print any rumour or gossip no matter how dire or harmful, unless it was accompanied by solid substantiated evidence. He had not expected instant remission but he had had the haunting feeling that he had left his friend even flatter than he had found him and he had certainly not succeeded in his aim of cheering him up.

****

"Let's get this absolutely clear. Run it past me one more time. Earlier today, Raymond Church phones up our James here, and asks him, in however roundabout a way, if we have anything at all on Robin McGoldrick, or are we looking for anything. Yes? Well if my years in this bloody job have taught me anything, it is that a question like that means you can be sure as hell about two things. There is something worth having, and there is something to be found." He waved the slim cuttings file in his hand. "The virtues of family life, by Scotland's leading Headmaster. This could get very interesting. I want us to be the ones that find it. Ten to one on, it'll be sex or gambling or drugs, always is. I want you to put two or three of our most eager people on it. The usual, Casinos, Escort Agencies, the big hotels, in Glasgow and Edinburgh, the top Bookies, fishing, trawls, the whole works. And fast. And yes, I want that 'Russian to sign for Rangers' angle worked up. First the English, then a black, then a pape, then a commie. There have been poofs there for years, and cripples, what's next? Maybe we could run a competition with suggestions. First prize, a Celtic season ticket, second prize..." Donald Dunne had a feeling he was onto something good from the moment he heard about Church's call to James Laird. He was seldom wrong when it came to that kind of instinct. He had a feeling this one could be a biggie. He had met McGoldrick a couple of times. Hadn't taken to him. Arrogant English colonialist bastard. Artistic, cultured, superior arsehole. No bottle. For all his dry posturing, he was the old kind of Tory, not the New Tory Right with whom Donald consorted. He knew McGoldrick was one of the Party's blue-eyed boys, but that was one thing about the paper under him, it wasn't colour prejudiced, it would pull down any kind of hypocrite. He had known McGoldrick despised his paper. He had been disdainful but too polite to say so. Probably never read a copy in his puff. If there was a story there, and his gut told him there was, he wanted it. He knew Scots loved nothing more than to see Dominies downed, even more than the English and vicars and knickers. He had run a small piece about McGoldrick's speech on family values, because it had fitted. It amused him that he might be able to do a bigger follow-up.

****

Robin sat in his car and looked out over the loch. He had always felt a definite affinity for this place. It was not what he would have described as picturesque. Its attraction was more emotional. The very first weekend in Glasgow, before she had even known he was already accepting the job; he had driven Francesca out here. He had meant to show her that less than 30 minutes from the area they would buy a house was a desolate place with a strange wild beauty. She had succeeded in showing him that everything had its price and he could have his way but would have to accept her terms. Its appeal thereafter had always contained elements of both promises for him, and each kind of desolation. Occasionally on warm late spring or summer Sunday afternoons he would go for an invigorating dip into the dark water. Mostly though, they would just walk round it together, hand in hand but silent, each in their thoughts. It was the kind of place that discouraged pretence of the soul. Its raw primitiveness pushed out trivial concerns and somehow unleashed more elemental feelings. It had always surprised him that Francesca liked it almost as much as he did, although unlike him she never came here alone. He had once forced himself to admit he was denying secret fears he had that she ever brought her young men here. That truly would be an act of infidelity.

He was proud of himself for his calm assurance. Maybe he was a man of action after all. He had not wavered in his resolve once. There had never been any doubt for him about where he would go. He had tidied up as best he could. All his affairs were in order. His will had been updated regularly, all his paperwork was in order and place. He had a sudden vision of how neatly the water would reform over the hole of his life leaving no real trace of its existence. Two of the books would be read as long as there were people interested in the education of children. Not as much of a written legacy as he had hoped. At least there were some who still read Wilbur's poetry, if not his biography.

Several years ago he had identified two main tasks for himself, in addition to his political career dreams, which he had hoped would be the major legacies he would leave his world. One was to sound the death-knell of municipal education in Scotland, the removal of the clammy hand of socialist bureaucracy and mediocrity. Opting-out, his contribution in Scotland, was the instrument that would achieve that in time. Not much had happened yet but he knew with a certainty that brought him peace that the logs were already on the move and could never be stilled. One day all schools in Scotland would be free, independent and competitive, funded directly and individually by the state. He had always anticipated that the major break-through on that front, the opting-out of the whole Catholic School sector, would also be the catalyst for the other main change he sought, the political realignment of the Catholic Church in Scotland and its most loyal followers to their natural home in his own Conservative Party. He was well-aware of the political history of this strange land and the irony that the dominance of his party had been eroded by the loss of influence and control over its followers of the rival religion, while the strength of his rival political party had been sustained by the greater loyalty and cohesion of his own Church.

His Church and its leadership, in Rome and in Scotland, was intensely conservative. Only his Conservative Party could ensure the safety of their schools, and their children, and thus their future. Conservatism was the natural defender of the Church's position on social issues, like abortion and sex education. Only his Party and its commitment to the Union could save his Church and its people from their fear of a Presbyterian Scotland governed by the worst strains of wee free morality and bigotry. His own election would have been part of that inevitable realignment, the one form of Europeanism he would welcome. Now he would never see it, but it would come.

He hoped he had taught Father Andrew enough to ensure he managed the transition to independence of the Catholic schools. As long as there were people like Hunter in the Labour Party in Scotland they would never be safe until that journey was made. He had absolutely no doubts that it would be beneficial for the schools and the children, and the Catholic community. He had shown in St Anne's, that a well-run Catholic school would always attract students, even outwith the faith. Despite the city-wide falling rolls he always had to turn parents away. He had shown Father Andrew the Coleman research from America, demonstrating the educational superiority of Catholic schools separated from the state sector, despite their relative under-funding. With opting-out the funding would not be a problem. It would come inevitably, as the Labour pressure on the Catholic state sector intensified. He had laid the foundations for that tremendous change, and the political consequences that would follow it. When the history of the times came to be written, his role would be acknowledged. He had hoped that it would be a more active and more political one but Hunter had killed that dream. Nevertheless the achievements were considerable.

These thoughts did not depress him, not any more anyway. If anything, they were a confirmation of the correctness of his solution. As was the telephone call he had received on his way out

189

of the door. He had almost not answered it, until he suddenly thought it might be from God. Not quite. It had been James Laird from the Sun. He had said only that he had done a small article on his piece about family values, and was considering doing a more in-depth piece, and could he meet to discuss it, but Robin had not been fooled. It had confirmed for him the accuracy of his analysis that he could not rely on Hunter's discretion, under any circumstances. He had been polite but noncommittal, while committing blasphemy by realising it was a celestial message indeed, if through a strange conduit. It was the green light, the affirmation. He knew his God was a kind and generous one, not mean or vindictive. Certainly different to the one the Scots worshipped. It was a sin, and rightly so, but his God loved sinners, forgave them and did not banish them from his domain for one understandable sin. He knew from his many trips to, and conversations with Wilbur, that he was safely in heaven, and his circumstances were not significantly different. He knew Francesca was the only one who would feel some pain, and he grieved for that hurt to the one he loved. But he could not deny she deserved some for her sins and it would pass, and anyway, he was partly doing it for her own good, to allow her to prosper. She had offered a sacrifice for him the other night, he was now rendering that unnecessary. He had seriously considered leaving her some written declaration of his eternal love, but that would deny her the greater comfort that would flow from his not doing so. He knew there was time for one last swim and then he must go.

Frank Hunter had had a wonderful weekend, his happiest, best and most active for many years. He had been in superb form in the pub on the Friday night, chatting, joking, laughing, planning, even talking. For the first time he had been enthusiastic about the forthcoming trip to Italy, investing a little in the prospect of further Army service if not in the hope of a dream coming true. And there had been the details of the trip to Barcelona to plan. Saturday had been a magical day. He and Joyce, and Danny and Sheila had gone to Millport for the day. It had been the last day of March, carefree and breezy, full of love and affection, companionship, sunshine and squawking seagulls, pints and pleasant conversation.

Sunday had been the football day, a day of two halves as they say in the trade. In the morning he had resumed his career with the pub team. His mood had been reflected in his play and he had shone, scoring twice and laying on several more as his ten man team beat Headley's nine Heroes 7-2. The afternoon was sadder stuff. A 3-0 gubbing for the Bhoys at Ibrox, a clear demonstration of the gap between the teams. He had persuaded Paddy and Gerry to go, on the basis that Rangers had at last done what they had put as the condition of their return and signed a Catholic even if it had been that one. Reluctantly they had agreed to go, and overcame prejudices as bad as their foes, to set foot and seat in the New Temple. Paddy was green with envy at the setting, so different since his last visit in 1971, and green with sickness at the slaughter he saw this time. They blamed Frank for making them go. Mojo scored, of course. At least he crossed himself. Frank enjoyed everything apart from the result, and that night, after a few quiet pints to relax and recover, had gone to sleep, on his own, happy that his life was back to normal, and that he had work to go to in the morning.

Frank Hunter had high hopes for his first day back at work. He had slept in longer than usual and had not got out of bed until a quarter past five, but that was a controlled process to maximise his energy. He had gone a short run through the park, and pushed himself far harder than for a long time. It felt good, now there was some point in being fit. He had stood steaming in the park, watching his breath go somewhere. He had taken his time in the shower, feeling for once that he had earned it. He wanted to be in the Mitchell prompt for 9:30am, so that he could put in a full eight hour day. He had already resolved not to go his usual walk at lunch time, or to have a pint, but to discipline himself to a brief trip to a cafe, a hamburger roll and a coffee and twenty minutes in the Magazine Room till the hour was up. He watched Sky News, rather than the morning TV. It didn't have the local news, but he could catch up on that when his Herald appeared just before 8am. He finished off the Sunday papers, rather than try to read a book. His Herald, Guardian and Record were late through the door and he just had time to glance at the football pages of the Record before sticking them in his bag as a treat for his first break.

He worked hard from 9:30 till 11. He was ruthless about the efficacy of the work he had already done in his non-believing phase and acknowledged that he would more or less have to start from scratch. The reading would not be wasted but the writing was not hard or focused enough for his purpose. He knew he had earned his tea-break. He folded his Herald under his arm, he would leave the other two papers for lunch, and strolled round to the cafe. As always he started at the back, and it was only as he was rising to leave did he actually look at the front of the paper. The headline halfway down the page reached out and thumped him. "Tory Headmaster in drowning accident". The pain was worse than the time he took a free-kick from Gerry O'Leary right where his hands should have been. They always were there thereafter but not when reading papers. The nausea racked his body, diffusing the pain throughout. Jesus Christ, what had he done? He read the full story as calmly as he could, then hurried to the Magazine room to read every single version of it. They were all basically the same. Gone for a swim in a loch he knew well. Competent but not outstanding swimmer. For reasons unknown had apparently got into difficulties and drowned. The body found by two anglers in a boat. Identified through the car and clothes parked nearby. No need even to say that there were no suspicious circumstances. All papers commented on imminence of selection as a Tory candidate. The qualities went on at length about his other excellence and what a tragic loss to Scottish, British and even, in the Telegraph, world education. Even the Sun had run a story, praising him in both educational and political terms, in greater length and prominence than might have been expected.

The numbing pain anaesthetised his feelings for a spell. He phoned Julie and fortunately got her. She had not heard his news, but heard his message that they might be in trouble, could expect visitors, if McGoldrick had left a note or anything identifying them and their recent contact with him. He rehearsed with her what line they should take depending on the nature of any contact. He could tell she was shocked about his death, but seemed more prepared than him to believe it might have been a genuine accident. She also seemed much more concerned about her own problems. Frank became slightly worried at her agitated edge. He picked up that for unspecified reasons to do with Flora, she needed to get her out right away. She had agreed the sale of her flat but was still several thousand short. By a thought process that only made sense to him later, Frank realised he would have little use for his own money, and offered her the loan of as much as she needed. They agreed to keep in touch and see how things developed.

Frank's own reaction was not instantaneous, other than the physical one. It took some time to sink into him how he felt about what he had done. He was instantly clear about what it was that he had done. He had killed a man. He knew with certainty that McGoldrick's death was his choice, whether he had dressed it up as that or an accident. Frank immediately resigned from his new job and went out for a walk to think. He linked what had happened to his decision to ignore the warning signs about his potential victory. His decision to plough on and finish the game was directly responsible for McGoldrick's death. Frank had no doubt about that. Suddenly he understood that the fundamental reality of his life was exactly the opposite of what he had allowed himself to believe for so long. What he had despaired of as negative and self-destructive impulses were actually protective devices saving himself from disaster and despair. His ignoring for the first time of that safety device had had fatal consequences. Some victory that. He realised with a sickening certainty even more painful than real or metaphorical kicks in the balls, that his victory would now have a more disastrous effect on him than any of his self-inflicted defeats. He had this sudden searing image of himself as a plastic inflatable man, with McGoldrick in his dying spasm pulling out the stopper with his teeth as he sank below the waves, leaving all the life, humanity, energy and wind to pour out the deflated remnants of Frank Hunter and disappear as bubbles on the water. Nothing left but a crumbled husk. He could not get over the reality that he had killed a man. Frank had always believed that people were directly responsible for the consequences of their actions. He saw no reason to exempt himself from that rule.

He felt sorry for himself. Frank never believed in harming other people. He always saw himself as a caring person. He did not need to like everyone, but he did need to care about them. Even his political and union enemies, which generally meant his own side, he would seek to beat but not injure. All his life he would swear he had never deliberately tried to hurt someone. He had not meant to hurt McGoldrick. He ran and re-ran the game he had set up with McGoldrick. The point had only ever been to make him make a choice, and thereby release Frank from the traumas of his own previous choice. Christ, he had set the thing up so loosely that if the man had held his nerve and called his bluff, made the right choice, he would have been completely unaffected. Or, even if he had made the other choice, the poor bastard would have been left only with professional success and eminence of an extremely high standard. But to fail to have the courage to make the choice at all, that had not been in his script. He felt an intense anger towards McGoldrick. He bet himself that when they cut him open for the post-mortem as they would be doing that very day, they would find out one strange thing for sure. The complete absence of a backbone. It was amazing how erect a man could seem without a spine, until it was required, then came total collapse.

Frank felt overwhelmed with a huge wave of depression. He knew exactly what was happening to him and knew he could not accept it, could not go down to that dark valley again. He had a clear map of his last journey in his head. The long, slow painful drift down the rocky slope, accelerating after the encasement in the ice of the pain of Elaine, till the freefall off the edge in the previous June. The reawakening in the black well of despair, the wallowing in the darkness and then the climb back up, clambering inch by inch up the cylindrical walls, wedging body and soul against the sides to force upward progress. He had made it to the top enough at least to peek out over the edge into the lit world again. The game with McGoldrick had been the final push for freedom. Friday he had vaulted the rim and enjoyed a weekend back in the real world. Now the beast had seized him up and was pushing him back down the tube again, into darkness. He knew he would never have the strength or energy to repeat that upward voyage, nor the weakness to remain again in the dark. He felt the hard fought inches he had acquired over the level of despair ebb away slowly. There was a constant drumming in his head. "I'm not going back down there. I'm not going through that again. I've killed a man. My stupid arrogance and conceit have had profound consequences I never legislated for. I must accept the responsibility and pay the price." Somewhere inside of him, he perceived the equilibrium involved in that price being the same as McGoldrick's. Even from the grave, the bloody man was reaching out and presenting Frank with another choice, one much more insidious but less subtle than the previous one.

Without realising where he was going, his walk had taken him to see his old pal Willie. Frank had been sitting on one of the benches at Willie's feet for some time before it dawned on him that this was the very same seat he had had that Hogmanay horror night in 1979. He wished a wish he never thought he would wish. That he was back in that awful dream again, rather than in the nightmare his life had become. This time he was undoubtedly sober. That realisation, and the fear of what might happen to the inside of his head made him make his farewells to his comforter, one last pat on the foot and he was off. It took him fifteen minutes to get back to North Street, but this time he went to the Ritz rather than the Mitchell, and sat down at a table on his own. Three pints in total silence, not even allowing a solitary word to be said to himself. Liquid filled his head with weird images of the drowning Head. It was not the way he would choose to go.

When he finally allowed himself to speak to himself, he wondered if he would get a visit from the police. He forced himself to go over all the arguments slowly, examining the logical lines between what he had done and a conspiracy to extort. He would not go to jail. That was not an expression of opinion, or an assessment of probabilities. It was a bald statement of fact. He had done his solitary confinement, from last June, and would never allow himself to be imprisoned again. If McGoldrick had named him, and left accusations against him of blackmail and extortion, he would be in deep trouble. The fact that the man had been driven to kill himself, would ensure that any accusations would be investigated very rigorously. Not independently, because the Establishment would want blood and bodies, revenge for its own. But sitting there, thinking about it, he felt a quiet confidence and serenity at least about that aspect. McGoldrick could not have it both ways, even in death. If he wanted his death to be an accident, then he could not appear to have been driven to it. If McGoldrick had had the bottle to go for him, he need not have faked his accident. Not for the first time in his life, he felt a gratitude for someone else's Catholicism. No, the only prosecution he would face would be his own.

He declined his offer of a fourth pint, walked down North Street without being tempted to call in for his tools and struck out for the river. He turned right and walked along what was left of the Broomielaw. If the Waverley had been there he might have walked on board and let it take him away. Paddling off into the horizon didn't seem such a bad idea. But she wasn't, so he couldn't. Maybe nothing from Sir Walter Scott could save him now. He admired the new houses. £140,000 grand for one bedroom. He was glad people were back living there, but he wondered how many of them would be Glaswegians, or even Scots. Not many, he would bet on that. He paused outside Off The Record. He knew newspaper folk, reporters and printers, often frequented that pub. He had sunk a few with the Father of the Chapel and other brothers in his time. He considered going in and asking if anyone had any gossip or theories on the McGoldrick business, but knew it would create more problems for him than it would solve. So he settled instead for a pint in the landlocked Waverley. It used to belong to, and be named after, one of Scotland's finest ever, wee Peter the boxer. Frank had been a regular visitor there when first a footballer, he and big McNair would plunk the Uni at lunch times and walk down Kelvin Way, cross Sauchiehall St and Argyle St, and along into this little hut on the river, for one of George's famous hamburger rolls and an ogle at the wee man's big son's wife's smile. They had really enjoyed talking to the old men, ex-boxers, who congregated there and told tales of fights and fighters. They had been secretly proud of the limited respect their professional status gave them, and returned it tenfold with a real respect for true sporting heroes. But the pub was sanitised and more upmarket now, or so it thought. If that was progress, he was glad he was going. He knew despite his efforts that he could not summons up the fighting ghosts of the past to help him now, he was too oppressed by the newest ghost of the present, definitely not a fighting man. He tried to envisage McGoldrick talking to his old men, but could not, the gulf was too great. They didn't talk the same language, his vocabulary was so much poorer than theirs, devoid of words like fight, and struggle, and getting up off the deck.

He went on along the new walkway, past the Rotunda, and the crane, and the SECC and the Pumphouse Restaurants, all the wonders of the new Glasgow, out along the Clyde as far as he could walk, until the deserted quays at Scotstoun would allow him to walk forward no further. He went right to the edge and stared down into the muddy waters. He felt a strange sensation urging him to jump. A realisation, unspoken but ever-present since the loss of his LDT job forced itself out a little more. There's nothing there, son. Come in Number Ten, his number, her number, your time is up, you're never going to work again.

He resisted the pressure of the water but absorbed the message. Part of the pain came from the knowledge that he could not, would not, talk to Joyce about it. He needed to, he knew that. He had genuinely wanted a relationship with her with no secrets, with everything shared. He knew he had denied that to Elaine, and been the loser, and had promised himself that he would give Joyce more. But he knew he couldn't tell her this. So he brought a told you so from his mother's haunted face and went and buried his own in Hazel's sweet chest.

Hazel didn't give a damn about McGoldrick, but she was alarmed at the effect of his fate on her pal Frank. He seemed stricken, and to have accepted full personal responsibility for the man's death. She tried to show him that the responsibility was not his, but McGoldrick's own. He had been given a choice okay, but it hadn't been a choice of life or death. He had chosen to respond in that way, so let him take the consequences of that decision not Frank. Frank listened to her but did not seem to hear. She cuddled him gently and watched dismayed as he disintegrated in her arms. He cried, and she guessed it was not for the dead man who was gone, but for the one he knew was soon to come. She had never thought of him as anything other than eminently sane from the first time she had met him in that hospital ward at Kamesthorn, but that early evening she began to wonder about the strength of his grip. She eventually managed to get him back together again, shakier in assembly but whole. She took him to her bed, naked, but it was to give him cuddles and rest rather than anything carnal, and the sucking of her chest that he gave her back stirred up memories of her Tommy rather than her Billy.

She walked him to his door, to make sure he went home. Once in, he found he could not leave, even though he was due to meet Gerry Robertson for a couple of pints. He did not want to but found he could not avoid sitting alone in his flat inhabiting once again the barren terrain of empty mindlessness that he had cultivated so fruitlessly for so many lost months the previous year. The landmarks had not changed and he screamed silently in despair at the awfulness of the return. He was still there, when Joyce let herself in about ten o'clock. She was horrified by what she found. He embraced her physically but thrust her away in the more meaningful sense. She could not get him to talk of what ailed him so. The point has gone, was all he said quietly, several times, I've lost it. An awful suspicion formed in her mind but refused to emit from her mouth, until at last the desperateness of the situation forced them out.

"Frank, did you ever do anything with what I told you? Did you have anything to do with McGoldrick's death?" They were questions that demanded the answer no. Underneath her quivering voice he detected all the layers that contributed to the request for a negative. He knew she would take a positive personally and he could not cope with that, so he compounded his betrayal of her and himself with another one and denied that source of his problem. He told her that in fact the news of McGoldrick's death was the one bright spot, but could offer her no clue as to the shape of the darkness. He wept for what he was doing. He was betraying the equality of their relationship, which had been his only hope. He knew he was doing it then because he accepted that he had already betrayed her by pursuing Julie on the basis of her information. It had not seemed like betrayal at the time, because he had not bothered to think about it, or her, in his blind determination to seek his revenge.

He tried to tell Joyce that he feared he was relapsing, that his depression was returning, that his carefully constructed grasp on a tenuous routine and reality was slipping. She was a skilled professional, who had seen similar signs in others many times, but she could offer him nothing that helped. She knew going back to Kamesthorn would not help, that a second admission, on the down, would destroy him. She suggested a game with Wee Ewan, she could arrange that, but Frank did not want to play. She took him to his bed, offered him the best she knew of the tricks of Hazel's old trade, but it was of less comfort to him than Hazel's therapy had been, although he did not tell her that. He did not sleep, and rose early to immerse himself again in videoed football.

The next two days were long, slow and empty. He read in the papers that after receiving the police and post-mortem reports, the Procurator-Fiscal had accepted the notion of an accidental death and had allowed the release of the body from the Greenock Royal Hospital mortuary. There were no suspicious circumstances and no need for a Fatal Accident Inquiry. He knew from the Glasgow

Herald notice that the funeral had been fixed for Wednesday in Edinburgh, going back to Mummy. Father Andrew was to assist with the service. Frank was still in that land of odd when Julie phoned. If there had been agitation in her edge before, it had seeped right into her core this time. She told him she had to see him urgently. The instructions she gave him about their rendezvous were pure Le Carre. Even then, if he sensed she were being followed he must pretend not to know her. He accepted her need, and her arrangements at face value, and agreed to meet her that afternoon. At least it would get him out the house and moving.

He watched her come into the Ritz. An intense pain and longing grew in his groin and surprised him with its urgency and vividness. This time she looked neither high class whore nor smart business lady. She dressed as she was, an attractive 24 year old woman, on a day's holiday, meeting a friend to share a problem. As she had arranged over the phone, she bought herself a drink and sat on her own for five minutes. No-one else came in, and she nodded to indicate it was safe for him to join her. He was pleased she kissed him but the pleasantries were minimal as she launched into her story. She had been visited by two reporters from the Sun, one of whom had set up a session with her, but like Frank six weeks earlier they had had other intentions than direct sexual gratification. They had told her that they had evidence from several Edinburgh and Glasgow hotel staff that McGoldrick and she had met on different occasions. They also seemed to know, although she had not asked how, that McGoldrick had withdrawn £5,500 from his account the day before she had made a significant deposit into hers. The essence was that she too had been given a choice to ponder, if not for long. They were going to do a story. Without her co-operation it would be that McGoldrick and she had a business relationship, with the strong implication that he had killed himself because she was blackmailing him and threatening exposure. If she co-operated, gave them details of their relationship and corroboration, then they would pitch their story as an expose of the Headmaster, defender of family values and hypocrite extraordinaire, who had killed himself out of fear of exposure. They would also reward her financially for her co-operation.

She had made her choice swiftly and decisively. No agonised balancing of dilemmas for her. She had made a deal with them. She had built on their own uncertainty about the validity and strength of the little evidence they already had, and their need for a great deal more to insure themselves against the censure associated with libelling the recently dead. She had offered them. She paused at that point and offered Frank what might have been an apology but seemed to him much more like an explanation. Before she had handed the originals over to him, she had made her own copies of the tapes of both the telephone conversation with McGoldrick and the pub interview. She had subsequently retaped them, using two machines, omitting the one reference that could have been construed as being to Frank. They were fortunate in McGoldrick's mealymouthedness and preference for euphemism. The description of 'our scruffy friend' fitted him all right, but also another million Scotsmen. The tapes would provide the Sun with incontrovertible proof of her relationship with McGoldrick and its nature. She had told them that she did not know the identity of the man who had approached first her then McGoldrick. He had said his name was Wharton, but he had never come back to her after that first contact. She had told them that she presumed that it was Wharton who had first alerted them to the story and therefore they would know better then she who he was and what his contact with her had been. She had told them that she had taped McGoldrick's telephone call because she taped all her calls. She had taped the Sir Walter Scott conversation to protect herself against any later accusation of blackmail or extortion.

She told Frank that she did not know how they had got onto her and the story. She did not know anyone else who knew of her relationship with McGoldrick, but they had used several hotels in two cities, so maybe staff had recognised him with the recent publicity and acted on their own initiative. It did occur to Frank, sitting beside her in that bar, that perhaps it had been her that contacted them rather than the other way round, but he chose to reject the hypothesis. He knew that he trusted this person, and that he was right to do so. The Sun staff had appeared to buy her story, before offering money for it. They had recognised the importance of the tapes, and had agreed to pay substantial sums of money for each of them. After that deal was concluded, she had offered them a bonus. She told them that she had got a friend of hers, who did not appreciate the significance of what she had been asked to do, to take photographs of her and McGoldrick leaving the Sir Walter Scott. For an extra £20,000 she would give them the negatives.

200

They had agreed to her terms. She said it was up to Frank. She assured him that whatever happened she would protect him.

Even if, as seemed likely, she was interviewed by the police, she would stick by her story. McGoldrick had approached her, without revealing who it had been that had approached him about their relationship. She had done the rest of the business on her own initiative: as she had seen his willingness to give her money for nothing. Julie told Frank the newspaper people had said that they would turn over all their material to the police, but it was their lawyer's view that she was safe from prosecution. Both she and Frank knew that the major weakness in this story would be if McGoldrick had left any note identifying him and his role, or making any link between Frank and Margaret Beattie. Julie felt that they would have heard from the police by then, if he had done so. Frank told her he was confident that McGoldrick would have hoped to take his secret with him to his place in paradise. He felt sure he had judged the man's personality correctly on that point. Frank felt a sudden exaltation inside himself at the realisation that the man's secret would be revealed. That would serve him right for fucking up Frank again. Another, better part of him felt a curious sorrow for McGoldrick and his wife and a deeper one for Joyce and Frank.

Julie told him, in words he believed, that if he didn't want the pictures used, that was fine by her. If he did, he could have all the money, that would be her gift to him. She had already been given enough to cover all her needs. He had offered to lend her money the other day, when she had really needed it. That had meant a great deal to her, that he would do that for her. He was her friend and she was his. Without being asked, she proceeded to tell him why she had needed the money, and what she was going to do with it, now she had it. He had already guessed most of it, which gave him some satisfaction.

Julie described how she had been befriended and helped at her lowest ebb, by Flora, a young Edinburgh girl caught up in drugs and prostitution. The story held no surprises for him, a friend of both Joyce and Hazel, the two slightly different perspectives. Flora had been a heroin user, amongst other drugs she was involved in. She had shared needles and pricks in a whirl of collective co-operation. She was HIV+, had begun to develop AIDS and would die. She was still held in some kind of thrall by her pimp, and owed money to some not very nice people. Julie loved her, she looked straight at Frank as she said that, as she had never loved

201

anyone else. He was ashamed of his immediate and ignorant thought, could a woman catch AIDS from sex with an infected woman. Julie had done what she could to help her, to take her off the street and off the drugs, to extricate her from the webs within which she had entrapped herself, to ensure that her last years were as peaceful and fulfilled, and as long as possible. She had worked on her master plan over several years. She had identified premises in Bridlington, a Bed & Breakfast establishment linked to the theatrical world. Flora had developed some expertise under Julie's guidance, in the making of costumes. They could have a comfortable and fulfilling life there, with a clean break from the worlds of drugs and prostitution. She had an option on the place, and a plan to buy it in the summer of 1991. It had come on the market earlier than expected. It had cost her more than she had budgeted to buy out Flora from her commitments, and even with the ten grand from Frank and McGoldrick, and the sale of her flat she had been several thousand short. The money from the newspaper had sorted that out, and she even had a little surplus to invest in her supply of AZT, which she obtained from one of her longest standing regulars.

As he listened to her, Frank knew two things as well as he had ever known anything. The fact that they were contradictory in some ways, only emphasised the complex nature of the universe. He knew he could trust her completely, and he knew that he could not tell whether the Sun had contacted her or she had approached them and had always intended to do so. The new choice he had to make did give him some problems, so he ordered himself another pint of 80/- and a gin and tonic for Julie. He was very clear in his own mind, always had been. He had never had any intention of shopping McGoldrick to the Sun. He hated the paper and everything it represented. Its hypocrisy, its moral sickness, its fervent loyalty to the Prime Minister and everything she stood for, the values it endorsed. He had never bought it himself, although he regularly read other people's copies, as well as voting for resolutions at the District Labour Party that the Council should stop purchasing it, so successfully that it was no longer available at the Mitchell. It was the same reasoning he used to justify buying the Sunday Times and reading the Daily Telegraph, know thine enemy, as intimately as possible.

Even if he had had no money he would not have been tempted by their pot of gold. Nor had he ever had any intention of giving them a story they would love, for nothing. It wasn't that he did not believe such a story should be told. He differed from some of his pals on that one. He considered the private lives of public figures were legitimate targets, if these lives impinged upon, or contained contradictions to the public one. McGoldrick had very definitely made himself a legitimate target by his speech on the sanctity of family values. McGoldrick had publicly set standards and expectations for public figures that he had not met himself. Frank had no sympathy for the man's public fate. It was the hypocrisy of the paper he could not abide, the offering of titillation in the name of taste, the deliberate masquerading of prurience in the name of propriety, the revelling in the lewd and libidinous while claiming sanctimoniousness.

He had a little debate with himself, shared to some extent with Julie, about the rights of the dead. On that one he felt that he and the editor of the Sun would not be too far apart. Being dead, should not confer on one rights not enjoyed while alive. He stifled the fleeting sympathy for Frankie McGoldrick with the rationalisation that it would be more liberating for her in the long run to know the truth than to spend the rest of her life with a leeching saint on her shoulder. The pint was 3/4 done when he made his decision. Julie could have the photographs. If the story had to be done, and it was being done whatever, then she might as well extract the maximum profit from it. He wondered if it would have been different if she had been asking for the tapes and his answer would affect the outcome. He reminded himself with a wry smile of Paddy McGuire's most fundamental rule of life, never waste precious time or emotional energy on hypothetical questions, there are far too many real ones to wrestle with instead. He told Julie she could have the whole of the money, he had no need for any of it. He almost told her why but some instinct told him not to expose that to her. She told him that he was a strange man, but that she was his friend and if he ever needed her, she would be there for him. He knew she meant it.

He had a brief fantasy of a menage-a-trois at Bridlington but it faded even as it formed, he didn't want to live in England. He did wish he had met her years before. He did know that it would have to have been before Elaine to be of any use. That would have meant she would have been 5 years old. No, even her own father had waited another 3 years. He did try to help her work out the implications for herself of her actions. He established they already had a photo of her so his action would not bring in a new dimension. He warned her of the dangers of this story destroying her, of its capacity to tie a label around her neck for life. She was way ahead of him on that one. The Sun would identify her as Margaret Beattie, an Edinburgh prostitute. Margaret Beattie would die the day the story appeared. Even Julie Henderson was not her real name, and that would go as well, although she did tell him that was who she would always feel herself to be, for both Flora and Frank. She told him voluntarily that the owner of the Bridlington Broadhurst would be Celia Warren, who had recently spent several years as an actress in the States but was now settling down to concentrate on her own career in England again. Her hair, which she knew Frank liked, would revert to its natural darker colour and shorter length by the end of the week. The blonde would be buried with Margaret Beattie.

She gave him a little present in return for his concern. She told him the names of some of her more influential clients, Edinburgh lawyers and establishment figures of the highest eminence. He knew she was giving him some hostages and leverage to use if he were ever persecuted for his role in McGoldrick's downfall. She was a remarkable person, and he felt a strong sense of gratitude at having got to know her. It wasn't just her intelligence he admired. He was used to the notion that women were as intelligent as men, and more sensible. It was the manner in which she had been able to shape events to suit her own purposes that most impressed him. He had treated her as an equal and she had shown him the fallacy of that equation.

He took her to where the negatives were hidden, then to his flat. She had insisted that he go alone to his car, drive round and pick her up several streets away once she gave him the all-clear. He had co-operated, as he had no wish to appear in the paper's story. It had crossed his mind that she might be taping their conversation but he had rejected the hypothesis. Although, as always, he had carefully considered everything he said. He gave her the negatives and some coffee. Without using the words she had offered him more, not this time as part of an unfulfilled contract, but as a parting gift from a close friend to someone she sensed was sad and struggling. He understood what sorely tempted meant from the pain in his scrotum, the desire in his sinews to mingle with her soft firmness was immense. He knew it would be a wonderful experience, but Joyce stopped him. He had betrayed her twice already, he could not add a category that was avoidable. As he did so he had a vision of her face reading the Sun, and wondered if his sacrifice was meaningful, but made it all the same.

He took Julie for a walk in his Park instead, and even that made him feel good and contented. Then he drove her to Queen Street and put her on the train to Edinburgh. When she was settled in her first-class seat, he kissed her mouth, wished her well and watched her recede into the night. Frank Hunter never saw her again, except in his dreams and fantasies, and in Friday's paper.

He didn't drive straight home. He went back to the park and talked to the man who had been there earlier. He was still doomed, the events of that day had confirmed that, but some of the pain had gone. He knew the dirt and shame he felt would flourish and grow in the Sun's heat and that he would be driven to complete the circle, but the knowledge of the timescale brought a degree of peace that had been absent earlier.

CHAPTER THIRTEEN - DESTINY REVEALED

One of the main benefits of the breaking of the power of the print Unions was that the next-day Sun now rose in time for Glasgow citizens to enjoy its first appearance with their late evening pint or stroll of the streets. Never buying it, Frank Hunter had not really internalised this information and was thus unprepared for Joyce storming into his flat late that Thursday evening with Friday's paper. He had assumed he would have the whole day to study it himself and prepare, before he would have to face her. Yet another sloppy assumption in a long line that was eroding his traditional claim to omnipotence.

One of the girls in the Group bought it, and of course, with that content, they soon all wanted a copy. Two or three of them knew Margaret Beattie or Julie. Joyce took Janis aside and quietly asked her if she had ever told anyone else what she had told her about McGoldrick and her friend. Janis, no fool, not only denied it vigorously but turned it back with a "I didn't, but did you?" and a funny look. Joyce prayed her denial was convincing, flat not indignant. In the toilet where she went for composure she vowed to kill the bastard. She knew Frank was involved in this somehow. It suddenly made sense of why he had been so depressed and agitated on Monday. The story had made no mention of him, but implied that McGoldrick was being blackmailed or threatened by someone other than Margaret Beattie, and that was why his accident might have to be reassessed. It had to be him. Although Janis would have said if he had approached her directly, that would be her style. Frank must have pursued the information some other way. Why had he done it? She knew he was not a blackmailer, and that he would not have wanted money from McGoldrick. Nor did she believe he would have done it to sell or give the story to the newspaper. He hated it with too much ferocity for that.

She knew that there had always been something personal about Frank's hatred of McGoldrick, it was more than just the usual distaste for a Tory. She knew a little of the events of 1970. She also knew that Frank had expressed concern that McGoldrick might do well in Kings Park. He had been particularly annoyed at the family values speech, even before he knew about the extent of hypocrisy involved. But none of that could remotely justify this. She felt a strong sense of personal betrayal. He knew how she felt about the importance of confidentiality and trust in her work with the Group, and yet at the first opportunity he had disregarded that and exploited the fact that she trusted him enough to share the strain of her work with him. Maybe he was no different to Brian Kirk after all, selfish bastards both of them.

The living room door burst open, as the noise of the front door being banged shut echoed through. It was her eyes that let him know the trouble he was in. The fierce light of injured innocence sustained by aggressive anger blazed out and pierced his gloom. He had always thought blazing eyes to be a stupid misnomer, now he was exposed to the reality he wished he had been correct. She threw the paper at him with impressive force. It landed front page up. He saw the main headline: "Dead Tory Head in Sex Scandal Shock". He was just commenting to himself on the arid predictability and lack of creativity of that when she launched her armada of words to sink him.

"You're responsible for that, aren't you, you stupid bastard." she screamed in rage. "What's even worse, you've involved me in this, this filthy thing. You exploited your relationship with me and betrayed my professional integrity, even though I begged you not to. You've used a paper you hate, to do something you despise, and now a man is dead, and you've killed him. And for what. Tell me that, you smart-arse, for what? I know it wasn't for the money. So what the hell was it for? Revenge? For what, for giving you six of the belt for nothing, for Christ sake. You destroyed a man for that? Don't try to tell me you did it for the Labour Party. That was a safe seat anyway. And don't tell me you didn't mean to kill him. Of course I know you didn't. But what did you expect, you stupid shite. He was a shy, sensitive man, and you took a very small and unimportant part of his life, how he harmlessly got some sexual release. Jesus, according even to that," and she spat a look at the rag on the floor, "he never even had intercourse with her. It should have been and remained nobody's business but his own. And you ensure it is to be broadcast to the nation. You must have known that would effectively kill him anyway. It would destroy his public life, make him a laughing stock for every tittering, lechering pupil and teacher. It would be bound to cost him not just his nomination, but his job and his reputation. What possible satisfaction could you have expected to get out of that. I can understand that he couldn't face that prospect. What I can't understand is how you could have done it. You're sick, Frank, sick, twisted and empty"

Empty, empty, empty, the word seemed to echo round his head, tearing through his brain tissue and consciousness like jagged razor slivers. His only consolation was that her judgement on him was far less harsh than his own. He stood, silent, transfixed, as her tirade poured out. On automatic pilot, his brain silently categorised her points, providing logical and rational or rationalised answers to the various strands, denying some, accepting others, explaining and correcting inaccuracies and false assumptions. But basically even his brain knew she was fundamentally correct, he was an arsehole. He also knew he had not been rigorous enough in his analysis of the options, and that he should always have realised that there was a fair chance that some kind of negative outcome like this would happen. His logical powers of analysis and prediction which had used to be his one true pride and joy, had let him down, with rather disastrous consequences. He could no longer predict and control the future.

He realised she was still in full flow. "I've had enough of you, and your games with people. Games, games, games, that's all your life is ever about. When it's not football, it's politics. When it's not either of these two, its even more stupid games, where only you know the rules. Maybe you are ill after all. Christ, you certainly need help to become a human being again. But I've had enough. You can bloody well help yourself from now on." Her last volley launched, she didn't even wait to see the enemy sink beneath the surface. She just wheeled round and stormed out, as noisily as she had entered. A strange calm descended on Frank as the reverberations of the slammed door died down. He walked over to the window and watched her dive into her car and drive off. No backward glance or upward look of regret or concern, just a Metro getting smaller.

The intensity of her anger took her through the drive home and her confrontation with him. It was only later, alone in her own flat, that she looked beyond her own hurt and pain to see the effect it all had had on him. She remembered how distraught he had been at the time of McGoldrick's death, how worried she had been about his mental health and the possibilities of relapse. The last thing he would need, with his guilt and pain, would be her giving him a hard time. Alone in her own bed, she wept for him, and despaired of him. He had given her things she had talked herself into believing she did not deserve and never would have. She loved him in a generous way. She knew in his own flawed way, he loved her and had tried to make it work. So at 3a.m. she phoned him up. The recorded Frank came on, not the real one, but she knew that didn't mean he wasn't there, or asleep. She told the machine and him that she was sorry she had lost her temper, and that she knew he couldn't be feeling very pleased with himself. If he wanted her to, she would come round and be with him. If he wanted to be on his own, she could understand that, but he was not to make it too long. Either way she would visit him on Friday about 7pm. He didn't pick up the phone, or call her back. She debated whether it was safe to leave him on his own, but reckoned it was. He was going to need her help though, but he would get it.

Frank too knew it wasn't the end. She was hurt, shocked, angry and annoyed, but she was not walking out on him. She was trying to hurt him, to reach him somewhere, somehow, and the good news was she was succeeding. She was a good person, too good for a shallowness of affect man like himself. He reckoned she would be back in a day or two, offering to talk to him about it and to help him with his feelings. She would try to help him get out of the mess he had created. He knew she loved him, and he wished for her sake that she didn't. She had done nothing bad to deserve him. He vowed that he would try to protect her as much as possible from some of the worst consequences of what he now knew to be inevitable.

After the echoes of her eruption finally died, he picked up the paper and read it carefully. It was on the front page. It was also all of pages 4 and 5. They obviously thought they had a good story. Page 1 had the big headline, the basic details and small pictures of both of them, the Headmaster and the Whore. Page 4 had the full gist of the story Julie had told him, only slightly expurgated for family consumption. There was a bold heading, Bend Over Beattie, with a smaller one Old Faithful Strikes Again, with a picture of a belt that was not even a Lochgelly. So much for respect for the facts. Page 5 contained the hard evidence, with extracts from the transcripts of both the telephone call and the pub interview, as well as a big picture of Julie and McGoldrick kissing. Frank felt a sense of pride at the picture, it was definitely a cracker. There was also an interview with Julie, referred to throughout as Margaret Beattie, a high-class Edinburgh prostitute. It didn't actually say she was English, maybe high-class meant the same. There was also a brief biography of McGoldrick and his achievements, highlighting his Tory career and his family values speech rather than his education record other than stressing this was a genuine Headmaster. There was only vague reference to a shadowy third party who was attempting to blackmail McGoldrick. It as good as said: he probably committed suicide because of fear of exposure.

The bit that most appealed to Frank was what passed for editorial comment, some kind of rationalisation of why the paper should run such a story so soon after the tragic death of such a respected man. It talked of a very difficult decision. Of respect for the dead, and for the feelings of the man's family, friends and colleagues. But all that had to be balanced against the public's right to know the truth. The paper had discovered a truth different from that published earlier in the week in all the other tributes and obituaries. The paper had information which would cause the nature of the cause of death to be re-evaluated, and it had passed this onto the relevant authorities. It was, and had to be, a matter of legitimate public interest that a man who spoke so convincingly and authoritatively about family values and public standards, consorted with prostitutes. It was, and had to be, a matter of legitimate public interest that such a prominent Headmaster, who had so profoundly influenced educational matters in his adopted country, had such fantasies and desires around the matter of corporal punishment. The editorial finished with a spirited rebuttal of the criticisms that it knew would be unfairly libelled against the paper by the Establishment, and all the other national papers. Their readers had the right to know, and were mature enough to judge for themselves.

Despite himself, Frank admired the tone and simple style, and decided he was definitely with them on that one. It was a legitimate story, and McGoldrick's public speeches had made it so. It was his hypocrisy that was the basic issue, not theirs. The fact that the paper was also hypocritical, and revelled in the libidinous and erotic details, was not an argument against the story being told, only against their particular manner of telling it.

The paper did not seem terribly interested in its own suggestion that McGoldrick was being blackmailed by someone other than Margaret Beattie. The paper admitted that it had paid Margaret Beattie for the story, and for the proof she had provided about their relationship. It took credit for revealing that it had thus helped her to give up her life of sin, and make a new and decent start somewhere else. Frank smiled at the statement from Margaret Beattie which said her Mr Ross was a very nice man, whom she

210

had never wished any harm, but that there was no denying that there was a side to him other than that which had appeared in his obituaries. There was a standard line of refusal to comment from his wife, his employers and the Tory Party Headquarters in Edinburgh.

After he read it, Frank sat silent and still for he knew not how long. At last he moved, and talked to himself. He knew that the appearance of the story had made him even sadder than he had been before. He knew with certainty what he would do, but he felt there was something missing, an aspect of purpose and destiny that would somehow make sense of the whole business. He knew it was almost there, to be found, just elusively out of his current reach. He took another decision and dialled Hazel's number. He woke her up, but she seemed tolerant. He didn't actually say "Hazel, can I come round and fuck you again for comfort" but he knew that was what he really meant and he reckoned she did too. She did say he sounded as if he could do with a cuddle, and also, since she hadn't eaten for two days could he bring something to eat. He retrieved two bottles of wine and a bottle of whisky from his collection, drove round to the shabby Indian Restaurant off Victoria Road that stayed open till 2:30am, bought two Lamb Pasandas and turned up on the doorstep where she was watching to let him in. While they ate, she read the newspaper avidly. She did not hide the fact that she found it highly entertaining. She was pleased at her own role in the enterprise and she asked him a question or two to fill in the details of how the tale which she knew, had lead to this story. She expressed admiration for the way he had set-up McGoldrick. She checked again her own presumption that he had never intended to give the story to the newspapers. "Some girl, that Julie." was one of her comments. "Pretty spineless man, your pal McGoldrick. He must have been a sad, weak and desperate man." was another.

They finished the two bottles of wine with their curry, sitting on the sheepskin rug in front of the coal fire in her one room. Then without words they made love slowly but furiously on the same rug in front of the same fire, naked and vulnerable like two little babies. After they finally finished they each put on one of her two cotton dressing-gowns, drank large amounts of malt whisky out of chipped mugs and cuddled, caressed and talked for hours. They both lied together in different ways as they talked about the future as if it existed, then they both lay together in the same way and made love one more time in the unspoken certainty that it did not, before drifting off entwined into a short and fitful sleep, safe in each others arms. He could not articulate it even to himself but he still knew that fornicating with Julie would have been an act of infidelity to Joyce, but making love with Hazel was not. And making love it was, no irresistible element of animal coupling, but once more two friends helping each other with their sadnesses in a form of love that was real but different.

Through the curry burning inside, the warm afterglow of the wine, the harsher tang of the peaty malt, the soft warmness of her skin on his, the occasional wet succulence of her cunt around his willie, the strong feel of her arms on his back, the tickly irritation of the sheepskin underneath him, the heat from the too-close fire, and the dry taste of her ear under his tongue, a chemical reaction took place over the long slow hours of that special evening and night that burnt the hurt and bitterness and despair out of his soul. It left the sadness untouched but purified. He awoke in the early morning a better man. One who still knew the essence of what he would do and why, but one much more at peace with the prospect. He thanked Hazel, cuddled her, kissed her forehead, cuddled her again and left.

Back at his own flat, he played back the message from Joyce. Oh Joyce, my lovely, lovely girl, what am I to do with you? The best I can. He had a shower then packed his bag for the Mitchell. He had not been back there since Monday. He knew his book was dead, but he wanted, needed, the discipline of work, hard work. He suddenly knew what to do. He would recheck his figures on the Daily Telegraph analysis of the next General Election, re-compute the results to see if the outcome could be any more favourable this time. He vaguely thought of the risk involved, of how depressed he had been the first time at the outcome, the inevitability of her getting back. But what the hell, he felt reckless. Maybe it would be different and he could have something good to hold onto. He packed his bag with great thought. There was the original article cut out and kept, his own political recordbooks, his fancy calculator, and the name and publisher of the other two textbooks he would require. He also packed his three newspapers.

He had already read them the moment they had arrived, but only for the McGoldrick stories. The Guardian had no mention of it, but the Herald and Record had been able to respond in their later editions. Both took a line of moral outrage and disgust at their rival's performance, and only outlined the allegations, as they called them, in the barest of terms. They both had more of a response from different agencies and other parties, although there was a curious confusion between those as to whether to say it could not be true, or even if it was true it didn't matter, and even if it did matter, it should not matter for someone so recently dead. Frank initially was totally dismissive of the curious argument that death bestowed a right to dignity and privacy denied in life. But then it occurred to him that his own point, once, had been to stop the man's hypocrisy. Now that he was dead, he could not be hypocritical any more, so a story could not claim to achieve that aim.

He remembered an argument with his Granny Jean, who had adored JFK the good Catholic, largely because he had been a Catholic. She had refused to accept or believe the tales of his promiscuity while at the same time trying to explain that powerful men must have powerful appetites. She had been adamant no good could come from blackening his name with tales of tail. Prissy puritan Frank had disagreed and lasciviously read every account of sordid detail, in the name of political understanding. Yet he knew his Gran would have been amused at the paper's story, and it would have been Shona who disapproved and felt pity for the man.

He arrived at the Mitchell later than usual but got comfort from his favourite seat still being vacant. He took out the reference books he required and set out his stall for the task ahead. The Telegraph a few months ago had produced a four page special spread proving beyond scientific doubt that not only could Labour not win the next Election but that the Prime Minister could not lose it. It had made its assumptions and arguments explicit and provided details of every single seat and the swings needed for Labour to win them. Frank loved articles like that, their minutiae were the food and drink of the political animal he was at heart, their arguments the wine that could induce euphoria. He revelled in the detail and small print of political life. When he first read the article, he was almost orgasmic. He had determined to obtain climax for himself, by testing out the validity of their hypothesis but using his own more valid assumptions.

He knew that the basic Telegraph claim was true. That the swing Labour would need to get even the basic 326 members for an overall majority far exceeded any swing ever achieved before, and massively exceeded any swing ever achieved by the Labour Party. Frank had spent a happy day, going through every single constituency with his own calculator and his own set of

213

assumptions and worked out the outcome. He had not liked his first outcome, but no matter how hard he had tried, and he did try hard and pushed the assumptions to the very limit of maintaining credibility with himself, the very best outcome he had been able to come with had been an overall Conservative majority of 14 seats. The result from his most realistic assumptions had been an overall Tory majority of 32. His orgasm had petered out in classic post-masturbation style and he had vowed never to play with himself like that again, before going out to the Victoria, getting pissed and making several bets with friends at generous odds that Labour would lose the next election.

Things had changed a little since then, and it was now possible for an optimist to alter the baselines of some of the psephological assumptions in terms more favourable to Labour. That bloody woman seemed to have finally lost her touch, even with the English. So Frank started out the exercise this second time with some expectation that he could maybe redeem this day with a more positive view of at least the political future. It took him a couple of hours to get everything set out, ready to start, with the new assumptions polished and ready to run. He knew it was probably two years until the General Election, 18 months at least. In that time, Poll Tax pain would fade, and interest and mortgage rates could be massaged down. Taxes could be cut again, and a Government generally improved in popularity in an approach to an Election. His assumptions took limited account of all that though, so that he knew in his heart that while they were valid for the here and now, they would likely overstate the Labour position for the future. He hung onto the current validity to obscure any self-accusation of cheating. Anyway, things might not get worse. They had so often over the past ten years, it had to end sometime.

Before launching into what he knew from his previous experience was about three to four hours graft, he went to the Magazine Room to see if there was a later edition of the Sun than the one he had seen. There was no official one but his estimate that someone would have brought one in was correct, but it took some time for him to get to see it. There was a queue of about six people and much hilarity from those at the top of it. Extracts were being read out, to much guffaws. The humour released was predictable, and very Glasgow. A right belter that one. Poor Alistair Beattie, a regular, was suffering the fate of all of that surname for the next few days. "Bendover Beattie" was destined to be a brief catch-phrase, as was "Buttocks or Palms". Old Faithful

214

had already entered into Glasgow folklore but was now elevated in prominence with a vengeance. People, including many who would never have been seen dead inside a Catholic school, were queuing up to boast that they had been assaulted with that very selfsame instrument. As Frank learned later that evening in the pub from Billy, Andy and the others, every school in the land had sent out for dozens of copies, every staff-room was full of it, every Headmaster's study, every playground toilet. McGoldrick had been right about one thing, he could never have coped with the consequences of the release of the story. It would need a man of sterner stuff, thicker skin and an actual spine to put that kind of public hilarity behind them and persevere on as professionally as possible. Most members of the public by the end of the day couldn't even remember the headmaster's name, although they all knew it was a Headie sure enough that had been caught.

But everyone in politics and everyone in education knew all right which one, and would never forget, and he could never have coped with that, never have lived with that reputation. The pub that evening had been even more full of teachers than normal. It had seemed to lift the morale of the profession a little, been a slight cause for celebration. There was no significant change in the later edition, only a bit more space to the outraged non-response of others. Frank returned to his work, chastened a little again by the reinforcement of the magnitude of what he had done.

****

The main man at the newspaper responsible was very pleased with his story. It was a minor classic of its kind and Donald Dunne knew it would enter the industry folk-lore. And unlike one or two he had swithered about and then let run, it had the advantage of being both true and provable. Not that the man himself could sue of course but he knew the wife wouldn't either, once his lawyers had a little chat with her lawyers. Some of the abuse he was getting within the trade was pure hypocrisy, envy at a great scoop. But there was also a genuine sense of upset at what the story would do to an innocent grieving widow, so soon after the funeral. Well, they could believe what they liked about him, but he had actually acted like a gentleman with regard to her and her sensibilities. He reflected on his good luck, a trade-mark of his, that he had sent out his trawlers armed with an Agency picture of the happy couple, arm in arm at some formal do. Out had gone the query, to every major hotel in the whole area, have you ever seen the man in this picture with another woman. And back had come the magic answer, from more than one. No, but we have seen the woman with other men. Donald, professionally, wasn't really that interested in sex stories. He had knowledge of several MPs and other public figures having illicit sex, but had chosen not to run with them. It was hypocrisy that was his main concern. The public preaching of one set of values and the private living of another. Well, McGoldrick had been exposed fairly and squarely as a classic hypocrite, and deliciously soon after a major speech on that very topic. But he would not let the widow cry foul, now that he had her measure. If she maintained a dignified silence so would he, and her secret would be safe with him. He had not allowed the slightest hint to appear. He had met her previously and actually liked her, much warmer and more human than her husband, even if she had not succumbed to his charms. An impressive lady. No, he would let her be if she did not push it.

He had been even more impressed with his star witness. One cool lady that one. She had sensed the weakness of the case they had taken to her, had not panicked as they usually did, and had extracted from him almost to the limit of what he had been prepared to pay. She had also delivered proof and evidence of the highest calibre, with great clarity and precision. Yes, quite a lady that one, he could understand what McGoldrick had seen in her, although why the hell he hadn't serviced her properly, what a poor sick bastard. But then Donald should be grateful, that was what made it such a great story.

****

The work was very tiring. It required a high degree of concentration and organisation. The effects of the long night, and all the alcohol still in his system gradually began to catch up on Frank. He forced himself to plough on, more and more narrowly focusing on his task. He knew what he wanted, needed, the answer to be, but he would not cheat, having set up his parameters. He wanted the Prime Minister gone, he wanted an end to that era and the promise of a better future to come. He ground on, crunching out seat after seat. His perception was that his altered set of assumptions weren't making much difference. The thing that depressed him most were the number of English seats where Labour wasn't even second. The inevitable Liberal Democrat

216

revival would be larger than he had budgeted for, and make matters worse for Labour. He disciplined himself not to count running totals, or to do summaries, until the whole process was completed. He decided not to go for lunch. He wanted finished. Everything else went from him, McGoldrick, the paper, Joyce, Hazel, the World Cup, Celtic's poor form, even Elaine, and nothing intruded into the relentless churning out of seats won and lost, column after column. At last he finished the final one, at 3:05 p.m. precisely. He always remembered that because he had looked at his watch to see if he should go for a quick lunchtime pint before counting them up and finding out the result. It was too late, he decided.

He realised something about himself when he found out which column he counted first. He wanted the Prime Minister out even more than he wanted a Labour victory, so he counted the Tory column. It was a Southampton seat that did it, that did for him. It gave the Prime Minister the 326th seat and another term. There were another 7 after that one. The Prime Minister would have an overall majority of 16. He felt something die inside him. These had been the most generous assumptions it had been possible to make with any realism. There were almost certainly over-generous to Labour and by Election Day whenever, they were likely to be revised downwards, providing better results for the Prime Minister. But even on those most generous negative assumptions, the Prime Minister had a working overall majority. Stick your 50% rating in Opinion Polls, it was only seats in Parliament that mattered, and no matter how those were counted, the Prime Minister would have enough to continue.

Frank thought he was going to faint. A funny light-headedness gripped him, quite out of line with his gut depression. An urgent desire to vomit became barely resistible. He staggered to his feet and tottered off in the direction of the toilets. The toilets in the Mitchell Library were very plush, more like those of a Brighton Brothel than a Glasgow public convenience. All the detritus of the past few hours, days, weeks and months seemed to want to leave his body. He held his head over the bowl, opened his throat, and let other forces do the rest for him. He retched and boked, puked and spewed, watching in detached wonderment at what came out. He recognised some of it, the curry, the red wine and the malt, but most of it was new to him. He was unable to put words or labels to the stream that poured forth. Long after the volume ceased, the process continued. First the green bile, then the froth, then nothing

217

not even that, but the heaving and the straining continued. He thought he was going to die there, and laughed silently at the irony of it all.

Finally the force left him and his head was his own again. He staggered from the cubicle to the sink, and pushed his face under the cold tap. The water didn't help. He pulled the roller towel and immersed his face in it. Slowly he realised he was not alone. He moved away from the towel and turned round to face in the direction he sensed his company was located. There before him, looking at him directly from the silvered glass was the face he knew so well, the face of the person to whom he had just given another lease of life, the final face from his old nightmare. He reacted as he did whenever that face came on his TV screen. "I hate that person. I don't know why someone doesn't just kill her." As the words crossed through his head, the face shivered with obvious distaste and went, leaving only emptiness and realisation. He ran his fingers down the mirror in pursuit and never forgot the strangled screech of nail on glass that resulted. It was a sound he would carry to his end, it was the death rattle of a dozen dreams and the birthcry of a nightmare. The sound scraped the last hope out of his heart. He had found the missing piece.

All his life, Frank Hunter had known he had a political destiny to fulfil, a major role to play in the only game bigger than football. He had originally assumed it was to be as an elected player, once he had hung up his boots after achieving a different kind of greatness. But over time he had realised it was not to be that, either part, nor a leader of working men in strife. Over recent years he had even begun to doubt the correctness of his certainty that there was this destiny waiting for him, although his recent meeting with Elaine had rekindled his faith. Now he felt vindicated. It had been there all the time. Revealed, it was so clear and obvious he wondered how he could have been so stupid as to miss it over these past few days. It was not perhaps the destiny he would have chosen, but he had rejected all the others after all, so maybe it was preordained. He was going to die anyway, but his destiny would be to take the Prime Minister with him, to be the one who would release his country from yet another unwished for, unvoted for term of office, and save it from any more of her ravages. That was why he had not become an MP, or a Union leader, his political destiny had been marked out in more dramatic manner.

A wondrous peace descended upon him, in that lovely toilet. He now knew how the rest of his life would work out. He recognised that all the elements had been there for months, especially his realisation that he would never work again. Well, he had one more job to do before he was finally finished. He realised that he was lucky, to be the chosen one. He knew that it was a pleasant fantasy, shared by the great majority of his countrymen and women, but for him this notion of killing the Prime Minister had now changed into a definite, irreversible and inevitable plan of action. He would be the one privileged to turn it into a reality. He smiled at the memory of the game he had often played in the pub, "If you found out you were terminally ill, and could take one person with you, who would it be and why?" The Prime Minister had spoiled the first part of that game in Scotland for the past ten years, with the who always spoken for and only the why and how for variety. Well, Frank Hunter was going to play the game for one last time, for real, and do his country a great favour into the bargain.

GAME TWO

THE HUNTER

VERSUS

THE PRIME MINISTER

CHAPTER FOURTEEN - ANSWER MAN

All his life there had been an edge and an uncertainty to Frank Hunter. A restless unsureness about who he was and what he was doing. The revelation of the nature of his destiny produced a resolution of that tension and left him with a peace unlike any he had ever known. It did not induce happiness. He remained in a state of some profound sadness; but the search, the quest was over. He knew at last where he was going, he could throw away the maps.

He retained the structure of his life in most respects. He sorted out his relationship with Joyce. The threads of mutual dependency and shared honesty that had threatened to bind them so tightly together had been pulled looser by him not her. He knew the relationship had an end in sight, given what was to happen to him. He had given strong consideration to the possibilities of keeping her away, of being cruel now as a form of later kindness, but had decided against it. He tried to imagine her response to the impossible question, if you were told what he is going to do and could not influence it, would you rather end it now, and came to the conclusion for her that she would prefer to have the last month or so than not. So he, very kind of him, let her come back, make their peace and resume their peculiar relationship. At least this time, if he had not let her actually make her own choice, he had attempted to consider the question from her perspective. He genuinely felt that was progress in learning the lessons of history.

He acted as if she was his close friend. He told her the truth, or as much as he could, of what had really happened with McGoldrick, of the choice and its antecedents. Of how he had never had any intention of going to the newspapers, of how he had definitely not done so. He told her of Julie's role and their relationship. She seemed assuaged by those explanations, a little, but still felt he had done a wrong thing. They became closer again though, with much gentle, generous, giving sex, and even more silent cuddling. He saw their relationship as akin to that of a dying child and his mother, but with only the child knowing the diagnosis. He encouraged her to maintain her independence and distance, though he knew she would have moved in if he had asked her. He knew he needed time on his own, and she needed a structure of life without him to enable her to cope better when the going came.

She acted as if he were ill, and needed her help, and she tried to give it as a friend rather than a therapist. She mistook the calmness of his mind and the clinical involvement in his project for signs of progress and underestimated the seriousness of his state. She knew there was a problem but she saw the love, care and concern with which he was treating her, and was happier than she had ever been before in her life, because she was in love with a kind man who loved her and needed her. Later on she would look back on those weeks with affection and regard them as a farewell present from him. Her view always was that although he had made her choice for her, he had got it right. He may have got everything else wrong, but he had got that premise right.

He was back in the pub routine from the night of the day the paper had appeared. There had been a higher turnout than usual that night. Every teacher he knew had seemed to want to talk about it and gloat. His southside pubs had a disproportionate number of teachers at the best of times. All good working class boys who were guilty that they had used the education system to escape, but who still drank in the same kind of pubs as their fathers and who could only see after the fourth pint that far from allowing them to escape the system had actually trapped them in the worst of all worlds. Frank knew dozens of them but couldn't name one that was happy in his work or in his life. They needed the pub, and the talk about football and politics and sex, far more than even the social workers did.

That night they had been cheered up. One or two felt sorry for McGoldrick but the overwhelming view was that it was hilarious, a source of joy, 'another fucking Tory hypocrite exposed', a bit of light relief in a dark world. Frank had been interested in Paddy's view, that they had him on toast. That if he had been alive he wouldn't have had a hope of successfully suing them, and the fact that he was dead was irrelevant to that. After that night, Frank cut down his trips to the pub slightly, to about five nights a week, maybe six, seven at the most. He valued the time spent over a quiet pint with his old friends. He knew he would not have long left to enjoy them, so he determined to make the most. So he enjoyed them to the full, and talked and argued and laughed and reminisced and drank. Days and nights were for working, but evenings were for him and his friends. And his friends were pleased about that, and thought their old friend Frank had come

224

back to them, unaware it was for a farewell visit. Paddy and Danny in particular enjoyed his company, and felt happier about him than they had for years. Maybe he would fulfil his potential after all, or at least be happy.

Like the good Leninist Frank wasn't, he identified the key questions that he had to answer. He had already sorted out the main two, who and whom. That only left three main questions to be resolved before the structure of his new enterprise was clear. The fourth, why, he left to the 3a.m. philosophy class shifts to sort out and concentrated on the how, when and where. The how was the easiest of them. He could not countenance any method like a bomb that would be likely to kill any person other than his target. Other forms, like a knife or handgun were too personal and intimate, and too dangerous. After all it was not really a person he was to kill but a symbol. It had to be by sniper's rifle. There were family reasons for that, genetic ones. Willie Hunter, the Black and Tan, had been proud of his efficiency with a rifle. It was one of the few things about him Frank knew for certain. Mary Ewing used to tell him that Willie Hunter often boasted that he could kill men, Catholics of course, at a range of up to half a mile, and often had. Among his claims was that he had been the one that shot Frankie O'Sullivan, one of the top IRA men, from a building off O'Connell Street. Mary had believed him. Frank knew that his father, Dave, had used a rifle in Italy. He had never talked to Frank about it, but Frank had heard from his Gran who had heard from Shona. Dave Hunter had taken no pleasure in his proficiency but it had been remarkable. He had apparently been selected for special duties on the strength of it. Even Shona had not been told exactly what they were but she had formed the impression that he had been an official sniper, with specified and important targets. Frank had never fired a rifle in his life, except at the shows of course. But he knew he had steady hands and excellent hand-eye coordination. He was a sportsman and an engineer. With the current state of modern technology anyway, you just needed to point them and the machines did the rest themselves.

He had spent some time that first weekend planning how he could find out what was the appropriate machine, and how to get access to one. He went to John Menzies and bought one of every magazine available. There was Guns Review, Gun and Accessories Mart, Guns and Weapons, Guns and Ammo, Target Gun, Handgunner, Shooting Times, Combat and Survival, Country Magazine and more. It cost him £22:95. He wondered who the

225

hell read all or any of them. There were far more magazines about guns than about football, but then the football fanatics got their addiction catered for daily. He went home and read them all. By the end of that he knew a lot more about what was available, what the law was, and how to go about getting what he wanted.

He did his homework in other places, too. The Mitchell for the more technical side, and several selected south-side and city centre pubs for the human dimension. By the end of that process he knew the ways he could obtain his gun. It would be easier than he had envisaged. Hungerford had obviously not made it totally impossible. Doing it without revealing his name would be more difficult. But he knew the basic rule, McGuire's law, would apply. 'If it's possible but difficult to do something legally, it is easier but more expensive to do it illegally.' There were four ways to get a rifle. The most popular seemed to be to break-in to or burgle a Gunsmith's shop. But that would be too difficult, too risky for an amateur like him, they tended to have very sophisticated defences. The second way, also very popular in certain quarters, was to carry out a housebreaking on the premises of someone known to have a gun or certain kinds of guns. That had more appeal to him. He knew Peter McColl would be able to point him in the direction of his high society pals with whom he went shooting. They would likely be strong supporters of the Prime Minister, and the irony of getting her with the gun of her one of her few remaining Scottish supporters appealed to him. He didn't rule that option out and added it to his list of reasons for visiting Peter.

The third way was to buy one on the black market. In the Glasgow of 1990 that was not too difficult. The fact that he was able to spend a lot of money would guarantee he would succeed. Legally it would cost around £2,000. He would be more than happy to spend five times that, or more if necessary. And he could use a false name. So he set in motion the processes by which to achieve success by that method. The final method, the slowest and the least reliable, was to attempt to gain one legally. He didn't have the time for that, apart from anything else, with the need to join a Rifle or Gun Club for a probationary period, and the application to the Police for a firearms certificate, giving reasons for ownership, and signed photographs. They might not be too impressed with his reason, or his social status. 'Unemployed labourer wanting an expensive gun for political and recreational purposes', lacked a bit in credibility that one. So he settled for pursuing routes two and three, simultaneously. If he ended up with two, that would be even better for the totality of his project.

He did the rest of his homework conscientiously. He went to the Mitchell and took out every book on rifles that they had, technical manuals mostly. By the end of the week there were few in the country who could match his theoretical knowledge of how these things worked. His favourite was the Gun Digest Book, Volume 5, Firearms Assembly/Disassembly-Center Fire Rifles by J.B. Wood. He learned how to strip down and reassemble every conceivable rifle that he might obtain. He went to the three best gunshops in Glasgow and talked to very helpful experts about what he could and should obtain and how. They were all very helpful and co-operative to Mr Robertson, especially the man from Crocket's. Frank reckoned that a gun that could kill a lady deer had to be able to kill a dear lady, so he said he was a hunter, and smiled. He ended up his homework with a short-list of the kind of guns he would prefer. They didn't include his initial favourites like the Kalashnikov AK47 or the Armalite type. He wasn't going to war, he only wanted to shoot one beast of prey, so in fact a hunter's gun was very appropriate for the Hunter boy.

Peter McColl was the only person Frank knew who used guns, and had guns. Peter had regularly over the years taken considerable slagging from Paddy, Danny and Frank over his use of and attachment to guns. He actually shot deer. Frank despised Peter for that. He had once told Peter that only Englishmen, Germans and bastards would do a thing like that, and he knew his nationality. The irony was that Peter didn't believe in shooting people, which Frank felt was the only legitimate use for a gun. He knew that Peter had several guns himself, and was involved in a gun club, and several shooting groups. So Peter was an obvious source for him of information, but he knew he would have to be cautious about how he used him. Frank had a funny relationship with Peter McColl. Basically he didn't like him, but he was still one of his best friends. Frank had known Peter since his own year at University. Paddy and Peter had teamed up right away and become very close. Frank knew that he was vaguely jealous, particularly as he did not understand why it had happened. He had funny contradictions did Peter. He was a socialist, more self-professedly so than Frank or Paddy but with even less clue as to what that meant in practice. Early on he had revealed an ambition to be rich, famous, legally successful and socially accepted. He had become involved with guns in pursuance of the latter aim, or the latter two. Frank's only explanation for Paddy's close friendship with Peter was that his was the only self-destruct streak even more rampant than Paddy's own. Peter would work long and hard ingratiating himself with people he didn't like but thought were important to his aims, then blow it all with an outburst of honesty and abuse. He was a working-class Catholic who despaired of his religion but kept it, although he desperately desired legal offices that even few aristocratic Catholics had held for over 400 years.

He was once engaged to the daughter of the Lord Advocate, a marriage that would have set him up for life and given him most of the things he had always said he wanted. Then he had called the whole thing off four days before the ceremony, after all the invitations were out and presents in, and publicity printed. He had found out that she did not love him, at least by his definition. He had been happy enough, delirious in fact, to marry on the basis that he did not love her, but he wasn't prepared to marry on the basis that she did not love him, although she swore she did. He had gone a bit wild sexually after that. He would shag a carpet if it had a hole in it, was one of the nicer things the puritan Frank Hunter had said about him during that period. He had a very low view of himself and despised any woman who found him attractive, so he never married and settled for becoming rich instead. He became a very successful Glasgow lawyer, capable of brilliant work when it was really required. His self-destruct streak ensured he would never reach the very top, but his talent ensured that he was always in demand. He was the most successful of that second generation of Glasgow Catholic lawyers who specialised in the criminal law rather than take the minor places behind the proddy big Civil boys. Paddy told Frank that Peter's salary was even greater than his, and must be pushing the six figure mark. For reasons even Paddy didn't know, which meant that Peter certainly didn't, he had held off the natural step of an application to the Faculty of Advocates, always being on the verge but eventually muttering only about waiting for right of access to the High Court.

In Frank's view, his sustaining grace, and the reason they were able to be friends, was that he had a genuine love of football. He had shared the same formative years as Frank and Paddy, nurtured on the Stein era, spoiled for life by 9 in a row before he was 21. He was also the only one of Frank's friends who shared his true international perspective on football. He was as interested in German and Argentinean football as in the Scottish version. He also had the money to pursue this interest, and he and Frank had been abroad together on many occasions. Peter had come with them in 1974 to Germany. He had been the only one of their crowd to actually go to Argentina in 1978. That had had a terrible effect on his already scarred and twisted personality, destroying another layer of trust. He had been with them in Fuengirola in 1982 and had almost persuaded the Elaine-less Frank to go with him to Mexico in 1986. He had gone on his own and survived the experience, apart from a mild venereal disease. He went to almost every Scotland away game, and since 1984 Frank and Gerry Robertson had generally accompanied him. He had been with Frank to the European Cup Final in 1985, 1986, 1987 and 1988, and gone without him in 1989. Although disqualified from full membership by a strange but typical inability to appreciate any aspect of the great man's game, he had become an associate member of SAD and went on every trip of that organisation. He had invested in Satellite TV even before Frank and each was the only one the other was able to talk to about the great range of treats this opened up for them.

If football offered enough common ground for some kind of friendship, politics should have done as well but it did not. Frank did not like Peter's politics, although to most people they seemed the same as his. Frank knew his dislike was irrational but that only made it worse. The Gas Shares row had somehow summed it all it. Of all their group of pub-drinking football and politics talkers, Peter was the only one who had bought shares at any of the privatisations. He had done so at all of them, to the maximum level possible. He was unrepentant, indeed aggressively positive. He and Frank had nearly come to blows in the Victoria Bar one night. He always remembered the speech Peter had made. "It's like mortgage tax relief, Frank. Put a resolution in front of me that advocates abolition of it, and I'll vote in favour. I've actually moved one or two like that in my time and tried to commit the Labour Party to scrap it. But while it is there, I'm bloody sure I'm going to claim every penny of relief to which I'm entitled and don't try to tell me any of you are different." He had them there right enough, every beer-swilling socialist one of them there that night had their own mortgage. "And at least with Mortgage relief the Exchequer would benefit from your refusal to accept, and there would be more there in theory at least for the poor and deprived. But with the Shares, it is not like that. Who do you think would have benefited if I had not bought these Gas shares?

Not your punter on Benefit that's for sure, just another share buyer, because they're all going to be sold, no doubt about that. I've voted against privatisation. I'll vote for re-nationalisation, with or without compensation, and because I'll have sold them by then, it wouldn't affect me personally which happens. But why should I pass up the chance to make some money when no-one deserving would benefit if I did? Why should I? Eh, tell me that." Frank had failed the challenge of demonstrating any moral, ethical, practical or political reason why not. Frank wasn't at his best at that time right enough. He didn't usually lose political arguments, but he didn't win that one. There wasn't a rational answer available. Any wrong there was lay with the Government for selling, not with the buyers. Even the wrong price was a further reason for buying rather than one for not doing so.

Drunk on his victory, Peter had not left it there, but had rubbed their noses in the contradiction of the wallet. He had pulled out from his pocket an expensive leather wallet and passed it round the table inviting them to feel its quality. "That wallet, a gift that cost me nothing, is worth at least £200. I am willing to sell it to you for £100. What is more I guarantee you that within one of its sealed compartments there is a £100 note, that can only be accessed by a new owner. So I sell it to you on that basis. How much does it cost? It has cost you nothing, to get something worth £200 but I still have your £100 in my hand to show as profit from the transaction, and to use for whatever good I choose. The wallet is still there, not altered or diminished in any way." There had been more but Frank had left it to Paddy and switched off by then, but it had not endeared Peter to him.

Peter lived alone in a big house in a secluded part of Baillieston. That was typical of him. He wanted to live in a big house, like all the other toffs, but he bought one not in Bearsden but in Baillieston, for Christ's sake. Although he did love that house. He kept his interest in shooting going, because he genuinely enjoyed that. He loved his guns if nothing and no-one else. He was probably the second saddest man Frank Hunter knew, and the unhappiest. So Frank resolved to visit him before their forthcoming trip to Barcelona, to test out against his friend's knowledge, some of the things he had learned about rifles and how to obtain them. He knew he would have to be careful how he did that, for Peter was both sharp and suspicious, and would not swallow any notion that Frank had suddenly taken a sporting interest in the topic. That would be a good challenge for Frank.

He had often fancied testing himself out in cross-examination with Peter. This might be the closest he would get to come to that.

With his homework, he had narrowed down the choice of rifle he wanted to three makes, Sauer, Winchester and Mauser. He had worked out a fairly elaborate scheme of how to obtain one of them, through the intervention of Harry Thomson, to whom he had been directed by the man to whom he had been directed by the man to whom he had been directed by the helpful man at Crocket's. He had a further elaborate series of pub meetings, terminating in the one round the corner from the other Victoria Bar, in the Bridgegate. He met a canny wee man, in the pub of that name. Frank had never shared Paddy and Peter's ambivalent fascination with the criminal fraternity. Frank was a true puritan and thought criminals were immoral cheats, not glamorous heroes. But he knew enough of the social ground rules to move in those circles when required. It would cost him all right, but what did the money matter now, and he would end up with one of the guns he wanted, the Sauer, registered in someone else's name. He made a cash deposit, to establish his credibility, but as well as confirming the deal, he wanted to check out with Peter, that there wasn't a better gun, or a safer way of obtaining one, or a soft touch he knew he could burgle.

So he visited Peter in his big house in Baillieston, on a Sunday morning. He wasn't that good a Catholic that he was likely to be at Mass but Frank had checked with him first anyway. Peter thought Frank was coming to collect a video tape he had made of a River Plate league game that Frank had also taped but forgetting to make sure the Satellite receiver was on the right channel. Frank had also said that he needed to sort out with him some of the administrative details and arrangements for the forthcoming SAD trip to Barcelona. Stevie boy had left Hibs, wise man, and returned to Barcelona to play for the other team Espanol, in the Second Division. He had worked out a good deal for himself, including a rumoured £5,000 bonus for every goal he scored. In January a euphoric meeting of the SAD committee in the Victoria had agreed that one last trip to Barcelona was called for, and it had been set up for the second last Saturday in April. They were to drive down to Manchester on the Friday night, spent the night in a hotel near the airport and take the early flight on the Saturday to Barcelona, where their old friends would entertain them royally on the Saturday night. They would go to the game on the Sunday, then fly home and drive back through the night in time to be ready for work on the Monday morning.

Peter seemed pleased to see him. He seldom got visitors other than the stream of young ladies who never stayed more than the one night, and were never invited back. Frank despaired of Peter's attitude to women. The fact that it reflected his attitude to himself did not excuse it. Frank genuinely believed that Peter was capable of being a serial killer of women, rather than just a breaker of hearts. He had used prostitutes, often, was quite open about it and said it was cheaper, quicker and cleaner than spending £50 on a meal for the same end product, and much less hassle. Less boring too, with no need for polite conversation.

His collection of video tapes was even bigger than Frank's. He had bought every pre-recorded football video and routinely taped every single game on Satellite or TV. He also bought tapes through international football magazines. There wasn't a major club or team in the world he did not have on tape. His library was immense, although it consisted entirely of books on football or the law. He had every single edition of the Scottish Football Book, and almost every other annual. The house did not look like a single man's, or at least like Frank's. It vaguely reminded Frank of a showhouse he had seen once, for young executives. All that it needed was for a human being to move in. It was soft and clean. The only consistent woman in Peter's life was Mrs Johnstone, who came in every day Monday to Friday and cleaned up after him. She did his cleaning, his washing, his ironing, his tidying and dusting. Frank had to admit she seemed like a good investment because he knew from various foreign trips together that Peter was not a naturally tidy or clean person.

Frank had carefully prepared ways of turning the conversation towards guns, but he did not need any of them. Peter raised the subject first and seemed keen to go on about them at length. Frank tried to look politely interested rather than keen, but in either event Peter kept going. Frank was extra-careful only to nod rather than seem enthusiastic when Peter asked if he would like to see his new pride and joy. He led Frank through from the sitting-room to one of his three studies. One, the smallest one, was for his law work. The largest one was for his football tapes, books, magazines, programmes and other memorabilia. The third one was for his guns and other sporting equipment. Frank had been in it before, but this was the first time he had ever paid real attention to its contents.

Peter must have had about twenty guns in all, displayed on the walls, mostly shotguns of various shapes and sizes, or old model rifles. He also had a reinforced glass display case about eight feet long containing ten handguns. The glass container was locked, and the guns on the walls were all attached by chains and padlocks. Peter ignored them all and went straight over to what looked to Frank like a small filing cabinet attached by a series of screws to the far wall. His engineer's eye could tell it was about 4'6" tall, 21" wide and 18" deep. "This is more secure than Fort Knox," Peter told Frank with real pride, "even Harry Herd couldn't get into this beauty. It's the very latest kind of gun-cage. Safe as they come." He patted it affectionately and walked over to his desk. Frank watched with interest as Peter contorted himself to reach a small, flat pouch stuck onto the back of the inside drawer frame. From this he extracted a folded plastic frame containing 4 small keys. He inserted them at various points in the cage and twisted the plastic handle twice forward, once back, then another twice forward. As the door of the cage swung slightly forward Peter explained that the theory of the cages was that opening them required two people, each of whom knew what to do simultaneously with both of their keys. He had paid good money to have it converted into a one man operation. Frank could see that there were three guns inside, two rifles and a shotgun.

Peter brought out one of the rifles and fondled it lovingly. "This is her, my new Parker-Hale M85, just made. I made arrangements to obtain one as soon as they were ready. I reckon its one of only three of its kind in the United Kingdom, probably the only one in Scotland. It'll be another 12 months before most enthusiasts get the chance to obtain one." Frank had read about this one in more than one of his magazines, but had reluctantly discounted the prospect of being able to obtain one in his timescale. "It is guaranteed to kill a stag at up to half a mile, no problem." "What about a human?" Frank asked, safe in the knowledge that from past arguments Peter would think nothing strange about the question. "Oh, yes. It would be even easier to kill a man with this than a stag, you know." It was obvious to Frank that at last Peter was in love. The tenderness with which he was caressing his new acquisition far exceeded any he had ever seen him show before. "As an engineer, you'll appreciate these." Peter said, as he showed Frank the sights that went with the gun. "With these beauties it is a bit like cheating. All you need to do is

233

set these sights, hold your breath for 10 seconds and squeeze. 100% accuracy guaranteed, certainly if you use a stand."

Peter told him the gun was very expensive, and he had had to pull strings and oil palms to obtain it. He told Frank of the special licence that was required for a gun like that. But he had the money, and the desire, and now he had the gun. He briefly explained the other two guns to Frank. The other rifle lay like a rejected lady in the dark. It had been his favourite until the Parker Hale arrived, now it had gone the way of all his other exs. It was one of the ones Frank had had in mind for himself. He was reassured to hear Peter say that while they were expensive, they were relatively easy to obtain. The shotgun was a beauty, a Churchill, another expensive gun and one Peter used for only the most prestigious shoots. Peter talked on, glad of an apparently interested audience, but his assumption was no longer correct. Frank was no longer listening intently to every word. He already knew what he would do. He would go ahead with the arrangements with Harry Thomson, but that would just be insurance and cover. The word alerted him to check that Peter was fully insured, for his whole collection which he was, and which he would need to be. He also got Peter to show him the ammunition that each gun used. Peter kept that separately in a box cupboard that did not even lock. He watched carefully again, as Peter locked the cage and put the keys back in their hiding place. He arranged with Peter that he would use his Mercedes for the trip to Manchester, that he would collect them at a central point on the southside and that they would then head straight for the motorway south, all in the one car.

Frank was very quiet in the pub that lunchtime after he left Peter. He was wrestling with a moral dilemma, or rather balancing up several of different weights and directions. He knew what he wanted to do, and how and when. He had gone there intending to identify a friend of Peter's from whom he could steal a gun. He had ended up identifying Peter's best friend, a logical progression. Frank overcame the initial feelings of guilt at the notion of stealing from a friend. It was no loss what a friend gets, is that not what they say. Anyway, Peter was not that much of a friend. And he would suffer no real loss. He could replace the guns with the insurance money. He could afford not even to have to wait for it to come through, so the time he would be without would be quite short, certainly before the deer shooting season began. Along with every other friend of Frank's, Peter McColl hated the Prime

Minister, but he did so with an intensity and a venom that far exceeded Frank's own. He never referred to her without coupling it with the common noun for copulation. For a man who by Frank's theory hated women, she seemed to have offered a repository and personification for that hatred in her own person. He seemed obsessed with her sexuality as much as her politics. He had often said that the one exception he would make about guns and people were if he could get her within his sights. So he should be pleased to have the opportunity to contribute to the success of Frank's venture.

And so he rationalised a further departure from the notion that Frank Hunter was a totally honest man who respected his own values above anything. Christ, if he could not even cope with stealing a gun, how was he going to be able to justify shooting someone? For the first time in his life, he had a mission that seemed important enough to justify such a failure of his own morality. He realised that he understood at last why religious people could be so immoral. Frank Hunter had always been clear from an early age that God did not exist. Or more accurately, God did exist, but only in the same sense as Tinkerbell, Noddy, Peter Pan, Elsie Tanner and the Tooth Fairy. A fictional character created by men, and believed in by other men either because it suited them better to believe, or because they were too stupid to know the difference. Frank had always been fascinated, as a political animal, how powerful people used the fictional creation to further their own ends. The most effective ones had to be those immune from the tendency to believe in their own fiction. They were able to rewrite the moral agendas to justify whatever script changes were required to achieve whatever ends they wanted. The same God gave the same permission to Englishmen to kill Germans, as he gave to the Germans to kill Englishmen.

The part Frank felt most bad about was his use of the knowledge that Peter would not prosecute him, or press charges, if anything went wrong, as long as he got his guns back. It would be put down as a prank, an unfunny joke or a mental aberration. But they could never be friends again. Any other way to steal a gun would be more risky and dangerous. The greatest danger to his project would be that he wouldn't get a suitable gun in time. The chosen date was only four weeks away. And he had a lot of other things he had to do before he could be ready.

The where and when of his enterprise had dropped into his lap like gifts from the gods in a manner that confirmed for him that

235

he was dealing with a destiny that could not be denied. It was the Tuesday morning and he settled down as always after his shower to read his three papers over breakfast. A conservative creature of habit, he always read them in the same order, the Record, the Herald, and the Guardian. As always, too, he started from the back. In all his life, despite devouring tens of thousands of them, he had never ever started reading a paper from the front. He wondered if football fanatics in France, Italy and Germany approached papers from the middle. Frank loved newspapers. So much for so little. The best value for money available, three for the price of a pint. That was his favourite combination, one pub, one pint, three papers. Or even better, if the papers were good, three pints. He read the main stories: Celtic gloom, Rangers boom, and the rest. He worked his way quickly to the front of the Record, then turned to the back of the Glasgow Herald. A slightly more sophisticated version of the same stories but Celtic were in just as much trouble. Then it caught his eye and the whole project changed up a gear. He knew that was it, a sign that it was for real and that he would do it. It was just a simple story, a few lines beneath another item.

"The Scottish Football Association confirmed yesterday that the Prime Minister had accepted an invitation to be present at the Scottish Cup Final to be played at Hampden Park on the third Saturday in May. The Cup Final will coincide with the final day of the Scottish Tory Party Conference to be held in Aberdeen that week." The Herald went on to add its own comments that on the last occasion, in 1988, that the Prime Minister attended the final, there had been a red card demonstration by a majority of the crowd in protest against the Government's attack on the National Health Service. It had been felt then that the Prime Minister would be unlikely to attend a Scottish Cup Final again. The Herald expressed the view that the Prime Minister had been strongly advised to attend by the Scottish Tory Party chairman, who felt that it would represent a reaffirmation of Conservative faith and confidence in its position in Scotland. Frank smiled absently at that last sentence. Arrogant little bastard; but his P.R. instincts were generally good.

The convergence seemed irresistible. It now seemed to Frank inevitable that his two greatest loves, football and politics, would merge together for his greatest act. The twin strands of his life, regularly interwoven would now combine in a climactic finale. He hoped Celtic would be there. It was fairly certain they would be.

236

That would somehow be appropriate for him. The main highlight of a dismal season so far had come in February when they had rather luckily put Rangers out the Cup. Then two days after Danny's own goal, the Prime Minister had considerably increased the likelihood of Celtic getting to the Final by going to Ibrox and making the semi-final draw that kept Celtic apart from Aberdeen and Dundee United, both of whom could be reckoned to beat the Bhoys the way they were playing. Celtic versus Clydebank or Stirling Albion, thank you ma'am. It is a funny old life indeed. Frank had been to every Scottish Cup Final since 1965, when King Billy's head had made him so happy. Well, his last one would make a lot of other people very happy, too.

Having settled the where and when, he became anxious to clarify the details and mechanics, so he ate up, did the relevant homework and set out for Hampden Park. As a boy in Govanhill, he had always walked to Hampden. When he and Elaine, he paused in silent grimace at the thought then forced himself on, when he and Elaine lived in Battlefield, it was heaven. Hampden on the back door step. Even in Shawlands, he always walked. From flat to pub, pub to Hampden, Hampden back to the pub, then from pub to home. But today he took the car. As he drove he went over in his mind what he was looking for, what he hoped to find. Ever since they had knocked down the old North Stand and left the side across from the Main Stand completely open, there were several rows of houses that had a clear view of most of the pitch. And more importantly for his purposes, a clear line of vision into the Main Stand. He knew where the Prime Minister would sit. That morning he had checked and rechecked his videos of all the previous Cup Finals and presentations. The pattern was always the same. The main VIP sat in the front row of the Directors Box, to the right of the centreline as seen from the touchline, in the third or fourth seat from the middle.

Frank had often watched the lucky families, hanging out of their windows, able to watch the match in the comfort and peace of their own home. Every other year, the Weekly News or some such rag would feature one of these families. His mind ran through various schemes for acquiring one of those flats for the occasion. They couldn't all be football fanatics. At least some would see it as a marketable commodity. Frank had heard various pub talk of them offering their site from anything from £20 to £100 depending on the match and the demand. That's what he would do, rent one such flat for the day. He could already envisage one or two ways of doing that without revealing his identity.

He could never approach Hampden without being attacked by bouts of football nostalgia. This morning he could not get out of his mind the awful game against England in 1966 when the 12 year old Frank had seen Scotland beaten 4-3. The game had been good and exciting, the awfulness had come from the realisation that England might just be good enough to win the World Cup after all. Baxter, Law and especially wee Jinky had all been brilliant, but they had been more interested in taking the piss than winning, and had finally paid the price. He still remembered the piss-taking more than the goals, so maybe they had been right after all. He parked the car in Somerville Drive. It wasn't strange for him to see the place empty. His evening walks had often brought him down this way to the deserted temple. He reckoned Somerville Drive was too near, too close, too obvious. Anyway, the police guarded the close doors, that wouldn't suit. He planned to walk round the square formed by Somerville Drive, Stanmore Road, Brownlie Street and Bolivar Terrace.

He soon saw exactly what he was looking for. He saw it from Somerville Drive, although it was actually on Brownlie Street. It was three stories up, off the back, looking right across to the Main Stand. A line from the middle of the window to the Directors Box would create an angle of around 10 degrees. It was a small window too, it must be either a kitchen or a bathroom. He went round to Brownlie Street to the close entrance. It was number 37. He walked slowly up to the top floor, on the left hand side. He felt a surge of adrenaline when he looked at the front door. Fate was still on his side, there were four different names sellotaped onto the side of the door. It looked like students, single people anyway. They would be more likely to be amenable to a good commercial proposition than a family. He surveyed the whole area thoroughly but found nothing else quite as good. There were no less than 54 houses or flats that had at least one window with a straight line of access, but the only other possibilities really suitable for his purposes were the back windows of two of the flats in Stanmore Road, although even there the distance was far greater and the angle more acute. He noted the addresses and the names on the door, though, just in case.

He was walking back along Stanmore Road to return to his car, when he made the discovery. It was a further moment of sublime truth, a realisation that he was no longer playing out a fantasy but on the verge of achieving an amazing reality. He paused at the top of Stanmore Road before turning into Brownlie Street and descending down the hill to where he had left the car. As he looked over at Hampden he realised he was looking straight into the Directors Box. He could not see the pitch at all but there was a direct unobstructed line right into the Directors Box. From a car parked right on the corner, he would be able to fire right onto the target. He didn't need the problems associated with acquiring and using any of the premises. It was an intellectual discovery of great magnitude for him. He could hardly believe it was possible, but it definitely was. He was so excited he sprinted down the hill and all the way to the car. He drove it right up to the spot and parked on the right-hand side of Stanmore Road, on the right-hand junction with Brownlie Street. There was not a building on the corner, just a low railing enclosing grass, with a couple of trees at the Brownlie Street top end. He rolled the window down, raised his binoculars and focused them. There was no doubt about it. There was an unobstructed line right to the very seat she would be in. He came out and went into the back seat. He nestled the imaginary rifle over the back of the front seat. It was a perfect line. He closed his eyes and squeezed the trigger, for the first of many times. He could fire from the back seat, then drive off. When he timed it later, he consistently could be on the M8 Motorway in under 7 minutes. He would be well away from the area before any road blocks could be set up.

He spent the rest of the morning with his tools, measuring out distances, angles and elevations. A germ had already formed in his mind which meant that he would still go for the Brownlie Street flat, although he would do the shooting from the car. So he worked out both sets of measurements and calculations. It was easy for a man of his work experience and skills. He felt like a working man again, with a job to do, and pride to be taken in doing it well. From the car, it would be a shot of 267 metres, downward elevation of 25 degrees. From the flat it would be a shot of 182 metres, from a downward angle of 13 degrees. He knew he would need a rifle that could offer 100% accuracy up to a range of 300 metres. He knew from his studying that most of the ones he had already considered would fit this bill. Certainly the Sauer and the Parker-Hale would. Frank had one other worry, about the wind, mindful of the Hampden swirl that had killed many a goalkeeper but could maybe save a Prime Minister. Like the Hampden Roar, it was probably a thing of myth, or at least of the past, but the issue should still be addressed. He had asked Peter in general terms about the effect of wind. Peter had given him a long technical answer but fortunately he had listened with genuine interest. The substance was that at full range, even a strong wind would make little difference, maybe 1/10th of 1%. At 400 yards, it would be significantly less than that, maybe 4 inches at the most, in a gale. Frank wondered how big a heart the Prime Minister had. Some said it was enormous, others said almost none at all. He would have to hope that there was no storm.

As he worked all this out, he could hardly contain the excitement he felt. It was feasible, very feasible. The realisation that it could be done from the car, on the street corner, seemed to him the final message that this was definitely where his destiny lay.

From that moment of revelation, he never looked back. He moved into a new phase in which he was totally committed to doing it. It was a real job he had this time. It absorbed almost all of his thoughts, waking and even during the little sleeping that he did. The depression and lackadaisicalness disappeared. They were replaced by devotion to duty, efficient planning, meticulous preparation and a vibrant sense of mission and purpose. He cross-checked every detail, several times. He assessed and reassessed his plans every day. He would modify, and test out. He was too busy to mope, too occupied to have time to be sorry for himself. Only the sense of profound sadness remained, but that had always been with him, even in the good times. Joyce and his friends thought he was getting better, that he was emerging fully at last from the black period. He looked better, more alert, more alive. He lost the aura of living corpse that had been present since the previous June.

He participated again in pub conversations, even started some. He provoked and led arguments, tested out propositions, played word and mind games. He talked politics in a way they had not seen for several years. They relaxed to see the progress and welcomed their old friend back. Only Hazel was suspicious of the new arrival, she still suspected he was planning something, and feared it would be bound to be something stupid. When he told her one night that it would be better for her if she were able to say she had never heard of Frank Hunter, or at least that she hadn't seen him for months, she was not much reassured. She continued to give him considerable comfort, but he never made love to her again after that Thursday night with the Pasandas. Twice more, on Tuesday nights, he had gently taken off all her clothes and licked her into the shape of a climax. But that had been for her not him, since she had seemed terribly depressed. It was the most he felt he could do for her without being unfaithful to Joyce, which he knew he would never do again. He worried about Hazel, she seemed without focus, without hope. He sympathised with her, but now felt himself to be different. He had had all his questions satisfactorily answered.

CHAPTER FIFTEEN - CONMAN

Christmas came early for Jim Morris in 1990. The 16th of April to be precise. He opened the two bills first, because he knew what they were, and opening them would be the only attention they would get. He left the thicker envelope with the typewritten address to the end. It held more promise. He saw the money first, and counted it before turning to the letter. 5 crisp new £20 notes. He pocketed them quickly before Ann-Marie could see them, but he had had enough time to check their authenticity. After his experiences the previous summer, he could tell a real £20 note with absolute certainty. Then he turned to the letter with some curiosity. Jim had a good imagination, so he was seldom surprised by anything. He noticed the letter had no heading address and no signature.

Dear Jim,

A mutual friend has recommended you to me as a man with the necessary tact and sensitivity to carry out a delicate task that I wish performed. This task is perfectly legitimate, and involves only the hiring of a certain commodity, but I have my own reasons for wishing it carried out by a third party. I will pay you a further £250 for performing the task, as well as giving you the opportunity to make some money by the efficiency with which you carry it out.

Please phone 041-556-7654 at precisely 8pm on the 17th, from your own phone. If you are interested in carrying out this commission, ask if Tommy Currie can be called to the phone. If you do not wish to get involved, and wish to return the money, less £20 for your trouble, ask for Danny Finlay, who will tell you what to do with the £80. From what my friend has told me about you, I am confident that you will do one of those two things rather than just pocket the money and forget about it. However, if it turns out that my friend is a poorer judge of character than I think, I would mention only two things. Pete Wilson and Gordie McLean. I look forward to an involvement that will be to our mutual benefit and satisfaction.

Once I have received confirmation that you are prepared to act on my behalf, I will send further instructions and funds to you.

He held the letter and the envelope up to the light. There was no identification or clue at all. It had a Glasgow postmark, from the Saturday. Jim felt a certain elation and a certain unease in almost equal measure. The money would come in handy, no doubt about that. He was having a run of bad luck at the moment. He was used to doing wee jobs for people. Nothing illegal, you know, but around the margins of normal commerce. Jim liked to think he had a good reputation. He had no illusions that he was in the big league, nor would he ever be. But he had enough good ideas every year to stop him from starving. He would like to think that the author of his letter was an important man, and that Jim had been recommended to him by another important man. He knew most of the important people on the southside, and had helped them out at some point. That was certainly one of the advantages of working for Charlie Spence, you came into contact with the right people, and were able to help them. You also got the chance for a fair number of unusual homers, which helped the income. This seemed mild, a doddle with no great complication. But he didn't like the idea of not knowing for whom he was working.

Nor did he like being threatened. He knew of Wilson and McLean. Two men from Govan who leant on people, often just for fun. It was not that long ago that they had beaten almost to death an old school pal of Jim's. For twenty quid each, so it had been said in the pubs he frequented. The remit had been to beat him up, the rest they had thrown in as a bonus. The police had been involved, by the Hospital, but his friend had had more sense than say what he knew. Every one else knew it though. What if this man didn't like the way he did the job, or if it went wrong through no fault of his. Or if it turned out to be illegal and he wanted to opt out, after he had spent his advance. He would have to rely on the man's friend, his referee, knowing he wouldn't touch anything too dodgy. He would make that clear to this Tommy Currie. It worried him that he didn't know either name, Jim knew everyone, it was one of his talents. Maybe they were false ones of course, or Proddies. Still, he wasn't in a position to turn down the chance of £350 quid for a little honest work, so he would give it a go. He tucked the letter into his pocket, he would read it again over lunch.

He had only the one run on, for the whole day. Business was poor just now, and he got paid by the job, not the week. That had been his choice, in the beginning, when he had been sure the driving was just to tide him over till he was working for himself again. By the time he had reconsidered, Charlie said he preferred it the way it was. Not that he could complain, Charlie had been good to him over the years. He would have to be too, with what Jim knew about him. At least he could afford a wee dram this dinner-time. Jim thought drinking malts in a pub was a sign of class, and indulged himself whenever he could afford. So with his Christmas present in his pocket he bought himself a double and sat and reread his mail. The man would not have reassured him it was not illegal, if he had not known of Jim's fastidiousness. What trouble could he possibly get into, hiring something on someone's behalf, with their money. He assumed it would be a car, or a van, that was his game.

He put the letter away, savoured his whisky and read his Guardian. He read the Record over the breakfast table, but liked the Guardian over his lunchtime drink. He liked to keep up with what was going on in the world. The letter seemed to make him restless. He went up to the bar and ordered another, a double again. He had been careful not to break any of the £20s with his first drink, but now the decision was definitely taken, what the hell.

He wasn't sure whether it was the whisky or the letter, but he was in a right mood to ponder. He always fancied himself as a bit of a philosopher, a bit of an intellectual. He never used that word about himself, but would have been disappointed if others didn't. He had become a fatalist too, recently. What's for you, won't go by you. He knew it was Ann-Marie's fault that he would never be rich. He always felt ashamed when he told himself that lie, but he also knew what he meant when he did. She had been the one great choice he had had to make in his life. He smiled at that, even he at his best he could not con himself into believing there had been a real choice. Even so, he had almost failed to make it, out of fear that she couldn't really seriously fancy him. That was why he could never be a real conman, he did not believe enough in himself, the true product of the genre artist. No, he wasn't a con man, he was a seller of things that weren't quite as they seemed, but he never really lied, or made people buy who didn't want to. He exploited people's greed and punished them for the fact that they were prepared to act on a belief that he was as stupid as he looked. Or he sold them cheap and harmless illusions that allowed them to believe whatever they wanted. Trinkets of the mind he would call them.

His greatest coup had been of that kind. He was fairly certain that 90% of the punters who had bought his Wembley turf off him in 1977 had known that it was unlikely to be genuine. That had not mattered, as long as they were able to say, "the man assured me it was genuine. He was definitely there and showed me a photograph of himself digging up the centre-circle." That photo had been an inspiration, the little touch of genius that separates out the great from the merely good. He had got Pat McDermott to take it, as he did dig out a far larger roll of turf than anyone else. Even as it was taken, he had seen the possibilities. Sure, it is a big piece, I've divided it up into twenty sections, and you can have one, for two quid, with its very own plastic base to ensure it survives. He had rushed back home, foregoing the usual Soho pleasures, to get to the Garden Centre early on the Sunday morning, and buy 48 rolls of best quality turf. All he could finance himself to, the day after Wembley, and that was with a robbing of the untouchable. Each roll was divided up into 12 pieces, each one given its own little plastic tray. Jim had thought the plastic trays were a wee touch of class, a sign that he was not a cowboy who had dug up the neighbour's garden. For the rest of the week, he had toured every pub on the southside, and a good few more, selling off pieces of history. He had cleared over £ 800. £812 profit, he had entered in the meticulous record he kept of all his enterprises. It wasn't the biggest profit he ever made, but it was the best, and the one that made his reputation. And the real roll? He had kept that of course, laid it in his own back garden. Occasionally he would still stand on the hallowed spot, pat it tenderly and re-watch King Kenny gliding over it on his way to score the winner. Jim had been 23 that year, still young enough to believe he might join him one day.

The memory always made him proud. It was the proof he used that he had it, that it was some other reason that had prevented him making it. This time the 'yet' never appeared. Since he had strangled it the last few times, maybe it was no wonder. No, it wasn't Ann-Marie's fault he wasn't rich. It was down to her that he had never been to prison, though. He had promised her he would keep it clean. She wouldn't have married him if he had not given her that assurance, on his solemn oath. And marrying her was the best thing he had ever done, or ever would. She was incurably decent, but no-one was perfect. He still loved her so much it hurt, and it still amazed him that she loved him. He knew he had fooled her, all their lives, and that that was the best and most important trick he had ever pulled, to make her happy when she could have had so much more. Given his assurance he would no longer do the bad stuff, the thieving, the extortion, the swindling, the reset, she tolerated his flirting with the edges. She had never needed to get an explicit promise that he would avoid the dealing, when that hit his friends. He hated enough what that did to people, himself. She had never complained that he had never had a real job, a steady job. She had worked herself. He had tentatively tried to stop her, but Ann-Marie was in charge of her own destiny. She made her own child care arrangements and his circumstances allowed him to help although she never asked him to or depended on him. She was working now, he realised, while he was sitting there drinking good money. He had always kept her and the girls from starving but there was no doubt her regular wage helped make life more comfortable, and minimised the effects of his dips. He was still a managing director, but. Since the bus finally packed it in, there was little to manage and less to direct. Morris Sporting Travel and Transport. We make the MOSTT of your trip to Europe, was his proud boast. Deregulation should have been his big chance, but he had let it screw him instead. He wasn't a planner, that was his problem, that and the fact that he wasn't a mechanic either, nor an accountant.

He was an ideas man. Short-term ones at that, manipulation of openings. He had heard a phrase once that summed it up for him, about jumping through windows of opportunity. That was him, a window jumper. To hell with what might be on the other side, he would be off and jumping before others even realised the window was open. He had often had soft landings, sweet smells and salmon sticking out of every pocket. But equally often it was into shite, up to the ears.

He was in the mood for savouring past triumph as well as old whisky, so he bought himself another double, of 12 year old, the year his company was formed. He realised with pleasure that the idea had come to him in this very pub. He'd been doing his usual, moving from group to group, on the fringes of each. The talk had all been the same. How many of them were going to go to Celtic's First Round game in the European Cup. The first leg had been at Parkhead, a 5-0 stroll against a bunch of young Luxemburgers. The size of the victory and the lack of quality of the opposition had meant that the usual agencies weren't running trips for the second leg. But some of the boys still wanted to go. It was the September weekend, too, they could give it a good go for only a few days off.

Jim was one of those who had wanted to go. He had been on a few magic trips when he was younger but there had been no real opportunity for several years as Celtic had lost to East German and Polish teams early on. He had heard the talk of hiring mini-vans, and pooling resources, and realised he had found the niche he was looking for, the gap in the market, the filling of which would make him rich. He would get to the games for nothing, as an added bonus. Pure genius. He had gone to the toilet and made a few calculations. For once he had been grateful for the hard toilet paper. He went back and announced the terms on which he could offer both transport, and accommodation, and sealed his fate by accepting several deposits on the spot. He had enough left of his Wembley money to stake him, to the hire of the van, the sleeping bags and lilos, the removable stickers, and the business cards. He had done League away games before, but only as arrangements for friends. There were so many Supporters Clubs too, all offering subsidised travel, that it had been very hard to break in and show a profit. Europe was different, he would have a clear run there.

The trip to Luxemburg went well. He made £27 profit, but had got his own trip free, and seen the Bhoys win 6-1 away from home. He started planning for the next three rounds, on a bigger scale. The draw gave him Austria, Innsbruck, wherever that might be. The first leg was tightly balanced, 2-1 to the 'Tic. Interest was good, so he sold more tickets than he had intended. He knew he couldn't let people down and survive so he had to up his scale, and take on another driver. That was when he realised his first profit had not included charging for his own services. But he had still been on for a reasonable return until the journey back went wrong. They lost the game 3-0, and were out. That was the best bit. His bus broke down, just refused to go any further. That was when he discovered his insurance policy wasn't comprehensive. £15 more would have covered him but he had cut that corner. Most of the passengers took it well. It was a nice place to be marooned and the beer was good, but enough made it clear that they were due back at work on the Friday and he could stand the loss of wages. It was the first time in his life he had felt really alone. Standing in that Austrian garage, without a word of the language, trying to tell a man about what was wrong with his vehicle, when he had no clue himself other than it wouldn't go, and ever conscious that he had no money to pay for whatever it turned out to require. The driver had to eventually ask the passengers for a whip round, to let him get his bus back. His book entry when he finally got home, settled what he owed the passengers, and repaired the temporary repairs, ensured the first year would show a trading loss.

He had invested his savings to ensure that he would have property of his own for the next season, forward planning he had called it, but he had overlooked one little thing. For the first time since 1962, when he was only 7 years old, Celtic did not qualify for Europe. Another victim of the Stein generation and their assumptions of superiority. He could of course have offered the same services to Rangers supporters but that would have been against his religion. And potentially dangerous, given his known IRA sympathies. It was a pity financially, as the Bears did have a good season and three perfect journeys, to Turin, Eindhoven and Cologne. The best Jim could make of it was to sub-let his vehicles, to a less purist Catholic, who made more out of the three trips than Jim had even envisaged as possible. The next year was better, after a nervous start when he disappointed himself by chickening out of trying to get to Tirana despite some demand. It improved with a convey to the old home land Dundalk and then a memorable trip to Madrid, where Celtic did him proud despite narrowly losing on aggregate. Thereafter there were triumphs and disasters in equal proportion though he never learnt to treat each the same. Getting marooned in Rumania was the worst, just. He learnt a litany: heartache in Hungary, ruin in Rumania, triumph in Turin, except on the pitch, angst in Amsterdam, sangria in San Sebastian, anguish in Aahrus. There was the one he made a real killing on: the nostalgic return to Lisbon, then the nightmare in Nottingham; beer in Belgium and vice in Vienna, and the unforgettable night when more Celtic fans went to Old Trafford than had gone to the game at Parkhead. That was the most places he ever organised, the organisational and financial climax. It had gone without a hitch, for the first time ever, he brought back exactly the same number of people as he took, but since it wasn't exactly the same people he dismissed it as a mathematical fluke.

It had soon got to the point that it was expected of him, to organise these trips, on a cheap and cheerful basis. And he couldn't have not done so without considerable loss of face. The costs of the disasters tended to outweigh the steady but small profits accumulated on the successes, but it was just something he had to do. And it certainly meant he developed his legend. Every southside Celtic supporter had his tale of drama on a Morris continental trip.

He never had to advertise the service. He toured the right southside pubs, getting emotional Celtic supporters to make the gesture of booking a place by paying a deposit. His happy hour was 9-10pm, when hopes were highest and optimism and adventure combined with ale made his proposition seem irresistible. Those whose wives or sober selves regarded it as a less good idea learned to write off their deposits as a penance for their lack of faith. Every time he made more from those who didn't go than from those who did. It didn't make him unpopular, either. He had a good memory, and every time he would remind his punters that they had lost their deposit last time and should maybe be more cautious this time. They respected him for that concern, and it seemed to serve a useful social function, since the same people signed up again and again. A small price for a dream, Jim would say, to himself. Michael Lavery was the record holder, eighteen deposits and never once made it on board. It became a matter of honour for him and for others, to sign up and hope. Enough did make it, at least once, to justify the faith of the believers. And he had his regulars who did make it on every trip, and many more who made a few of them.

But it was the one he didn't do that convinced him he was not marked out for true greatness. He could have had it too, assured himself of at least a permanent footnote in the verbal history of Scottish Football, of an achievement that would still be talked about as long as enough Scotsmen had enough breath left to fill the bladder of the last pig. It had been the virility test of his generation. Argentina 1978. With Ann-Marie with the first due, on the day of the Final, there was no way he was going to pass as a soldier. No wonder proddies believed in family planning. But work, that would have been different. So he had looked at different ways of doing it, but couldn't solve the problem of getting his vehicles across the water. Then it had come to him, talking to some American sailors in a bar in Greenock. He always swore, even to himself, so it must have been true, that he had the submarine idea before anyone else. He had even realised that it would never even need to have to happen to make him rich. The myth would be enough. All he needed was to float the idea that Morris Travel was organising it, and he would be immortal. People would have paid good money for tickets, just to say to their grandchildren they had had them. He cursed his procrastination. 'I'll do it next week.' Those words had cost him dear. So had the bragging ones of the notion he had foolishly shared with Charlie

Spence on the Friday night. Charlie hadn't meant to scupper him, he was sure of that. He had just been boasting about how brilliant his pal was. To someone with a clearer killer instinct who had given the story to the Evening Times as his own scheme, the next day. Jim hadn't pursued it, because he didn't want to be thought a copycat: that wasn't classy behaviour. So he never launched his submarine and stayed marooned on the dry arid land of minor riches and small legend rather than sailing off into superstardom. And he learned the wrong lesson about the speed required for window jumping.

His attempts to develop a more consistent trade fluctuated from the mildly successful coup to the disastrous set-back. Sometimes the odd driving job for Charlie Spence had been his only source of income. Other times, he had employed drivers, and mechanics of his own, and only obliged Charlie for old times' sake. He did well in Spain in 1982, moving for the one and only time into the accommodation business as well as the transport. Charlie had tied up that end, but he did all right by Jim and they had cleared four figures each, even after Jim had had to write off two of his vehicles and fly the punters back on a plane that was even older than the better bus that died outside Malaga. Jim had his own integrity. It was a matter of honour for him that he got everyone back, except for the ones that chose to stay. He was amazed and envious, of the number of southside Celts over the years who had liked places enough to say, "see you later, lads.", and just decide to go no further. In the pub, he ran up the total in his mind. Nearly 20 in 12 years. Most of them had shown up again, anywhere from weeks to five years later. Not one ever admitted to regretting getting off his bus.

He had lost the chance to cash in on the World Cup in Italy. That still rankled with him. He blamed the fat Councillor for that, even though it wasn't his committee that had denied him his licence. It was his cronies though, and Jim would bet good money the fat wee bastard had put them up to it. Jim had never hated anyone in his life. He had always been popular, everyone's pal; but there had always been ill-will between him and McGuire. He could remember its origins, right from primary school when he had set the wee roly-poly up for ridicule on account of his shape and the wee man had taken it badly and given him a doing. They had clashed many times after that, although Jim had been careful never to make it physical again. Wee and fat maybe, but a hard bastard for all that. Verbally they were more equal. McGuire was harder, more intellectual, more cutting, but Jim had similar quickness of thought and a lighter turn of wit and abuse. At football they had always seemed to manage to be on opposite sides and kick lumps out of each other. The boys picking the sides knew it would be useless to have them on the same team, and anyway it was more fun the other way. The wee man may have been more skilful, and more solid, but Jim had had the advantages of speed and mobility. Politics had been the real battleground though. Jim had early on signed up with the Charlie Spence mob, while McGuire was always on the other side, with Frank Hunter at first then on his own.

The first time Charlie had tried to get a seat, against the Shopkeeper's widow, Jim had feared it would end up in murder. Every other tactic and inducement had been used and still McGuire had succeeded in defeating them. Hunter had done most of the work, although McGuire had been the hatchet man, but Jim never had the same problem with Frank. They weren't close, but they had been to games together, and had supped many pints together in common company, and would pass a civilised word, usually about football, whenever they met. Frank had been on several of his trips, but the wee man had always refused to consider it. Jim had taken his revenge all right, after the licence fiasco. Maybe he had gone a wee bit over the top, but it had been his livelihood that had been affected after all. Even so, he did feel a small measure of shame. It wasn't really his style to fight that dirty. He should have realised that it would be bound to hurt Christine too, and it wasn't really her fault her man was such an aggressive little bastard. He knew Ann-Marie wouldn't be proud of what he had done so he had never told her. Still, what was done was done, and maybe that could be the end of the matter. He certainly felt it was quits now on his side. He didn't think McGuire could realise it was him that had dished him, but one or two others did and he would likely find out sometime. Then Jim would have to watch out.

Jim had stayed in the Labour Party, to be of use to Charlie when required. Even now, with a safe seat elsewhere in the city, the man still pulled some strings locally. But Jim's heart had never really been in it after the Young Socialist days, and he put his emotional energy into Sein Fein, and Troops Out and supporting the Bhoys. He smiled at his memory of the one time when these strands had come together. What a laugh that had been. Jim had got to meet the Prime Minister, Sunny Jim. He had come to

Glasgow to address a rally in the Shopkeeper's constituency, and who had been put in charge of stewarding but Charlie Spence, who had promptly recruited all his lads from the Cavan Club, to protect the Prime Minister from the IRA. Jim had always wondered what Special Branch had been playing at, and whether they were looking for an own goal or not. He had heard the wild talk but had been very glad when it had come to nothing. The rally had gone like clockwork, and both he and Ann-Marie had been invited to meet the Prime Minister for a drink afterwards. They still had the photo on the mantelpiece. He was almost as proud of it as he was of the one of him with Sean Gilligan, the number two man from across the water, that he kept in the drawer.

He remembered the one strange time he and McGuire had been on the same side, when Charlie had finally made it as an MP. Right up to the end they had been unsure whether it was for real or whether they would be betrayed. They had relied on Frank Hunter being an honest man. Charlie certainly would never have made it without their help. McGuire and Hunter must really hate those Trots to do that. Jim realised that McGuire's assistance in that venture had been the beginning of the end for Jim. Charlie didn't have the same need or use for him in his new career. Jim had hoped to able to pick up some of pieces, and had been disappointed and hurt when Charlie had given most of it to others and left him very little. That had been the start of the bad times.

Still he had Ann-Marie to keep him warm, and the four girls. One after another they had appeared, every year of his married life until she had surprised him and Father Andrew by saying no more, and capping it all, she didn't care that none of them were boys. Until this season he had thought that meant that no child of his would play for Celtic, but the precedent was there now. And they did have Irish grandmothers. He loved his girls, all five of them, and knew he was the luckiest man alive. He had his final glass, a single, and walked home to do the hoovering, with his belief in Santa Claus intact.

So he made the phone call, as directed, prompt by habit. The number turned out to be the Elcho Bar, a pub he knew slightly but did not often frequent. He knew Gerry the barman, of course, and the man knew him. The barman didn't know Tommy Currie, but he confirmed there were a few strange faces in that night. So the message was shouted out, "phone call for Tommy Currie, Tommy Currie wanted on the phone. Is there a Tommy Currie in the night? Last call for Tommy Currie. No, sorry, Jim, it seems you're out of luck, son." The barman didn't know a Danny Finlay either, although he thought the name rang a bell. He described for Jim who was in that night. Willie Hastings and his brickie pals, Harry Muldoon and two or three others from St James' School, the Williams brothers and their cousin, Gerry the Union man and three of his mates, Liam Houghton and another lawyer, and some more names that meant something and nothing to Jim. There was also two lots of strangers, unusual for a pub like the Elcho with a regular trade. He had directed his shouts to them but there had not been a flicker, although they had heard all right. He could make the dead hear that one. Gerry told him he would issue a call for Tommy Currie every hour for the rest of the night and if he turned up tell him there had been a phone call for him, but not mention who.

Jim wasn't too concerned. He had held up his end of the arrangement. At the worst he would get to keep the £100. As long as there was no misunderstanding. He would not like the consequences of that, indeed not, so he rechecked the number for the 4th time, and against the directory. Yes, he had dialled the right number, and it was the Elcho number. Maybe only Finlay was there, in the terms of the letter that was all that was necessary, he could give the message. He was in his own pub by 9pm, catching up on lost time, and beginning to wonder if Santa really did exist after all, but he was still drinking the proof. He shared his fortune with his pals, to the tune of a wee goldie each, but kept the nature of his windfall to himself. None of them believed in anything but fairies, they watched enough of them every Saturday.

The second letter arrived on the Thursday morning, in a thicker envelope. He pocketed it unopened to study away from Ann-Marie. It was worth the wait. It contained 7 £100 notes, again definitely the genuine article. The letter was once more unheaded and unsigned. He recognised it as done on a wordprocessor. He had bought one himself, for his business, but never really learned to master it. He knew different typewriters left their individual trace but wasn't sure about PCWs, probably not.

Dear Jim,

I am very glad that you decided to co-operate, and join me in this venture. I want you to arrange the sole and exclusive use of 37 Brownlie Street, Top Flat, Left, from 10a.m. to 7p.m. on Saturday the 12th May. I am entertaining a group of colleagues from Aberdeen and wish to have a base in which to offer them pre and post match hospitality. I do not wish my name used. I leave it entirely to your discretion as to whether or not you use your own name. I do not wish any other premises, only that specific flat. I estimate that £500 should be sufficient to ensure the lease. I instruct you not to go below £300 even if the occupants appear willing to do so. However you may keep any difference between the figure you negotiate of £300 or more and £500. The remaining £200 is the next instalment of your fee. If you have to go above £500, I would be very surprised and disappointed, but I would still expect you to do so out of your own funds, and reimbursement would be provided to you. I want the full fee paid to the occupants in two instalments. Half immediately you make the arrangement, and the other half at 6pm on the night before the Final when you confirm the arrangements and obtain the keys. I wish the key to the back close gate as well as to the flat front door.

I need to know by 27th April that you have been successful in arranging the lease. If you have been successful be in Neesons Bar at 8pm on the 27th, when my colleague Mr Finlay will phone you. In the unlikely and unfortunate event that you are unsuccessful, be in the Albert Bar at the same time, and wait there until Mr Finlay contacts you and makes arrangements about the return of the money.

You will receive one more communication from me, with the final instalment of your fee and instructions on how to earn it, on the morning of the 11th of May.

I expect you to maintain absolute discretion about our business. Complete compliance with my instructions and requirements, should lead to further and more lucrative opportunities for you in the near future.

Jim relaxed considerably after reading the letter. His role would not land him in any trouble. He was already £100 up. He reckoned the flat could probably be obtained for between £200 and £250. Still, he would not be greedy, if the man wanted to pay £300, so be it. That would still leave him with a £200 bonus on top of his £200 fee. £500 with a promise of more to come, for a simple and legal operation. Santa was not only a gentleman, he must be a Catholic too. Jim didn't believe the business about entertaining Aberdeen supporters, but that was nothing to do with him. His bet would be a little drugs party, before the match, which would explain the secrecy. But he could not be done, even at the worst, for allowing his premises to be used, since they would never be his. The less he knew about it the better. He would do his bit and give it a wide berth.

Jim was never one for deferred gratification, and had given up procrastination, so that afternoon he did his homework. He sussed the outside first. He clocked the window, with its clear view over the pitch. But it was too small to allow a party to watch, it couldn't be that. It was certainly handy for the ground. One minute walk to touch the walls of the Temple. He walked up to the top of the stairs and read the names on the door. He wrote them down, then sat in his cabin and memorised them while waiting to see who came home. Four of them, all male. That meant probably students or young men. It also meant £75 per skull, just for a few hours rent of your living room. By 6 o'clock he had reckoned he had clocked them all in. Definitely students rather than real workers, although not university types. That was all right, they would sell their granny for less than £75.

He came back the next morning with the car rather than the lorry. He followed the three of them that came out together. Discreetly. He had done it once before, for Noel and the boys at the Club, in that terrible McCabe affair, when he had nearly got out his depth. That had been more serious, deadly serious. He still broke out in a sweat just thinking about it, but this was different, just a game. It wasn't a long journey. Down across Cathcart Road, up Bolton Drive, over the railway bridge and down into the back of Langside College. As he watched them disappear into the main building he decided he might as well go that evening. Get it done and his money earned. He dressed with care. Jim always felt that appearances told a lot about a man. He always strived to let his tell a tale of a smart man, a man with class and style but not ostentatious. He put on one of his managerial efficiency suits, pale blue, with a £48 Carswell shirt and a darker blue silk tie. Expensive leather shoes, freshly polished for the occasion. Although it was a mild night, he decided to carry his best coat, for effect. Ann-Marie smiled as she kissed him goodbye. She knew her Managing Director husband on the occasional outings he made. She was pleased to see him again, she had worried that he had lost his confidence and hibernated. He told her he would go onto the pub without coming back to change. He liked the boys to see him in his best working gear. It got him that little bit more respect. He was looking forward to coming back home too though, and the look on her face when he gave her the £150 and told her there was more where that had come from.

It was easier than stealing sweeties from weans. He had been kicked on the shin last time he had tried that. This time he was given a great deal of respect. With his charming personality it was no great challenge. He told them he was representing a group of Celtic supporters, who were looking for a base at which to congregate for the Cup Final. There would be six of them, no more. All they would want would be the use of the living room and the bathroom and kitchen. He checked there were no locks on the bedroom doors. It might be sex as well as, or even instead of drugs, but the boys didn't need to know that. The natural leader wanted to know the key answer. Four pairs of eyes looked at him greedily. He knew his penpal had taken the fun out of this for him with his bottom line. He started them off at £50 each and was dismayed to see their jaws drop in ecstasy. He was sure he could have swung the whole thing for a £100. Instead he had to commit the sacrilege of upping his opening offer despite their too apparent willingness to accept. Indeed he had to be quick to use the stunned but eager silence to reluctantly increase with a final "oh very well, £300 and not a penny more". He could tell they thought they had won the pools, particularly when he peeled out his wad of notes and paid them the first half in advance. It was the little touches of having it ready in piles of ones and fives that made him proud of his mastery of psychology. They would have given him a key then, but he insisted there was no need, nor for any written agreement. He could trust them. He would be back for the key, with the balance, the night before the game. None of them were intending to go to the game anyway. Jim despaired of the youth of today.

In the Club he felt pleased with himself. £500 already earned, and a wee bonus likely on top of that. He would be happy to be one of Santa's little helpers any time. The atmosphere in the club was happier than it had been for some time. Celtic getting to the final had saved the season, and offered up some grounds for hope. Jim felt ashamed of the treacherous thoughts he had harboured since it had become obvious the Cup was the only route left into Europe next season. He had actually found himself wishing that Celtic would lose in the final, so he would not have to resuscitate the European Division of Morris Sporting Travel and Transport. Blasphemy indeed, but that was how bad he had got to, in his first mid-life crisis. His new job brought with it a more optimistic frame of mind, and he began a tentative plan or two for obtaining the vehicles. He might be able to get his licence back by then. In the Club, he got a few offers of deposits, based on the new-found confidence. He declined, but assured them all he would be back in business in time, if they won. There was some excited talk in the Club of who might be coming over, from the firm, now the Bhoys were definitely in the Final. Some big names were mentioned, top rankers.

"Jim, you're wanted on the telephone, some Irishman." The barman in Neesons was no softer spoken than his counterpart in the Elcho. The man said one word only. "Well?" Jim confirmed that the arrangements were made, and there were no problems. He tried to draw out the other person, get them to speak but they didn't fall for it and had already hung up. The barman confirmed the caller had a distinct Irish accent rather than a Glasgow Irish one.

He got one final letter, the morning before the Final. It contained 5 more £20 notes. Automatically he checked them but they were all kosher.

Dear Jim,

Thank you for the efforts you have made on my behalf. I am grateful to you for the efficient way that you have carried out my exact instructions. There are two more actions I require of you in order to earn the money I have given you. Once you have read this letter, and absorbed fully the instructions in it, I wish you to destroy the letter and envelope, and any of the previous ones of which you have not yet have disposed.

Pick up the keys at 6pm on the 11th and pay over the remainder of the fee. Reinforce that part of the terms of the lease is that there is exclusive use. Under no circumstances must they return to the premises between the agreed hours, no matter what they have forgotten. Remind them also that they are likely to receive a visit from the police, most likely on the Friday evening but possibly early on the Saturday morning. They will be asked who is likely to be in their flat for the period of the final. Instruct them to reply no-one other than themselves, and likely not even that. Emphasise those instructions with an additional £40 bonus. If all the arrangements work out to plan, go from the flat to the Cavan Club and remain there till at least 9 pm. If there is any problem, be in Neeson's Bar for the same period.

On the 12th, I wish you to visit the premises at precisely 10:30am, go inside, satisfy yourself that they are empty, close every door and leave the keys on the top rim of the Storm Door mantel. You should then go to the Cavan Club for 11am. If all arrangements have gone to plan, wear a Celtic rosette on your right lapel. If there is any snag, wear it on your left lapel. If necessary, you will be contacted there by telephone. In either event, at exactly 1pm, leave the Cavan Club and walk round to the Victoria Bar, where the barman will have an envelope for you that will contain a final bonus. Flush the envelope down the toilet. That will be the last act under our contract.

If I am satisfied that you have carried out my instructions exactly as requested, and matters proceed as I intend, then there may be one additional bonus for you. An all expenses paid holiday for four in an exclusive establishment. I would thank you again for all your co-operation. It is very important to me that my venture goes exactly as I have planned it, and I will reward you well for your role in achieving that. I would stress the importance of carrying out my full instructions to the letter.

Jim wondered again who his correspondent might be. He had made a few discreet, at least he hoped they were, enquiries but there was no word out about any special parties before or after the game. Maybe it was Aberdonians after all. Those mean bastards would keep tight-lipped. Maybe he should check his farmer contacts to find out who had been asked to provide the live sheep.

CHAPTER SIXTEEN - BARCELONA

Frank Hunter continued to spend most of each day in the Mitchell Library. Only he substituted work on his new project for further effort on his book. He read about many different things. He read everything the Mitchell had on guns, rifles and the art of sniping. He read all about terrorism, and the political use of violence. He became an expert in Arendt, and a fierce and dismissive critic of Wilkinson. He found out many useful and interesting things but none which impinged on his determination to fulfil his destiny.

One of his first major decisions to make was between Avis and Hertz. As usual he settled for second best. He phoned up on the Wednesday and booked a Maestro for a week, to be collected in Manchester on the Thursday, and returned to the depot in Glasgow on the following Thursday. He used his own name, again on balance it seemed the safer and simpler way. He took the shuttle to Manchester on the Thursday morning and picked the car up from the airport. A ten minute drive took him to the Ringway Air Park in Cheadle Hume where he booked his place from 6a.m. on Saturday. After doing his shopping, he booked into a small hotel near the airport and spent the evening practising not drinking. At 1am precisely he left the hotel and set off on his round trip to Glasgow. He was back in the hotel shower by 7am, and at 9:15 caught the morning flight back to Glasgow. He put in two hours at the Mitchell then went home to pack his bags for Barcelona and have a quick sleep. He was looking forward to the trip, and the chance to say his farewells to Stevie, and to Isabella, Eloisa, Jean, Jose-Luis and Maria. There were five of them going, Danny Campbell, Gerry Robertson and Andy Rogers, as well as Peter McColl and himself. Only Peter's Mercedes was large enough to take them all comfortably. It had been agreed that he would pick them up at the Victoria at 5p.m. and they should be in their hotel in Manchester for 8ish, the way Peter drove.

Frank enjoyed the journey down. The chat was good, full of reminiscences of previous SAD excursions, of games seen and arguments had. They were all excited about seeing Barcelona again. To stroll down the Ramblas, to have another of those fabulous 4 hour meals they specialised in, then the singing, the sad haunting singing, and the excited talk about football and politics, all night long. Then they would spoil it all by going to the game. But even that might be tolerable. Second division fare, but the Premier League had been no great shakes this season. They were all conscious that it might be the last chance they would get to see the man himself in action. They had all met him. Danny knew him first, from when he was dropped by Clyde and would stand in front of the Stand and talk to the few supporters. Frank and Gerry had met him several times through the Scottish Professional Footballers Association. The whole group had met him once on one of their trips to Barcelona. They had deliberated then decided not to give him the SAD news. He might have mis-interpreted it as piss-taking rather than homage, he was known to be a sensitive and touchy soul. So they had just said they all happened to be there on holiday, visiting friends and were looking forward to watching Barcelona. Only Danny said it would be good to see him play again. It is better in life to keep a healthy distance from heroes.

Frank knew that his major problem that evening was how to stay sober enough to drive to Glasgow and back through the night, and remain alert enough to do his business. It would look very odd if he did not drink at all, on the other hand he could not afford the risks in having too much. He reckoned that over the evening he could afford to have three pints, maximum. The rest would be consuming 6 to 8 pints or more. He solved the problem by inventing a bladder complaint that had him going to the cludgie regularly, often with glass in hand, ready to tip it down the loo. He also made a point of moving seats a lot. No-one seemed to notice. Around midnight after 8 pints bought, and less than three consumed, he pleaded tiredness and upset stomach and went off to bed early. He got a slagging but he got away. Up in his room, he poured several cups of the Hotel coffee inside himself and took three cold showers over the next hour. By the third one, he was ready for what he wanted to do. As the organiser he had arranged that they would all get single rooms this time. They could all afford it these days, even Danny. Andy and Danny had started to moan, so he had offered them the opportunity to be different and sleep together, but they had declined. He changed into his track-suit and trainers. Nike, to be sure. Apart from the comfort, if anybody came looking for him early in the morning, he had to be out for a run. They were used to him doing that on his travels. He put the Do Not Disturb sign on his door, switched out the lights and slipped out the Hotel as silently as he could manage. He walked in 3 minutes to the car park where he had left the car after being reassured it had 24 hour access.

He headed along the M62, then the M61, onto the M60 until it joined up with the main M6 road to Glasgow. It was almost totally deserted and he made even better time than on his trial run the night before when he was not absolutely sure about the tangle of roads. His dummy run meant he did not panic when he hit the temporary roadworks on the M61, he knew he would be clear in a few minutes and that it was the only such problem. He found no difficulty in filling his head on the run. He went over 100 times what he had had to do when he got to Baillieston. He knew this was a turning point which would take him into new territory of criminal activity. He repeated his rationalisations as to why it was permissible to steal from a friend. He definitely did not like that bit. But he came back to the same conclusion, if he was not able to steal a gun then there was no way he was going to be able to fire one. He arrived in Glasgow at 3:38am, 7 minutes ahead of his schedule. He cut the lights and ran the car gently into Peter's drive. There were no neighbours to see anyway. He used the seven minutes to blank out his registration plates with masking tape. He checked he had all he required. Brick, gloves, masking tape, screwdrivers, bag, carpet, torch. He assembled them in order. At 3:50 he walked round to the back of the house. He had worked out the smallest, most sensible window to enter, one of the few not double-glazed. The trick with the masking tape worked even better than in his practices. The glass broke into large pieces but did not fall. He removed the segments one by one until he was able to get his hand in and unlock the window locks. He knew that with that make, any key unlocked any lock, so he had bought himself a set from the same store Peter had used.

It took him less than five minutes to get inside the house, although it seemed far longer. He was amazed at how hard his heart was pounding. He knew he wasn't cut out for this business. He dreaded being caught with a fear far greater than any he had ever known before. All it would need would be a nosy neighbour, or a passing police car. Unlikely, but his fantasies were flowing. He discovered something else too, of interest to him with his anal obsessions. The folk tales of burglars shitting in peoples homes as a form of desecration and humiliation. Not true, sheer bloody fear and terror. He wondered if they could do DNA tests on toleys. Probably, so he kept it to himself. He kept repeating to himself the statistics he knew, that Peter had told him. 85% of Glasgow housebreakings are never solved and of the 15%, 10 of them are fitted onto the 5% genuinely caught. Most of them are young kids. An intelligent adult like him would never get caught, unless he were very, very unlucky.

Once in, he made right for the appropriate study. He checked the wall- screws on the cabinet. As he had thought, it might be the most secure device in itself, but its level of attachment to the wall was not particularly sophisticated. It only took him a few moments to separate the cabinet from the wall. He laid it on the floor then went to the desk where he had seen Peter hide the keys. He smiled wryly as he told himself this was the key moment. If they were elsewhere, his whole strategy was in trouble. But fate remained on his side, there they were, taped onto the underside just where he had seen them go. He extricated them and unlocked the cabinet, checking it would not automatically re-lock on closing. He blocked the lock with tape just to be on the safe side. He returned the keys exactly where he had found them. He then opened the desk drawer and took ammunition for the Parker Hale and the shotgun. After a moment's hesitation he also took some for the Mauser. He was annoyed with himself for that as he had repeatedly stressed the absolute necessity for not departing from his master-plan in the slightest detail, but it was done and he couldn't see any damage. He wrapped the cabinet in his blanket and carried it to the entry window. Made of steel plate, at over four foot long and more than a foot wide and deep, it was not light and it proved harder than he thought to move on his own. He swung his bag out first, then lowered the cabinet down, and finally let himself out. He shut the window and adjusted the tape. Even a nosy neighbour might think only that Peter had cracked the window and repaired it himself.

He put the cabinet and the bag in the boot of the car. Then and only then he checked his watch. It was 4:11a.m. Four minutes ahead of schedule. He was glad he had learned to live without sleep. Sometimes over the last year that had been a decidedly mixed blessing, given the thoughts and discussions he tended to have on the night-shift. But now it was a boon. He didn't feel tired. There was a quiet but intense elation. He felt good with the adrenaline pumping through his veins. It was less intense than the feeling of scoring a goal, more like the satisfaction of a good pass. As soon as he cleared Baillieston and hit the motorway, he knew he was clear and away. As long as no-one looked in his boot, there was nothing to tie him into the robbery, which wouldn't be discovered until Monday anyway. Peter would find out early on

262

Monday morning when he got home after dropping the others off. Frank would have the perfect alibi, not that he would even be asked to provide one. He drove down the dull roads, A74, M74, M6, M60, M61, M62. His elation subsided but was replaced with quiet satisfaction. He knew his enterprise was definitely for real. He spent the journey rehearsing the remaining stages, satisfied that the greatest difficulty was now behind him. He determined to proceed with his plans to obtain the Sauer, despite the success of this venture. There would be a role for it in his master plan. He didn't return straight to the Airport. This time he took the car onto the M63 to Cheadle Hume, to the Ringway AirPark, where he had made a booking the previous day. He gave his false name, and a real flight different from his own but leaving Saturday morning and returning Tuesday morning. He knew that this was where he was most vulnerable, if the car was stolen or anyone looked into the boot, but he had been assured earlier by the firm that neither ever happened, and they were absolutely secure, with lockfast premises and close-circuit cameras. Still, he knew he would be anxious on his return was his thought as they transported him to the airport in their courtesy coach, as they had promised him, getting him there in under 10 minutes from his arrival at their premises.

It was 7:13am when they dropped him at the Airport terminal. He jogged vigorously to the Hotel to work up a sweat and was in his hotel room by 7:28am, two minutes ahead of schedule. He took the sign off his door and had a leisurely shower. He was feeling rather pleased with himself, at the smoothness and success of his mission. By 8 o'clock he had been told to eff off by each of the four others in turn and went down to breakfast on his own. Each one finally arrived down looking worse than the one before. No doubt about it, he was the brightest and most alert of the bunch. The benefits of a good night's sleep, he assured them. They were in Barcelona by 12:22pm, and were met at the airport by Isabella and Jose-Luis.

It was a truly wonderful couple of days. Frank was nicer than normal to Peter, and they all enjoyed themselves thoroughly. After the 2 hour lunch, Frank opted out of the siesta and wandered off on his own into the centre of Barcelona. He had seen many cities, and liked them all, but Barcelona was the one that came closest to replacing Glasgow in his heart. It was very similar, maybe a little less cultured, but a little more clean, and warmer, the people as well as the climate. He knew the city well enough to complete the route in his head without a map or guidebook. He knew it was a farewell tour he was making, but he was happy, at peace. He started from the waterfront, the harbour he loved. He amazed himself again at the smallness of the Santa Maria, the bravery of the men who had voyaged so far in so little a craft. He said his quiet farewell to big Christopher. He had used him in the past as a substitute for his friend Willie but this time it was just a pat and a nod. He wandered up the central promenade of the Ramblas, overcome as always by the sheer excitement and bustle of it all. In his heart he knew Argyle Street and Sauchiehall Street weren't in the same league. He bought one Argentinean football magazine and two Spanish ones, two cups of coffee and a beer before he was clear. He had resisted the temptation to wander into the Gothic Quarter to his right. He was going to his own cathedral. He lingered in the Placa Catalunya, paying his homage to the Goddess. Talking to statues was the one area of his emotional life when he revealed more of himself to men than women. The cold look on her face reminded him too much of Elaine post-1984 for comfort, and he preferred Desconsol in the Cuitadella though not for conversation.

But he didn't have time for that detour so he moved on up the Passeig de Gracia with its beautiful street lamps. He paused for a moment to take in the Casa Mila, La Pedrera, almost as beautiful as some of the Victorian Glasgow buildings he had learned only recently to appreciate on his walks from the Mitchell. He turned left onto the Avinguda Diagonal and lapsed into his own thoughts and memories as he neared his destination. Along the Travessera de les Corts, and there it was before him, the Nou Camp, the most magnificent stadium he had ever seen. Truly a temple of the gods. Frank had never liked churches, they made him uncomfortable, he fretted about the waste of bricks. But football stadiums met the same needs in him that Cathedrals seemed to in others. And this was the finest. As well as the games he had been to there, he had been round it several times on non-match days. They had a museum to the club, a celebration of their history that was wonderful to behold. He went round the tour for a further and last time. He was amused and pleased to see the video of Dundee United beating them in the Nou Camp. He enjoyed the carving on the toilet wall, Whitfield Welfare were here, 2-1 ya bass. Coming out the museum into the directors box with its view of the Stadium was always a special moment. Frank knew now that he would not have his ashes scattered over Parkhead, or Hampden. Maybe it was as well, neither might be there in a further ten years. He would like to think his soul would reside here though, or the other place he had never seen, the big one, the Maracana in Rio. He had a picture postcard of that he held dear and had often promised himself a trip there one day. A sadness descended on him at the realisation he might never make that now. He took a last look at the panorama below him, and saw once again Stevie score into the far right hand goal. He closed his eyes as the ball hit the back of the net, kissed the pillar and walked out leaving his soul behind to wander forever in bliss in the finest setting for the finest game in the world.

Their friends entertained them in splendid fashion, an orgy of food, drink and animated conversation. Frank did little talking but listened as Danny argued the toss about the bits of the Welfare State Catalonia should emulate. He listened as Andy compared notes on the education of children. As Gerry debated the role of organised labour in modern society. As Peter compared the Scottish legal system more favourably with the Spanish than the English. Their hosts were eager to compare notes, and advance their own notions, of nationalism, of socialism, of welfare. They teased their guests about being ruled by the Prime Minister and argued that Catalonia was already free-er than Scotland, and would remain that way. It was only when the conversation returned, as it always did, to football, that Frank felt he could enter as an equal. Trips like this always reminded him of the wrongness of the Scottish myth that they are the most football-mad people in the world. The average Catalan, and almost all Italians took a much more serious and intense interest in football than most Scots. Frank loved to talk to people who cared about more than the Old Firm, who loved the game for itself and took an intelligent interest beyond their own parish. They had a fabulous argument about whether Koeman or Rijkaard was the best sweeper in the world, or the best midfielder, or the best goalscorer. Then the singing began. Sad soulful songs that fitted Frank's mood although the others thought they were just songs. He did go to bed happy though. He was happy enough that in the bed provided by Isabella he toyed with the notion of emigration rather than death. If he could get clean away, undetected, and came here, he might be able to carve out a new life for himself in this city where politics and football truly were the founts of life. But he knew it was an idle dream, for he would bring with him the one thing he needed to escape from, the essence that was himself. The wine must have been very good for half-asleep he had another fantasy that had half-haunted his mind for several days. He would go to Rio, with his guns, and become a hitman, hiring himself out between football seasons. The ludicrousness of that notion amused even him. He knew he was temperamentally unsuited to the notion and trade of hurting people. It was not part of his moral code.

The football the next day was good. They had spent the morning in the city with their hosts, had a light lunch, then gone out to the Sarria Stadium. The Nou Camp it wasn't, nor even Ibrox but it had atmosphere, and a good crowd, and two teams that wanted to win. Two years before Espanol had thrown away the UEFA Cup after winning the first leg of the Final 3-0. The shock and heartache had been so great they were relegated the following season, but they were now fighting desperately to return to the top. The man they had come to see did not let them down. Stevie Archibald had turned it on, almost as if he somehow sensed that his devotees were on a last trip to the shrine in motion. He earned himself a £5,000 bonus, laid on another, missed the obligatory sitter or three and was generally the star man in his team's 3-1 win which put them on course for the promotion they so desired. The SAD conclusion was that he could still do a job for them in Italy. Only Peter McColl dissented and claimed it was a ludicrous notion, although no worse than some that seemed likely to happen. Frank at least knew that he had seen the slim hips for the last time, seen his last easy miss and his last magic goal. No more SAD days left for him. It was, SAD, one of the ideas he never regretted having. If only that header had gone in at the European Cup Final in 1986, it would have been perfect. Still, the boy had done not bad, for a wee lad from Clyde.

They had flown back to Manchester, subdued but satisfied and driven back through the early hours of Monday morning to Glasgow. Frank sat up front and talked to Peter while the other three slept on a drive home which was much quieter than the trip down. Peter dropped them all off at their front doors and made his way back to his violated premises, content with his weekend.

Tuesday morning Frank was off on his travels again. He told Joyce on the Monday night that he felt a few days in the Lake District on his own would help him sort his head out. He seemed much more stable and she was pleased he was taking an initiative. He took a taxi to the airport and caught the morning shuttle to Manchester. He was getting to feel quite cosmopolitan with all this travel. He had with him a case packed with all the necessities he had in mind for the activities he was hoping to pursue. He arrived at Manchester Airport in good time and settled down in the lounge to await the arrival of the plane he had indicated he would be on. Once it was checked in, he telephoned the number at the AirPark and let them know he was back. Within 20 minutes their minibus had him back at their premises. The car was still there. He had a real fear of being jumped on by Special Branch but everything went to plan. He paid his £18, a very good investment, and he was soon on his way back towards Scotland. No-one tried to stop him and no-one appeared to follow him. He drove at a more leisurely pace to the M6, headed up north but turned off the motorway at Keswick and meandered into the Lake District. He had made a booking at a hotel in Hawkshead where he had once spent a blissful weekend with Elaine. He denied to himself the obvious truth that that had as much to do with his choice of venue as its proximity to Grizedale Forest. It was only when he was right in the middle of nowhere did he allow himself the mental comfort of opening the boot. He had briefly checked at Ringway that his sellotaped hair was still in place, but they could have been crafty and replaced it. Everything was exactly as he had left it, the blanket, the case, the bag of gear, the rests. No sign that the cabinet had been opened and shut again. It was a much more relaxed man who drove into Hawkshead and parked as near as he could to the Queens Head. He didn't know why he had used a false name when he had phoned to book the room, and for a horrible minute he couldn't remember who he had said he would be. Then he remembered his clue. There's only one King Billy, that's me, Mr McNeill.

He had asked for a double room. Fortunately or not, they gave him a different one from the one he and Elaine had used. He spent the entire afternoon and early evening driving and walking through the Forest at Grizedale, with his ruler and protractor, until he found exactly what he wanted, where he wanted it and how he wanted it. Satisfied that he had enough possibilities he drove back to Hawkshead and had a quiet evening. Two pints in the Red Lion, two pints in the Kings Arms. Then back to the Queens Head for a further two, all the while quietly and happily reading his book. Still slightly paranoid he took great care to avoid letting anyone see what he was reading, just in case. He had read it before, and seen the film. The visual image of the pumpkin disintegrating had lingered with him long after the rest had gone. He had turned to the book again, to see if there were anything he could learn in a technical sense, given his new role. There are not exactly many handbooks for would-be assassins around. He rolled the word around his tongue, and lengthened it. It was an ugly word. but then it was an ugly deed. He hated crossword puzzles and seldom tried them, but he had been unduly pleased by one he had tried and got. 15 Across. The likely outcome when two fools rule a land (13).

Did it seem the likely outcome when one mad lady ruled a nation that had rejected her? The book didn't really offer much practical help or hope. After all, if a professional expert like that failed in the end, what chance would a first-time amateur have, especially one who had always doubted if he were capable of killing, even in a war.

He slept fitfully once the book was finished by 4a.m., with one ear on his car boot which was parked close to the window. The next morning he drove off in the opposite direction, found solitude and isolation and played with his empty gun. He got to know it intimately, in various states of undress, until he could strip it cleanly and reassemble with his eyes closed. All his homework at the Mitchell came into play then. He learned to understand the corny line about a gun becoming an extension of a person. It was a beautiful piece of machinery, stylish but not elaborate. Classic simplicity and great efficiency. He would have preferred one of the camouflage fibreglass stocks, but Peter, being a classy fellow, had gone for the walnut. It was a 7.62mm x 51mm calibre bolt-action rifle. He was surprised by the weight, with the bipods it was about a stone all told. He was glad he wasn't going to have to run away carrying it. The sights were something different, a complex work of wondrous majesty, a marvel of skilled engineering. He replaced the good ones Peter had for the gun with a better pair, the best, Schmidt & Bender 6x42 which he had purchased in Manchester along with a Viane sound modifier, once he had been persuaded that it would not affect the accuracy in the slightest. And the best sights mounting system, Apel rings. There had been no problem about ordering and collecting these extras, no certificate was required for them, only money. The sights were better than any binoculars he had ever seen, he loved the sensation of setting them on a target.

He went back to Hawkshead for his lunch. He deliberately had two pints, the least he reckoned he would be able to get away with on Cup Final day. He might as well simulate the exact conditions under which he would be performing. And it was good beer, Castle Eden. Over the next two afternoons he used his four selected sites, two a day because he didn't wish to return. He needed to be able to do it from the car so he concentrated on that but also simulated from a bathroom window and standing free, for comparison purposes. He folded the front passenger seat right down. He constructed a set of rests, that complemented the Parker-Hale bipods. They fitted in the back seat and over the front one, and allowed the gun to rest pointing out the back window at the angle required. He set the pictures up on trees. He did not use pictures of the Prime Minister, in case he was disturbed and had to leave in a hurry. He didn't want to run the slightest risk of raising an alert. So he used instead pictures of Graeme Souness that he had bought, £20 for a dozen, from the Rangers shop after making sure no-one saw him enter. The Shop had not regarded it as an unusual request. It was Frank's idea of a joke. He liked and admired the man, as a player and a manager. Hard but unfair, with his own kind of integrity. It was an appropriate choice given he was Scotland's most successful exponent of the Prime Minister's philosophy. And if he were discovered, it would be within the acceptable Glasgow tradition of eccentric tribal behaviour.

He wasn't caught. He wasn't even disturbed and never saw another soul either day. He learned to master several arts. The tinting of his windows, the erection of his rests, the placing of the gun, the setting of the sights, the holding of the breath, and the squeeze of the trigger. And the reverse sequence at speed. Then it came time to try it with the rifle loaded. He felt a real sense of fear grip him. He did not know what to expect, in terms of noise or recoil, or emotional block. He knew that he needed a very high degree of accuracy to allow him to continue with the project. He had already promised himself that he would not proceed if he could not guarantee hitting the target. Even a 1% error was three yards. That could kill a few other people, especially the Lord Provost who was likely to be sitting beside the Prime Minister. He knew her through the Labour Party. There was no way a gentleman like him was going to risk killing a woman.

He had read much about ammunition, but he need not have bothered. It only helped confirm that Peter had obtained the best possible, hand-loaded 168 grain HPBT Match bullets, with a muzzle velocity of 2710fps. He had obviously underestimated the seriousness of Peter's commitment to his new love. The first shot was surprisingly quiet, the recoil almost unnoticeable. He wasn't even sure he would need the ear-muffs. He pulled the binoculars into focus on the tree. Graeme was still smiling that fixed hard grin of his but his Rangers crest was split, right where his heart was rumoured to be. He did six shots in all, from the elevation of 25%. What a cluster. Not one missed the crest. The variable wind seemed to make no difference. Paddy would have been proud of him, only one would have missed the heart, and that only by a fraction. The gun truly did seem incapable of missing. He realised it was the gun when he tried it without the bipods and rest, hand-held. He did all right, hit him most times but the margin of error was unacceptably high. He improved with practice but it would take too long for even a natural like him to acquire enough proficiency on his own to guarantee doing as well as he needed to do. He went back to the rest and the results improved dramatically again. He did three more, one to the heart and one to each elbow, all were near perfect. He had even better results with the shorter range and lower elevation. He felt a sense of elation greater than any he had known since he was scoring goals regularly. This enterprise was not only possible, it would succeed. He went to another part of the woods to clean his gun before returning to the hotel.

The next afternoon he replicated the performance, but from different sites. He also replicated the results. In the interests of scientific experiment he had gone without a pint at lunchtime but it had no adverse effect on his performance, nor a beneficial one. By the time he finished the second session he was fairly certain that he would be able to guarantee hitting the target with the first shot with fatal results. There would be no time or need for a second shot, it would just increase the risk to himself and others. He also shot two bottles to death with the shotgun. One from ten yards, and the other from ten inches which proved to be a rather stupid thing to do. He started a collection of empty bullet shells, including two kept in vacuum-packed conditions.

He enjoyed his wee holiday in Hawkshead. Apart from two days in Arran with Joyce in November, it was the first real holiday he had had for almost two years. And he knew it would be his last, so he enjoyed it, once his work was done. There was a quiet peace about the place that soothed him. And a pleasant ordinariness. There was no sense of tension or aggression in any of the three pubs he frequented, just good beer and good food. He realised he had no problem at all with English people, other than their choice of leader.

The major choice he had to make at the end of his trip was about a balance of anxieties, to do with where he should plant the

270

guns. To use his own place ran several risks, his house could be broken into, Joyce could stumble over them, or the police could tie him into the McGoldrick business and turn up with a search warrant. Against that, if he stored them elsewhere, in Left Luggage or whatever, he would have constant insecurity about whether they were still there, or worse were still there but had been discovered and were being watched to see who would pick them up. He made the decision driving back up the A74. He decided he could live better with the insecurities of the known and resolved to hide them well in the attic of his own flat. Joyce nor normal burglars would never look there and if it got to the point that the police were taking out search warrants on him, then he might have to revise his plans anyway. He drove the rented Maestro back to his own flat, and moved all his gear including the gun cabinet in its blanket, up into his flat. No-one seemed to notice. He didn't have particularly inquisitive neighbours. Now if it had still been the Battlefield flat, Mrs Callaghan would have been able to give the Court sworn statements about the colour of the car, the fabric of the blanket, what he was wearing, the exact times of arrival and departure, the weather conditions and what he had for breakfast. He put the guns securely away in the attic and nailed them in. He knew he would not need to look at them again until he would have to use them, for real. He returned the car to the Avis depot in North Street and walked back across the bridge and up Victoria Road for a well-deserved pint in the Victoria Bar to catch up on all the news.

He did get a visit from the police, early one morning. He had expected that they would become more rigorous, in the light of the information about a potential extortionist. Detective Sergeant Tolmie and Detective Constable Rowan were his visitors. "Good Morning, sir. We are conducting an investigation, routine in the circumstances, around the drowning and death of Mr Robin McGoldrick." Pause. "We noticed from his school diary that you had appointments with him twice in the week prior to his death. Is that in fact correct, sir?" He was impressed with the politeness and respect shown to an unemployed labourer. "Yes, Sergeant, I was at his office on the Tuesday, and then again on the Friday." "Would you mind telling us why, sir." "Certainly. Some friends of mine in the G&M branch that covers St Anne's told me there was a vacancy coming up for Assistant Janitor in the school, and that McGoldrick preferred to fill these things quickly, without advertising. So I phoned and asked to see him, and he agreed to see me on the Tuesday. I asked him about the job, he said he would think about it, and give me an answer on the Friday." He paused, to see what would happen. "Go on, sir." "I went back on the Friday and he said he had considered the matter and I could have the job. He said I would hear officially in the next week or two. You can imagine how I felt when I heard he'd drowned. Jobs that good don't come that easily, you know." "Did anyone else at the school know he had offered it to you?" "I don't know if he told anyone, I had hoped he did. I certainly told Mrs Little, his secretary, when I came out on the Friday, but that's about all." He hoped he was getting the tone right, flat but not pathetic.

"How well did you know Mr McGoldrick, and what made you think he might offer you a job."

"Well, he was my old Heady, you know. I was the captain of the School football team that won the Scottish Schools Cup in his first full year as Headmaster. Apart from that I only knew him vaguely through local politics. I would bump into him at meetings an' that. Not that we spoke to each other. We were on different sides, you know. He knew my mother better, though. They were on various church committees and things. She died last June." The sadness in his voice was not part of the act. "He came to the funeral, with his wife. He said, I know everybody always does anyway but, he said that if there were ever anything he could do, just to let him know. Frankly, when I heard about the job, I thought I would try and take him up on that." He deliberately sounded a little apologetic about that. "I've been unemployed since the LDT closed last June, you know."

"What sort of mood did he seem to be in? Did you notice any difference between Tuesday and Friday?" "No, not really. On the Tuesday, he was your typical big Headie, I'm in charge, Its up to me kinda thing, you know. He made one or two comments about how he'd never had any industrial relations problems in his school, hinting that he feared I might contaminate his staff with union militancy. I didn't really think I had much chance. But then he talked of my mother, and what a good woman she had been. Then he had dismissed me, as if I was still one of his pupils, and told me to report to him again on the Friday. It was a bit eerie, as if I was back at school again, subject to all that discipline shit, know what I mean."

There was no response other than silence, so he went on. "On the Friday, he seemed more relaxed. Although he did enjoy playing the white man. He told me he had decided to offer me the job, but he stressed it was on a probationary period. Just to make sure I didn't immediately bring them all out on strike." He laughed wryly. "I've never led a strike in my life. I even told him that, I'm sorry to say. No, he seemed okay to me. Didn't appear to be a man with major problems, or one about to do himself in. I was quite taken aback when I heard about the accident on the Monday. Then of course I read the Sun on the Friday. Quite a bombshell that. I suppose he must have known the paper had the story, eh?" They seemed to regard it as a rhetorical question, so he continued. "Some story too, eh? He didn't seem the type, but obviously you can never tell. I've been belted by that belt, you know. Old MacDonald had it before him. Aye, many's the time, I felt that thing on my hands." Sergeant Tolmie didn't seem interested in his reminiscences, and moved the interview on, to more dangerous territory. "Have you ever had any contact with a Margaret Beattie?" "Bend-over Beattie, you mean, her that was in the paper. A right little belter that one, eh. No, chance would be a fine thing though, eh. A bit out of my financial league, that one, I think. No Sergeant, I've never met anyone called Margaret Beattie, I'm afraid to say."

"Bye the way, have you done anything about seeing if the job is still available?" That was one he'd anticipated they would ask, what they call pursuing the logic of claimed motivation, so he had the right answer ready. "Yes, I phoned up the Deputy Headmaster, but he said he knew nothing about it, and the job would be advertised in the normal way in due course, and that I should apply for it then along with everyone else. I don't reckon I've got any chance under those circumstances, I'm afraid." The interview fizzled out in general chat. The constable was a supporter of the wee Rangers as a boy, and had seen Frank play in the Juniors several times. The Sergeant had a couple of friends who had been in LDT, and he expressed some sympathy at its closure and its effects. Frank knew the friends vaguely and asked if they had been any more successful than him in getting another job. One had moved to England, to a poorer job, the other was still unemployed, and struggling. Frank realised that underneath the chat, the sergeant was fishing for something he knew was down there, so he put what he thought was wanted on the hook. He told them how hard he had taken it himself, how he'd virtually had a bit of a breakdown and even spent a couple of weeks in Kamesthorn, but he was a lot better now and desperate to get a job and get back to work.

They seemed satisfied and thanked him for his co-operation. He assessed it afterwards and was less than totally satisfied. It had gone more or less as his "A" script had anticipated, on the assumptions that McGoldrick hadn't fingered him, nor had Julie. But there was always the possibility they were playing it smart, the bastards, and letting him hang himself. He hadn't been under oath, or asked to sign a statement, but he had failed to tell the truth. Still if it were acceptable for the Prime Minister's Cabinet Secretary to be economical with the truth, then it would be all right for the Prime Minister's hunter to use the same technique. He loved that phrase. He knew that it didn't mean telling lies, as public mythology now had it, but it meant telling only portions of the truth as known. If they did come back at him, he would have to change his tack, and use his tape to defend himself. He was fairly certain McGoldrick hadn't left any evidence of the true nature of their discourse. It would be inconsistent with an attempt to sell the notion of an accident. But he would be vulnerable if Julie cracked. He knew she would be subjected to some strong interrogation and pressure. McGoldrick's friends would want some blood, he was sure of that. She had a strong vested interest herself in not revealing anything about him. Without that link, there could be no charge of conspiracy to defraud. She was a tough lady and he trusted her. She would remain cool under pressure, he was certain of that. She had told him she had carefully edited her tapes to take the slightest reference to him out, then destroyed her originals. He hoped that was right. She had phoned him once, to say the police had finally let her go, to England, although they could still come to interview her. Her lawyer, paid for by the Sun, was confident that there would be no charges, and even if there were, they could not stick. Frank knew he would destroy his own tapes, just before the Cup Final but not until then.

Frank had no problems with the police, unlike many of his Labour Party colleagues. He knew they were just working class blokes, doing a job. Bloody good job they were doing it, too, It always amused Frank how dependent on them their critics became when crime or violence threatened to impinge on their protected lives.

He reckoned two days was his safety margin. If the first interview was a dummy, and they were really working on script "B", then they would run it past the Superintendent and the Procurator-Fiscal and be back at him for real within 48 hours. He sweated a bit but in vain. He didn't get another visit from the police. They didn't have any link, and it never occurred to them that he might have the drive and motivation to mastermind such a plan. He knew that they might review that later though, in the light of his project. Julie phoned again to tell him that her lawyer had let her know that the Procurator Fiscal had decided that it would not be in the public interest to prosecute her. The official verdict of accidental death was not being revised either. They were both home and free, safe, and he could concentrate on his project.

Someone else he knew who should have, didn't get a visit from the police. One dog didn't bark in the night, and the silence strengthened his resolution and his belief that fate was with him. Frank didn't see Peter McColl the week they came back from Barcelona, nor did Paddy mention anything about him. It was only some ten days later, when they all congregated in the pub for the midweek home league game against Aberdeen, did he meet up with him again, along with Paddy, Gerry Robertson and Danny. "You look fed up, Peter, what's up with you?" Frank had asked. The answer wasn't quite as he expected it. Peter said nothing but Paddy did, "While you lot were all away in Barcelona the weekend before last, some bastards broke into his house and stole some of his guns." Frank asked if the police thought they had any chance of getting them back, as he knew how attached Peter was to his guns. There had been an awkward silence broken eventually by Peter admitting he had not told the police and he would be grateful if none of them talked about it. Paddy deflected the anger directed at him by stressing that Peter could trust these three. Peter explained that he didn't have a licence for one of the rifles, the kind you were not allowed to have as a functioning gun after Hungerford. He had bought it in a hurry, unofficially and hadn't got round to getting a firearms certificate for it, although he would have done of course, when the gun became officially available. He could hardly report it stolen, in his position as a lawyer it could finish him.

Frank had tried to compute the implications of that information for his enterprise. He concluded it would not really affect it one way or the other. In fact, it would be better, they couldn't trace any link back to Peter and therefore his circle, once the calibre and kind of bullet was identified. Peter might wonder, if and when Frank's role came to light, but that would be his problem. Initially he had toyed briefly with the notion of fitting Peter up for the job, but had dismissed it. He didn't really like him, but Christ, he was his friend, and anyway it was politically less sound, and a lot less

275

amusing, than the alternative he already had under control. He knew Peter would be in the same position on the day, same alibi, same contacts. He might be vulnerable if the gun link was made. No, he strengthened his resolve that initially at least, he would leave things pointing firmly in another direction, to those bastards he hated so much and wanted to finger.

He now realised why Peter had looked at him so funnily when he had asked him how easy it would be, how possible, given money, to get a gun like that without people knowing and without having to register it. Peter had said at the time that money could buy anything. Lawyers needed to be extra careful but often aren't, like policemen and vice. Even after he had known what he would do to Peter, Frank had proceeded with his plans to get a rifle on his own, without any reference to Peter. He had decided to obtain the Sauer from Harry Thompson. He had already done the series of deals, involving three middlemen, which ensured he would obtain the gun, for £5,000. It had been easier than he thought, the ease with which money buys things. And the fascinating glimpse of the men who occupy the world where such things can be bought, discreetly. If the route was traced to him, the gun would be found, unfired. That would confuse the bastards. He had already made arrangements for Peter to be left enough funds in his will to replace the three guns and the cabinet. Let Peter make of that will what he will, Frank regarded it as an act of friendship, and atonement.

CHAPTER SEVENTEEN -THAT BLOODY WOMAN - THE HATE DEBATE

Frank Hunter had an old fashioned sense of manners, inherited from his Gran, which meant that if he were planning to be intimate with a lady he should first get to know as much as possible about her. He would actually have preferred to think that his planned transaction was not of an intimate nature, that it could somehow be depersonalised and thereby made easier. But his respect for the truth meant that he had to acknowledge that the insertion of his lead into her flesh was about as intimate as any gesture could get. So he became, in his usual thorough way, an expert on the lady in question. His days in the Mitchell were full of intense study. His evenings were spent in pubs, testing out his learning and new theories in the heat of argument, then a few hours rest, recuperation from the alcohol and even occasional sleep before his early mornings spent in assessment of the results of both processes. It was those early morning shifts where he honed the justifications for his whole project and considered whether he had base enough to proceed.

He read every single book written about her, from crude hagiography to cruder hatchet job. It was not a project designed to do much for his mental health but he enjoyed it more than he had feared. By the end, he was confident that he knew more about her than she did. As the son of a devotee of Coronation Street, it was a help to him to place her as the daughter of Councillor Alf Roberts, shopkeeper. Other than that the books told him remarkably little about the real person, or even whether there was one.

He had started out with a hypothesis, that she was hated, justly, because she was evil and that she carried responsibility in herself for many injustices and wrongs. Therefore she deserved to die, and her enforced passing would improve matters. If he could prove those three steps to his satisfaction then he could proceed with his plan and his destiny.

So much of his considerations were political ones, about effect and outcome, but there was an underlying thread of cause, of human input. In truth he was not able to kid himself as to why he read all those boring books, especially the positive ones. He was desperately looking for the human core behind the politician, the example or revelation of humanity that would disable his will. His

277

mother and grandmother had taught him well, that present in all human beings was more good than evil, and that everyone should be respected for their capacity for good. And even when they exercise their capacity for evil, they do not forfeit all rights to kindness, understanding and forgiveness. So he had ploughed through these human histories, partly hoping to encounter some spark of humanity, some feeling if not of a warm and caring human being, at least of a person worthy of dignity and life. None of them, friend or foe, provided that for the finished product. No trace of humanity ever emerged. There had been some once, he had had to admit that, but they had all been edited out over the period 1976 to 1979.

His reading and analysis led Frank to a remarkable discovery. That as a conscious act of political choice the woman had been slowly, part by part, replaced by an automaton. A machine with programmed responses that allowed it to ignore dissent and disagreement, and travel on in a straight line, safe in the inputted assurance of its own correctness. His later political reading confirmed this thesis, with its evidence that the machine had worked perfectly at first, at least by its makers specifications, but since about 1988 it had increasingly started to malfunction, and was now deteriorating fairly rapidly, with successful spare part surgery unlikely. So if he proceeded with his plan he would not be killing a woman, he would be destroying a malfunctioning machine, and doing everyone a favour.

That theory saved him from having to seriously consider another, advanced in different forms by some of the more psychoanalytical of the analyses he read, about the sexual nature of her power over men. He remembered in particular the babblings of two once-Labour MPs, one a prominent broadcaster, the other of more poetic bent. They had talked in explicit terms about her sexiness and attraction. Frank had to fight off vague fears that his own desire to penetrate her body with a slim bullet was some kind of fantasy of repressed sexual desire. But he dismissed the possibility as extremely unrealistic, and also any oedipal alternatives. There was no doubt his victim suffered from a perverted form of that, over-love of father and dismissal of mother, but she was not his mummy, or his lover, he left those fantasies to Tory males.

He noted in passing the surface similarities to his own mother; born at the same time; same outside lavatory and unplumbed bath;

same choice of older husband at the same age; same one-birth concession to motherhood if for slightly different motivation; same commitment to excellence at career. But a different kind of woman. His mother had warmth, humanity, wit, compassion and above all care. A life outside work. He knew which he would recommend as role model, and chose to seek a cuddle from. He noted the likelihood that if her beloved father had been based in Glasgow, then with his commitment to municipal service he would probably have become a Labour Councillor. Not exactly like Frank's grocer, true enough, but a strain well represented in Glaswegian Labour local politics all the same.

He found it a funny thing, that he had started the exercise with two faces of her in his head, the one from his 1979 Hogmanay conversation and vision with Old Willie many years ago, that had appeared to him in the mirror in the Mitchell, and the updated but paradoxically more youthful-looking version familiar from his TV screen. The more he worked on the project, the more he read and learned about her, the more faded both visions became and the harder he found it to put any kind of face to his foe. He never again looked in a mirror and saw her, but another funny thing, he seldom saw himself there either. But he heard the voice often, during all his reading, the grating hating voice that he could never thole, the voice that always reminded him of the real nature of the enemy, the harsh strident shrillness of superiority and deafness.

After the personal, came the study of the political. Again he read every book on the subject of the nature and effect of the Prime Minister's rule, and whether the ism that bore her name was real, substantial and had an existence outwith her, or her public relations. Much of it was familiar ground to him, the meat and drink of his every day discourse and thought for the past twenty years. But it was a useful discipline to approach it as an academic exercise rather than partisan polemic. Again, being an honest man he was not able to hide from himself the surprising truth of much of his research, the conclusion that almost disabled his will to proceed. The Prime Minister was not to blame, personally and politically, for all the ills of the world and was innocent of many of the charges laid at her door. She was guilty of others though. His conclusion did not come as a total surprise to him. While he started off the exercise convinced that he hated her, he had always been against personalising it too much. He had never blamed the Prime Minister for everything as some of his countrymen did. It seemed they all hated her. Not just his working class friends, and the first generation middle-class that many had become, but every level and class of Scottish society.

Paddy and Peter McColl confirmed that the hatred extended right into the heart of the law hierarchy, so conservative by instinct. Frank knew personally no Tories, and McGoldrick was dead wasn't he, but Frank knew from his observations and his newspapers that even most of the faithful in Scotland hated her, for her arrogance and what she had done to their kind of Conservatism and the standing of their party. "That bloody woman" was the universal national sense, and only a small band round her wee man valued her positively. It wasn't just deep dislike either, but a tangible hatred. Ministers of the cloth, and priests, men of love and forgiveness, set the national tone in the harshness of their hate. And it was reflected by all other leaders as well as the masses. In the course of his studies Frank asked everybody he met what they thought of her, every single person used the word hate, many used much harsher ones. Several said that they often prayed someone would shoot her, and Frank would hope that they wouldn't feel guilty that they had given him the idea. But when he asked them all, "why do you hate her?", the responses were not very productive, or helpful to his project. It was almost as if it were a conditioned national reflex, a tangible focus for collective bile.

All the same he was surprised and alarmed by the nature of his academic conclusion, that the extent of hate for her was not rational but childish. He had expected it to be easier, given the hate, to be able to produce a bibliography of bile, a catalogue of crime, a detail of deviancy, a litany of loathing, a justification of the judgement of undeniable demand for death. But what he got was a sense of shame, his own at the immaturity of his rage, and that of his people, his nation. The closest he could get to understanding the phenomenon, and it was his deduction never actually articulated to him, was that over and above the political causes, which were legitimate for hostility but not hate, there was some sense of national rejection, a return of antipathy doubled in intensity, a basis for unity but an unhealthy and negative one. A rejection of the bossy English Nanny, finally personified. A response of a Scottish desire for national expression but distorted in the worst old way by negative attachment to a poor English model, embodying all the patronisation and bullying of the mythical foe. He was amused too at her genuine puzzlement at the rejection of her values by the Scots. She believed that it was Scots who had first articulated her philosophy, and that her values were in tune with everything that was finest in the Scottish character. But instead they rejected her with a hate most intense, and believed that she despised them. It was the Scots who read contempt there, in her face and in her voice, in their national search for an external bogey to blame.

He learnt the hard way a further note of caution on his hate, through the reaction of others, not Scots or English. Through the Union he had met many delegations of workers in G&M type Unions in Europe, particularly the Eastern Bloc. It had been a shock to him and a source of thought, the extent to which they were disturbed by his hate and offered other words, love and admiration, instead, and an envy for being under such leadership. She represented to them hope and means to convert their corrupt systems into something more responsive to their wishes. The Bulgarians and the Poles in particular had been her admirers.

He also came to the conclusion that it was unfair to blame her for the mean-spirited nastiness of the times. If the fields of London were full of unpleasant and obnoxious weeds that was not entirely the fault of the main gardener. She did not make them weeds, only provided some of the particular manure that allowed their special qualities to bloom so fully. It was silly, weak politics to direct the anger against the weeds, to hold them up ambivalently to the light rather than help the better flowers to bloom.

If he was to proceed to kill her, the honest man in him feared that it would not be because of the soundness of his hate, but solely because he was going anyway and wanted to do some good in his going, that would make him famous.

But there was one person who considered the matter more objectively, without the obligatory filter of hate. So he revived his lunchtime walks, with the talks with Willie taking up more of his interest than the visual delights of his city. He needed someone to bounce some of the dilemmas he was uncovering off against, and only Willie could be guaranteed to listen calmly and rationally, and provide sensible responses. He used those talks to get his perspective, a Prime Minister's angle that might excuse or explain otherwise aberrant behaviour. Willie was not a great admirer of hers, it turned out, although he had respect for her courage. Not his kind of Tory though, although he found it hard to believe Frank's claim that he did not know a single person, friend or acquaintance who did not hate her.

Willie reminded Frank that he had been against women getting the vote, to protect them from themselves. How right, how wise he had been, was his modest assessment, given a century to reflect. He had predicted that if once they got the vote, women would not settle for that, but would eventually want to be MPs and even Ministers of State. But even he had never envisaged that one would take his job. Never. Or that even more inconceivable just as he had sought a fourth term in 1892 one would try for similar in 1992. They had a good laugh together, though, at the irony of her evocation of Victorian values. That it was to his values and economic virtues she looked, rather than the paternal care and concerns of his old Tory rival. That amused Willie greatly.

Willie also reminded Frank that the Tories had once been even more unpopular in his time than in hers, that in 1885 they had had only 7 MPs in Scotland. Until Willie had given them a break, with his home rule obsession and his disestablishmentarianism, and pushed the Church of Scotland to switch from its traditional support of the Liberals into the Unionist and therefore Conservative camp. So Willie wasn't that much help to him, and made it clear he could not condone any act of violence.

Deprived of the anticipated easy transition from hate to justification, Frank had to work much harder to find a rationalisation that would allow him to proceed. He looked in vain for a personal edge that could bring the imperative of the vendetta. Frank had to acknowledge that the Prime Minister was not to blame for his unemployment, or even his factory's closure. Whether she was to blame for anyone's unemployment was a more difficult question than it seemed, since Frank had the disadvantage of not being a believer in keeping dead jobs going. His own earlier studies for his LDT book had not lead him to the conclusion that all those closures were her fault. Take the loss of mining jobs. Was that her fault, or Scargill's who had rejected a favourable deal in June 1984 to keep alive a national strike for which he had no constitutional mandate? Was it really a sin that so many fewer men would now have to do such a hellish job? Overall her instruments of slaughter had been too crude and unsubtle, and too many people had lost productive and defensible jobs, and then been made to feel socially worthless in their waste. A heinous crime, an evil disgrace, but he doubted if it was a capital one.

One proof that the hate was not rational was the permanence of much of her achievement and the impermanence of other parts. Frank had no quarrel with her sale of Council Homes and was glad

282

his party had learned to live with that. Likewise he recognised her translation of the nationalised industries into private firms, and the creation of a new generation of share-owners was an irreversible but not regrettable act. His own experiences at LDT where he had encouraged the remuneration of his people by shares in the stock of their own company had removed any ideological tangle. It is a short step from shares in one company, even your own, to shares in many, and many of the LDT workforce made it. His own failure to apply that knowledge to his political response to the major privatisations was a result of confused emotionalism and disgust at the bribery element rather than anything more noble. Peter McColl had been right. On Trade Union reform, Frank had always been in a minority, with John McLure, and knew she had done less and more favourably, then they had once proposed. Even the movement recognised that itself now and was not lobbying for massive return to the bad old days. Much of the rest, the froth-inducing stuff, was style not substance and would vanish with her.

Given what he had in mind, he particularly wanted to come to a conclusion that she was to blame for deaths, specific identifiable ones. At the time he had definitely blamed her for Mary Ewing's, and that was before the full hate developed. Now, he was less sure. Mary had died of hypothermia, in early 1980, under a Prime Minister who hated welfare benefits, but she hadn't yet cut the real value of what Mary had subsisted upon. Though that came later, it was too late to harm Mary, so others had to share the blame including Labour. But Mary had not been the only one to die, many thousands came after her, and the Prime Minister and her benefits policy could be held accountable But it lacked the personal immediacy.

Nor could he easily lay the blame for Billy's death solely at her door. He had met Billy in Kamesthorn and struck up a strange kind of protective friendship. After Kamesthorn Billy would occasionally turn up at Frank's door, at odd times in odder states. For a while it had seemed as if love might save him, the best hope of all screwed-up Glasgow boys, that a good woman might rescue them with their greater strength, but strong and hard though young Linda was, her inability to cope with his excesses had soon vanquished that hope and sent the downward spiral into a more vicious spin. Billy sought relief from his boredom and frustration in a series of chemical cocktails. Not heroin, because he was frightened of needles, but the NHS had taught him well of the range of alternatives open to him. He was a jelly baby, at £3:50 a tablet. He pioneered the rediscovery of coffee mornings on the southside, with his two bizarre personal electrical possessions, a liquidizer and a coffee filter, that followed him wherever he found a socket. Not that it made him perky, a drowsy peace was the best he could ever manage. Through him Frank became familiar with a whole new vocabulary, of Buprenorphine, and Temazepam, Temgesics and Triazolam, and young people who lived and died on a diet of eggs and jelly.

Billy paid for his supplies by the fastness of his hands and the cheek of his spirit, doing his bit for redistribution on the retail side. The shopkeepers' enemy, the nearest to political action he ever got. He never dealt. As he kept telling Frank he had some principles but he would often supply his friends as well as himself. His false sense of how to conduct himself meant that he was often cheeky to those who did the supplying, not men noted for their sense of humour. His redemption was beyond Frank, and he always induced a deep sense of despair, at the inevitability of his doom.

Billy had spent most of life in the care of the Social Work Department. He once asked Frank to help him, he wanted to break into his Social Worker's office to steal his file. He had been amazed when Frank had told him about an easier way, to ask his Social Worker to let him see it, and had not pursued the matter. He got comfort from Frank's anger and despair, it pleased him enough to provoke more. They had one or two good afternoons together when Billy's head was not too scrambled, out in the hills or along a beach, but Billy never took Frank up on his invitations to join him in pubs. That kind of sedate chemical abuse bored him.

One week after McGoldrick's trip to Loch Thom, Billy also went for a swim, in the Clyde and was pulled out in front of the Pumphouse restaurant. It was never established whether he fell, was pushed or jumped, although the official verdict was accidental death. An accident of birth. Frank was too busy to mourn properly, or even wonder what might have happened if he had been in on the Friday to take Billy's last despairing call, but he went to the funeral with Hazel, and wept for the waste. Billy had been denied an income by that bloody woman's assumption that he would have a family to support him. Rather a sloppy assumption for a young man careless enough to have the Director of Social Work for his daddy. No, what she had done to that 16-17 year old age group was truly criminal, the worst single crime of the many of which he found her guilty, but it could not really be said to be murder, the responsibility for Billy was wider than her.

Some of his reading taught him, if he were the type to believe what he read, that her very accession to power was the fault of Danny Campbell, and his fellow NUPE Shop-Stewards, whose failure to bury the dead, except under piles of rubbish, in that 1979 Winter of Discontent, had brought her hopes to life. Maybe he should just shoot Danny. It would be a lot easier to organise. But having won, she had proceeded to demonstrate her convictions, so he sought out his own consensus about which of them merited the ultimate sentence.

One major crime of which he found her guilty was a general indifference to the plight of the poor, after some plea bargaining from the original charge of creating and fostering poverty. The rediscovery of poverty in the late sixties was something of a source of droll amusement to a working class Glasgow boy like Frank who had never realised that it was lost. Not that his family could be described as poor. Both his parents had worked, always and hard, and one had earned a good wage and the other a good salary. They did not have expensive tastes or hobbies, and most of their money was ploughed back into making their small home very comfortable, and their one child even more comfortable. They were both believers in thrift and savings. They could have bought a house of their own but never wanted to do so. They were in a good close, with good neighbours and were happy with their lot. But Frank had always been well aware that many of his friends were not so fortunate and that he was a privileged young man in comparison to many. He knew the hard realities that Labour Governments from 1964-1979 had not been able to mitigate, despite a commitment to the welfare system.

He was always well aware of the strange ironies and patterns of the eighties, with most wage-earners becoming significantly better-off but the poor getting poorer, and more frequent, in his area at least. He had often ruminated on the ironies of all his friends and colleagues in the Labour Party and the pub, despising the Prime Minister who ruled over a period where their income and wealth had increased considerably. And himself, with well over £100,000 in the bank from his mother and his redundancy, spiritual disasters they may well both have been, and cost him plenty in terms of his health and well-being, but poor they did not make him. Yet, as well as the anecdotal evidence of his own eyes, he consorted with Social Workers enough to know that real desperate poverty was the lot of a considerable number of his neighbours, and that the

285

changes to the system encouraged by the lady's mentality made that poverty more humiliating and more enduring. He knew of the mothers who chose between shoes for their children and food for themselves. Of the revival of jumble sales as the source of supplies. Of the wonderful logic of the Social Fund where if you were eligible for a loan then by definition you were too poor to be able to repay it. Danny had given Frank a copy of a devastating report "Poverty in Strathclyde" which showed graphically the increases in poverty and misery for almost a million of its two and a half million residents. The unemployed, of which he was one, if an immune variety, fared particularly badly, along with single elderly and lone parent families. It was a more effective exposition of the horrors of her times than anything the Labour Party ever produced.

Frank also knew from Paddy and Peter, from their pub talk of their caseloads, the daily tales of the resort to criminality taken by many of the more desperate and deprived. The champion of law and order seemed unaware of her role in pushing many to the point where desperation eroded their own restraints on their behaviour. The worst part of all was the extent to which too many of the generation below him, the generation that only knew her regime, had been pushed by poverty, hopelessness and despair to seek their salvation in the sickness of white hope.

But it was the total indifference to all those casualties that seemed the worse part of her nature. No human concern for the consequences of the deliberate widening of the gulf between the poor and the rest. She had summed it up best herself when she had come to the General Assembly of the Church of Scotland and told them, who had once been her natural constituents and her party's strength, of the religious base she was drawing on when she said that she did not believe in the concept of society, that there was no such thing. It was an incredible performance, of arrogance verging on the insane, of a mediocre mind being led by fawning circumstance to believe itself capable of rational and creative thought. A confusion of will and intellect, the proof that strength of one was no guarantee of health in the other. Frank had gone to the Mitchell and reread that Sermon on the Mound several times. It was all there. Her defence of the creation of wealth, her scriptural backing for the necessity for self-reliance and the evils of dependency. The responsibility of Christians to make money. The ultimate rational defence of her recent budget that had given the rich billions and lowered the living standards of the poorest. I know it because the bible tells me so. "If a man will not work he

286

shall not eat." Well he would not work but he would eat her heart out and feast on her brain.

Despite himself, he had been amused at her heresy for that audience, that Christianity was not about social work, but spiritual redemption. And amused by her other notion that it was his money that had allowed the Good Samaritan to become memorable not his intentions. From her full text he was consoled by a wonderful piece of political theological philosophy that the press had not reported. She had confessed to initial misgivings about the injunction to love neighbours as yourself, obviously a problem for her. Then the solution had been shown to her, you often hate yourself, therefore it is acceptable to treat your neighbours the same way. It was an elegant defence of her feelings of hatred for lazy working class trade unionist scroungers like himself, but no use in his search for a way to turn his own hatred into a murderous edge. He had learned the uses and limitations of self-hate long before her insight.

That speech had crystallised for him the nature of his opposition to her, and where he stood politically. For all his political erudition, or perhaps because of it, he had always struggled with the notion of exactly what he meant when he called himself, as he often did, a socialist. As a youngster there had been several glorious nights when Frank Hunter had woken at 3a.m. with the secret of the nature and meaning of socialism clear at last in his head. Crystal clear, never a diamond in shape, more a logical parallelogram of rational construction. The following mornings he would always search desperately the insides of his head for the remnants of his creation. The joy he occasionally felt on each rediscovery of this slumbering revelation was always surpassed by the dry taste of crumbling dust in his mouth the following morning as the insights collapsed in the caverns of his subconscious. But he always believed it was still in there, somewhere, a meaningful definition just waiting to be defined. Frank Hunter never did find it. Nor was he alone. It was not true to say that no-one in the Labour Party knew what they meant by the word to which they were so attached. The Trotskyists and other Democratic Centralist infiltrators did; but they were a tiny minority representing no-one but themselves. The vast majority of Labour Party supporters called themselves Socialists, but in an emotional and religious sense rather than an intellectual one. There was, and could be, no real sense of what the meaning of that was that would be acceptable to them, the kind of fundamental reorganisation of society that real literal socialism represented. That was not what the Labour Party's supporters and voters wanted.

That was why the Left hated her with a particular virulence for what she had done to them. Expose the lie they lived to themselves, that socialism had a future. And expose the lack of principled leadership, with vision and commitment, only empty vessels mouthing empty doctrine. She had succeeded in her stated aim, of destroying socialism in her country, or rather she had forced the Labour Party to acknowledge that it had been dead in their heart for some time and could not be revived. Frank never tired of telling his pub friends that the Labour Party had not been formed as a socialist Party, but as a labour one, to further the aims of collective solidarity, a different matter. So it need not matter that socialism was seen to be dead, as long as there was awareness of a coherent moral alternative. And he had found that on his 3a.m. shifts, the waking ones. She had helped him with her notion that there was no such thing as society. Frank was not a Marxist, never had been. The only writer who had helped him in his search was Andre Gorz, and even he didn't get it right. Frank had moved from an appreciation of the evils and defects of State Socialism, where the State is everything and society nothing, through the Prime Minister's negative echo that there was no such thing as society and that the state should go the same way. Frank developed the realisation that society is the important thing and the state is only a subservient creature of that society. The issue was not the ownership of the means of production and distribution, but the controls exerted over that ownership, by society in the interests of society.

It had come clearly to him one night. He was not a Socialist, he was a Societalist. He had a belief that Society could be and should be organised rationally and democratically, to meet peoples needs and enhance their potential in a way that reliance on markets alone cannot ensure. That did not require the ownership of the means of production and distribution, and anyway social ownership had not proved an efficient way of producing wealth, but it did require the political control and regulation of the worst excesses of private and corporate ownership. The state, as society's representative, should seek higher goals than purely short-term economic ones and put the economy in the service of those higher priorities, of a social, ethical, cultural and ecological nature. That was the kind of vision the Labour Party needed to recapture, not the perverted bastard-son notion of better management of capitalism that was the best the morally bankrupt current leadership could aspire to. Society owed every citizen a reasonable standard of living, but they in turn owed society the responsibility to contribute, by their work and behaviour, in maintaining its health and strength.

He wished he had the time to explore these themes further, to finally finish his LDT book, which would outline his philosophies at length and explain why things were as they were, rather than as they used to be thought to be. He had made arrangements to leave his copious notes with Mary-Ann Ewing but even though she was her grandmother's granddaughter, and a prize-winning political journalist in Canada, he did not know if she would be able to make sufficient sense of all of it to make the book coherent.

So after the Prime Minister was gone, and him too, the dispute would no longer be about socialism or not, but about societalism or not. And she had never come close to winning that fight on a longer-term. Her thesis that society did not exist had been rejected. Despite all her efforts, there was still a great recognition of the role of society, and a preference for collective support and action, for good quality public services. The real issue for the future would be not who manages capitalism better, but who identifies and implements societal concerns better. The state would stay, as the positive instrument of society's collective will to care. She may have succeeded in her stated aim of killing off socialism, without ever realising it was already dead, but she would undoubtedly fail in her more important goal of killing societalism. That was how history would judge her ultimately, a failure in her most important goal.

He loved the irony that in the attempt to destroy socialism in her country, she had succeeded in also destroying conservatism in his country. So his awareness of what she had done, and why she had done it, helped create in him an understanding that he had been using the wrong term, that he was now and always had been, a Societalist. His political faith rested on the acceptance of the notion of society, and the consequences and responsibilities that followed from such acceptance, including a definite commitment towards the welfare of all members. It was not the ownership of the means of production, distribution and exchange that mattered, but the acceptance of the commitment towards all members especially those faring worst in the ownership and distribution struggles. The enemy were those who would deny that commitment, and she was their flag-waver. She had led her party away from the tradition, however patronising, of Willie's great rival, that there was a society and one nation lived in it. That was her great crime, but whether it was a capital one was open to debate. She had at least led him into a greater understanding of what it was he believed in, and did not.

He hated her adherents perhaps even more than he did her. He never forgot the night, in a hotel bar where their conference was taking place, he had literally bumped into one of the four Young Conservatives in Glasgow, with a tee shirt on his scrawny chest with the message Hang Mandela stamped upon it, and a hat upon his superior head with We Love The Lady around its trim, and on his lapel the ubiquitous badge of the North British beast, Scotland says No to Devolution. It had taken all his willpower and his memory that he deplored violence to avoid exterminating the vermin.

There was some amusement among his pub talkers that her Poll Tax was proving such an own goal. There was a certain pleasure that it had been the Scots Tories that had lured her into that false play, with their complaints about the rates. But the insistence on it, with its known defects, costs and weaknesses had been all her own work, the most personalised political product of a warped personality. And now it was threatening to destroy her, might do even without his bullet. She would find it hard to abandon her own baby, had shown no desire to do so. Any replacement would get rid of it immediately, whatever their own craven acquiescence in its birth. Hearing intelligent Tory Cabinet Ministers defending the indefensible tax had confirmed for him his hatred of all politicians, and his knowledge of why he could never have been one. So his project would kill the Tax as well as the Lady. That irony would upset rather than amuse his Militant enemies, since despite their rhetoric, those liars loved the Tax, relished every warrant sale, blessed their corrupt god every night for its introduction.

Frank's major concern was not so much his intention as his timing. He knew that if he had embarked on his project just after the third victory in 1987 he would have almost unanimous approval, but he had a strong fear that he had mis-timed it and the tide had turned, leaving the hate as a high jetsam mark but taking the political danger away with its ebb. There was a general unanimity amongst his pub pals. For all they hated her, they reckoned she had become a liability, Labour's best weapon, that bloody woman, and that any other Tory leader would do far better. Gerry Robertson posted the one note of caution on that scenario, that they were applying a Scottish perspective to a UK scene, and they should not underestimate the degree of tribal loyalty she could inspire in the south. But the general view was that she had lost the place. Frank translated it all into his new hypothesis, that the machine was malfunctioning, increasingly mis-aligned to modern requirements on Europe, South Africa, reform of the Poll Tax, and would be unable to improve its performance. He knew that if the malfunctioning became even more pronounced there was a real possibility that the Tories themselves would take it out of service, they were so much more sensible and ruthless about those matters than the caring party. And even if they did not do it before the Election, they would do it shortly after one. So why continue with his project, when inertia on his part could soon see her out anyway, rejected by the people, his or hers.

There was even the prospect of a horrendous own-goal, with the current prospect of the Prime Minister left alive, losing the election, compared with a new reality altered by him to a replacement Tory Prime Minister winning the Election partly on a sympathy vote. He answered that for himself easily enough, with three powerful arguments he found convincing. The main one was that even if another Tory leader, imposed by him or them, might do better, since the bottom line of his calculations was that she would not lose, arithmetically could not lose, then leaving her there would not offer Labour victory. And in a Scottish context, since the Tories would get hammered whoever the Leader, it would be best for Scotland and its thrust for Independence the greater the Tory victory in Westmister. And new leadership would be far more likely to let them go. Then there was the final factor, that inertia would not secure his place in political history. He reckoned too that Gerry was not far off the mark. Frank's own final view was that her own disappearance would be fairly neutral in its net political effect, and would not greatly affect the outcome of the next election, and that any marginal effect was as likely to be positive for Labour as negative.

The sessions in the pub were important to him, not just for the analysis and argument. He never had more than two or three pints, four at the very most. He needed a clear head to remember all he had read during the day and early evening, and all he talked about in the pub. His friends were delighted that the argumentative Frank was back. He would walk home, and if Joyce wasn't with

291

him, watch a football video or two until his head cleared then a little light reading before catching a couple of hours sleep. On waking he would resume his serious study. It was the one disturbing similarity he found with his foe, the ability to exist on a few hours sleep and devote the rest of the time to work. Maybe she shared his own insomniac sadness.

As well as the personal and political aspects of his lady friend, he read much about the select activity he was about to endorse, the world of the political assassin. He wanted to know what sort of company he was about to keep. Most of the stuff about violence and terrorism was not directly applicable to him. He found out with some relief that he did not match the profile of a terrorist set out by Scotland's leading expert. He was very disappointed in the quality of this man's work. An international reputation on the basis of those slight works and sloppy conclusions. Frank knew he could do better as an explainer of that aspect of political activity, and toyed again with the notion of going back to University and becoming an expert. There was actually very little history of individual political activity of the kind he was planning. Most political violence was a collective matter, carried out by movements. His was to be an individual act. A form of political commentary adopted by an individual as a conscious alternative to the other more conventional forms accepted by most people. It was slightly more extreme than the placing of a cross on a piece of paper, but still an act of that ilk, a political rather than a personal comment. Many of the so-called political assassinations by lone perpetrators that he studied were not in fact political acts. Certainly few could be described as conscious choices by rational men. Most of them were almost random acts by lunatics, irrational acts of mentally ill people. Wilkes was maybe the one that came closest. And Frank realised that his scenario at least would offer the same kind of question to the husband, "but apart from that, Denis, what did you think of the game?"

The rest didn't offer any real role model or inspiration. From his readings, particularly Professor Ford and his classic text on political murder, Frank learned that there were very few if any examples of an individual committing an act of political murder that achieved the end it sought, other than revenge which was not his primary motive. But it was an old tradition, as old as politics itself. He had to admit the classic justification, that the target be a tyrant who usurped or misused power and that no other corrective route be open, didn't apply in his case. Also he knew from his own analysis of the likely consequences that it would not really change anything. Although it did confirm a route to immortality for people who would never have been remembered by even those who met them. Sirhan Sirhan, Dimitri Tsafendas. Both guaranteed a footnote in the history of the world, while hundreds of millions of far better men go unmentioned and unremembered. Killing a world leader was a certain road to eternal fame and international renown. Frank Hunter could attain immortality. Nothing else in what was left of his life could ever assure him of that. It would be the only thing he could ever do that would make the film he always made in his head of his own actions one that would be wanted to be seen by others. It would be up to his chosen scribe to make sure that his act was seen as political, and understood in its own terms. But that was assuming he wanted the knowledge of the authorship of his act to become public. He had soon come to the conclusion that there was a degree of choice about it, an option to seek to do the deed but to keep his name out of it. The possibility that the value of the deed lay in itself and not the accreditation of responsibility. He had already learned from his studies and his rehearsals how remarkably easy it would be to kill anyone who appeared in public. The difficulty would be in escaping detection and arrest rather than in executing the deed.

One thing he was clear about was that he would not go to prison. He had been in a black dungeon the previous year, of his own making perhaps, but never again would he thole such restriction. If he elected for exposure it would be on the basis of implementing his own exit plans first. He had read many of the books on the Kennedy killings. He did not attempt to read them all or even any more although he returned to the best and spent spring Summers nights revising what he knew. He knew the whole saga from Warren Whitewash to Congressional Committee "Conspiracy" and was clear in his own conclusion that at least one person, possibly two, had shot dead the President of the United States and got away without even being identified far less caught and punished. He wondered what they did with the rest of their life after an achievement like that, or whether that problem had been taken care of for them with a bullet for their own brain and throat. Sweden offered an example to him nearer home, of the feasibility of killing a Prime Minister and not getting caught. It also offered another model to him, of how the wrong person could eventually be charged with the deed if not convicted.

These considerations allowed a seed he had planted himself to flourish with some vigour. Its main shoots were that he could not be caught, but he wanted the credit for his political gesture. But only eventually. He would not be adverse to the notion of others getting the immediate credit, particularly if it allowed him the time to implement his own end on his own terms. But he wanted his place in history, so the truth would have to be allowed to emerge sometime. The project was getting more complicated the more he considered it. It would truly be a fine test of his intellectual and organisational abilities. He had had several doubts to overcome before firmly accepting the conclusion that he did want the credit for his act. One was the fear of the jail. He could not cope with that. In his post-pint musings he used to wonder where they would put him if he were caught. Peterhead, Barlinnie. There would be problems with both. He would be a hero, the man who shot that bloody woman, they could not have that. He would not want to go to an English jail. He did not hate the English, or even dislike them but he had long ago ruled out the notion of living there. He wondered if he could apply for political prisoner status, but that was not British. Maybe he could petition the European Court of Human Rights. He had a horrible vision of Carstairs, maybe that was the most likely outcome. But he always returned to the inevitable conclusion that it was academic, and to his new motto, "they'll never take me alive", or the vow that if they did they would not keep him that way. He did some research on the mechanisms for guaranteeing the success of these promises to himself. Again it was easier than he thought. He could guarantee he would never be arrested, far less imprisoned. He might be caught, he knew the first 2 minutes after his act would be his most vulnerable for detection, but he wouldn't be captured alive.

He had a worry about the effect of such fame for him on those who knew and loved him. He knew his background would be exposed to rigorous research and digging. Fortunately his parents were dead and would not be disgraced. He had no wife to live the rest of her life under the cloud of his fame or shame. Elaine was sufficiently far away from him not to be too compromised. Best of all, he had no children who would have to grow up living their life not as themselves but as the child of someone notorious. Joyce would get some publicity but at least they were not married or even living together, so she would escape the fate of a wife. His friends should find it an asset rather than a hindrance. He knew who he wanted to tell his real story, and knew it would be done well and

294

fairly. If Mary-Ann Ewing were given a head start, she could lay the tramlines for others. He liked the notion of being a hero. Scotland had few enough modern ones. He had failed to become the football hero he had dreamed of being as a child, but at least he could settle for second best and be remembered as a man of action. In his wilder ramblings he even saw himself as Willie had warned him, cast in stone and raised up beside him. The pre-Independence hero, who had shown how important it was to Scots to be free. An inscription "Frank Hunter 1954-1990. He died that we might be free." that would do nicely. It would be ironic but nice if they wrote a song or two about his deed. They could sing it in the Jungle as a change from the Irish ones. He saw and liked the graffiti, and the tee shirts, "Frank Hunter was right" or "Frank Hunter did it for us". He was too young to be victim to the "Where were you when you heard Kennedy was killed?" syndrome. For his generation it had been "Where were you the night of the Iran game?". But he quite fancied a "How much did you celebrate the day Frank Hunter shot that bloody woman?" Yes, his place in Scottish history would be secure and positive. Frank Hunter. He liked the name, for its literal meaning, the seeker after truth. He had tried to live by it, now in his death he would reinforce its validity, the hunter as much as the frankness, and that appealed to him.

There was one worm that threatened his more pleasant fantasies of his life after death. Two weeks, that was all it had been, but that might be all that it would take. Two weeks that weren't even necessary and had achieved nothing. Okay, it had helped him in the process, but a process he was managing himself anyway and would have managed fine without them. And okay, he would never have met Hazel, Billy and Mary, and that would have been a major loss, especially Hazel. She had enhanced his life, knowing her, so okay that would have been his loss right enough. And okay, he might never have got it on with Joyce; although he might still have anyway through Danny, but maybe not, okay probably not, and that would undoubtedly have been a very major loss. He did love her and she had liberated him in some ways, and made him a more whole and better person. Okay, but for that, and because of those two small little weeks, he might never be the Labour Party activist, the trade union leader, the ex-professional footballer that he undoubtedly was. But instead might be dismissed always as the ex-Mental Hospital patient, the mentally ill person, the man with mental health problems, the loony, fruitcake, nutcase, head-banger, lunatic, madman, person of unsound mind, mental case, confused, deranged, unhinged maddy, screwball, aff-the-heid, daftie dooley and every other like kind label that would take away the need or likelihood of anyone having to take his actions seriously.

Kamesthorn Man. It would be so unfair, so untrue. He was not mad. He was perfectly sane and of sound mind. He knew exactly what he was planning to do and why, and they were rational acts, both parts. Okay, he was not happy, and had not been so really, since 1984, but sadness was not madness. Indeed it was a very sane response to a mad world. And he had had good cause, very good cause for his special sadness and difficulties of 1989. He knew too that the McGoldrick business had reawakened many of his sadnesses and despairs of that period, and reinforced for him the nature of his personality and weaknesses. But it was a calm and sane choice to decide that he did not wish to carry on, did not intend to struggle anymore to overcome, did not wish to risk returning again to the depths he had seen previously. He knew that his concentration on his project had stilled those demons, shut a lid tight on the turmoil and pain within to allow him to concentrate and to succeed, but the lid could only be shut for a defined period and he did not wish to cope with the bubbling uproar of its release. No he was sane all right, and had always been so. He knew that he would need to show calm cleverness in action to offer proof of that to those who would rush to judgement, and that consideration was one of the vital determinants in his decision to go for the more complicated route to credit and glory.

He worried too, about any possible adverse impact his planned action might have on Glasgow and its new image as the capital of Culture. He saw it as his own contribution to the European Year of Culture. The Assassination, a Tragicomedy in two Acts, by Frank Hunter. But he would not want it to detract from the overall success in moving away from the false image of mindless violence. Glasgow was miles better, than it used to be, and than anywhere else he would rather be. It felt more alive than he did. He drew life and vitality from it, in a reversal from previous days when the city achieved its own life only from the generous contributions of its citizens. He was proud of its new European role, and rejected the false-proletarian purist snobbery that sought to decry the achievement. He welcomed no longer having to apologise for his origins, or accept the sympathy of others. He was proud of his Glasgow and did not want to do it wrong. He reckoned this was a different kind of violence and would not revive the razor image. Indeed, if the automatic reaction was that it was the IRA, then the city would get a deal of sympathy. No-one thought the worse of Brighton for what happened there. Even when or if it later became clear that a Glaswegian had done it, it would be seen as a political gesture rather than a cultural one. That would also be part of his challenge, to make that accepted. He was not a violent man, not in action or in capability. He had not been in a fight for over twenty years, never as an adult had he hit another. Nor was he a hard man. He had a degree of mental toughness, and never shirked a tackle, but nothing more. Frank Hunter had always believed that violence was a defective way of resolving problems and making points. But he knew for all the progress, his city was still too prone to outbreaks of vicious and pointless violence. So he was very conscious of the irony that he was now contemplating using violence to make his most important life-point. Maybe he was a more typical Glaswegian than he knew, a son of the old city after all. He tried to convince himself that what he was planning to do was a political gesture not a physical one, and he preferred to avoid thinking of its physical manifestations.

CHAPTER EIGHTEEN- WHAT A DUMMY

Frank Hunter rose early the day of his dummy run. He rose early every day. He was still existing on about 3 hours sleep a night, maximum. This Saturday morning he departed from his normal routine and didn't read a book. He prepared himself for the trial run, the dress rehearsal. He had started the night before by ensuring Joyce hadn't stayed the night, although she had been in an affectionate mood. He would make up for it this evening, if not on the final one. He was grateful for once to BSB. Not his system, he was a Sky man, but due to the BSB arrangement, the Celtic game due that Saturday was postponed for a few days so he was free to attend another game without suspicion. With some difficulty he had rejected Danny's offer to go to see Clyde, and Jack's invitation to watch the Hearts with him. He knew he had to run it exactly on schedule as if it were the Final a fortnight later, so Queens Park versus Berwick Rangers it would have to be. The sacrifices he was prepared to make in the cause of destiny.

He checked all his equipment methodically. Tinted paper for the windows with sellotape to secure it. It was surprisingly effective, made the car look good and ensured passers-by could not see into it. He checked the four parts of the gun rest he had made himself, which clamped onto the front and back seats and secured the gun in a vice-like grip. He polished the binoculars, which he would need to check he had the right target in the right seat. He wasn't using the real gun. He had bought a model rifle from Victor Morris and adjusted it to make it the exact size and length. He was going to use the real sights though, and he caressed them lovingly before packing them. He was pleased with the state of his golf-bag. He had bought a top model with his wealth before realising that even then he would never fancy this game. But it looked the real McCoy. He had considered various other methods of carrying the gun, including the two he remembered from the movies, the violin case and the carpet. But he finally settled for the golf-bag with its zipped hood. Finally he packed the range of goodies for No 37. He hadn't collected most of them yet so he used replicas, fitted neatly into his Adidas bag. Then he checked his case for the later trip.

He did one practice of his quick change. He was tickled with as well as by his beard. He had bought two from the Theatrical

Outfitters on the corner of Gibson Street, next to the Blythswood Cottage. The pub hadn't changed much since his university nights, and he enjoyed a quiet pint wondering about what might have been. He had always wondered what he would look like with a beard. The only one they had that matched his black hair was fairly bushy, and it didn't have the attractive effect that he had always imagined a real one doing for him. Still, it looked authentic enough, it should at that price and with the pain involved in removing it. And it made him look quite different. Not better but definitely different. He then added his glasses. The lightest tint of sunglass he had been able to find, which looked like ordinary glasses with a trendy tint. He would be able to wear them without affecting his vision. He had also bought two football hats, a Scotland one for the dummy run and a Celtic one for the real thing. He never wore anything on his head normally but he would make an exception this time. He stuck his big anorak up his jumper and put his wee one on top. He looked in the mirror and was pleased to see a fat, hairy, specky stupid-lookin' bastard staring back at him. Excellent.

He then did the other things exactly as he planned to do them on the 12th. He set the video to tape the whole game, including extra-time and penalties just in case. He tidied up the house exactly as he wanted it left, and exactly as he wanted Joyce to find it. He ran through each act four times, timed each part of the process every time and noted down all the timings in his wee book. He checked and double-checked to make sure he had thought of absolutely everything. Then he read his book until it was time to telephone for the taxi. He gave the taxi firm an address in the next street, waited three minutes, then walked down the stairs, out the close and round the corner with his golf-bag over his shoulder, his case in his right hand and the bag for No 37 in his left. The taxi came a further 3 minutes later. It wasn't likely to be that much slower at that time on Cup Final day but he allowed a reasonable margin to cover that anyway. He told the driver to take him to an address in Cumming Drive, the street below Stanmore Road. The fare was £1:30 so he noted that and gave the driver exactly £1:50. He didn't want remembered for generosity or meanness. It was 11:50am when he was dropped off. He was inside the car by 11:52. He had spent considerable time in the last few weeks observing the parking habits of the natives. Fortunately none of them seemed to regard that space on the corner as theirs. It was absolutely crucial to his plan that his car must occupy exactly that space. Everything else followed or fell from that centrality. He had got into the habit of checking every night he could. Only once was it occupied at 7pm and then it was clear by 9pm. No-one ever left their car there overnight. So he had started to do so once or twice. No-one seemed to mind, or even notice, though he couldn't be sure whether any of these curtains on the other side of the road hid a Miss Callaghan or not. It might prove important later.

He had swithered about taking the risk of driving over early on the morning of the Final. It would do away with the need for the taxi. But the risk was just too great, and unnecessary. He would leave his chosen car there on the Friday. He knew it would be safe enough there, near a lamppost and flats. He bought a flash steering lock clamp to discourage young boys. What he could not risk was leaving anything, particularly the guns, in the car or car boot overnight. Except for his two small carpets. No, the car Friday, taxi Saturday morning routine was the safest and most thorough. So before five o'clock the previous evening he had driven up Stanmore Road and left the car parked on the corner with Brownlie Street. He had checked for the 481st time that he was not imagining it, that he had a clear line of sight right from the window into the Directors' Box. He had been grateful again for the brutal surgery done to the tree in the corner plot, reduced to ugly stumps. He had previously thought such action was an act of cruelty and barbarism, but now he blessed the barbarian. He also asked forgiveness for the two bushes he had vandalised in the corner to ensure they did not obstruct his line. He had been able to park exactly in the right spot on the corner, to hit the key gap between the lamppost hood and the rails and get the pure straight line into seats three and four. He put his case in the boot and laid the golf-bag flat on the backseat floor and covered it with one of his two carpets. He put the other bag on the front passenger seat, and settled down to await his next deadline.

Which car to use had been one of his first problems to solve. He had learned enough to be fairly certain that one of the consequences of the additional security likely to be employed because the Prime Minister was to be in attendance was that the police would check out the registrations of all cars parked in the immediate area overnight and early morning. They would make further enquiries about all of them not registered to local residents. Although he lived within walking distance, he still lived too far away to come into the category of local resident. So he could not use his own car and own number plate. His initial bright idea had been to find a local resident with the same make and colour of car as his and replicate the number plate. But none of the neighbourhood seemed to share his taste. So then he had decided that if they wouldn't replicate him he would replicate them. He had toured the rectangle of streets until he found the ideal one that met his specifications. It had to be a hatchback with the right kind of rear windows to suit his primary purpose. And it had to be an easy car make and year to hire. And they had to have a lock-up in which the original would be off the street at the appropriate time. He had found several that fitted all three conditions, but settled on a white Maestro 1300 - which was why he had hired that make for his Manchester trips. The owners were an elderly couple who lived on their own in an adjacent street. Getting duplicate plates made in their registration number was even easier than he had anticipated. He wasn't even asked for the proof of registration that he had "forgotten" to bring.

That still left one very real risk, and one more minor one. The main one was that both cars would feature in the police trawl. They might regard that as interesting. Observing the couple's behaviour patterns, he found out that Mr would put the car away for the evening around 7pm. Saturday mornings he would bring it out to take his wife shopping and sometimes leave it on the street when they returned about midday. That pattern would be sufficient for Frank's purposes but could he rely on it? He wished to eliminate every single risk. He swithered about providing them with some aversion therapy to street parking by smashing a window every time they left it out. But eventually he settled on a more ambitious scheme that would also remove the lesser risk that one or other of them might pop out to the shops or a friend and pass their own car. He had had considerable reservations about embarking on that plan. With his own personality and life experiences he was well familiar with the concept of iatrogenesis, literally defined as the doctors' art of scoring own-goals, where the response to an identified problem or risk ends up creating an even greater problem or risk. He felt an affinity for that word, maybe he should ask for it to be scratched on his tombstone. Here lies Frank Hunter, iatrogenic genius. He was aware that every extra tentacle he created for this monster was one more possibility that could strangle him. But the risks attached to this particular scheme were not really great. If it worked he would eliminate both risks entirely, if it didn't he could still revert to a late course of aversion therapy.

So he set up his elaborate game, through a Travel Agent that Mr Currie approached in person with his beard on and paid in cash for a gift from a friend who wished to remain anonymous at least until they arrived. So Mr and Mrs McCallum were slightly surprised but pleasantly so when the Travel Agents contacted them with the details of their all expenses paid weekend for two in the Marine House Hotel, Troon, and confirmed that they would drive down there on the Friday afternoon and stay till after Sunday lunch. Frank put considerable artistic and creative effort into the letter of explanation he arranged to be left for them at the Hotel foyer, to be given to them with the champagne over Saturday dinner. "You probably will not have any memory left of this, but you once long ago did me several extreme kindnesses at a time when I was very down, and now that my circumstances have altered considerably I have decided to share some of my good fortune with the people who demonstrated their true worth. Please enjoy this weekend as a small recompense from me for your earlier acts of charity, and drink the first glass to my memory, Your old and grateful friend, Jimmy Brown." He wished he could be there to watch them read it but he would have more pressing priorities by then.

For his dummy run, he hired the car on the Thursday, for four days. He did everything else exactly the same as he would on the real thing. The trip down the Ayrshire coast to Ardrossan on the Thursday in the hired Maestro. The leaving it in the car park and getting the train back to Central. The leisurely drive back down in his own car on the Friday and the changeover, driving the Maestro back up to its date with destiny in Mount Florida. The only thing he didn't do was the switch of number plates, although he stopped in the shady lane outside Dunlop for the required amount of time. No point in taking that chance for a dummy.

In the car, he waited for the period of reserve he had given himself and at 12:05pm precisely he swung into action. He put the tinted paper on the windows then transformed himself into his hirsute friend. Then he got out, locked the driver's door, went round to the other side, took out his bag of goodies, locked that side and walked down the hill towards Hampden. He went right into the close at No 37, up the steps without pause and climbed the stairs to the third floor. It was too early for the policeman on duty outside the close to be there yet. He went straight to the far door, of the top flat right, and studied it intently for 5 seconds. Then he turned and walked back slowly gently kicking the mat outside the top flat left as he passed it. He estimated his business inside would take him five minutes maximum so he adjusted his timings accordingly. He walked briskly down the three flights of stairs and out into the street. He bowed to his left in homage, then made his way back up Brownlie Street to his car, where he put the theoretically empty bag into the boot. He went back into the front seat and transformed himself into Frank Hunter again. Then he took down the tint. The less time the car looked flash the better. Some of these sickos could see that as reason alone for smashing the window. At least there would be no bluenoses around on the day.

He left the car at 12:22pm to head towards the Victoria Bar where he would be expected at half past. He got there at 12:35pm, which was fine, since once more he would have a drink problem: how not to drink too much of it without arousing the suspicion of his friends. One and a half hours they would be in the pub. Fortunately after a couple of bad experiences Paddy had started insisting they leave early for big games, so they would be out of the bar by 2 o'clock. Maybe he could extend or delay his walk to the Victoria till about quarter to one. Then he could comfortably drink or appear to drink three pints or more while only actually consuming about two. This time none of his regular mates were there. He spoke to one or two people at the bar before taking his pint over to sit by himself in his favourite table at the corner of Allison Street and Victoria Road. He had put the papers in his anorak to explain the bulk if asked, so he settled down happily with his pint to read them in his usual order. He was amazed how cool he was. Some kid this, he told himself admiringly.

He was joined for a while by Tony Dixon, who had dropped in for a quiet lunchtime pint. Tony worked with Danny. A rabid Spurs man, he had been an eager recruit to SAD but had pleaded poverty and given the recent trip to Barcelona a miss. He was keen to hear all about it again, especially the blow by blow account of the goal. Any remaining doubts Tony had about Frank's sanity were confirmed when he heard he was going to see Queens Park play Berwick Rangers. Tony hadn't adopted any Scottish team to his heart, preferring to spend his money going down to Moffat every Sunday to watch some decent football. When absolutely desperate for the real thing, he would go to Ibrox and admire the Stadium, and count the Englishmen. Frank liked Tony unreservedly. He had often felt ashamed at the response of some of his friends and colleagues, at the less than totally friendly aggression that had been directed at him solely because of his Englishness, in both the pub and the Labour Party. Not that Tony needed protection. He always stood his ground and could generally generate a spark of shame of his own by saying that he had always thought Arsenal fans were the worst racist bastards around but they had nothing on the Scots. Tony bought Frank a second pint but left without taking one in return, so Frank found it easy not to drink his third pint. He could keep his renewed bladder complaint for the Final.

He left the pub at 2pm on the dot and walked the route they would take to the Final. He knew he could rely on the fact that they were creatures of habit, remarkably conservative in most ways, and the route was always the same whether they left from the Victoria, Neesons, the Queens Park Bar, the Albert or the Hampden. Down Langside Road to the bottom, left through the Queens Park Recs. to Cathcart Road. Right down to Somerville Drive and along to turnstiles M at the Celtic end of the North enclosure. Hampden was completely deserted. It was ludicrous whatever way you looked at it. The biggest ground in Scotland being used for a game that would attract 500 people at the most. There would be more than a hundred times that for the Final. Frank remembered being part of a crowd of 134,000 on several occasions, great days. It didn't bother him that he was early, still 40 minutes to go till kick-off. It gave him time to do his strange thing and pay for admission twice. If once was verging on the insane what did twice make him? He went to the Stand first, as near to the Directors Box as he could get. He had underestimated if anything the number of flats and houses with a direct line. But he had chosen well, he could see that vividly. He could see his car clearly, without glasses. Yes, it was remarkable but he was right. It could be done.

He made an excuse and left, back round to the North Enclosure. He found it hard to get a gate open to get into the Celtic end of the North Enclosure, where they would be for the Final. But he was in and on the open terracing with 15 minutes to spare. Frank could never be lonely or bored at Hampden, not with all his memories and ghosts. Frank had always had the football-intellectual's capacity for remembering games in detail, for being able to rerun whole segments through the internal video in his head. So while he waited he thought not of the Prime Minister and their future interaction but of Cup finals he had been at, of great games he had seen, of magic moments that had warmed him

304

forever. He remembered in particular his first Cup Final, against Dunfermline. Christ that was nearly thirty years ago now. He could still remember the impact on the little boy of the first few moments coming out from underneath that Stand now long demolished. The noise and the colour; the atmosphere of joy. It had been like an injection of football fever, a lifetime dose. He remembered fondly the sad wee boy he had been, crying himself to sleep after the replay, his mother and Gran trying to console him despite their own pain. There would be plenty of time for crying after this one, but it would be other people who would do it.

Standing there, on his own, leaning on a barrier, he felt happy again, like a child. These had been the good times, the Stein Cup-winning teams; the Leeds game; Scotland qualifying for Germany. He had had hopes for a golden future. He had always seen himself on that pitch, doing the business. He remembered the games he had played on that turf, for the Viccies. No-one could take that from him. He had played at Hampden, scored a goal into the Celtic end nets. Now he was going to play another kind of game there, and maybe earn himself the fame that had been so cruelly denied him by his knee. At that precise moment he found it hard to believe, he was so happy with his memories. Queens Park broke that spell for him, replacing romance with reality. Amateurs against professionals. For once he identified with the amateurs, since that was his new role. It was terrible stuff. He did not believe he could not do better, even at his age and with one and a half legs. Enjoyable enough in its own way, but then he enjoyed watching park games. Berwick were two up by half-time - so much for the amateurs.

At half-time he said his farewell to his friends and went looking for his Uncles, down nearer the halfway line they would be. He departed from the routine to get himself a pie and a Bovril. There would be no chance of that treat at the final. While queuing, he took in the toilet arrangements, eight portacabin cubicles for the number twos, eight more than there used to be. In desperation, at the Argentina game last month, he had worked up the courage to use one. Not only was the toilet roll still there, but there was soap in the sink. No towel but. The pie and Bovril gave him a warm glow that the game had denied him. The second half looked no better from his new vantage point, but even so he felt a faint sense of regret at having to leave before the end. Still, he disciplined himself and at 4:12pm precisely he went to the toilet. There was no queue this time but he had to legislate for at least some wait on the day. He locked himself in the cubicle. It was tight but not impossible. He put on the beard, and the sunglasses, and the Scotland hat pulled right down to the ears. He stuffed his first anorak up his jumper along with his papers and put on the light weight one. In his wee mirror he looked definitely different. The whole transformation took less than the normal time for a shite. He didn't want to draw attention to himself by poor time-keeping. There would likely be a queue. He wondered again if anyone would notice if someone went in clean shaven and came out with a beard. He could just hear the Glasgow voice. "Some shite that, son, I've heard of them putting hair on your chest, but on your chin, that is truly fucking impressive." He was relying on people queuing having their mind on other things. They tended to do so. Getting out of the ground proved harder than he had imagined, but eventually he found a steward who obliged. What were his chances of getting exactly the same one in a fortnight? Slim, he hoped. And even then why should he remember. It would be a busier day.

He was up at the top floor of the Brownlie Street close by 4:20, did the same pirouette and walked back up to the car with the imaginary carpet under his arm. He still wasn't sure about including this bit. At first he had been depressed at the general consensus that yes the police outside closes did extend round the corner to Brownlie Street at least up to the junction with Cumming Drive, which was past his one. But the more he had thought about it, and explored the vicinity, the less of a problem it had seemed and the more of a bonus. The peculiar geography of number 37 helped, right enough, with its unusual high staircase up to the close, and its long hall with the turn downstairs concealed round the corner. If the policeman stood at the bottom of the close steps, as he would, he would not be able to see anyone coming or going by the back close. The back close door had a lock, although the old bolts meant that it would be easy enough to pull open without the key. He had decided to acquire the key, though. It would be useful for that knowledge to be known. He had envisaged at first an undignified scramble over a back wall but there was none. Entry could be had, unobserved by any stationed policeman, off the lane from Bolivar Drive, or through 148 Stanmore Road close, without the need even for opening a gate. So even if he went back to the flat, he could do so unobserved and would have the choice of leaving past the policeman or more discreetly. He still had a fancy for the former, so on his dummy, he entered via the lane and left by the front stairs, but then it dawned on him that if the policeman was bored he might follow him with his eyes and see him stop at the car. The man swearing that absolutely no-one came out at all would not count for much once they clocked the back position. And if he didn't need to be seen leaving, maybe he didn't need to go back at all. Although the later he put the bullet shells there the better.

The street was empty when he got to his car. He quickly retinted the windows and then set to work. It did not take long to set up the rests. He was very pleased with them. They provided an echo of his old skills and precision. He took out the dummy gun and placed it in the rest. He noticed his throat had gone very dry and his breathing was becoming restricted. This man was less cool now. He wished he had done the toilet in the cubicle, maybe that was one lesson he could learn from the day and adjust the timings accordingly. He wound down the driver's window and looked out. No-one coming either direction. It was too soon for any one to leave the game. He checked with the binoculars from the front seat. Seats three and four from the centre on the right hand side as he looked at it were occupied. It would be one of those two seats, he was positive of that, almost certainly the third. It was taken by a fat man in a smart suit. He would never know he was about to feature in the sights of one of the most lethal rifles available. Frank checked again, no-one coming his side, only an old lady with her shopping bag on the other. Since there would be no noise this time he could let her go. No-one coming up Brownlie Street. That would be the danger, anyone else would have to be right beside the car to see inside, but coming up the hill they would be able to see the barrel of his gun. He had always reckoned his main danger would be in leaving it too tight, too late and have a flow of early leavers. Celtic were playing badly enough to remind him of 1963 and the mass walkout that had had such a moving effect on the young boy. This time there were no early leavers but he might have to bring everything forward five or ten minutes to be sure, to be sure.

He set his stop watch, left the driver's side and entered the car on the passenger side front door. The seat was already folded right down. He rechecked the sights one last time. Seat three was his choice, the man continued to look unperturbed. A real contact, not a distant inhuman image. He could see from his tie what the man had had for his dinner. Frank felt a strange sensation that he knew to be fear, his own. He waited until the imaginary helicopter was the optimum range away, then refocused. He held his breath and then two seconds longer than the plan he squeezed the trigger. He would have to work on the mental problem and eliminate those two seconds, they were about three minutes long each. He didn't wait to see the effect of his squeeze. He rolled over into the front driver seat, switched the ignition on, put the car into gear and drove off down Stanmore Road. His previous practices had shown him he could be down from the crest of the steep hill into the main road in well under 30 seconds. That would be about the time he would have for the Police Control Room to realise the effect of his squeeze, monitor the hellytelly and get word to the helicopter to swing back. He was fortunate that it was a steep hill. 1:7 the sign said but the engineer in him reckoned it was even steeper, it would block the view from that angle. Cathcart Road was a busy thoroughfare, even with the match on, and he knew if he could use the hill and the angle and the gap to get onto it before the hellytelly could focus on movement in the immediate vicinity, then he was free. They would not pick up and follow cars on the main road, they would be looking for activity in the side-streets. 24 seconds it took him this time. Then straight down Cathcart Road, left into Allison Street away from the police traffic men, then up into Pollokshields away and free. He was on the M8 motorway in seven minutes and in under an hour was paddling in the warm waters of the gulf stream. He would not have missed the boat.

He had a long walk along the beach, then a quiet contemplative pint in the Brown Bull in Lochwinnoch on his way back. When he got back home, he packed everything away methodically then sat in his bath for an hour trying to work out why it had gone so well, and why that made him feel so peculiar. It could not be that easy, could it? He asked himself a question he had often considered on his late shift tutorials. He asked himself if it was that easy to kill the Prime Minister, why had the IRA never done it?

He reassured himself that they had tried, and come damn near it too, in Brighton in 1984. He was always amazed at how little impact it appeared to have on the national consciousness, just how near they had come to killing her that night. The outrage had passed soon with barely a ripple left. Maybe that was why they did not repeat the attempt. Maybe they realised that she was so unpopular that killing her would be seen as a release and a bonus rather than the final unacceptable straw that would provoke withdrawal. Maybe after that they had decided it would not be good politics to kill her, it would make too many people happy, not

308

the desired result from their viewpoint. They tended to use bombs and missiles, and handguns, rather than rifles. And the rifles they did have were not the same as any of his, but he did not see that as a problem. Because he knew the truth gleaned from his homework: it is incredibly easy to kill any target who appears in public, if a rifle and rest are used. The difficulty lay in escaping detection, either immediately or later. He wondered again what special security arrangements would be in force for the final, other than the normal parking restrictions. There would be the helicopter, with its camera and film. Would there be film of the parked traffic they could examine later, or of moving traffic? Would they do any vetting at all of premises overlooking the ground, other than their perfunctory check of the residents? Would they have film of the windows, a camera constantly monitoring them? He had made many enquiries of the security arrangements likely to be in force, particularly with the guest of honour. Her immediate protection would be taken care of by her regular people, a team of Personal Protection Officers from the Royalty and Diplomatic Protection Branch of the Met. But the Strathclyde Police would work with them and keep full responsibility for the overall security. He could imagine their weary despair, life was hard enough without her adding a further dimension to their workload.

Frank was fairly confident he knew the realistic answers to these and all his many other questions. They were more relevant to the success of part B of his plan than the main objective and he still wasn't sure whether that was just an optional extra or whether he would proceed with it for real. He did like his little jokes did Frank Hunter. It never bothered him that few other people found them funny, too dry and ironic for most tastes. Since it was just a joke, he knew he would have to ensure that after sufficient time to make his point, someone explained the nature and humour of it to the appropriate people. He needed to do a bit more work on that side of it yet, but he had already decided whom he would use. Generally though, as he lay soaking in his bath that Saturday night, he had an ominous sense that the whole enterprise had taken on a life of its own and that he could not stop it even if he were to wish to do so. He was prepared to bet himself good money that it would be successful, a sure sign that it was a sure thing.

CHAPTER NINETEEN- SCOTLAND THE WHAT

Alone in his bed, Frank kept returning to the notion that he was doing this for his country, for Scotland, and that somehow there would be benefit to that land in his action. Through the dark Eighties Frank had remained true to his dream of an independent Scotland. The development of the Prime Minister's rule meant that he knew he had been absolutely correct in his 1979 assertions to Willie that the establishment of a Scottish Assembly, even the weak creature then on offer, would have inevitably lead to conflict and struggle that would have ended sometime after 1987 with the Scottish Assembly declaring Independence. The Labour Party in Westminster had proved totally unable to protect Scotland from the excesses of the Prime Minister despite their vast number of Scottish MPs. But a democratically elected Assembly representing the will of the Scottish people would have strived harder to do so and would have polarised matters to such an extent that there would have been no option but that a crunch would have come. However it had not happened, because of the No people, so detailed speculation of the process was only torture and self-abuse.

Frank had taken a degree of cynical amusement, a First Class Honours, in watching the effects of the Prime Minister's style of government on the attitude of many of his countrymen and women, especially those bastards who had voted NO in 1979. One by one those people who had killed the notion of Home Rule then, came out strongly in support of it. Frank had had to adapt his Hunter's Law of Scottish politics that had been so applicable throughout the seventies. It had stated that the commitment of the Labour Party to devolution of power to the Scottish people was in direct proportion to the strength and electoral standing of the Scottish National Party. While this Law still stood as valid in itself, as was demonstrated by the Govan By-election and subsequent responses, the more complex realities of the 1980s meant it had to be supplemented by other truths. So Frank had re-christened it Hunter's First Law and added Hunter's Second Law which stated that the Labour Party leadership's real as opposed to public commitment to devolution was in inverse proportion to the current likelihood of it forming the next government in Westminster. Frank also added the Special Case Third Law which stated that the commitment would equal, or be worth, zero, in the event of a Labour Government with a very small or non-existent majority.

Labour remained a Unionist party and its commitment to the needs and wishes of the Scottish people remained secondary to its commitment to the Union and its desire to see a Labour Government in Westminster. The arguments for a return of democratic control of their own affairs to the Scottish people were essentially the same as in 1979. Frank had little faith that it was the merits of these arguments alone that had wrought the change in the party's stated attitude to devolution. It was the recognition of the political realities of the United Kingdom, and in particular the hatred of the Prime Minister and her powers, that caused most converts. He knew that with a Labour Government in Westminster, the desire of many Labour people for a separate Scottish Parliament, fired by opposition to Tory policies, would not sustain itself just for such a Parliament to pass the same Labour policies that could be had directly from London. If Labour were to win they would desert again, fearing the loss of Westminster MPs and the reaction of their Northern English own, the ones who would prevent them delivering from a position of weakness. Then they would suddenly find, to their intellectual amazement, that the Mandate argument no longer applied, since the Scots would have the kind of government they had voted for. Conveniently they would forget that Labour in Scotland was a minority party, benefiting ludicrously well from a corrupt electoral system. That was why Frank would always argue that the real issue was not the mandate argument but the sovereignty one, but most of the new converts couldn't see that they were different which is why they failed to realise how much ground they had sold to buy the Claim of Right.

Despite his disillusionment, Frank had stayed in the Labour Party, and still attended its meetings, regularly failing even to get a seconder for his motions that Independence might be a good thing. Frank was depressed by the lack of understanding in his own party about the religious factor in the success or otherwise of their campaign against the SNP. Much of the concern about Govan had been dissipated in the celebrations about the turning of tide in Glasgow Central without the realisation that it was the differential commitment to Labour of the two rival working class communities that was one of the keys. It was only two or three generations ago that many of the Protestant working class in the West of Scotland automatically followed its Church into the booths on behalf of the Tory Party. That was the main reason why Frank was able to win pub bets from his less literate Catholic drinking mates about which was the only Scottish party to get more than 50% of the votes in a post-war election, the Tories in 1955. Although after that, more predictable class divisions became reflected in the voting, the commitment and loyalty of the Protestant working class to Labour was much less disciplined than that of the Catholic community. The proddies were more likely to be encouraged to desert Labour and embrace the Nats than their Catholic neighbours. Frank had always known that was one of the great unmentionable truths of Scottish politics, and was a major factor in Labour's unwillingness to grasp the school segregation issue. That was why he also had little truck with the sentimental nostalgia for working class values of the past that some of the leading Scottish artists and intellectuals wallowed in.

The morality and logic of the few Independence people in the Labour Party depressed him. They wanted it both ways, to win under the old rules, but if they lost to immediately say they weren't playing any more and change the game. Frank, instilled with his Union discipline, felt if you weren't going to accept the decision you should not take part, but if you did take part then you were committed to accepting the decision. Nor was he impressed by the logic that said the best possible outcome was a win by her because the Scottish people would not tolerate that and would rise up. He had heard that before 1983 and 1987. Doomsday was a mañana date, and Scotland was not an occupied country, but maybe content to remain a mañana republic. He wanted to make his point, as an alternative to a vote in a game he rejected, to provide the example and basis for political myth, for a Scottish political identity wider than the SNP vision, for Scots to grasp the need for direct action.

He had often asked himself why he stayed in the Labour Party in preference to joining the SNP. He knew it was partly tribal loyalty. The Labour Party was still to him the party of organised labour and the Trade Unions. He preferred the philosophical basis of Labour's social policies to anyone else's. For all his commitment to national independence he never felt himself to be a nationalist. Also the leadership of the SNP were so consistently petty and stupid. No movement whose major intellectual basis appeared to be hatred of the English could expect his support. The SNP leadership had consistently got every major decision they had had to make wrong. They had been anti-Europe in 1975, ironic in light of their later commitment. They had failed to support the Assembly cause enough in 1976-79, preferring instead the futile purism, or puerility, of "Independence Nothing Less". They had turned back to their traditional habits in the early 80s and had expelled or exiled all those whom Frank had any time for. If he had joined in 1976 say, he would have been ones of those expelled.

But the worst betrayal of all, the most craven refusal to learn from the lessons of history, was their failure to stay in the Constitutional Convention in 1989. The decision to abandon the Convention was the one that depressed him most, reeking as it did of their old arrogance that they were the only true voice of the Scottish people. It was self defeating and did the wider cause they claimed to represent no good. The basic issue was, as it always was, the notion that the Scottish people have their own sovereignty, and that that basic principle must inform the government of the land. The Constitutional Convention was bound to endorse that notion, but would have done so more vigorously, clearly and credibly with the SNP on board. The stance of the SNP was actually detrimental to the aims they professed to hold most dear. If the 80% or more of the Scottish people believing in some separate expression of that sovereignty united to demand it, then either it would be given or it would be taken.

Once that expression was consolidated into an Assembly then the rules of the Westminster game changed. The SNP has always made the mistake of playing by those rules, and saying that Independence could only come when they won 50% of the Westminster seats. Yet the Westminster electoral system would mean that they would always fall far short of that total even when a majority of the Scottish people wanted independence. Under those rules they could wait for ever. However, as Frank would scream to the few nationalists he talked to, if an Assembly were created the rules would change. The Assembly, directly and democratically elected, would be the representation of the Sovereignty of the Scottish people, and all that would be required for the moral authority for Independence would be a majority vote of that body. If that body did not wish that, fine, but the Labour Party and the other Unionist parties in favour of an Assembly could have no quarrel with the notion that its wishes must be obeyed. Yet by opting out of the Constitutional Convention the SNP turned their backs on that route to the expression of the wishes of the Scottish People in favour of their own partisan model. This was rightly seen by many Scots as rejection of their best interests and their popularity slumped. Not only did they lose for themselves the chance to build on the Govan victory, they lost the chance for their ultimate cause to be seen as a Scottish one rather than a party one. Tommy Gemmell and Willie Donnachie could teach these people nothing about the defence of Scotland.

Whilst they had overcome their earlier anti-Europeanism in time to benefit from the Scottish awareness that a European community now existed and changed the rules of the game for good, making the old separatist fears no longer the potent bogey they had been twenty years before, they had failed to grasp the most effective way to project that reality and their demands. They had got their slogan wrong, missing the positive point and confusing the people. It should have been "Independence at home, Interdependence in Europe", not the incorrect and confusing "Independence in Europe" that they did adopt.

He did not like the emotional and nasty nature of many of their activists, with the talk of traitors, and vilification of all things and people English. And their unpleasant greed. They were often the worst kind of Scot, with their moaning self-pitying complaining. A dour depressive race of greetin' faced girners, searching for the cloud in which to encase every shard of silver. The ones whose idea of sportsmanship was to score an own goal whenever a game looked dangerously like being capable of being won. And not the kind of creative own goal favoured by Paddy, Gerry, Danny, Peter McColl and all the rest of his self-destructive friends. Their own goals were spectacular, wondrous entertainment to save the fans from goal-less boredom. These others would score their scrappy own-goals to avoid the responsibility for coping with victory and to allow them the preferred option of wallowing in the complaints of robbery and injustice. Yet at least they had voted YES, so there were worse than them around, even more negative and vile.

He hated the SNP anthem too, with its anti-English obsessiveness and its violent tone. He always enjoyed the memory of Gerry Robertson's outburst at the Scottish night of the G&M conference in Brighton, when towards the end of a booze-filled evening the rabble had broken out into full flower. Gerry had grabbed the microphone and insisted on full attention while he challenged all of them, any of them, to prove to him that they owned any wee bit of any wee hill or glen. Not one of them could of course, but the stupid bastard had ruined it by pushing it too far, turning a productive guilt into a defensive protectionism. That was the great thing about Scotland, your friends were more dangerous

314

than your enemies. And he didn't have a better anthem. In the end they had all been worn down, past a point of redemption and even the SFA had conceded that song its place. He preferred the words, "welcome to your gory bed, or to victory", but it didn't fit as well to the musical mood of the Tartan Army. The more Frank studied the psychology of his country the more he felt the suffocating restriction on his soul. He could not stand to stay and choke, it was only possible to prosper away. He understood why some of the best had gone, to new lands far away, to escape the limitations of their own. Well, he was going to escape too, seek his own warped release and leave the survivors to draw the lessons from his gift.

He had known casually one or two of the wilder madmen on the lunatic fringe of the SNP, the Scottish Liberation crowd. Daft bastards the lot of them though he had had pleasant enough pints with a few of them. He was not allying himself with them, that would need to be made very clear to posterity. His protest was of a different order, ordure to their silly shite. They might try to claim him as one of their own but he would leave his denials in place before he went. The Scots were not an oppressed people held down by violence and authoritarianism. They were subjugated only by the weakness of their own will, not the strength of others. Therefore they had no right to use violence against others, especially not the English, who genuinely believed they were doing them a favour by having them as partners. Frank always had a sound grasp of the morality of political violence. It was only permissible when other democratic means were totally denied. The Scots claimed that they had rejected the Prime Minister three times but had had her policies forced upon them on each occasion. A democratic deficit indeed. By his calculations it could and would happen a fourth time, in 1991 or 1992. That would still not, in his book, justify a violent response because each time they had played the game by the rules, taken part knowing these rules, and hoped for a different outcome.

If it came to the point that they decided not to play the game any more, opted out and claimed their own separate sovereignty as a basis for playing their own game, and that request was denied by force, then and only then could violence be countenanced. And he did not think that such a violent denial would take place. He did not believe that the thoroughly unfriendly process would be as unfriendly as to extend to violent suppression, and he had generally won the pub debates with the more pessimistic who believed it would. But he had always said that if he were wrong

315

then he would be prepared to fight. Just as the oppression was not worth killing to remove so the benefits were not worth killing for to protect. Ultimately the English state would let them go without a physical fight, once the political one was lost. His political instincts had always been correct in matters like this and he was certain of his correctness on this one.

He had always believed it was not worth killing for, this independence he wanted, unless people were killing to prevent it, but the question for him now was it worth dying for. Because that was how he wished his act to be seen, as a political protest for which he was prepared to die.

He spent more time talking to the crumpled and faded picture of Jan Palach he had carried in his wallet since 1969 than he had done for many years. At last there was a model for him, not an assassin but a political suicide, one that had a profound and moving effect on his country. Jan had committed suicide on the 19th January 1969, when a 21 year old student, by burning himself alive in Wenceslas Square, in that "one dreadful act that highlighted the disillusionment of an entire generation." The young Frank had been impressed that Jan was one of a larger group and the decision that it should be him had been made and accepted by the drawing of lots. His sacrifice had not been in vain. His death and its horrific manner had become the symbol not just for his own country-folk but for the world, of the refusal of the Czechoslovakian people to accept the reality of Soviet domination and of their desire to control their own destiny. They had kept his memory alive during the hard times, burning candles before a photograph similar to Frank's, and now in victory there was Jan Palach Square. Frank's hope was that his people would understand that only one had to die, that killing the Prime Minister was not a murder, the incitement to further slaughter, but a demonstration of the seriousness of a nation that would require only two deaths, hers and then his. Both acts would then be political rather than just the first. Being able to reach that conclusion gave him considerable satisfaction, making his sense of destiny seem ever more positive. That became important to him.

He had a further Czech connection in his argument with Havel about whether a man's destiny could be divorced from his character or whether one was always the victim of the other. If Havel was right, given what the years had revealed about Frank's personality, how could he possibly hope for anything but a negative destiny? But his would be positive, he promised that to

316

himself and his crumpled photo. Frank knew what the man meant, and agreed rationally with it in general terms, but without compromising his rejection of both religion and fatalism he also knew that he had always known that Frank Hunter was marked out for a major destiny, and that early knowledge had had a profound effect on the development of his character and personality.

He kept the concept of the two time scales going, the immediate aftermath and the historical reality. He proved to himself, since it was a joke he could not yet share, that his sense of humour was still alive as he developed his concept of the initial decoy. He wasn't quite sure what the lesson of Lee Harvey Oswald taught him here, possibly contradictory things, but he was certainly proof that people are not necessarily what they seem, and the tying-in of representations of what they seem into the likely time and place can cause initial certainty and later confusion. So he happily sowed his plans to ensure that others would be given the initial credit for his actions and that he would get the time thereby to execute his own end with his own end.

It helped that he had always hated them, with such a venom, bordering on the irrational, that he sometimes wondered if it could be a Mendelian inheritance from Willie Hunter that had skipped his dad and shot straight into him. Except that he knew he hated the other side just as much. They were murdering bastards, both lots of them, but his particular venom was reserved for the ones that pretended that their murders were politically positive acts.

He had lived and been active in the political southside of Glasgow long enough to well know who their main men on the mainland were, which particular permutations of Irish Glasgow and Glasgow Irish gave their allegiances to which sections of the movement and to what degree, the ones that just gave them sympathy, and the ones that gave that little deadly bit more. He knew that was one thing he had against them, and one element, one layer of humour to his joke. They regarded themselves as Irish rather than Scottish, even the ones whose great-grandparents had come over with Frank's own ancestors, Peter Coyle's parents and Jean Rogan's parents, in the last decades of the previous century. Frank wasn't Irish and neither were they, except that by believing so they became so. They would go to Hampden and wave the tricolour, for fuck's sake; and support Eire against Scotland. They all supported Celtic which meant they were on the same side as him, and they all sang the same rebel songs, but they marched to a different tune.

317

Many of the less extreme of them also joined the Labour Party, at one time or another, to help Charlie Spence or to support the Labour Committee on Ireland or whatever other front they were sponsoring at the time. He hated them for that, almost as much as he did the Trots, for using his party for their own nasty and vicious ends rather than its own positive aims. They often drank in the same pubs as him, with him often enough if he were honest. He knew many of the milder ones from school, Celtic Supporters Clubs, and travel to away games, and numbered several of them among his casual friends with whom he was happy enough to share a chat and a pint. The harder cases were another matter, with a lower profile and regular spells back in the old country. He knew them but did not like them, and tended not to drink where they did.

Frank had a degree of conscience when he worked out who his main victim would be, because he had had a genuine affection for him, and real respect for his wife. They had been to many games together, over the years, many Labour Party meetings together, and if they were seldom on the same side there, they were always able to share a pint and a laugh together later. But he would never forgive Jim for what he had done to Paddy. The bad blood between the pair of them went back as long as Frank could remember, and he had often defended Jim from Paddy's vicious tongue - but maybe Paddy had been more accurate in his assessment. For very little personal gain Jim had knifed Paddy and cast a major shadow over his standing in the Labour Catholic mafia family that determined who would prosper and who would stagnate. The cloud with his putrid piss in it had hovered low over Paddy's head and had even threatened his District Council base. It had certainly rained a damper on his prospects of further advancement. Well reckoning time was near, and Jim would find out what happened to those who hurt the ones Frank Hunter loved. Unless their name was Frank Hunter of course, but it was now established that his own punishment was to be capital so Jim might be getting off lightly. It was only a joke after all.

There were one or two books in the Mitchell that helped with the forensic aspects of his subplan. Amazing what could be done with sellotape and imagination, but in the main it just required nerve, organisation and a resort to drinking with a slight change of company. He knew there were several dangers to this little diversion. There was the physical element. If he underestimated their intelligence or, more likely, overestimated his own and they worked out what he was doing, there would be a little knee-capping or worse. They might just think it was theft, the stealing of an anorak here, and a pair of gloves, a spectacle case, and a supply of glasses. He had no illusions about what they were capable of, the harder end, if they guessed anything of his wider aim. He knew of one or two of their Scottish operations, as well as their involvement in the real thing. His knee had ended his football career, he didn't fancy it doing the same to his political one.

There was a more subtle fate that he considered an even worse outcome: that he would be too clever by half and end up creating an end rather than a means. He was a Irish Catholic Glasgow man the same as his targets after all, and he would be seen, surveilled was the word, frequenting where he was planning to go. Maybe the Oswald illusion would backfire, he would have to do his external homework well to avoid that conclusion. That truly would be an own goal if he got the credit after all but they kept it too, and his was only part of theirs.

This aspect of his plan had required, for the covering immigration of his choicest target birds, Celtic to be in the Final, not a certainty the way they were playing that season. But he had found it a source of some amusement that the lady herself helped his case and chances by conducting the semi-final draw personally and giving the Bhoys the easy option. Given that assistance they did not let him down, and by the 14th of April it had been done, they would be there against Aberdeen, and the cross channel migration could be expected, with certainty.

He had tried to talk to Gerry, Paddy and others about the political implications of a Scot killing her rather than the Irish, but none of them took the hypothesis seriously. He did; but could not foresee unacceptable consequences. He knew that nationalism clouded the analysis of the morality of violence and its relationship with democracy. Democracy can incorporate the permanent subjugation of the minority by the majority. Democracy might be incapable of reconciling competing demands. There was no democratic solution to the Irish problem, perhaps there was none to the Scottish one either. He knew it was possible, if very unlikely, that Scotland could remove every single last one of the ten Scottish Tory MPs in 1992 and yet still end up ruled by that bloody woman, with their separate legal, educational and social systems under further threat and erosion. Yet that would be legitimate by the rules of the unionist game they had never refused to play. Salvation would only come when they withdrew from the game and played their own in Edinburgh. He could not see many of the Labour MPs of 1992 having the desire to do that, or the capacity to provide moral leadership to the nation. They had long ago as a party lost the sense of what was morally correct. Every issue in the 1970s was judged on the basis of what was best for Labour not what was right, morally. In the early 1980s it had been even worse with every issue assessed as what was best for the left or the right of Labour. Leadership election formulas and every other issue were supported or rejected on that basis rather than on independent consideration of its moral merit. It had become a habit from which there seemed no escape.

He found he could read a political tome during the day at the Mitchell and then decide at night which pub to go to pursue an argument on its thesis. Glasgow was still a city where its drinking classes had a regard for self-education. Not that he bought the myth that every savage with a pint was noble. Many of them, especially in the Rangers pubs, had not even read the beer mats, although they would still give you an argument. But he did know enough philosophers to assure himself that his theories could be tested with people who had some knowledge of his source material or similar. A part of Frank Hunter had always believed that he was, if not the cleverest fellow alive, the cleverest one that he knew. He never met anyone to whom he would bow in recognition of superior political analysis, although he gave way slightly to the wee man at Keir Hardie House when it came to the ability to walk down a street, smell the air and know which way a town would vote, to within a few hundred. But he had never felt that he had ever really tested his powers and stretched his abilities. He knew this project was a challenge worthy of him. To work out exactly what he was going to do and why, and how he wished this achievement to be viewed, then and later. For the first time in his life he enjoyed his work, and would awaken, when he slept, with a sense of anticipation and joy, looking forward to the challenge that lay ahead.

He knew his little joke would be a test of the separate Scottish legal system. That was part of the joke, that it was different, and his lawyer friends had been saying for years that certain defects of the English system just could not happen north of the border. If it passed his test then it would prove its inherent superiority. In addition, he would have a safe backup just to make sure it did not fail. He had wrestled with his conscience about the morality of his joke. He knew that it was the hatred of the IRA that had led to the wrongful arrests in Birmingham and Guildford, and the scandal of innocent men being locked up for years. But he was talking about months at the very most. And they wouldn't be entirely innocent, that was one of his wider points, active sympathisers bear some responsibility for the murders of the organisation they support. He hated their habit of apologising for their fatal mistakes in the fatalistic way they did. Two children dead, very regrettable, but their parents did chose to live in Ireland. One aspect of his joke was to show the potential price of that support. Another was to restore some faith in the legal system, ultimately. Definitely a very moral joke.

CHAPTER TWENTY - MORE IMPORTANT THAN THIS

His evenings in the pub became very important to him, an integral part of his project as well as a joy in themselves. They were usually in the Victoria. It had always been one of his favourite pubs, one of his 14 favourite pubs. He had a catholic taste in pubs, a bhoy could get beaten up in the other kind, but towards the end he plumped almost exclusively for the Victoria. His commitment to it had even survived the purple paint. He liked the soft old fashioned leather benches, the good Guinness and the fine company. It was a democratic pub, not divided by crude tiers of social class into public bar and lounge, but only by a more subtle front and back section. Frank was a front man. His favourite seat was in the corner, at the junction of Allison Street and Victoria Road. He knew where on the wall he wanted the small brass plaque to go "Frank Hunter drank here". On a good night, and there were many of them, his friends would take up all three tables in that small corner. They would be shut off from the rest of the pub, except for a clear view of the bar, by the sets of heavy mirrors that topped the leather backs. Frank's favourite manoeuvre, when sufficiently well-oiled, was to align himself in exactly the one spot that could provide the right angles for reflections of himself. Images within images into infinity, a mind-blowing experience worth any three pints. He reckoned the happiest nights of his life were spent in that small corner, sipping Guinness and swallowing football and political arguments.

For his project he revived the pub games he used to enjoy so much, like the Greatest Scotsman of the Twentieth Century, and the Greatest Living Scotsman. The same man got Frank's vote for each, and generally ended up the winner. Kenny Dalglish. He often wondered if it was down to significant chance, or merely the rutting cycles of West of Scotland Protestant Males, that he and Kenny Dalglish shared the same birthday. It seemed too significant to ignore or dismiss as chance, a line with God. He looked for other lines of comparison between himself and the man, the same height and weight, the same magic left foot, the same keen football intelligence - but he seldom pursued it too far, it was the one form of blasphemy that bothered him. "Kenny Dalglish plays on water." His mate Gerry Robertson had spray-painted that message onto the wall of the Mitchell Library after one particularly intellectually taxing evening in the Ritz, the favoured bar across the road from the G&M head office. He was then 37 years old and had not held a can in his hand for 24 years, but he had succumbed to an overwhelming need to pay tribute. Gerry always gave him his vote too.

The winner of these games had to be a footballer. Think about it, Jack Reilly their philosopher would say, who else has created national identity and awareness and pride by their actions? Not a politician in sight, despite the voters' commitment to that art. They had read John MacLean's speeches instead of just buying the legend. Wheatley and Maxton got a mention. Frank and Gerry had toyed with the notion of the book that needed written, the three who failed to make a revolution, the Scottish Wolfe that didn't howl in the night. All three were admired in part but their failures and failings were too great. Of the rest of the dead, not a one, a Johnston or a Ross, could even get a mention far less a proposer. Ramsey Macdonald got the cynical vote, as the most typical politician. The current lot got a mention. Smith, Brown, Cook might be destined for greater glory, only none of them except for Jack believed they would ever get real power far less use it well enough to qualify. If one of them had the guts and heart to lead a move for an independent Scotland they would have a late chance but it was generally recognised that they didn't have that kind of bottle. The group did not share the old Scottish trait of veneration for scientists and engineers, but this century had not produced them as in the past anyway. The Arts and Literature fared no better with these educated philistines. None of them could thole MacDiarmid with his primitive and brutal politics, and his unreadable verse. There was no other contender, although the dour depressive Glaswegian sometimes got a vote or two after the fifth pint took effect, and the subtle wordsmith got grudging respect despite the convention to claim that his brother was the better writer. Sean Connery got a vote or two from the receders for losing his hair with grace and dignity, but that tended to be it for the arts.

Andy Rogers, with his Aberdonian wryness had created a near-riot one evening by proposing very seriously that for the greatest living Scot it would have to be Michael Forsyth. "School Boards, compulsory testing, opting out, privatisation, Health reorganisation, and that's just for starters, lads. Wait till the wee man gets going after the election, there'll be nothing left unprivatised in Scotland. He's the man." It was certainly a record of legislative achievement none of the non Tories could match, but eventually amid uproar he was disqualified. Jack, the referee in these matters had accepted Tommy Little's objection, "We hate the bastard. You can't have a winner none of us respect or admire." But it left an uneasy feeling and spoilt the taste of the pint.

Denis Law regularly got a minor placing in both categories, as much because of his behaviour on the afternoon of the 1966 World Cup Final as for any ball or body he had kicked. Jim Baxter was the other player who came close, but he would suffer from the fallout of the argument Danny and Jack always had about who was the greater, him or Beckenbauer. Baxter was a genius. Even every Celtic fan acknowledged that, but at the end of his too-short career what had he won, only the Scottish trophies. Beckenbauer with no better gifts had won the European Cup thrice, the Cup Winners Cup, the European Championship and the World Cup. It wasn't that winning was the only thing that matters, they all rejected that philosophy. It was that there had to be a purpose to the exercise other than just being brilliant, otherwise they could have designed the pitch and the rules without goalposts. So you had to play with style and class, but you also had to win, and to win at the highest level. Dalglish had done that. It was a source of grievance to all of them, but especially the European Frank, that Kevin Keegan - the Prime Minister's values in a football strip - had made the most of his limited abilities, by hard work and dedication, and become European Footballer of the Year twice. While King Kenny, a far more talented individual, and as dedicated a grafter, had never been given that recognition. They admired Keegan, but Dalglish was worshipped.

The only ones who ran him close were the trio of managers, Busby, Stein and Shankly. Frank used to wonder what it was about the Scottish character that had produced three such outstanding, strong and successful managers. There was a book waiting to be written there, three who made a revolution. But great as each man was, and they were, especially Stein, they found the final balance went against them and to the King, because they had demonstrated their genius off the park rather than on it. Kenny had been the last true genius on the park and none of the stars of the past that Jack Reilly and others waxed so nostalgic and lyrical about could touch him for consistency of genius at the highest level. So Kenny it had to be every time. Gerry Robertson had a theory, which meant it was regularly shared with the whole pub, that the English response to Kenny was the most graphic illustration of their subtle colonial superiority. The man inspires their best team, is the best player for a ten year period, wins the double in his first season as a manager and nearly repeats that three more times. Yet the English only made him footballer of the year twice, and most of the time instead of continuously lauding his genius they sneer at the incomprehensibility of his accent and mock his taciturnity, while idolising the inferior but home-grown Keegan. Talk about separate societies with different values.

For those who grew up with his nine in a row, and most of Frank's friends came into that category, Jock Stein had to be the greatest manager ever. Busby was admired, if not liked, for the attractiveness of his teams. But Shankly was the one they loved. He was the one who never managed the national team, maybe his good luck, or SFA stupidity, but he was the one who captured the national football soul. The one who gave them their motto, in his immortal words, "no, football was not a matter of life and death, it was more important that." For Frank the man spoke the truth, and truth was the most important thing. He might give a new meaning to the man's words, with his project.

Tony Dixon would sometimes respond with his own trio of great managers and argue his case for equality. He had nearly caused a riot the night he would not yield to his claim that Alf Ramsey was the greatest manager ever, having taken two hopeless cases to the top, Ipswich then England. Frank did not share the narrow view that it had been the FIFA Organising Committee that had won the 1966 World Cup for England not Ramsey. After all he had been there at the 4-3 game and had feared what was going to happen. But Ramsey was too cautious, as were his teams, to win true greatness through grace. No manager who left out a fit Jimmy Greaves could qualify. Jack supported the case for Don Revie and even claimed he loved the man, but while his team could be admired they were too mean of spirit and cautious to be loved, a reflection of their chief, so he was disqualified too. Clough they liked, he could come close, they would let him manage Scotland if he wanted. He was proof that they could admire an Englishman, they were not racially blind, but he was just not quite as great as Busby, Shankly or Stein.

Evenings of discussions like that always awoke some of the never dead pain in Frank about the premature end to his football dream. He had more natural talent than Keegan. He had as much dedication and commitment as the man. But he had been denied the other ingredient, of luck. If he had been allowed to try and had failed then that would have been painful. But to never be allowed even to try. That was the festering wound that he would take to his grave. All his close friends who did make it had stopped playing now. Derek Duncan and Tommy Gallagher were coaching in England, Tommy Little was a Social Worker. But they all had their memories, their sense of glory, of the knowledge that they had been able to pursue their dream as far as it would take them. They could die happy but he could not. At least he had found a way of believing that his death would do a little good for football as well as fulfilling his political destiny.

Very occasionally, after such a night of discussion in the pub, and then his own sad soliloquy to himself at home, he would wonder if there was something fundamentally mistaken about his sense of priorities, his evaluation of the truly important things in life. He was never really able to convince himself that politics was significantly more important than football but very occasionally on the far edges of his consciousness would seep in the uninvited visitor, the possibility that perhaps there was something even more important than either. Not some abstract concept like the truth, which he did believe in intensely but which he knew inhabited football as much as politics or any other aspect of life. But a more personalised notion like people. But people were surely an inescapable part of football and politics just like the truth; and he generally sent the intruder away.

Once, just once, in those busy days of his project, he caught a glimpse of its true shape and nature and wept into his beer for the way it had passed him by. There had just been the three of them, Danny, Gerry and himself having a quiet couple of pints. He loved them both, Gerry having gained promotion many years before, but he knew he could not tell them that. He tried to that early evening. Ran it through in his head several times. Just put his pint down on the table top, get their silence and then say quietly, I love you both. But he could not do it. The words came out as I love Celtic and I love Scotland and they were not in the least embarrassed or surprised. He looked at Danny with his two wives, his three live-in lovers and his several other ladies. But the only people he had ever admitted a passion for were men with names like Haddock and Herd, Coyle and Currie, Robertson and Ring. And Gerry Robertson. Oh dear. Gerry like the good boy he was, loved his mammy all right, the one affection allowed to all Scotsmen. He really loved her and even told her so, once a year. But not another living soul, not once, not ever and his fixation for sixteen year old cuntlicking was partly to ensure he never would. Yet he loved something called GoodfellowHilleyHarleyGrayandMcInnes with necrophiliac devotion and regularly followed the real love of his life all over Europe. Paris to him meant the eleven men in blue at the Parc de Prince, Vienna the Prater. True despair for Danny was the regularity with which Clyde were relegated rather than he separated. A broken heart to Gerry was the death of Third Lanark. The worst humiliation of his life had been Argentina 1978, not the other more personal candidates.

And then there was Jack, dear Jack. The worst disasters, the greatest pain in his life, were the two Hearts near misses, when they had only had to avoid defeat on the last day of the season to win the league, and failed. Come the great Post-Mortem in the sky when they cut Jack open and examine his heart they would find two deep scars, one dated 1965 and the other 1986. Neither had proved fatal, just, but Jack himself often acknowledged that if he had followed his father's dream and become a Thirds man, their death which killed his father could also have proved too much for the vulnerable young man he had been then. Gerry, from a harder mould, had survived the death of his first love, had survived the failed Thistle transplant and found some solace in sharing the love of his friends for the Celtic. But when his capacity for loving relationships was examined closely, then maybe the death of his first and main true love had done some irreparable damage after all.

Frank always remembered a conversation between Danny and Jack where Danny, in that cruel way even kind Social Workers have of transmuting their own pain by forcing other people to face theirs, had made Jack consider the possibility that his rejection of the Thirds had been a subconscious rejection of and desire to hurt and punish his father. Jack had been mortified, perhaps by some hidden understanding of the truth of the thesis, but he knew he could not have hurt his father deliberately, and he was still very grateful for whatever impulses had made him reject them and the fate and hurt and devastation that their embrace would have brought him. Danny, in a bad time, had expanded on how easy it was to survive the loss of a woman, and find a equally good replacement, but how none of them could really survive the loss of their one real first love, the true affair of their heart. Jack never would have survived that loss, but then he was the one who would never survive the loss of his wife either.

327

Frank knew with a different kind of sadness to his usual that he was no better. Worse certainly than Danny who did at least try to talk to his male friends about feelings, love and hurt and got in return only denial hiding anger and fear. Frank was far worse. He did not have feelings that could be expressed, only slogans. Elaine the never ending pain. Joyce the still voice, of denial, betrayal and sharing. Celtic for the Cup. Scotland the Brave. Jock Stein for pope. He was truly the number one SAD man. He realised the cause but not the solution. He had seen then with a chilling clarity that made his beer seem warm in his mouth what his problem was. And what their problem was. And the problem of every Scotsman he knew. All his life he and they had been taught by their sick society that emotion in men is wrong, a sign of weakness. The only acceptable avenue for expressing it he ever had access to was football. It was all right to cry when your team got beaten, and rejoice in victory. So football had become his sole focus for emotional identification and expression, and fulfilment. All his life the main emotions of love, happiness, despair, fear, joy, anger, disappointment, triumph, hope and aspiration were defined in terms of football. The relationship with club and country, the first loves, remained more important and deeper than any other. The old Glasgow Rangers supporter to his wife joke, "Love Rangers more than I love you? Listen, I love Celtic more than I love you" seemed more apt and more sad than he had ever found it before. Maybe not love, but certainly the object of more expressed and shared emotion.

They had been talking the previous night, the three of them and some others, about the harmful effects of Scotsmen placing their political national identification so firmly into their national football team, and how stronger Scotland might be if that identification could be transferred to political institutions. But he saw for the first time that there was an even more serious problem. He tried to share his new understanding with Danny and Gerry but it came out too much like a second-hand McIlvanney throwaway for them.

"You know, the problem with Scotsmen, the really sad thing about them, is not that they substitute football for their sense of national identity, but that they use it for their emotional sense of identity." "Yes sure Frank, sure. Isn't it your round?" But he knew he had found the key to something. It was just a pity the door was bolted.

It was not just his need for Celtic to get to the Final that brought football into being an integral part of his project. The more he read and studied, the more he became aware of the importance of the relationship between national identity and sport. He had always been aware of that but he learned more about its relevance to his project. The decision of UEFA to admit the Faroe Isles and San Marino into full membership was one strand. The realisation that East and West Germany would soon be one state with only one team and one champion was another. For all his claimed political acumen he had been as surprised as most at the speed of the disintegration of the Soviet Empire in East Europe and the release of national feelings involved. He was not at his best that autumn of 1989 as it crumbled and fell, and was too depressed to benefit from the real joy he felt at the death of state communism. As he got better he was able to work out the political consequences and likely sequences. He was particularly pleased for the Czechs and had had one or two conversations with his old friend Jan Palach.

That had been his final disillusionment with the Labour Party. Sitting in his misery trying to cheer himself up by watching the 1989 Labour Party Conference live on television. No wonder he didn't get better quickly. The painful bit had been the defence debates. Not the final burial of unilateralism, but the failure to grasp the significance of what was happening in Eastern Europe. Against the clear demonstrations available that the Warsaw Pact was over, that Poland, Hungary, Czeckoslovakia and the rest could no longer be seen as Soviet Union's Military Allies, far less as any threat to the West. So what did the Labour Party do: ignore Frank's exhortations whispered down his set, and commit itself to increasing conventional defence spending to stop any such invasion or threat. At a cost of alternative social welfare spending. What depressed him was his realisation that none of them in the leadership had the grasp and vision to see what was happening in the world and how that could change everything.

He acknowledged it was partly his fault. He had been part of the consensus in the G&M to get rid of the Lavatory Man to Parliament that had helped him get his seat, although he took no responsibility for the amazing decision to make him a major party spokesman. He wasn't called that because of his moral constipation but because he had made the mistake of patronising Frank in the toilet of a Union Conference once too often. Frank had grabbed the man by his lapels before remembering his hatred of violence, but it had been enough time for the man to wet himself. The Labour leaders had drawn the wrong lesson from their perception of the public's distrust of unilateralism. Nuclear or conventional defence was not the issue, it was the nature of the threat that was, and that, never great in practice, was now non-existent. But the leadership, frightened by the fear of an impression given to the public by its defeat, had thrown their weight behind a resolution seeking a major commitment to increase conventional defence spending. Watching that was maybe the nadir of his depression. After that he wanted to get better and started to do so, but not to live in a world of their making.

He knew that the Baltic States would be bound to be free, and he could foresee further national developments with major political and football consequences. He envisaged the draw for the European Cup in 1992 with first round ties like Jalguiris Vilnius versus Spartak Moscow, but also Dynamo Tbilisi versus Dynamo Kiev, Red Star Belgrade versus Dynamo Zagreb and probably and sadly even Sparta Prague versus Slovan Bratislava. The consequences for Scotland were twofold, a political strength and a major football danger. It would be hard for Scots themselves to see small nations all over Europe claiming or reclaiming their right to exercise their own sovereignty within a nation state, and still claim or feel that it would be impossible or unthinkable for Scotland to do so. It would be a powerful thrust in the raising of the credibility factor of a free and independent Scotland exercising its responsibilities within the European community.

But there was also a danger and one that began to obsess him and provide him with further motivation to proceed with his plan. He had always realised the close connection between politics and football in Communist states. How Celtic's nine in a row was still a world record because Dynamo Berlin had had their ten bought for them by the Stasi. How a Romanian had become Europe's top scorer and Golden Boot winner because other teams were ordered to let him score against them. And how Steaua Bucharest had gone a year without defeat at home because everyone else was scared what would happen to them if they beat them. He knew the realities of the brave new world would have football as well as political ramifications. It had always been an historical anomaly that Europe and the world tolerated the existence of the Scottish, Welsh and Northern Irish Football Associations without a corresponding state behind them. That anomaly would be increasingly unacceptable in a world where the number of genuine

330

national associations in Europe increased markedly. The Africans would become even more aggrieved and the European defenders would no longer need the extra votes. There would be renewed pressure for the rationalisation of the position and the recognition of only one United Kingdom Association. That was already the position in many sports, and, most importantly, the Olympic community.

If that were to happen, the Scottish Football team would no longer be an International team. It would no longer be able to enter the European Nations Championship. Scotland would no longer be able to enter the World Cup, which would mean the end to his greatest dream, that one day the Scottish captain would collect that gold trophy and lift it skyward along with the hearts of a joyous nation. One day, my friend, one day. It would also mean that the Scottish champions were no longer able to enter the European Cup. It would mean that the English clubs, with Tory chairmen, would be able to field as many Scots and Welsh as they liked and would no longer be handicapped by having to include 12 Englishmen in their pool of 16 for European competition. Rangers too would benefit, being good enough to qualify for Europe within Britain, and not having to restrict the numbers of Englishmen they could play to three or four. They could then recruit more Europeans in addition. The people in Scottish football she would listen to would not support the old system. For Rangers, her team, it would be the logical outcome of their espousal of her philosophies, to be in a British League.

Looked at from her point of view it could have major attractions given her logical thought processes. Okay there would be pain and discord at first from the nasty Scots at the loss of their national toys, but they would soon fall in behind the efforts of a United Kingdom team to qualify for the 1994 World Cup. They could even play one of their games at Hampden, or better still Ibrox. This removal of the separate Scottish team as a focus for nationalist feeling, and the switch of allegiance to a British team, could defuse the emotional nationalistic feeling in Scotland and aid identification with the Union. It depended on several assumptions about the identification of Scots for their national teams. The evidence was clear that Scots were as enthusiastic in support of UK teams in other sports as any other part of the Union; but was their centring of their national identity on their football team a good or a bad thing? There was one argument, that it deflected it from having a more political focus and was thus a safety valve for the Union. The opposite view was that it kept alive an identity and a feeling denied a political outlet, a storage jar for a sense of separateness and a constant danger to the Union. The threat to remove the substitute could lead to a strengthening of the Union or it could lead to the strengthening of separatist political activity. He knew which way her logic would take her, and also the personal satisfaction she would feel about punishing the Scots for their blasphemies and their sins, by depriving them of their precious toys and giving them one of hers to play with instead. It was the ultimate logic of a polarisation of the Union or Independence, one that would have the benefit of increasing identification with the Union, and stopping that stupid song being sung.

The more he thought it through, the more terrified he became that the same thought would occur to her. Even if, on the worst predictions, she were bound to go a year or two after another Election victory, any other scenario but his would give her the time to set that in motion before she went. It would be her perfect parting gift to the Scots, a return with interest on the hate invested in her, but one that made logical good sense in her terms. No other Tory Prime Minister would have the rigid logical blinkers required to see such a measure through. By his projected action Frank would not only make a political point he would save his beloved National team and keep alive the possibility of a Scottish World Cup victory. The favoured version of his last surviving dream had Elaine's Michael supplying the cross for Jack Reilly's son Willie to head the winning goal for Scotland in the 2010 World Cup Final. Frank would die so that the dream could live on. He liked that very much, it somehow seemed to make even more sense to him than the somewhat confusing outcomes of his political studies.

And so he worked his way through the academic part of his project and came to the conclusions and reasonings and rationalisations that would allow him to proceed. To make his mark and move on to face his destiny. The practical bits were all in place, the plans drawn up. They had survived the test of the final trial run and subsequent re-evaluation. The approval to proceed had been earned by hard endeavour and much intellectual wrestling. He had considered his final decision long and often, and changed his mind three times at least, but at last he knew clearly what he would do. Only time would tell whether his decision was going to win him the place in the footnotes of political history that he craved, whether it would be a glorious strike that would lead to freedom and independence for his people, or be another of the own goals so endemic to his race. Only time would know if he were about to reap the glory denied to him as a footballer, and as a leader of men. It was time to say his goodbyes and get on with the rest of his life.

CHAPTER TWENTY-ONE - GRAVE TALK

Frank Hunter held the last review of his situation on the late shift on the Friday night. Plan E, the cop-out provisions, had not worked. He reran the play again to see where it had failed. By the Thursday it had got to the point where he knew that there were only two things that could stop him, those that loved him and those that hated him. The latter were easier dealt with, he gave himself a stern talking to. He had known he would have to say his goodbyes to the other category and that involved certain risks to his enterprise. A part of him had hoped that the process would produce some better alternative, that someone would somehow love him enough to offer more than he was preparing for himself. But he knew that was too much to load on them, loving him was hardship enough. It had been harder than he had imagined, organising all his farewells. He had had to realise that there was a sentimental side to him often denied beneath the sad and cynical exterior.

Some had been easy enough to organise, if not undertake. He had made his last visit to Mary Ewing, going for once to her last resting place rather than summonsing her before him. He had realised it would be more in the nature of an away match for him. In truth he had also lost the power and energy to call her up and needed what strength he had to survive her wrath. He had been pathetic in his apologies. "I'm sorry about your letters, Mary, but I've made sure they are safe, and passed them on to the one person I know can do them justice better than me." She had cried him a stupid bastard, a gutless wonder, a snivelling coward. He had been taken aback by the vehemence of her abuse. "Hate, you don't know the meaning of the word, son. You've never hated anyone in your life, except maybe yourself, you mollycoddled big arsehole. You may despise the Prime Minister, but that's not hate. Now your grandfather, there was a man who knew what hate was, to give and to get. And your father, poor bastard, at least he hated your grandfather. You, oh don't make me laugh. I had high hopes for you, son, but you've disappointed me sorely. You had the chance to do so much, but you've done so little. And now you're going to call it a day at that. Ye never had the bottle, did you, when it came down to it. And don't kid yourself that shooting anyone is a political act, or a courageous one. Aye, there's maybe the Jessie in you after all, giving up instead of fighting on. Away and lee me alane."

There had been more in similar vein. He had been hurt by her rejection, largely because of his recognition of the truth of what she said. She had not been interested in his rationalisations and justifications. She just saw the surrender and despised him for it. She had never surrendered even once in her life, despite facing higher odds and greater hardships than he had ever known. She had taught him to despise leaders, particularly of their own side, for their surrenders in power. She regretted most never having taught him the responsibility to accept the burden of leadership when the talent and opportunity was there. She reviled and despised the rationalisations he used for his failure to meet these responsibilities, the biggest treachery of all. He had wept at her, at his pain for the lost man, and especially for the great lie that it was because he could not tell a lie. But she did not soften, would not caress his head again with her twisted old hands and finally left him weeping on the ground. He knew how much of what was left of her would die again with him, and continued weeping, but this time more healthily, for the wisest and bravest person he ever knew.

He had walked round later to where his paternal grandparents lay. It had been Mary Ewing that had shown him where. Even in death they were not quite together. He did not have the power over them that he had with the rest and neither offered him advice or solace. He felt a deep aching loss for the emptiness on that side of his soul, and a feeling almost of affection for the memory of his beleaguered father. For the first, only and last time, he acknowledged Willie Hunter as his family and felt an affinity stir within him for what he was about to do. He remembered the photographs Mary had shown him of Jessie, his grandmother, the overwhelming sense of sadness and inner despair that shone through from the face in them. He would take something of her with him. He remembered also the wedding picture of the young soldier, younger than him and harder. Well, Frank was going to enter his league now.

No matter how difficult and painful the session with Mary Ewing had been, it was in some ways easier to take than the reception he got from his mother and grandmother when he had visited them on the Friday forenoon. They had told him what he was about to do was a sin, and begged him not to do it. It had

335

taken him a minute or two to realise that they were not talking about shooting the Prime Minister but the next part. They were worried that he would not be able to join them. They tried to offer him hope for a future that was a better alternative to what he planned to do. It was hard on the football front, their first attempt. Even though they now got into Parkhead free, they still felt they were being robbed, and could not offer much hope there. Nor did they believe any more than he did, that Italy-90 would offer any real joy. They were more optimistic politically. His Gran, who had hated the Prime Minister vehemently in the months before her death, told him the working classes were coming to their senses at last and would unite to do down the Prime Minister, without his help. It just proved to him how much she had missed in the last ten years. His mother had hated her too, in a more sophisticated way, for what she stood for as much as who she was. She had despaired of the Labour Party herself but didn't see what would be wrong with letting her stay. She was past her peak and was a liability rather than an asset. She had urged her son to be logical, but the problem with that tactic was that he had been and had come to a logical conclusion.

His mother urged him to consider going back to University. She had always been very saddened by his withdrawal. "You can afford it now, with my money, and might enjoy it better." "Then what", he had asked her, "become a bloody Social Worker, no thank you". One of the problems about where they were was that they had seen him together with Hazel, as well as him with Joyce. So there was an ambivalence in their attempts to tell him that he had a good lass there, one who would help him through his bad patch and stick by him. He knew his mother didn't really take to her, too cold, too sad, too distant, too serious for her taste but she acknowledged Joyce was trying to help her son, she gave her that. They would both have preferred him to have five kids by Hazel, but accepted that Joyce was his choice. "I've let her down, mum," he tried to explain, "we could only have ever made it if I had been able to share everything with her, to trust myself to her entirely, but I couldn't, I didn't. I know it's my fault not hers, but the equality I need is not there". He didn't explain why he and Hazel were wrong for each other.

So he left them sad and unhappy, grieving for their wee boy, their pride and joy. He cried when he left them, a different taste of tears to those he had left on Mary Ewing's grave. He loved them both, beautiful, beautiful women, the best he had ever known. He knew they were there still but that he wasn't going to join them. It wasn't that he was going anywhere else. He was clear about the reality that he was going nowhere other than into fish fingers, but with him going they would die too, because now his mother and his Gran only lived on in him, in his head and in his heart. He prayed to their God that he was wrong and they were right but he knew they were wrong and he was right, in that at least. He had always been clear about that. When people's bodies died, they lived on all right, but only in the souls of those survivors who loved them, and when they died too, the original people died a little more, until the final end when no-one was left alive as the custodian. He realised this meant he would kill his father since only four people had ever loved him and three of them were already dead, but all big Dave said to him, a long speech by his standards right enough, was "It's up to you, son, do what you think is right." and Frank was too tired to push him for more.

Partly because he was there anyway, and partly because he needed something more positive than Mary Ewing gave him, he had gone to pay his last respects to old John McLure, the man who had helped open his mind to a world beyond his own. John had suffered a great deal of abuse from his own generation and the following ones, for his Europeanism, for his belief that unity in Europe was the best road to ensure working class peace and prosperity. He had used his extensive reading and knowledge of the rest of the world to help Frank put politics in a wider context than a Gorbals, or a Glasgow, or Scottish or a British one. He had been the first person Frank had ever heard argue for membership of the Common Market, and for some time after that the only one until Frank had realised he agreed with him. He knew he owed an enormous debt to John for the fact that his own Europeanism was based on more than enthusiasm for the European Cup. John had also been his early guide not only to the history of Trade Unions but to their future, a much more hazardous journey. He had been a good Trade Unionist himself, who had worked his way up from the shop floor, self-educated, to become a full-time official in the days when you had to be tough and hard instead of merely acquisitive and pushy. John had seen and understood what almost everyone else Frank knew had missed. That Unions did not have any divine right to exist, that they were defensive organisations, not instruments for revolution or social change and that in a democratic society they must operate within a framework of law and accountability. John had vigorously supported "In Place Of

337

Strife" in the year Frank had joined the Labour Party. John had suffered dog's abuse from his friends, and much worse from the rest of the Party, of comrades. He was denounced as a class traitor, a fascist, a government toady, by people who did not know the slightest thing about Fascism and Trade Unions. It was Frank Hunter's introduction to the fury reserved for those who challenge comfortable orthodoxies, and to the moral arithmetic that being in a small minority does not make you wrong. John had conducted himself with dignity but Frank knew that the vehemence of the abuse hurt him.

He had been further hurt by the personal attacks on his pro-Europeanism in the 1975 referendum campaign. Frank had parted company with him before then on the issue of Scotland and its place in the world. John had been consistently anti-devolution or any concession at all. He believed it was a madness to move in that direction when a push for unity in Europe was possible. He had played an influential part in the 1979 No campaign and in the climate that had led the Labour Party and Unions to betray the cause in the preceding years. In vain, Frank had tried to get him to see that his allies were the very bastards that had so vilified him over his stance on Europe. And that so what if devolution was bound to lead to an independent Scotland, that was a reason for supporting it rather than opposing it, and an independent Scotland could be a willing participant in the new Europe. Their close relationship never really survived Frank's bitterness at what he saw as a wasted opportunity in 1979 and his view of every No voter as an enemy, to him and to his country. John had even had the inconsideration to die before Frank had matured enough to heal the wounds. He regretted that bitterly and standing there in front of John he gave him the gracious apology he had denied him in life.

Frank found his consideration of matters political helped ease the pain of his more personal conversations and he lingered on to relive some of the conversations and arguments he had had with John, of the successes they had managed at elections, on the streets and in the committee rooms. He remembered the best speech he ever heard John make. He was not a great orator, he relied on other means to get what he wanted normally but on this occasion he was so outnumbered that words were his only weapon and he had utilised them so well. He still got gubbed of course. It had been an evening when his two great themes combined, Europe and Trade Union reform. There had been over 100 people in the hall,

all of them alive too, just for a Branch meeting. They had good meetings in those days, when people had actually listened to the arguments and made up their minds rather than arriving disciplined to follow the faction line. Militant may be dead and gone but they had killed the old soul of the Party before they expired. The 1969 by-election had just been won and a feeling of power and progress, and complacency was in the air. John had moved a resolution in favour of the Trade Union reforms, quoting the European context and pointing out that even in all those European countries with Socialist or Social Democratic Governments or traditions, the Trade union movements operated within a legal framework much more rigorous than Wilson was proposing. He was right, in what he said and what he proposed, but he did not convince his audience.

Most of the members were of the generation to whom a foreign holiday was a trip to Skegness and where memories of the War and its devastation of the Continent still lingered. One fierce old lady, no fool in her own terms, had turned on John. "Don't give us your foreigners as a model, John McLure. My husband was over there just after the War and I know for a fact, a fact I tell you, that the Germans, and the French, eat rats. And as for the Italians you talk about, they even eat rat shit." There were few brave enough to snigger at Jessie Murray in full flight, she weighed 15 stone and had forearms fatter than a man's thigh, but Frank Hunter was one of them. But she had had the mood of the meeting better than John, and he and Frank had been well and truly gubbed. Won the argument but lost the vote. That was why John McLure never really bothered with fancy speeches and generally preferred to have the votes stitched up before the debate.

Frank smiled again as Jessie Murray's words echoed across the years and ears again. He had thought of her then as an old woman, but he realised that she was younger then than the Prime Minister was now. The only power that Jessie had ever been allowed to exercise had been in her right hook. Yet often over the last few years, when ever he heard that bloody woman talking about Europe, he had thought of Jessie and the vehemence of her outburst. He often realised that her views expressed then were only a more sophisticated version of the anti-Europeanism still being exhibited by the Prime Minister and her cronies. At least Jessie had been able to articulate graphically what it was she didn't like about them other than that they were foreign. That brought back to him why he was there and broke the spell of happy reminiscence.

Standing there on the green hill overlooking Cathcart, Frank realised how right John had been that night. If Wilson had kept his nerve, if Callaghan had not been an opportunist looking for a base, if the world hadn't been round we would have all fallen off the edges long ago. Frank had often despaired of the failure of the Trade Union movement to have any leader with the vision and education, in the best sense of the word, of a John McLure. His own Union had been particularly badly served, by a procession of snivelling fools and ignorant self-serving egoists. The whole movement had paid a terrible price for the poor quality of their leadership and was now almost bankrupt, intellectually and morally. He knew, the bruises were still there from the previous day, that Mary Ewing would tell him it was a case of put up or shut up and he had declined the chance. One person had not missed. The reading and research he had been doing recently had brought home very clearly to him just how successful the Prime Minister had been in exploiting that intellectual bankruptcy and gelding the monolith. Yet all she had done had been to do less than what the movement should have done to itself a long time before. And she had agreed that her government should pay for much of it. Yet because it had been her that had done it, too many people were still pretending it had been wrong and that it must be reversed. That was one of the problems of the emotion she generated, it interfered with the vision.

Frank quietly acknowledged some of the debts he owed to the lump of dust and bone beneath his feet. In the arrogance of youth he had tended to assume that all his views were not only right, but also entirely his own work. Now maybe he could acknowledge that many of them had roots in that soil below. Frank reckoned that maybe there had only been three things they had ever disagreed about. One had been about the morality of working with Charlie Spence and his methods, and Frank reckoned John would have a wry smile down below at Frank's role in the campaign to get Charlie into Parliament, a campaign that was not the cleanest on record. Frank had kept his own hands relatively clean, but he could hear John ready for an argument on that one. The most serious dispute had been about Scotland, and the need for it to take responsibility for its own destiny. Frank tried to ask John if he had done as many of his allies had and changed position on this one since his act of treachery in 1979, but it seemed that it was only the dead women in his life that talked back to him.

340

The third area had been about whether politics was more important than football. At that Frank raised his eyes and saw far beyond the distant hills in search of a view and a landscape he had often sought in the past. It wasn't lost on Frank that if he had taken John's advice in 1970 then his life might have been so much different. McGoldrick might be alive today and Frank would not be forced by his great weight of sadness to measure his destiny in a farewell act of destruction. He realised that John would tell him that even what he was about to do now was being done for football rather than politics, and increasingly Frank had come to recognise to his surprise that that was right. He wondered whether John would accept that in either sense Scotland was worth the sacrifice.

He remembered that they had buried John with a pile of his beloved books so that, as Father Andrew had quoted John's own words, he had enough to read on his long wait before they let him in. Father Andrew had upset some of his flock by publicly enunciating and endorsing John's theory, that purgatory without books would be Hell, but with books, who would need Heaven.

Talking to John had put him behind in what had been a very tight schedule. He had arranged that people would arrive at Joyce's flat for 8pm, to eat about half-past. It was later than usual, but he had things he had to do. At 5:30 he met Gerry Robertson. He had arranged to meet him in the Granary, a modern pub they seldom frequented, because he did not want them to be joined by anyone else. He knew he would see Gerry on the Saturday, but that wouldn't be the same. Frank knew he had to maintain a balancing act. The sadness was there, his normal plus the realisation that he would never enjoy Gerry's company again. But he needed to inject an element of despair, and despair did not make for good conversation or company, so he settled for maudlin instead. Frank had a genuine despair for Gerry, for like himself his opportunities had passed him by. Gerry had had a couple of years flourishing in the General&Municipal in the inter-regnum years but now that the new regime was established, Gerry's star was on the wane. He had recently been removed from his Union's seat on the Scottish Executive of the Labour Party that had given him some power and influence over the turbulent years of the mid-eighties. He could still expect promotion within the Union, but only if he were prepared to move to, in the G&M's quaint phrase, another region than Scotland.

For reasons slightly different to Frank's, Gerry was not prepared to move out of his own country. Some of that was to do with his elderly mother in Braidwood, whom he loved dearly. He had missed the boat in 1985 and 1986 when several less-talented and less-connected Union officials had jumped into the Labour Party seats available. Gerry would have made a good M.P. and with his G&M backing and political links it should have been possible for him. But he had made too many enemies in his own Union so other Trade Unionists resented him for the sins of the G&M and the G&M resented him for resenting and resisting the sins of the G&M. Frank and Paddy had urged him to go for their Constituency's nomination in 1985 but he declined on the promise and premise of another safer option and by the time that fell through Gerry had said it was too late and they were committed to Reid. Now it really was too late, there weren't all that more seats to be won, and women would and should get those of them not already sown up. With the G&M having settled its leadership tussle, Gerry would pay the price for not being on the side of the winner. The longer he was off the Scottish Executive, the more his residual influence would decline. Both Gerry and Frank knew his only chance was a Scottish Assembly seat in the early 1990s, and neither felt that was more than possible. Frank knew it was also the most likely next step for Paddy, if his own plan came to full fruition.

So Frank's was not the only sadness seated round that trendy little table as they drank their 70/- ale and talked of football rather than politics or Unions. Frank had learned to trust and admire Gerry's judgements and his detailed knowledge of Scottish politics. It had mainly been past Gerry that he had principally ran most of the notions of the political implications, for Scotland and the United Kingdom, if the IRA or anyone else were to murder the Prime Minister in Scotland. Gerry had been dismissive of the notion of a Scotsman doing it, even from the lunatic fringe of the SNP, despite the universal hatred felt for her. He had not felt that an IRA killing would have any effect other than probably to lessen the intensity of the Tory opposition to any form of devolution. He had felt that assassination by a Scotsman, as a hypothetical notion, would lead more English Tories into saying let the bastards go. Gerry believed that the Tories were going to win the next Election. His view was not based on the kind of calculations Frank had made in the Mitchell, but was a product of an acute political instinct and a depressive personality. The death of the Prime Minister would not affect that outcome one way or another. Gerry was not a believer in the Doomsday scenario. It hadn't been true in 1983, or 1987, 1992 would be no different.

There was no sign of Gerry ever marrying, or settling down with a woman. He still seemed fixated around the young girl stage, although it became more and more incongruous as he reached the forty mark. He was having to make greater and greater efforts to seem younger than he was, and the effect was becoming slightly ludicrous. He had looked vaguely like James Dean when he was twenty, but twenty years on was in danger of looking more like Bill Dean, in a leather jacket. He was also taking the biker bit too far. In an outbreak of adolescent fantasy he had returned to owning a motorbike, a huge Honda 1000cc, a massive and frightening brute. He did not buy it for its effect on wee girls, that was just a bonus. Get a 1000cc throbbing between their legs for a wee while and they can't wait for you to bring it to a conclusion for them, he told Frank several times. So he called his beast The Vibrator which appealed to the sense of humour of those few of his 16 year old victims who understood it. The rest just enjoyed the other use of his caustic tongue. He would pick up young girls on Glasgow streets, frighten the shit out of them on the motorway, generally literally, then take down their knickers in neighbouring woods and bury his head between their legs to finish off what his bike had started. When it was too wet for that, he would take them up to his smart bachelor flat and in his sophisticated terms commit cuntilickies with them.

He didn't care what they looked like, which helped considerably in his recruitment drive. His philosophy was flat on their backs, in the dark, with their legs over his shoulders they're all exactly the same height of the ground. Many a too fat, too thin, too spotty or just too plain girl was overly flattered by the attentions paid to them for the first time by a charismatic adult male. They seemed to love getting licked off. Even they knew they couldn't get pregnant that way, and it was good for them too, unlike what most boys their own age were trying to do to them. He never repeated himself, "never drank out the same cunt twice", was his depressing boast. As far as Frank could tell, and though he had long ago decided he didn't want to talk to Gerry about it he sometimes was subjected to Gerry's need to talk, Gerry seemed to have given up ever inserting his penis where his tongue had been. He settled instead for them wanking him off, or when he could persuade them, for a return of the oral favour.

Frank's own experiences with Hazel had helped him to see that pattern as slightly less bizarre but still, basically, he felt his friend was not a totally healthy person, sexually. Gerry always seemed uneasy in the company of females over the age of 18. Women, especially mature, sophisticated and intelligent women like Joyce and Sheila, terrified him. He was more comfortable, just, with the more motherly type like Christine and Vera. The Feminist wing of the Party despised him with an intensity that distressed Frank although it seemed to please Gerry. At least they weren't likely to try to engage him in social intercourse. Politics, Unions, football, bikes, books, beer and people were all he ever talked about, but fortunately for his friends he was extremely knowledgeable, articulate and interesting, at least about six out of the seven. He must have been, like Frank, a mid-night reader, because there was hardly a book on any these topics that he had not read and critically dissected. Frank both loved him and despaired of him. So whole and so incomplete. Frank was certain Gerry would die one day, in pieces. He drove his bike in an increasingly reckless way as if to invite it. He had been warned by the police several times for being with 15 year old girls. Aim for 100 16 year olds in a year and you're bound to misjudge in one or two cases, was his own view on that. Gerry was a prominent activist in the Civil Rights movement and knew his own rights well. He was convinced that the police would love to get him for political reasons. It was he who had first alerted Frank to the fact that Frank's phone would be bugged as an active Union leader. His own had been for years. Frank believed him about the phone but not about the police. They could have had him, and ruined him, for lewd and libidinous practices, if they had been so inclined. Maybe they were saving it for the most effective moment, was Gerry's retort to accusations of paranoia. Still he had no intention of reducing his vulnerability by changing his lifestyle.

Gerry was also more depressed than the rest of them about Celtic. He had long ago given up the Jags in favour of company on a Saturday. Like many late converts he became passionate in his devotion. He feared that the Celtic problem was worse than it appeared, more serious, and that their decline was long-term, absolute and likely to be irreversible. It was a serious matter for all of them, Frank, Paddy McGuire, Peter McColl, Gerry and many thousand more of their fellow drinkers. It took up more discussion time, analysis and personal emotional investment than any other issue in their life, certainly much more than the state of the nation they worried about the state of their club. That early evening in the pub Gerry had run over once again his favourite political parallel. Celtic was like the United Kingdom without the benefit of the Thatcher revolution. Full of charity and care, compassion and goodwill, but hopelessly out of date, ill-managed at all levels, ignorant of market realities, with a management structure devised in the 19th Century and unaltered since, ill-equipped to deal with European competition. Rangers, on the other hand were the epitome of the results of the correct application of the Prime Minister's medicine. They had had temporary pain but were now equipped positively for the challenges of 1992 and beyond. They had the most modern, and best, stadium in Britain, the management structure at club and team level to back it up, and had built a team that would dominate indefinitely.

Even the managers epitomised the difference with brilliant clarity. Souness with his hardness, his ruthlessness, his lack of care for the human casualties, buying and discarding people within months, his nakedness of self-interest as the dominant force, always working for the future, trampling over the past ruthlessly as it stood in the way, appealing to it only in the longer way, the same recourse to Victorian values, and Churchillian times, the Iron Curtain days, but identifying their own more recent past as part of the enemy to be conquered and defeated. And on the Celtic side, good old King Billy, Labour voting, Party Political Broadcasting, living on the glories of the recent past, "never mind today, hurrah for 1967, we were the best then, we can be the best again. We don't need to change structures, tactics or systems, just evoke and rely on the old spirit and tradition." Never mind his record in England, two teams managed, two teams relegated, he's the embodiment of the glory of the past and that will be enough to take us forward. Hail Caesar, we who salute you are about to die.

Gerry revelled in yet a further irony. The hatred and contempt that Souness was held in by the great majority of the Rangers faithful, and the universal love of the Celtic legions for King Billy. Souness betrayed their traditions to enhance their future, and they hated him for that. And because they knew he despised them. And King Billy betrayed their future in the name of their traditions and remained worshipped, because they knew he loved them. Gerry saw that as telling its own story about the essential worth and decency of the two respective families, but Frank was less sure.

Gerry had had the pub in uproar the night he had first advanced this thesis. They had been stunned by the vehemence of his analysis and denunciation. But they had found it hard to argue with, or to challenge the answer to his question about which set of fans were happier. Most had only made the equation Rangers equals the Prime Minister and given themselves another reason for hating them, but the more sophisticated had grieved at the political as well as the football implications. Frank had always known that a European League was inevitable, and regularly constructed it in his head on the basis of his wide knowledge of the European game. Celtic had been for a long time in his first division but now had slipped almost out of sight. He knew that if they didn't get the ground and the team sorted soon, they could miss the escalator and only have one direction to go. He could not bear that, could not live with permanent inferiority. Gerry and Frank both knew Celtic would have to open themselves up to new arrangements. They discussed possible methods whereby Celtic, given the best of their history, their tradition and their support, might be able to offer a slightly different and better model than the Rangers one of private capital, but they found it difficult to be specific about an alternative. They both knew that business as usual was not an option with any merit. Frank had seriously considered at one point investing his six figure wealth in the Club and becoming a player in the game, but he didn't have enough to be effective. The talk moved on more specifically to the game the next day. Neither of them believed that the Celtic tradition, the Celtic spirit would win the Cup Final but it was the only thing likely to, the team alone certainly were not good enough. Their God had let that be enough once, in their Centenary Year, but he owed them no more favours.

Frank had begun to worry that Gerry might be more likely to be seen as possibly suicidal than himself. He had never seen the big man so depressed, so low, so down, so lacking in any aspect of optimism. Frank told Gerry why he had to get a grip. He pushed him to acknowledge that he did want to be an elected representative rather than a Trade Union official, and begged him to start planning now for a nomination for a seat in the Scottish Assembly. He told Gerry he was getting really depressed himself and worried that he was getting like he had been the previous year again and how he couldn't face going back through that again. He told him that he was going to go away, alone, immediately after the game, for a few days to see if he could work out things for himself.

Frank left his sad friend with a spontaneous cuddle, and walked down to the Cavan Club with his bag to complete his collection. There were one or two personalised autographs that would have arrived off the boat by now, that he wanted just to add a touch of external authenticity. There was the frisson in the air that was always around the Club when any of the main men in the Firm were in town. Frank always felt the name was a misprint, or mis-translation, of Cave or Cavern. The main bar was a large barn of a place which could hold 300-400 on a good night and this was promising to be a great one. If he hadn't been making an effort to be around more than usual in the past few weeks he probably would not have got in. They had the special stewards on and the steel doors barred, and no casual trade was getting access. He hadn't needed to stay long, to get what he needed. He hadn't taken his baggy jacket and gloves off, but the big barn was cold enough even on a spring night for that to pass unnoticed. He bought a round of drinks, took the tray back to the bar with empty whisky glasses and pint tumblers and borrowed a quick look at a Belfast paper with a crossword puzzle half-done in a distinctive hand. He was aware of the risks he ran. Some small still part of him half-hoped they would catch him at it. Take him down the stone steps to the poky toilet underground and knee-cap him, or up the grotty stairs to the wee back room where the serious business was done, and a confession beaten out of him. He could then watch the game on the Hospital TV and not have to follow-through on his project. Escape plan 14. But it proved as easy as the collection of the other parts had been and no-one paid much attention. The life there seemed so normal, drink and talk of football, that he had a momentary attack of conscience at the confusion and disruption his little joke might cause but then he reminded himself of the other bits and the reasons he hated them, and knew he would go through with it. Always game for a laugh, that Frank Hunter.

He dropped his souvenirs off at his flat and walked round to Joyce's flat. He wanted a quiet time alone with her before the others arrived. He made sure she was aware that he was going away for a few days immediately after the Final. He had to tell the others before Saturday so his behaviour on the day would seem understandable at the time. But he wanted Joyce to feel that it was a plan they had shared together rather than something sprung on her at the same time. He knew he wouldn't see her on the Saturday. She had decided not to go to the game, even though Sheila was and had encouraged Joyce to accompany her. Frank was very glad of whatever force had helped him by arranging her refusal. He had helped in a subtly manipulative way. She had decided to go to East Kilbride, and once she knew he would not be there on the Saturday night, she decided to stay overnight with her parents. He had done that for her, given her her family back even if he was denying her a new one. Frank knew he would be very tired and emotional by the end of the evening and that he would have to be up by 5am. So he knew he would make love to Joyce and say his non-verbal farewells, let her sleep in his arms for an hour or two and then leave her to go round to his own place for cold showers and hot final thoughts before he was due in action.

He told her things while they finished off the preparations for the meal. The real things he wanted to tell her she would have to read, but he had already organised that. He told her he felt he needed a wee holiday, a break to give himself a chance to think a few things through, to make a few decisions about his life. Joyce had been very pleased with his state in the past month or so, since their make-up after the McGoldrick article row. She had known he was ill, and in trouble, but seemed to think he was fighting it well. There had been a calmness about him, a sense of purpose, a clarity of thought and deed. He had been more open, more animated. He had obviously enjoyed the SAD trip and his holiday in the Lake District. He was working hard at the Mitchell most days, on his book she presumed as that was what he told her. He was more forthcoming in pub conversations, more interested in political arguments, less was seen of the passive space traveller he used to become in company.

Despite some signs of relapse in the past few days, she felt he was making slow but steady progress and was still hopeful. At that particular point in time, she was more worried about the meal than about him. Their deal had been that he would do the preliminary work but that she would finish it off and dish it up. Joyce was most impressed by the preparations he had made for the meal. He wanted it to be an occasion they would remember later with happiness not sorrow. He had stinted nothing, to treat his friends to a last supper. He had gone to the best fishmonger on the southside, to the best butcher. He had bought many bottles of the finest wines. He had prepared the soup so it only needed heating up, the pudding so it only needed mixed. He had gone for nothing fancy, nothing saucy, just simplicity with quality. He had had no difficulty in persuading them of the sense in celebrating the night before the Final. Three of them, himself, Paddy and Sheila were Celtic fanatics. Danny was a Celtic sympathiser, being a Social Worker. Jack, as a fair-minded man, wanted Aberdeen, the better team, to win. They all felt that would be the almost certain outcome. Joyce had never organised a dinner party before in her own flat, and Brian Kirk had not approved of such bourgeois behaviour. Frank knew that he would encourage Joyce to take full credit for the meal, not only to boost her confidence but because he was vaguely aware that there was an inconsistency in the detail of organisation and control required to deliver such a meal, and the image he was trying to project of a man slipping down into a pit of despair, apathy and helplessness.

It was the kind of irony Frank always appreciated. He had deliberately spent much time over the past week, particularly with Joyce, in projecting an image of a man on the slide into black despair, while all the time he felt more in control of his life and destiny than ever before. Here he was that evening, on the verge of killing himself, and wanting to give the impression of someone on the verge of killing himself, and having to plan to act unnaturally in order to give a falsely correct impression of himself. Things were seldom as they seemed to be with Frank Hunter. Most people Frank knew told lies and tried to convince people they were telling the truth. It had always been one of Frank's favourite games to try to tell the truth in such a way that no-one would believe him. This time, he would use a lie to tell the truth.

Danny and Sheila arrived first, as Sheila was aware of Joyce's nervousness and need for moral support. It gave Frank some time alone with Danny as the two women disappeared into the kitchen.

Danny, oh Danny boy, how he would miss him. It had been a hard choice at the time of his wedding, which of them would be his best man, between Paddy and Danny. He had been best man at both their weddings. Frank had nearly asked Derek to avoid making the choice. But he had really known the hardness was in the way Paddy would take it. Danny was the best man he knew. If it hadn't been for women, he would have been near perfect. Frank knew Danny would be horrified at what he was about to do. Danny hated the Prime Minister as vitriolically as anyone and everyone Frank knew. Mostly because of her complete indifference to the casualties of her policies, the human beings Danny worked with, day and daily. But shoot her, never. Danny did not believe that shooting or killing anyone could be justified, in a British political context. And although he believed in the need for an independent Scotland, he did not regard the Scots as an oppressed people for whom political violence was justifiable. Danny hated violence. He despised the Glasgow myth of the hardman and the kind of behaviour that resulted from attempts to live up to it. He despaired of the use of violence as a response to problems. As a Social Worker, he saw too many of its victims, both givers and receivers, to invest it with even the slightest vestige of glamour. He would refuse to accompany Paddy and Peter McColl on their trips to boxing matches, and refused to acknowledge it as a sport. He believed in the rule of reason, combined with care for others.

Frank knew that Danny would be even more devastated by the second part of his plan. Danny was more open and honest about his feelings than Frank or Paddy and regularly embarrassed them by telling them that he loved them. Paddy had retorted the last time that if he had been as fastidious in letting his women know, his relationships might have survived better. Danny had taken Frank's decline into despair harder than anyone else, including Frank. He did not believe Frank was or had been mentally ill but he recognised that his friend had needed and still did need help, and was distraught at his own inability to help him and restore him to his former level of operation. He had tried everything he knew, including all the tricks and techniques of his trade which he always compared to nothing more than what a good and intelligent friend would do anyway, but nothing had seemed to work. He felt he had failed Frank, and tried to replace trick and technique with pure love and affection, with little better response. Frank found Danny's guilt slightly oppressive but loved him too much to tell him. He never told him that either.

So they talked about football, and football matches. Danny had found his own fears and vulnerabilities reawakened by the pictures from the Hillsborough Disaster. His dreams had returned to go along with his permanent nightmare from Stairway 13 at Ibrox. He had tried to talk to his fellow-survivors, Frank and Paddy, about it at the time but Frank had been to busy with his LDT campaign and Paddy had no problem. Danny had been sufficiently concerned about himself to seek out the services of a colleague who had been involved in the Social Work Department's contribution to the Piper Alpha and Lockerbie aftermaths. He had spent the first few sessions doing little but crying for all the faces in his head, then two or three more pulling himself onto more secure ground. He had repeatedly tried to persuade Frank to go, and later enlisted the help of Joyce, who was a friend of the colleague in question. But they never succeeded in persuading him to give it a try. Danny made no secret of his view that suppressed feelings about that awful afternoon from 1971 might be a factor in Frank's problems. That night he talked to him about an article he had just read, about the number of Hillsborough survivors that had committed suicide just before or around the first anniversary. Frank wondered if Danny knew anything at all, or just felt the vibrations in the air. He asked more about the article and talked a little of Stevie McGrath, their friend who perished in the crush, but declined yet again the offer of an appointment with Danny's colleague.

Paddy and Christine, and Jack and Vera arrived together, and his collection was complete. Friends worth dying for, he was definite about that. But worth living for, that was a different and harder matter. He had racked his brains to find a way to transport them and him safely far away, to some oasis where life could be one long happy session in the pub, followed by slow curries and fast chat. He was the only one who knew the real purpose of the evening, the others thought they were there to relax and enjoy themselves for tomorrow was only another day. Frank wanted to avoid talking about politics, for once, since he had done enough of that over the past few weeks, and it would not be that way they might change his mind. Football would leave three of them out the conversation, so he made sure they talked of memories and myths. Paddy was softer than usual, he was glad of that. He and Frank always argued rather than talked. It was their way, even though they agreed about almost everything almost always. They had different approaches to arguments. Paddy relied on slicing through the spine with swift sharp verbal karate chops until there was no backbone left and the foe collapsed. Truly a brutal wee bastard. Frank preferred the longer rope approach, tying people up in logical knots until they went whichever way he pulled. He would point out that as they believed in A and B, it followed that they must also believe in C, and they would confirm and believe they did. Then he would point out that they also had said they believed in X and Y, so presumably they must also believe in Z, and they would confirm they did. He would then demonstrate that C and Z were logically incompatible and a complete contradiction, so one set of beliefs at least must be wrong, generally the one that most suited his current purpose.

He and Paddy admired each other's technique, and occasionally even used it, but each believed his own was superior. Together they were formidable, complementary and hard to resist. Though many found their personalities quite resistible. There was an anger to both of them, always had been, that was a constant source of fear and concern to Danny. It was not fear for himself, as they never turned their anger on him, except Paddy whenever he left a woman. No, it was fear for their souls that troubled Danny. They handled their anger in different ways. Frank was always cold, disciplined, dispassionate, distant, turned inward in search of Christ knows what. Danny had feared last year that he had finally found it in there somewhere. Paddy was generous and giving with his anger, almost anyone could have some. Tories, the Prime Minister, Rangers, Rangers supporters, the English, Protestants, and fools got the greatest share. The day Terry Butcher met the Prime Minister at Ibrox Paddy nearly expired with pure impotent rage. No matter how much he gave away his wee fat frame always seemed ready to burst forth with an excess.

If anyone in their group had ever been pegged as a potential killer, it would have to have been Paddy. Frank knew there was a large part of Paddy that would be jealous about what he was about to do, that he had not done it first and better. There had always been a competitive edge to their friendship. Paddy had never really forgiven him for being a more successful footballer and had seemed almost glad his career had been terminated prematurely. But they were blood brothers, literally. They had stood behind the factory sheds at Polmadie and, shivering with fear, solemnly sliced open their thumbs with hesitant scratches of the Swiss penknife Paddy had got for his ninth birthday. It had taken Frank three goes before the blood trickled out, amazingly painless. So Paddy had done it in two. Pressing their bleeding thumbs together had meant

352

something to them then; and still did now as Frank talked about it. That was the kind of conversation he knew he wanted that evening. Joyce and Sheila were impressed that they still had the scars, running right down their left thumbs. Danny may love them each more but their bond was more primitive.

They had worked together well over the years. They had taken over the Young Socialists, the Branch, the Constituency. They had worked together in the District and Regional Labour Parties, at Scottish and National Conferences. They had even worked together in Union alliances, although Paddy as a lawyer had had the sense to join a different manual workers union, the Transport&General. They had been a formidable duo in various devolution fronts and campaigns. Neither was a follower by nature, but a subtle change had taken place over the last few years. Frank had been the early leader, the driving force, the number one man, with Paddy the hatchet lieutenant. Frank had masterminded Paddy's selection and election campaigns. But then he had declined and Paddy had bloomed, and Councillor McGuire somehow left Comrade Hunter far behind. Frank's trip to Kamesthorn and the preceding period had eroded what little equality had been left. They both recognised there had been an element of choice at one time, but that it was now irreversible.

Paddy never really understood why Frank never took the opportunities he had, and saw it as a weakness in Frank and a criticism of himself. Frank knew he had run away from his political responsibility to fight most effectively for his beliefs. He knew that was a moral failure of the gravest kind. Down inside himself he knew all the reasons and justifications he put up were just clever rationalisations and that the simple truth was that he was afraid of himself, of what he would do with responsibility and success if he ever exercised one and got the other. Paddy had accepted his responsibilities, and was doing well. He was flourishing under the current City regime. Frank hoped he had taught him well, and that Paddy could do enough for the pair of them. He would have to now. He was the kind of leader Scotland would need. Brave, clever, with the kind of recklessness that gave away penalties rather than scored own goals. A subtle difference but with a similar effect.

So they reminisced about old times and happier days and shared triumphs. They swapped stories and tales, true mostly, of their times in the Army together, in Germany and in Spain. Frank was strangely silent as they planned the Italian campaign. At least it was poetic if he were shot for desertion, as long as the truth came out one day that he did it so that there would be future battle honours, and that the great dream, of ultimate victory, might be realised one day: when Willie Reilly would score the winning goal from Michael's pass. That would be worth living to see, except he had to die to secure and ensure the opportunity.

The highlight of the evening for Frank, was the reliving of the farewell to arms, when the three Musketeers from the Young Socialists recreated the cabaret with which they had delighted the known world at the farewell concert for old MacDonald in 1969. Frank had written the script, Danny had been the MC and front man, and Paddy had masterminded the action and acting. Frank was surprised but delighted that he got the other two willing to help him recreate it. Jack and the women were receptive to being a sympathetic audience, Christine for a second time. The title was Animal School. The basic premise was that Old MacDonald had a school. And on that school he had some pigs. And Paddy and one or two others had come on dressed as male teachers, crude and brutal. And on that farm he had some hens, and Paddy had orchestrated girls dressed as fussy old women, jabbing people with knitting needles. And on that farm he had some dux, and a rather cruel parody of the school swots. And on that farm he had a bull, with Paddy in a brilliant over the top impersonation of the school stud. Then the one they rather regretted now, advance of social sex consciousness, on that farm he had some cows. They had actually persuaded one or two of the fourth year to act themselves in slight exaggeration. They were all too frightened now of Joyce and Sheila to do more than a sober strut in embarrassed re-creation. There had been a further range of animals all with identifiable and libellous school connections.

Each scene had been linked with the chorus, to which the whole audience soon cottoned on and joined in. Old MacDonald had a school, ee aye ee aye oh. And in that school he had a belt ee aye ee aye oh. With a whack whack, here and a whack whack there, here a whack, there a whack, every where a whack whack. Davie had lent them his belt, which Paddy had laid about with great glee and gusto on surfaces which produced great noise, and everyone had known or thought, it was their final tribute to Old Faithful, farewell old friend and they could afford to laugh and be nostalgic. They had woven into the script subtle political parallels with Orwell's text, with all animals being equal except some pigs were more equal than others, with farewell speeches to Napoleon

354

and a welcome to Snowball. The comedy had been rather more effective and obvious than the political satire but they had felt at the time that it had been a great success, a triumph for the Young Socialists over the system and a message to the old bastard that he had failed to crush them.

They hadn't talked about it for twenty years but the three of them went right through the whole sequence, in order, without falter, till after the final chorus when they collapsed in each others arms in tears of laughter and joy. Great days, good memories. It led onto excited chatter. Danny made the point that if Old Faithful had been retired then, McGoldrick might still be alive and Frank noticed Joyce looking at him anxiously, but he appeared indifferent to the thought. As they compared notes on where all the animals were now they pondered some of the funny rules of life; that the best looking women were not sexy at 15 years old and those that were fade before twenty; that there is no direct relationship between social success at school and in life; and that schools spend a lot of money to fail to teach anything other than a sense of relief at leaving. The re-creation gave Frank what he had been looking for and created a collective mood of nostalgia that sustained him through the evening.

He had a couple of relapses during one of which Christine found him crying in the kitchen and cuddled him gently to her generous bosom. He went further back with her than with any of them, than anyone. Like the big sister he never had. She had always been there, up the same close. He had taken her knickers down once, when they were six years old and didn't know why, but other than that their intimacy had been more sedate, and more reassuring. For all its innocence, neither had dared tell Paddy about their little experiment. So Frank cried in her arms while he asked her to look after her fat wee bastard for him, told her to cover his self-destruct button and make sure he went for an Assembly seat rather than a Westminster one. That helped get him in the mood for the serious part of the proceedings towards the end of the evening when he told them that he had been feeling that things were getting on top of him again, that he could not stand the thought of another spell like he had had in the second part of the last year, that he could not bear to go through all that again, he would not go through that again, and that he was going to go away for a few days immediately after the end of the Cup Final and see what he could sort out. He felt ashamed of himself at the obvious care and concern they showed for him, the worry that they were in danger of losing him again. His act was good enough that the possibility that it might even be for ever clearly flickered across several of their minds, as did the valedictory nature of some of his comments to them individually.

Somehow he survived the rest of the evening and saw them all off, with a special kiss of farewell for Christine and Vera. As he watched those two women leave he felt envious of Paddy and Jack. Those two proved that the marriages that survived, the relationships that lasted, weren't the ones moulded in the furnace of lust and looks but those built on long mutual respect, care and admiration. He persuaded Joyce to leave the tidying up and take him to her bed for what he knew would be a last physical act of love. He did not know what to say to her. His letter had said it all but she would not read that for some time to come and he knew he could not tell her any of it then, but did not want to end on any kind of lie, so he said nothing but let his tongue and hands do his talking for him. The tender ferocity of his desire to have and please her, pleased her. Afterwards she talked and he listened. Joyce was very pleased about how well her evening had gone. She talked of having the confidence to do it again and he began to weep tearlessly into her black, black hair. She knew he always woke very early and got up once awake. He warned her he would leave in a couple of hours. She fell asleep in his arms, for the best and longest cuddle he ever gave her.

He did sleep much to his surprise, he had budgeted for a night without but got a bonus two hours. He woke, dressed quietly then ensured she was alive enough to hear his rehearsed farewell apology. "I do love you, Joyce, my pal. I'm sorry I haven't been as honest and as open with you as I should have been, but I do love you, and I did try. Just remember I've given you more of me than I've ever given any other living soul. I'm just sorry it wasn't enough. You deserve better. I'll explain it all properly to you later. Goodbye my darling. Take care." He lent over the bed and kissed her cheek lightly, cuddled her briefly when she said "Bye, Frank, honey" in a sleepy voice, then tiptoed out past her books and her bookcases, seeming to pause momentarily, then through the dining area with the debris from his farewell to his friends, and out into the dark street to begin the journey towards his destiny.

Although it wasn't quite the quickest way home, he found himself drawn once more to Queens Park and the path to the top of the hill where he paused again at the flagpole and looked at his sleeping city. At this time of goodbyes he found it hard to forget the morning six years before when he had stood in this same place and said his farewells to Elaine. Oh why, oh why, oh why, the incessant question came even though he knew his answer, carved forever on the stone surround of his heart. He had wrestled for weeks with whether he should, could, risk seeing her one last time. She had said in the cafe that afternoon he had met Michael that he should arrange, good code word that, to come round some time to see wee Shona. But he never had and never would. He had been to his lawyer and seen Michael all right, but he did not have the courage to square his mother. He could hear her cold tones echoing in his head and could not risk the original. "Sorry for what, Frank? Thanks to you I have a wonderful husband, two lovely children, a back and front garden and a future. Why should you say sorry to me. It is me that should be sorry, for you." In some of his versions she had ended "but I'm not." and in others "and I am." and he never knew which was the worse. He had decided not even to write to her, the only person of his heart that was not to receive a letter of true farewell rather than the fake performance of the past week. He composed the letter in his head all the same and it hurt.

At least he had done his duty by Michael. He knew Michael was his child. Of that there was no doubt. His procreation was the direct result of a physical act by Frank Hunter. The cold slap in the face he had given Elaine had led to her impregnation as surely, more surely, than any insertion of his penis and sperm would have done. Michael was the fruit of the essence of Frank Hunter, the only remnant that would bear his trace through future generations. He knew Elaine knew that too, and loved her even more for her understanding. In acknowledging that openly for the first time, he released the spirit from the body and the death of the love that never died allowed the love to live forever.

As he left his flagpole and walked home, he thought of the content of the other letters. The easiest letter had been the one to Mary-Ann Ewing since he had not had to lead her to believe anything else, or apologise for misleading her. He still had had to apologise but found it easier with her than any of the others. For various painful reasons, Frank knew that although Elaine was the one true love of his life she was not the ideal partner for him. An older Mary-Ann or a far younger Mary would have been. The two weeks he had spent with Mary-Ann may have been full of sexual passion, but they had also been about more and he had often returned to their memory. In his letter he gave her some advance notice about gifts to come. Including detail of access to the key of the safe deposit box where he had placed her grandmother's letters, with a request that she do what he had so sadly failed to achieve, and edit Mary Ewing's wonderful words. Frank knew that she had inherited her grandmother's power over language. She had become a political journalist with vision and integrity. She had regularly sent him the best of her work and he had been genuinely impressed. He offered her, before he did it, the exclusive story of his deed, subject to certain conditions about timing. He made only one small request about content, that she was to stress that he was not a madman, but a sad man; not a lunatic but a patriot; not a hater but a waiter. He also asked her to do two other things for him and for Joyce. He asked her to accept his judgement that they were both acts of kindness, which she might otherwise have been inclined to dispute. He had posted the parcel to her, airmail, on the Tuesday lunchtime. He would post the letter in the post office in Victoria Road, on his way back to the Victoria Bar tomorrow. He had already told her when he would phone her, if things went to plan. The first letter to Joyce would be posted in his favourite letter box in the world on Monday. The second one to Joyce and the only ones to Danny, Paddy and Gerry were already in the elaborate system that he had set up with his lawyer Paul Ross, with triggers and time-locks. He had a fail-safe system for all of them if his project began to go awry, but Mary-Ann's was not in that system. She had another role, as his personal historian. That was one book that would be written.

As he walked down the hill towards his flat he regretted the one other letter he had decided not to write. He wished he had taken a different decision about Hazel. She might be grateful about the money but he reckoned she would rather have an explanation. She might not even take the money. He had offered her the chance of a job with Peter Sludden. Hazel knew the story of Frank's mother and her rise, but declined his offers of a similar start. She chose to remain a cleaner, as part of her planned programme of self-abuse. He was seriously worried about her mental health. He had spent his last time with her earlier that day, at lunch and early afternoon. She had been so flat, he had been concerned for her. Her mood matched her own description of her pre-Kamesthorn admission days, and left the impression he was trying to generate for himself. Indeed he had drawn heavily on her performance for his own, but hers was the real thing. No spark, no fight, no motivation. She was overwhelmed by her own sadness and despair.

She seemed devoid of motivation to continue. He had considered again, whether he should take his mother's advice, marry her and save them both. He could get a job, an ordinary job, and she could bring up their four or five children. He could go out with his pals several nights a week, and she would not nag. They would have good sex, regularly and often, and give each other much comfort. Money would be no problem, and they could have a comfortable existence. If he got bored he could afford to go back to University, or write his books. When the children were at school, she could get a job at Sluddens and become his mother again.

He had indulged this fantasy a few times recently, in his search for alternatives to the course on which he seemed locked. In one, he had even been happy to take on her own children too. It would not bother him to bring up another man's children. And if they had their own children it would perpetuate the Hunter line. Otherwise it would die with the single son of a single son of a single son, who had not a single son. It would also keep the Coyles and Rogans happy, and give Shona the grandchild she had been cruelly denied. But pleasant as he found the fantasy, he knew that was exactly what it was. They were too similar to be compatible. They each separately had a terrible burden of sadness that would always threaten any partner free of it with drowning, swamping, sucking into the quicksand of blackness. Together no relationship they created could possibly bear the combined weight of that sadness, of their heavy knowledge of the true nature of the world and their own weaknesses.

Hazel had recently signed away her children. Agreed to a pompous old Court Officer that they could be decreed Freed for Adoption. Frank had talked to her about the possibilities of taking them back, or at least fighting for them. But she had been clear in her own mind that it was too late. She had been away from them too long and she was a stranger. She knew the couple who had them and was certain that they loved and were loved in that household. And anyway, she had to be punished for her sins. She had forfeited her right to be a mother. Frank knew from Danny and Joyce the child-centred arguments about security and attachment. But he also knew Hazel, although her version was less strong than his. She was scathing about what she had to offer, no home, no good job, no secure income, no future, no prospects, a past lifestyle of drugs and prostitution, balanced against only the love of a mother who had proved inadequate to the challenges they had posed. Frank had argued she could provide the home, he could help her furnish it, she could get a better paid job, she could rebuild her relationship with them. But she knew she had lost the strength somewhere between Govan and Kamesthorn, and would never find it again. And he was in no position to upbraid her for being a quitter.

She had shown him her letter to her children. And being a recent expert he recognised a suicide note when he saw one. The timing just convinced her God was still punishing her. She was asked to sign the forms on Debbie's birthday. And on Tommy's birthday, her Social Worker, a good one who had only recently finally accepted her decision not to seek their return, asked her to write them a letter that they could later use to make sense of their background and why their mother let them be adopted. She had spent the remainder of her limited stock of emotional energy on that letter. She had known that it was her exit visa, that it ruled out the one challenge that could have sustained her through her black valley with the promise of a hint of spring sunlight over the hill on the other side. The letter extinguished the slightest ray and left her soul in total darkness. In a sense it had been a release, from the burden of parenthood and the responsibility that had put on her to survive. Released from that burden and that responsibility, she was now free to float gently down to whatever level of despair awaited her.

Frank had read the letter and cried. It was a lovely and a loving letter. It was not written for them now at their age, but for later. It was written for them to read and grow into and return to again and again, for the rest of their childhood and the rest of their lives. The letter had talked of their conception in love. That whatever else their parents were, they had loved each other and wanted and loved the products of that love. She had written in plain and simple language. She had addressed to Tommy the story of his father and the mistakes he had made. She had talked of the good points but had used his tale to warn of the dangers of greed and the harm of the acceptance of the Glasgow myths of gallusness and hardness. She asked him to do her the favour of being strong enough not to try too hard to be strong. To learn from his mistake and show the other gentler side of his personality that his father had been ashamed to own. The letter explained in unsensational and unglamorous terms how drugs and perverted dreams had killed their father. It also revealed the romantic ambition in him that she had found so attractive. She told Debbie of how good-looking her father had been, and gave examples of the tenderness and kindness of which he had been capable but so rarely showed. She tried to leave them with a view of a man, full but flawed. She tried to explain that mistakes and errors of judgement were not the same as badness. She shared with them the little, the good, that Billy had told her about his family, which had dissolved before she met him. He had been in care too, so that was one experience they had shared with him. She had built from that her gratitude to Mr and Mrs Lyons for giving a loving family home to her two children. She told them she had no resentment towards them, only thanks, for doing so well what she had been unable to do. That family was her last gift to them, so they should use it wisely and treasure it.

She had told them about herself, about her childhood in Motherwell, and her own family, which would always be theirs as well as their new one. She told them of her Aunt Harriet and her fourteen cats, and how Uncle Tommy, her favourite and the source of Tommy's name, had played for Shotts Bon Accord and could have done better with a bit of luck. She talked of how her parents were young enough likely to be alive still when the children came to be old enough to go looking, and where to look. She mentioned her first marriage in the passing but only to stress how much she had loved their father in comparison. She had stressed the love between them, and the love of both of them for their children. She told them how much she had loved them from the first time she had felt their presence in her tummy, right through and beyond the final kiss and cuddle she had given the small strangers on the final visit her Social Worker had allowed her to make. She stressed the beyond. Her love for them was real, and would endure throughout their lives, always and forever. She talked of incidents they had shared together, that she hoped Tommy at least would remember, reinforcing the memory and supplying the background detail. She knew Debbie was too young to remember any of their time together, but she gave her details of comic and touching incidents, where her personality had already been clear.

She told them of the mistakes she had made, for love and from weakness. She acknowledged to them that she had done things she would rather not have done, and would not want her daughter to do. But mistakes are only mistakes, lessons to be learnt from as an aid to growing up. And she had done two wonderful things in her life, and she would be happy if they grew up, those wonderful things, able to draw on the knowledge that they were lucky enough to have four parents that loved them rather than just the two of their less fortunate friends. She referred to two photographs she had given to go alongside the letter. One was taken on her wedding day to Billy, a lovely couple whose joy on the day hid all the realities. The other picture was of the four of them, in Bellahouston Park on about the only occasion they had been out in Glasgow together. Frank had seen the photos before they went. He had recognised Billy's face in the wedding photo, not that he had ever met the man. It was the face of the Glasgow chancer, a wideboy, charming, likeable and unreliable, that could switch from friend to killer in one blink of a cold eye. Not a man whose drink you would want to spill. Hazel had been beautiful that day, radiantly attractive, desirable, and slim. By the second photo her decline was apparent. It was a good photo of the two babies, but both adults had a haunted look, as if their faces already knew of the fate that awaited them both.

Hazel had told Frank that the Social Worker had found the letter moving, and had even cried. But she had failed to see its true significance and cried for a different reason than Frank. The Social Worker failed to see that despite what she had told Hazel about later rights, this was not the letter of a mother who envisaged ever seeing her children again. Frank knew what she missed, that it was not an apology for deferment, but a final goodbye, because there would be no mother available to come looking for. That was why Frank cried, he knew his friend was almost as dead as him. How could he fight her, stimulate in her a desire, a will to survive, without being hypocritical. And what would be the effect on her of his action? He had tried not to ask himself that question, far less answer it. She had to be responsible for her own destiny, she had to make her own decision.

As ever words had failed him and he had resorted to actions. He had meant to cuddle her goodbye, hold her close and insert his life-force into her without her noticing, so that she would have twice the chances. She had said nothing, asked for nothing, but he had sensed she wanted and needed more, and so almost without realising it he had taken off all her clothes and given her what he could without breaking his promise to himself not to be unfaithful to Joyce. She had been frighteningly passive while obviously consenting, as if she knew it was the last time they would and she would be intimate. He had used his tongue and his hands to offer her comfort and love. At climax she had given a squeak rather than her usual shriek, a timid mouse quivering. When the gentle shuddering subsided he had rested his head on her stomach. He had declined her offer to blow his mind. They had had a long cuddle on her floor, two vulnerable, sad people. During that cuddle, they had experienced what they both needed, a greater intimacy than any generated by the mingling of organs and orifices. Finally he had kissed her and left. Walking down Battlefield Road he knew he could not leave it at that and the will. He would have to trust in making it across the water, when he would have the time to write a proper farewell. All the others were already written.

He had a brief sensation that his friends had let him down. Part of him had always felt that his whole enterprise was a joke, an exhibition in the Frank Hunter Museum of Ironic Art. But on that walk home he knew the cage was open and the beast had broken free, never to be returned. He had a feeling of inevitability, of having walked too far off the end of the pier to avoid getting wet. He really was going to do it. Every trick he had tried to derail himself had failed, or even strengthened the attraction of the notion. His trips to the cemeteries had not produced an endorsement but there had been no veto either. That had just left his close friends. And they had failed him, failed to stop him, the bastards, their pity and their patronisation offered no hope of a better alternative. His anger was at them, a relief from himself. "Well at least I tried", he found himself saying. Then he had a sudden memory of the wee man from George Square who had crystallised Frank's hatred of No bastards and their pusillanimous rationalisations of their cowardly failure to do the right thing. "It wasnae ma fault, Jimmy, honest, I'm a helpless victim on the tide of destiny". He remembered the girning tone and how much he had despised him. "Rubbish," had been his response that Hogmanay night twenty years ago, and "Rubbish" was his renewed response. With a final shake of the heart, he reasserted control of himself.

He was going to do what he was going to do, because he wanted to do what he was going to do. It was his destiny, marked out for him maybe by his character and personality but his nevertheless, by choice, not blindly allocated to him in a random manner. One accepted by him as his, because it fitted him and what he was and used to be, not what he might have been. The understanding comforted him. Frank Hunter was still in charge. So all his farewells had been said, all his analyses made. His destiny was clear, as was his destination. He was truly alone at last, and ever more would be. Sartre was wrong. Hell is not other people. Hell is yourself.

Subsequent accounts and re-constructions of the death or final disappearance of Frank Hunter all turned out to be inaccurate. That was because of their assumption that it must have taken place sometime after he was last seen in public. That proved to be a simplistic, erroneous and sloppy assumption. In truth, the real Frank Hunter, son of Shona Coyle and Dave Hunter; grandson of Jessie and Willie Hunter, and of Jean Rogan and Peter Coyle; eternal lover of Elaine Duncan; friend of Paddy McGuire, Danny Campbell, Gerry Robertson, Jack Reilly and Hazel; soul-mate of Mary and Mary-Ann Ewing; too late lover of Joyce; passionate supporter of Celtic and Scotland; number one SAD man; passed away down the plug-hole at 5:05a.m. precisely on Saturday, 12th May 1990.

At 5am he finished his reverie of great friends I have known and loved and prepared himself to meet his destiny. He knew he needed a cold shower. Not only to drive away the residue of alcohol in his system, but more importantly, to flush away the last remnants of the sentimentality and nostalgia in which he had been wallowing for the previous two days. Plan E had failed to protect him from himself. Now he needed a clear head to concentrate unemotionally on what had to be done. He knew exactly what that was and why he was going to do it in the way he was going to do it.

He had his shower, watching in silence as the remnants of his relationships were washed off and away, swirling down the exit to the same sea he had in mind. The best of the real Frank Hunter went with them, prematurely, slithering down the cold body, out through the round grid, down through the Glasgow sewage system, then into the River Clyde, along down to the Atlantic Ocean and the last reaches of the Gulf Stream, where it would search out again its missing parts with a view to reintegration. It left only a pathetic hunched naked human wreck huddling on the floor of the shower watching in awe as the machine, cold calculating and professional, took over. That wreck was condemned for the rest of the day to hover in detached amazement in corners of rooms and roofs of cars, as the remnant machine went through its ordained routine, a spectator at its own finest hour. It was always the role Frank Hunter did best.

The man of destiny dressed with care, then checked his various bags. The golf bag was first. He checked and rechecked the Parker Hale. He had cleaned it several times, most recently on the Thursday, but he did it one more time for luck. He also checked the shotgun, less fastidiously. He put in most of his golf clubs. He placed the ammunition in the side pockets of the bag. Then he did a final census on the bag for Brownlie Street. It was important that it coincided with the list he had already posted. He did a final check on his trip bag, remembering to add the writing paper and envelopes, after his resolution about Hazel. Then he sorted out his flat, conscious that it might be others than Joyce who would get there first. His affairs were in order. His will had been updated, all his bills paid, all the seed money planted in the necessary places. Not that he could truthfully say that he did not owe anyone anything.

With all his preparations done, and redone, he still had time to spare, but something didn't seem right. It took him a while to realise what missing. The buzz that always accompanied Cup Final day whether or not the Celtic were playing. He had been to his first Final at the age of 7, an experience that nearly broke the heart of the young boy he had once been. He had returned at 9 to witness the walkout and his introduction to the power of collective action. He had been back at 11 for the happiest day of his life, when King Billy gave them the Cup. He had not missed a Final since then. 25 in a row, today would be the 26th, not counting 5 replays. Celtic had been in 16 of them, 12 times as winners. The sight of the Celtic captain lifting up the Cup was a special thrill that never failed to move him deeply. But even when the Bhoys weren't there, Final day was holy, a tribute to the great day in a great game. He was worried about the risk of defiling it. Was shooting the Prime Minister there, then, an act of blasphemy, akin to or even worse than, than what? He tried to imagine a similar act of literal blasphemy but struggled to come up with a parallel. He remembered but didn't quite equate, Tommy Gallagher farting in church with the school, and old MacDonald's response. No, his deed was of a slightly different magnitude. But would his success smell any sweeter?

He remembered the conversation he had had, or rather not had, with Jack the previous evening. Frank had done his old party piece, the two simultaneous conversations with the one person, only one of which the other party was allowed to hear. Frank would talk little in one, and do the talking for both in the other, which was always why there was such a gap between his perception of how talkative he was, and every other buggers. Frank tended to regard the conversation only he was able to hear as the real or more important one, which explained another set of divergent opinions. Frank had known that he wouldn't see Jack on Cup Final day, since he was taking Willie to the stand. He was overprotective to that boy. Willie was nearly 10 years old, and already fulfilling all the promise of his earliest days. Frank was sorry that he would miss the full flowering of his talent. It would be nice to believe that he was going to that heaven his Gran and mother occupied, where you got a free view of every game and could discuss them at length with your visitors. But you needed the right visitors for that. Jack would visit him, Frank was sure of that, but he also knew the conversations would be on Jack's terms not his, and that would be too positive an agenda for Frank's taste.

Frank knew, because his Jack had told him so, that Jack would never forgive Frank for what he was about to do. Not the Prime Minister bit, Jack despised her as much as Frank did, more probably, he was certainly always more virulently abusive about her. Indeed she was the only person on earth who ever seemed capable of producing a negative reaction in Jack, now that Hiddleston was roasting in hell. No, it would be for defiling the Cup Final that Jack would attack him. For betraying the sense of history and tradition, the sanctity of the Final as Scottish Football's special day, the highlight and climax of the season. Like Frank, Jack had never missed one since they had been given their own special day. It never mattered who was playing, Jack would be there honouring the game. Unlike Frank, Jack could, and for the price of a pint often did, name the finalists and score in every one of the 104 Finals. He could name the teams and the scorers too. He had met almost every living survivor who had won a medal. He would definitely see Frank's act as a form of blasphemy. It was not even that Jack didn't mix football and politics. He had enthusiastically red-carded the lady at her last Hampden visit, and would roundly boo her this time. He had waxed lyrical and romantic nonsense for months afterwards about what a moving and effective political protest that had been, the Scottish people united in showing her the red card. Frank had argued the previous night, in vain, that a red card, or 40,000, was one kind of message, and a bronze bullet another, and that it was a matter of degree, of

367

relativity not an absolutely different kind of act but even his Jack had remained unconvinced. "Say ma boy sees the blood, takes it bad, is traumatised or terrified" had been one consideration, one that had never occurred to Frank till then, with his sanitised conception of the purity of his act.

Jack hated violence, hated that side of Glasgow's underbelly, the simmering ever-present possibility of pain and disruption. He was a pacifist who didn't approve of shooting anyone - certainly not a lady. He had an old-fashioned view that women should be treated differently and better, not as equals but as superiors. For all his genuine hatred of the Iron Lady, she was still a lady and should not be physically abused.

But Jack's real concern was more fundamental. The red card protest had not affected the game in the slightest, but Frank's act ran the real risk of impinging on the Final itself, and that would be unforgivable. To be fair to Jack, this had been a major theme and concern for Frank himself, one to which he had given considerable thought. Jack had a thing about abandoned games, ghost games as he called them, and the unfairness involved in them. He had once seen Willie Bauld score two of the best goals ever seen in a game against Falkirk that had been abandoned with 10 minutes to go, due to fog. He always believed that Bauld should have been allowed to keep the goals. They had been scored fairly, how could they be erased as if phantom. Denis Law once scored 6 goals in a cup-tie that was abandoned before the end, and people had to pretend it never happened. Logic and justice demanded that abandoned games should restart at the point and stage they had been abandoned. Sensible sports like golf and tennis behaved that way. Jack told Frank that if the Cup Final were to be abandoned because of his act he could be creating a major injustice. He drew Frank a picture of someone peaking at the final, McStay perhaps, and scoring two great goals, then finding that career peak performance turning out to be written on sand because some madman, and Frank winced as his Jack used that word not once but twice, some madman pulled a trigger with 5 minutes to go. Say it cost his Celtic a victory, and they went down to defeat in the replay. Could Frank live with an outcome like that? Would his Grandmother ever speak to him again?

The use of these arguments by someone else, even second hand, was somewhat of a relief to Frank. He had been concerned about the morality and even sanity of his own concerns. Here he was busily planning to shoot someone, end a human life, and his major dilemma and moral consideration seemed to be the effect his action might have on a game, a football match. He had resolved it for himself, eventually, by reassuring himself that if he got the timing right, middle to end of the second half, then in the interests of public order and safety they would allow the match to finish. They would whisk the victim away out of sight in minutes. Very few of the crowd would know what happened. They would just assume it was an attack of boredom, or a slipping away to Aberdeen before the end. Christ, after all, they had played the whole match at Heysel, with 39 dead before the kick-off, in public safety terms. Surely to God they would finish a match with ten minutes to go for only one casualty. Even her supporters wouldn't want to run the risk of a joyous reaction from the crowd. No, the rationale was as strong as the rationalisations, the match would be allowed to finish. He wasn't quite as able to reassure Jack as himself, so he had moved the conversation back onto securer ground and finally integrated it into the other one which was about whether Willie Hamilton really could have been a better player than Baxter, Law and Dalglish. The real and animated Jack, assured them all he had been the greatest Scottish player ever, and more typical of his race than the other three, in that he had allowed drink to deny him, a passive victim, more than merely minor fruits of his talent. But those who had seen him in his prime knew and would never forget. The other three men had seen him, near the end, good yes but that good, no. For once Jack's judgement could not be relied upon or his version of history accepted whole.

Over the meal the previous night, they had gone on to talk about their favourite project, one that Councillor McGuire was now in a position to influence positively. If the Year of Culture and its promises of permanent momentoes was to mean anything, then surely the climate was as right as it ever could be for the establishment of a temple to the true Glasgow culture, for a football museum, a Hall of Fame. They had all denounced the money and subsidies going to music, to ballet, to opera for the benefit mainly of a privileged and unrepresentative elite. A fraction of that sum could create a shrine, that could reflect what was the best in popular culture, the true reflection of the Scottish creative artistic endeavour. For years it had been confined to pub talk, but at last they were starting to make it happen. They had welded an alliance, Paddy had interested some of his District Council colleagues, Gerry Robertson had brought Scottish Trade

Union Congress support, Tommy Little had the Scottish Professional Footballers Association behind it, and even the Scottish Football Association had made some positive noises and appeared to grasp some of the potential. Jack had offered his professional services for free, whether it was to design a brand-new building, or as more likely, to assist in the conversion of an existing structure to fit new purposes. He would give it his best, which would mean that it would be excellent. Jack had thrown his soul into the venture. He had used a business trip to New York to check out their Baseball Hall of Fame, and bored them for months with his enthusing about the possibilities and lessons. The job of caretaker or Director was made for Jack, or vice versa. Frank had felt impotent about his lack of involvement. He no longer even had a role in the District or Regional Labour Parties, no resolutions to move or support, no resolution left.

Jack already had a considerable library of tapes of Scottish games, compiled with the help of his friends in the BBC and STV. As a special birthday present, he had once got for Frank 12 minutes of highlights of the Viccies-Hibs cup-tie replay of 1974, transcribed onto a VHS tape, one of the best presents he had ever received, although a mixed blessing. Jack always promised him that if they got a Hall of Fame, he would ensure Frank's winning goal that night would be included in any anthology of great goals. For Jack, any goal that beat the Hibs was a great goal. Frank's most urgent contribution to the discussion that evening had been to remind him of that pledge. He felt he was allowed one act of vanity, especially given what he was about to do for Scottish Football. Replaying his conversations with Jack generated a degree of interest in him in the coming game. Not that he was confident. He was sure Celtic were going to get beaten. Gerry had been right. King Billy was a dumpling, his two main signings weren't even going to be in his own chosen team. So he wasn't too optimistic about Escape Plan 31. Still, it was a Cup Final, and his last one.

His thoughts soon turned back to the task in hand. He ran through again the exact sequence of events he had planned for the day ahead. He knew it would be important not to deviate. He reminded himself of the conclusions he had finally come to about exactly what it was he was going to do, and why and when. The what had remained largely invariable but he had surprised himself with the outcome of the why. At least it was grave enough to justify the venture. He switched on the video timer and went round the flat saying his last goodbyes. It was easier than he had feared.

He had never been happy there, and that was where he had spent the Depression. Wherever he was going had to be better then that. He was surprised at his calm flatness. He wanted nervousness, knew he would need the adrenaline surge for later, but there was just a quiet emptiness broken only by his own recollections, no tenseness in the stomach, no dryness in the throat, no monkey-wire round his neck. The machine was immune.

At last it was time. He phoned the taxi firm, giving the same address in the adjacent street as last time. The next three stages went like clockwork. He was inside his car with 6 minutes to spare. It had not been interfered with overnight. And at 12:05pm precisely he moved into stage 4. He had been right, the police constable was not yet on duty. The keys were where they should have been. He was not too disappointed. If they had not been, only his little joke would have been aborted, not the grand plan, but already it was palling a little for him. Maybe he wasn't so funny as he thought after all. Still, it was there, so he went inside and distributed his little collection of items around the flat. They hadn't made any great effort to tidy it up, so he didn't have too much to do to make it look well-used. He made the right marks on the bathroom window sill. He didn't see anybody watching him as he looked out right down into the Directors Box. The view was breathtaking, a magnificent panorama of the ground. Could it really be that easy, or was he overlooking something fundamental. Well, he would soon find out. They were bound to do more than normal with the Prime Minister coming, but the game must go on. It took him longer than the 5 minutes he had estimated, but the excess went in thought not deed. He memorised it well and set his little test so that he could be sure when he came back that no-one else had been and seen. The last thing he did was switch on the TV, loud enough to be heard but not loud enough to cause complaint. No-one saw him on the close stairs and no-one seemed to be particularly interested when the rotund and bearded gentleman re-entered Brownlie Street and strolled back up the hill to his car. A few minutes, and he was the remnants of Frank Hunter again. He checked everything was in his big anorak pockets, beard, glasses, wee anorak, hat, vacuum pouch, keys for 37, then set off for the Victoria.

He arrived at 12:38pm. Late but not disgracefully so. Danny, Sheila, Paddy, Peter and Gerry were already well into a round, so he bought another and made the right noises about catching up. The pub was buzzing with the excitement of the day. Most of the

371

punters were regulars but there were many casuals including a few wearing red. The atmosphere was friendly and good-natured, with the usual warnings about the lamb stew being the nearest thing to aggravation. His performances of the previous day must have been successful, for they seemed solicitous about his health and state of mind. As he sat there, at his favoured corner table with some of his favourite people, he asked himself the one question he had been avoiding even posing for weeks. "Am I mad, or what? I could be facing the prospect of watching my team in a Cup Final, and here I am planning to make some kind of political statement with a gun and end the world as I know it." He decided the answer was what, but he wouldn't have liked to put it to a vote, even to the limited electorate inside his head.

Various people they knew well or casually would drop over to their table and exchange insults or jibes. Andy Rogers brought his old mates from Aberdeen into the pub but the banter remained harmless. It was building up nicely to a good final day. There was some talk of the nerve of that bloody woman, and a general reaffirmation of the hatred that the mere mention of her name inspired. There wasn't a repetition of the red card business planned but it was obvious that she was going to be in for a dose of the verbals. Someone actually said, and by Frank's count that was the 23rd time since he started his project, "Why doesn't someone just shoot the bitch and do us all a favour". Frank smiled grimly to himself and thought, anything to oblige, Jimmy, anything to oblige.

He was becoming quite an expert in the art of not drinking. He bought or was given 4 pints during his spell in the Victoria but consumed barely half that amount. Well within his target to avoid jeopardising the enterprise. Bang on 2 o'clock Councillor McGuire, leader of men, had them out the door and marching off to victory. The streets were fuller then, of both shades, many buses from the far north parked on their route so if anything they encountered more of the enemy than friendly forces. But it was peaceful stuff, quite unlike the Old Firm antics. Frank saw one act of madness that reminded him of his earlier favourite suicidal impulse. One wee Celtic supporter, about 16 or 17, 5'5" if that, walked right into a crowd of about 30 or 40 Aberdonians singing at the top of his voice "Sheep-shagging baastards, sheep-shagging baastards, you're nothing but sheep-shagging baaastards, sheep-shagging baaaastards". He emerged from the other side of the group unscathed, untouched, unbowed. The Aberdeen supporters

372

knew how to humour the mentally handicapped. Frank felt some amusement at the Glaswegian sense of geography, economics and romance that assumed Aberdeen residents saw more of sheep than they did. Their tickets were for the Celtic end of the North Enclosure so they parted company from Andy and his pals at Somerville Drive and made their way to their usual spot just off passageway 25. Creatures of habit, conservative, a word they loathed but lived.

A storm of booing alerted them to the fact that the Prime Minister had taken her place in the Directors Box. She really was hated with a venom that was tangible. It was not exactly her kind of constituency, but Frank knew that the hatred for her was one of the few Scottish feelings that bestrode all class and occupational divisions. They had had the sense not to get her to do the presentation of the teams and attention was soon diverted from her presence, although Frank clocked that she appeared to be sitting according to his plan. As the teams kicked the balls about, Frank felt some of the normal pre-match excitement and nervous tension and almost forgot what he was there for, until he put his hand in his pocket and felt hair. That sobered him up, it was maybe Labrador after all, and the opening 20 minutes did the rest. After one initial flurry, Celtic never looked like scoring and were very lucky not to be two goals down. Frank even at that stage of his decline couldn't help correcting himself and changing the assessment to twice lucky not to be one goal down. Pedantic to the last. The remaining 25 minutes of the first half, he spent preparing for the break, his with his friends. He had done all that bit, but this time he had to do it again, in a different way, just in case he was caught.

He had already warned them that he was going to do it, so they weren't too surprised when he announced as the whistle blew for half-time, that he was off to try to find his Uncles, Sammy, Rosaleen and their child, who were keeping the family tradition alive in a different part of the North Enclosure. He said he might be back if he couldn't find them, but reminded them that he wasn't going for a pint after the game as he was going away for a few days. He resisted a strange impulse to cuddle them, or even touch them, the machine was winning, and left with merely a shifty and dishonest "see you all later then." The crowd that opened to let him through closed again immediately and they were gone forever. His next problem was to make sure he didn't meet his relatives, some of them at least would be there although Des had obtained some Stand Tickets, Centre Stand of course. It dawned on Frank that with Des's prominence and influence these days, he might actually get a grandstand view of his favourite nephew's last performance. He had always told Frank as a child that he had a dear wish to see him covering himself in glory at Hampden. This was probably not what he had had in mind. He did meet one group he knew vaguely and made a point of talking briefly to them so that they would be able to swear he had been there. By the time the second half started he was where he had wanted to be, ready to go to the toilet when the call came.

The time on his own allowed him to consider one final irony for addition to his collection. He had started off being aware that something was missing, then he had realised what it was. There would be no Scotland-England game in the weekend after the Final. It would be the first year of his life there would be no such game. And he was pleased. It was a sign of the maturity of his country that what would once have been unthinkable and unacceptable, was now welcomed. Scotland would measure itself no more only in terms of a narrow comparison with England. The internationalisation was complete. Scotland would judge itself in relation to Europe, and the World. They might even qualify for the European Championship, now that was their primary target. Yet here he was, about to shoot the Prime Minister in the name of the freedom of the Scottish International Team, and he couldn't even arrange matters so as to go to Italy to watch them pursue his greatest dream. He had opted in, in the months after his recovery, the period October to March, to the plans for the invasion of Italy. He had been sure, and touched, that some of the enthusiasm of Danny and Paddy had been on his behalf, in a healing attempt to recreate the wonderful atmospheres of 1974 and 1982. But he had been a reluctant conscript to the Army, not a joyous volunteer. There had been no enthusiasm, no belief, no map in his head. Then that weekend he had defeated McGoldrick, he had felt the stirrings of a dream of Italia 90, a hint of possibilities. He had taken part in planning discussions, positively, started to put his shape on the plans, made an emotional commitment. Then the bastard had died and ruined everything. McGoldrick's death had also been the death of Frank's last dream. The man had screwed him up one last time.

The second half conformed to the pattern of the first and it was obvious to his professional eye, that while Aberdeen were the better team, they both could play all day and all night and never

374

score. He was glad there wouldn't be a replay, that way he wouldn't miss it. He knew with an absolute certainty what would happen, how Celtic would lose and even which player would be guaranteed to miss the vital kick, the one with the family name. He remembered at first thinking how proud his Gran Jean would have been, how eagerly she would have pursued her beloved Parish registers looking for some link that would tie Wanton into her dynasty, proof of relationship and bloodline. But after a couple of Old Firms games he had realised she would have done the search all right, just to prove there was absolutely no relationship, no responsibility. With that realisation fled the last of his escape clauses, Plan 31 the hope that Celtic would be playing so well, or Plan 32 that the game be so enthralling, that his primary instincts would predominate and football desires overcome political destiny. But they had both failed to deliver. In truth, almost blasphemy, certainly once unthinkable, he was almost bored with the game and glad of the excuse to leave. So he took his leave and turned his back on the game, and went to fulfil his life's true meaning.

He had taken it at first as a by-product of his depression, his growing boredom with live football. But he was one of the first victims of another more modern disease, SFV, satellite football videoitis. To cope with all the football on his satellite, he recorded every game, even the live ones, and watched them later on his video. He had mastered the art of distilling a 90 minute game into a 30 minute experience. The ball was out of play for 30 of the 90 anyway, and much of the rest could profitably be watched at double speed. This actually gave a clearer perception of the pattern of the game, of the ebb and flow. It added to and aided his professional analysis. He kept normal speed for the occasional flashes of skill and individual brilliance, sadly in decline. At a real game, he would become increasingly frustrated at his ability to move the dull action on, irritated by his loss of control.

There was only a small queue at the Portaloos and nobody joined behind him. This time he took his own advice and had a quick shit first, shades of the turmoil in his gut of the time in Peter's house. It fair took it out of you, this criminal activity. Somebody was waiting when the fatter and bearded gentleman vacated his cabin but they registered no surprise at his appearance and their only interest appeared to be in the accuracy of his aim. If only they knew how crucial that would soon be. It was easier than he had feared to find a Steward, a different one, and be ushered out into the almost deserted street, without offering any explanation that might be memorable. It took less than two minutes to reach the outside door at 37, via Bolivar Terrace and the back lane, unobserved by any policeman. He quickly established that no-one had entered it in his absence. He had a quick stand at the window, with his hat pulled down over his face. Yes he could definitely see the front row, and the third seat lady, although he got a better view of the game on the still loud TV. He wondered if his appearance at the window was being caught on film anywhere, or otherwise clocked but saw no sign of surveillance. A final check that everything was in its place, exhibiting signs of a quick exit. Two cans left unopened, that was his master touch, to go with the empty cans and bottles from the Cavan and the ones the contents of which he had poured down his own sink earlier that morning. He hadn't wanted his joke ruined by some smartarsed Glasgow forensic scientist pointing out the unusualness of a party where the toilet contained more alcohol put there directly than via a human conduit. He opened his vacuum pouch and placed the second empty container at the foot of the window.

He gathered up his second carpet and held and carried it in such a way as to give an impression in hindsight that it might contain a rifle. He passed no-one on the close stairs. The police constable did turn to look at him as he exited but he caught his eye and nodded and the man turned away to resume his watch in the direction of the ground and the noise. There was a wee lady bringing home her shopping at the next close door and two young boys in Brownlie Street but no-one seemed to see him reach and enter his car. He was grateful for the efficiency with which the machine took over, putting up the tinted paper and then assembling the rests without the need for thought or contemplation. Without getting out the car he moved to the back, got the gun out of the golfbag, placed the sights in position and then fitted it carefully into place on the rests. It was 4:25pm. He was cutting it fine. He knew from the car radio that it was still 0-0 and it was unlikely spectators would be starting to leave, but he had always known that it was likely that the Prime Minister would leave before the end, with a plane to catch to Aberdeen and no interest in the outcome. He wound the front window down and looked out. No-one in Stanmore Road, and more importantly no-one coming up Brownlie Street.

He picked up his binoculars and focused them. There she was looking thoroughly bored. He would be doing her a favour, putting an end to her torture. The sensation of closeness was a funny one, even on TV she had never looked real before. This was no monstrous machine, just a tired old lady. His glasses absorbed all the detail, her smart blue suit, the obligatory flowers, the black handbag by her side. He could even see the detail of the badge attached to her bag by some sycophantic acolyte. "Scottish Tories say", around the top, a big "NO" in the centre, "to Devolution" curved round the bottom. Her famous hair was unadorned but a smart blue hat sat in her lap. He couldn't see her shoes. He had known, in an act of primitive faith in fate, that he would get one final sign to point towards his destiny. He had known for weeks the truth of what he could and could not do, but he had never wavered from his intention of claiming his place in history with his act of destiny. Now was the time. He put down the glasses, rechecked the roads, still clear, and went into the other position leaving the back window down.

His sights gave a sharper, clearer view than his binoculars. She seemed even more tired. He concentrated on her face first, then on his target. He lifted his head, checked for the helicopter to reach a position far away from his steep decline, checked the policeman was still facing the ground and re-focused his sights once again. No. Yes, Go. He felt only cold calmness, the quiet satisfaction of reaching journey's end on schedule. He had proved something to himself, that he was capable of achieving any goal he set himself. Time to make his mark, or else he'd miss the boat. He held his breath and then squeezed the trigger.

It was Jack Reilly, a plainly decent human being, who best articulated the sense of unease felt by several of his better friends. "What kind of city is this, what kind of country is this, what kind of people are we, when the news of the shooting of an elderly woman can provoke such scenes of joy?" Because joy it was, the reaction, when the rumour swept the Southside post-match pubs that the Prime Minister had been shot. Spontaneous cheering broke out in all of them, in Paddy Neeson's, Heraghty's, the Victoria, the Elcho, the Albert, the Queens Park Bar, the Queens Park Cafe, Dixon Blazes, the Mally Arms, the Allison Arms and a dozen similar, when a TV newsflash confirmed the news. Celtic supporters grabbed it eagerly, as a form of comfort and consolation in their pain. At least the Bhoys in the IRA hadn't let them down. Aberdonians regarded it as gilding on the cake of joy. Neutrals saw it as some solace for an otherwise unrewarding afternoon.

There was a genuine sense of despair and disillusion when the news followed some minutes later that she was not dead, not even wounded, just shaken and stirred. The Celtic fans while more disappointed were more philosophical, not only their forwards couldn't shoot to save themselves. The Aberdonians were more worried. Was their moment of glory to be tainted by a popular wave of sympathy that would make her more secure, and drive their triumph off the front pages. The general consensus was deep regret that she would survive, that it would have been better to see the blood of that bloody woman. Others more cynical got their confirmation that it truly was the Iron Lady, and lead just bounced off.

The usual Glasgow experts and know-alls surfaced in droves to explain, on the basis of their having been there of course, exactly what had happened. Some swore she had screamed "Oh, God, I've been shot", others that she had calmly stated that it might be better if they went below. There had been a brief flurry of activity, she had been gathered up by her detectives and hustled out of the Box and into the safe Boardroom below, then the show had gone on, just as if she had slipped off, on schedule to fly back North to her more sympathetic crowd. Few around had known the seriousness of the situation. Some said she was merely bored and had had the bottle to leave, lucky her, others that she had been taken ill, nothing trivial they hoped, and the game had soon reclaimed full attention. There had been no dispute then or later, with the decision to allow it to continue its course, even its extended one, without public announcement. The TV cameras had not sensed the minor commotion and there were no pictures to compare with the ones of Stein being carried up the tunnel that haunted so many sensitive Scots. The first pictures were from the Victoria, the adjacent Infirmary rather than the pub. She had been taken there, as a precaution, but nothing more than mild shock was diagnosed. The details had emerged slowly over the next hours. She had been shot, by a high velocity rifle, from outwith the stadium, but fortunately her large handbag had got in the way and absorbed the force of the bullet. There were rumours that in fact there were shots from two sources or locations but uncertainty as to where the second bullet went.

The IRA did not deny the responsibility immediately attributed to it although it was the Sunday before it half-acknowledged it, by which time the Police were also publicly looking for several prominent terrorists rumoured to have come over to Glasgow, using the game as cover. Several Glaswegian supporters were soon assisting police with their enquiries as well as the ones from Ireland who hadn't managed to fade away on the news. Most papers, at least the Scottish ones, had wallowed in a particular kind of hypocrisy. The guilt induced by their recognition of their own and their readers ambiguous joy and disappointment had been converted into that peculiarly Scottish brand of sanctimonious moral indignation demanding punishment of the guilty, but only the guilty of deed not thought. It became an Irish problem not a Scottish one, and its resolution was to be an English one not a Scottish one. And anyway, she had asked for it, and Scotland would not mourn her passing when her time came. One inspired editor had even seen the irony of it, saved by her anti-devolution stance, and highlighted a picture of her handbag with the bullet smashed badge buckled in the centre from a direct hit. All agreed, that while of course they were glad she had survived this attempt, by the evil Irish, to get rid of her, there would be no popular backlash of sympathy in Scotland. One paper even produced the graph of her popularity in Scotland following Brighton, a downward spiral which never re-ascended. The English papers took a different line, which only emphasised to the diminishing number of Scots who read both, what a separation there was in the national psyches.

The Prime Minister had had to be restrained from proceeding to Aberdeen that evening but had made up for it the next day with a performance that showed both her ability to maximise the advantage to herself, and an indomitable courage and determination that only the five million most perverse Scots refused to acknowledge and appreciate. Even in England her nearness to death and assassination was not really absorbed into the national consciousness and political life quickly returned to normal, which meant she was soon exposed to much more deadly dangers.

Paddy McGuire later admitted, only to himself, a little guilt at the venom of his joy and the extent of his immediate disappointment. He hated the IRA, for personal as well as political reasons, and while he was often an angry man he was never a violent one, except with his tongue. He had been exultant at the rumour of her death, and bitterly disappointed when the vista had been eroded before he had had long to enjoy it. A little later, hard political reality reminded him of the conclusion he had reiterated often in the pubs and chambers of the last few months, that it suited Labour to have her alive, well and the enemy. One of his initial reactions had been to wish that his pal Frank were there, to join in the celebrations and the calculations of impact. Frank had seemed to have developed a few theories of his own about all that recently. Sheila had demonstrated that responses divided on political and national lines not sexual ones. Sheila really hated that woman, although she consistently refused to chant "Ditch the Bitch". Danny Campbell had been less exuberant but had still fallen short of an attitude that would have reassured Jack Reilly. Frank Hunter had been accurate enough in his silent prediction that Jack would be as distressed about the location as the act. Danny maintained that Jack's dismay at the reaction of others was just a manifestation of his own guilty thrill, and that moral superiority was not claimable.

Joyce had been watching the game with her father, a fervent Aberdeen supporter for the day, when the news had come through just shortly after the final resolution. Her Dad had been upset, because he hated the IRA even more than he hated the Lady. The real lady, Joyce's mother, was most upset. She took the attack on her heroine personally and used it as her excuse to trot out every bigoted conception she had about Irish, Catholics, Socialists and the unemployed. Joyce was very glad Frank was not there with her, and wished fervently she were wherever he were. He hadn't said where he was going, the man-child's version of "out", so she had no way of contacting him. She would have liked to have talked to him about the events, and wondered what would be hurting him most, his team's defeat or his foe's survival. He had become a bit obsessed about her recently, and had talked of little else. She was disappointed but not surprised or upset when he didn't phone her on the Saturday night or Sunday, at her parents. He had said not to expect him to and that he wouldn't get in touch till the Tuesday, but she was slightly concerned that he did not phone her at her flat on the Monday night. She hoped his rest was doing him good, because she had become increasingly worried about his mental state in the last week or so. Still the next day was the one he had promised, so she could rely on that. And he kept that promise to her, although he broke the other one in doing it.

Joyce had left that morning, as always, before the post. It never bothered her because she never got interesting letters, so she was surprised to find one lying there waiting for her when she got home. The satisfaction she got from recognising his handwriting was the last real pleasure Frank Hunter ever gave her. One sentence in and she was crying, by the second and last page she was sobbing violently. "Oh no Frank, oh no my darling don't, please don't." It was a pathetic letter, in every way. It told her he would be dead by the time she read it. She had checked the postmark. Lamlash, Isle of Arran, Monday 10:15am. He was going to leave his room, hire a rowing boat, take a last walk on his Holy Isle, then go for a swim. He did not mention the echo of McGoldrick, but she heard it anyway, rolling back off the bleak island and drowning her hopes. Justice in symmetry, what a stupid notion. Basically, and his message was both curt and basic, his reason was that he had become more and more depressed over the last few weeks, had tried to fight it but failed, had felt himself slipping beneath the waves again, could not face the prospect of a return to his black valley. He was sorry for the pain he knew he would cause her, but he no longer had the courage to face the pain that failure to do this would cause him. He reminded her of a cheery conversation they once had had in happier days about each other's preferred funeral arrangements. It might be a long time, if ever, before his body turned up, so he begged her not to wait long but conduct the other arrangements along the lines he had indicated. He was relying on her to deliver for him. There was a little more, but she did not absorb it.

Although she heard his voice pronounce every word, it didn't sound like her Frank. There was a difference between flatness and depression, there was a tone that did not quite seem right, and most crucially, as she later realised, he had not said goodbye to her. None of that meant he wasn't dead though, so she continued to weep for him.

Being a decisive creature, she did something. She phoned the police at Craigie Street. They were very good, despite being obviously busy with other things. After a few basic and sensible questions, they got in touch with the local constabulary. She waited quietly amidst the bustle and activity for what seemed an eternity, before getting the confirmation she feared that that was how long his peace would now last. The Lamlash police had checked the hotel mentioned in the letter. He had arrived on Saturday off the last boat, the 5:35pm. She reckoned that meant he must have left Glasgow before all the excitement, it had taken them well over an hour the last time they had driven down. He had stayed in his room all day Sunday except for a brief sortie about 4 o'clock to pick up Sunday papers from the shop beside the Bowling Green. He had gone out early on the Monday and been out all day. It turned out he had hired the boat on the Monday, for the whole day Tuesday, and had insisted on paying in advance. He had been seen at several points in the day, at Holy Isle, apparently collecting large boulders, but had gone round mid-afternoon to the far, blind side of the island. The Police had found the boat, floating deserted, with a trailing anchor. No sign of him or of a body. The next bit surprised her. They had found a gun in the boat, one which seemed to have been recently fired once. A Sauer 200 they said, but the name meant nothing to her, although it later seemed to be a source of relief to a white Peter McColl. There was some blood splattered over the side of the boat. There was also cut rope, and one or two smaller rocks. And a large fishing bag and gear. The initial assumption was that he must have tied weights to his body, and then shot himself in such a way as to deliberately fall into the water. They gently told her to abandon any hope. If anything was found, and it would be the next day before a proper dive could be undertaken by their sub-aqua team, it would be a body not a boyfriend.

She had known he was dead the minute she had started to read the letter, but the official confirmation of it did help. She agreed she would go over to Arran the next day, to identify his things, and any body that turned up. They were flying in CID staff from Kilmarnock given the circumstances, as there were none on the island. She walked from Craigie Street round to Danny and Sheila's flat. Devastated would not adequately describe their reaction. Danny wept and Sheila cried. Then Danny got angry, which reminded him to phone Paddy. Stupid, stupid bastard was the consensus view. They all took her round to Frank's flat but it offered no clues, other than that the video was on. Danny checked and discovered Frank had taped the whole final, and allowed for extra-time and penalties. Not the act of a man not expecting to be back was the conclusion of both Paddy and Danny. There was no farewell note or message.

The police were waiting for her when she got back to her flat. A Sergeant Tolmie, who claimed to have met Frank recently, and two others who weren't introduced and who said little. They had no further news, but asked some more questions, some of which seemed of no relevance to her. Sergeant Tolmie was very kind. He talked about Frank, and how depressed he had seemed at the LDT outcome and being out of work. He knew how hard Frank had taken the closure. He told her "It's this bloody Government, and that bloody woman. It's a wonder there'll be anybody left at work soon, but you Social Workers and us police." He also talked about how good a footballer Frank had been, and how better he might have been, but for his injury. They took her key to his flat and she did not have the energy to insist on accompanying them. After all there was nothing of interest or relevance there. Sheila and Christine came round, despite her saying she wanted to be on her own, and they had to physically restrain her from going to her Group. Eventually she agreed to let Sheila go to tell them she wouldn't be in herself. Actually she was relieved as she knew somehow it was the Group's fault Frank was dead. Well, her's really. If only she had never told him about that conversation with Janis. Why had she done that, and what a punishment for a minor breach of professional etiquette.

She had not told the police about the link with McGoldrick, and knew she would not do so. The waters had now closed over both of them, and nothing was to be gained by rippling them. Her friends plied her with whisky and tea in equal measure and then poured her into bed where she wallowed in guilt and grief in similar doses. Sheila stayed with her and was there to help her up when her alarm went in time for her to catch the early morning boat. Danny, Paddy and Sheila had all offered to come with her but she was vehement that she would cope better on her own, and since there was nothing to be done for Frank they let her go. It took her an hour and a quarter to drive to the pier at Ardrossan. She had a major relapse from her controlled calm when she spotted his car parked near the water's edge. The car park attendant remembered him arriving, late, on the Saturday evening, since he had nearly missed the boat and had had to run up the gangplank as they were disconnecting it, with his case in one hand and his golfbag in the other. That surprised her too, as Frank had only played golf once in all the time she had known him, and had come back muttering about a stupid game and never again.

Going across the water on the boat she sat in the lounge and remembered everything Frank had ever told her or showed her about Arran. It was the one place he ever got animated about. His parents had always eschewed Rothesay and Millport and gone to Arran every Fair, except for one abortive excursion to Scarborough that had merely reinforced the joys of home. They always stayed in the same place, Lamlash, in the same hotel, a big white house overlooking the whole bay. Frank had become fixated on Lamlash, would never acknowledge that the rest of the Island even existed far less had any merit. He loved Holy Isle, stuck across the end of the bay almost blocking it entirely, a wild and deserted island where a young boy could blissfully spend all day walking round the shore and exploring the caves, while his parents climbed the hill in pursuit of the view. She smiled despite herself at how upset Frank had got when telling her the story of how, many years after, his mother had told him that the top of that hill was the one place and the one time she could ever persuade her husband to make love to her outdoors. Frank had regarded that as an act of desecration of his holy ground and had not been too amused when Joyce had asked which, land or body.

Frank had taken her to Arran just the once, in the November, before he had been restored to full vigour. It was out of season and the white house had been closed, so they had stayed in a nice wee hotel on the front. Frank had seemed to get much peace of mind just from being back in the quiet sanctuary and they had had several silent but good walks around his memories. They had not been able to get a boat across to Holy Isle, so she had had to settle for his descriptions of its magical powers, its caves and chapels, its square and round lighthouses. He had told her that he had discovered a crack at the back of St Molio's cave, where a young

384

child, but only a young child, could slip through into an internal cavern. She had seen the whole experience of being there do him good and restore a degree of inner peace to her tormented friend, so she had been grateful to it for that.

At Brodick Pier, she had got on the bus to Lamlash and cried again as it slowly climbed up the hill. Deliberately or not she had sat in the best seat to capture the first glimpse of Holy Isle as it came into view as the bus started its descent. Frank had always assured her that that was the best view in the world, his favourite sight, He had several posters and cards of it, and had always talked about getting a proper picture. Well, he never would now. On that May day, she felt she appreciated why it had meant so much to him, and distressed the nice couple in the next seat by sobbing uncontrollably all the way down past the golf course and into Lamlash. By the turn at the bottom of the hill, where the whole of Holy Isle was exposed to her, she had composed herself sufficiently to work out where she wanted off the bus for the Police Station.

They were expecting her and were very kind. The team of divers from Oxford Street had been out since first light but there was no news as yet. They took her to his hotel room, where she identified his stuff. There was a note for her there but to her relief and disappointment it was a business request to settle his bill to the Wednesday, and to reimburse the boat firm for any damage or loss. There were no clues as to his state of mind, no farewell note, no diary. She did recognise the golfbag and clubs as his. The police had pulled together a picture of his spell on the island, except for a large missing section on the Monday, but the only thing they added to what she already knew was that he had spent the whole of Monday evening in the Pier House Tavern, quietly drinking several pints of draught Guinness and reading a book. He had not appeared distressed, more like a man calmly at peace with himself. The only book in the hotel room was his favourite Silone. She had opened the cover but quickly closed it when she saw the inscription, "To my darling Frank on our 6th wedding anniversary, may the sadness of this book, which I know that you sometimes feel, be compensated for by the strength of our love for each other, for always, love Elaine XXXX". The Policemen probably misunderstood why she began to cry again but they were very good to her. It did not take her long to pack his few clothes and possessions in his suitcase, and they helped her put them into the police car from where they would take care of them.

385

She stayed for two days on the Island, in the same hotel she and Frank had stayed in, but a different room. The divers never found the body, or anything else, and the official estimate seemed to be 'with the currents out there it could be months, particularly if the body were weighed down.' The blood turned out to be human, the same type as his. With no parent alive, they could not use their fancy DNA techniques but the medical records confirmed the sameness of type. The Herald and the Record both ran a short news item, Glasgow man dies at sea, and both quoted the same official statement that there were no suspicious circumstances and the police considered the matter closed. The Sun did not even run that and Joyce concluded that they could not know or even suspect of any connection with their Headmaster. She never for a moment doubted that he was dead, it was the only thing that made sense of the last week. She had been a bit surprised at the presence of a gun, but she had remembered him saying, in one of his interminable ramblings about McGoldrick and his death how he could not envisage the passiveness of a death of that nature and how he would not be able to rely upon himself not resisting the temptation to keep on or to resume swimming. He would require a method that removed that option.

So she had returned home and prepared to implement his wishes, and massage her guilt. She had worked out her liability while resting in Lamlash. She had failed as a Social Worker to prevent a suicide, despite over six months of the closest casework. She had failed as a lover to offer an incentive to live, despite the full investment of her personality, body and soul. She had been instrumental in creating the situation and events that had pushed him over the edge. At his weakest and most vulnerable she had abused him and attacked him instead of supporting him. In vain did Danny and Sheila spend much time telling her she was Not Guilty on all four counts, that at worst she was Guilty of giving him love and comfort that had lightened up his last few months and recreated for him the kind of personal happiness he had always believed he had thrown away and lost for good. A much more critical jury found her Guilty, the one that inhabited her head.

The one that inhabited Paddy's came to the same verdict, despite himself. After all he had to blame someone and the obvious recipient was no longer around. He had never forgiven her her Trotskyist past, now he found her guilty of at least her own charge of failing to give him sufficient motivation. Cold Protestant cow.

Christine and Danny argued in vain, Sheila fell completely out with him but he had his comforter and wouldn't let it go. Gerry Robertson didn't blame her in the slightest. He knew which son of a bitch was to blame, and blamed him every night for the death of the only real friend he had ever allowed himself to have.

The lack of a body confused things slightly. There could be no Post-Mortem, no Inquest, no Fatal Accident Inquiry. There was not even a legal presumption of death, so technically at least Frank Hunter was still alive and the Will he had laboured over so thoroughly and rigorously could not be implemented. He had had the foresight to anticipate that possibility, that once more his body could fuck up his best plans, so he had given his lawyer a written authorisation that in the event of his non-appearance by a certain date, he was instructed to dispose of his assets in certain ways, similar to but not identical with the will, but close enough to avoid any question of discrimination to anyone by the implementation of one rather than the other. The lawyer, Paul Ross, the next of kin Des, and the Executor, Paddy all knew each other well and were all separately and jointly satisfied that the arrangements Frank had made represented his last wishes, so Paul had felt free to implement his instructions on disposal, with the backing of the "no prejudice" agreement of the other principal parties.

Similarly, there could be no funeral, not the simple graveside service he had sought, before being laid to rest beside his mum and Gran for an eternity of chat and cheer. Although he had never said that bit, Joyce knew he would want her to, and with the permission of Des, put up a small stone alongside the big one, that just said, In memory of Frank Hunter, lost at sea 1990. However the real service he had wanted, a memorial service rather than a funeral one, could proceed without the body. So they gathered for his farewell performance, in absentia. Joyce directed along the lines he had requested. No fucking priests, although he would allow friends in the cloth, as that. They could even speak as long as they did not plead for his soul. Two came, Father Andrew who came to mourn the further death of part of Shona, and cousin Peter who took his bar on performing far harder than the pragmatic Andrew. The fact that there wasn't a body actually helped the proceedings, more time for the memory rather than the reality. It cut the travelling time too. Affected by the memory of Mary Ewing's leaving, he had requested that his friends talk about him formally, as the footballer, the politician, the trade unionist and the man. Danny got the first and fourth, Paddy and Gerry the middle two, although

387

they both cheated and blurred boundaries. Then they were all to get drunk at his expense.

Over 100 people turned up, to the old hall in Govanhill where he had once attended Labour Party meetings before he changed constituency. Elaine came, although she did not stay for the party. None of her family came, although Derek Duncan phoned Joyce and explained he would have if he could but his club had a match on. Joyce liked him the few times they had met. She knew how important to Frank it was that Derek still acknowledged him despite what he had done to his sister. Joyce liked Elaine, too, although they had never been close. She was glad Elaine turned up, she knew how disappointed Frank would be, have been, might have been, whatever, if she had not. Elaine gave her a cuddle that said it all. Hazel was there. Joyce had visited her to make sure she knew the arrangements and had been horrified how depressed Hazel had seemed. Without it being articulated, she had gathered that Hazel saw Frank's desertion as a proof to herself of the futility of fighting on. She had not been going to come and Joyce had to work hard to explain that it would be important to Frank not only that she come but that she maybe say something. Any residual resentment and jealousy she might have denied she had, had disappeared at Hazel's obvious distress and unhappiness.

Joyce had phoned Mary-Ann Ewing to tell her about Frank's death. She had said she would be over soon, and would meet her then, but that she would not come to the memorial service. She had been calmer than Joyce had expected, maybe it was the North American in her, or maybe Frank was less important to her than he had thought. She had found liaison with the Coyles rather hard. Des, whom Frank had always regarded as his official next-of-kin, was very kind to her and did not interfere with the arrangements she made, but she could sense the collective family sense of disappointment that it was her affair, not theirs and God's. She had dreaded it, worried about her ability to cope with the emotion and the pain, worried about letting Frank down by failing to realise his conception. He had hated polite Scottish funerals, where the dead were barely mentioned, and then only as an example of God's generous grace. His was to be about him, no matter the pain.

She took the lead role at the beginning, ignoring Paddy's mutter about Mistress of small ceremonies, explaining that Frank had asked her to be the custodian of the proceedings that he wanted. Many of them, certainly the closest, had heard him talk about Mary Ewing's funeral and how moved he had been by the form that had taken. So it was no great surprise when she explained that several people would make formal speeches then everyone else who wanted to would be invited to say a few words, although no-one should feel obliged to do so. Then they were to consume vast amounts of Frank's favourite beers. He had left instructions and funds for the beer to be supplied by the Bon Accord and the food by the Anarkali. By the time Danny, Paddy and Gerry were finished most of the audience were emotionally exhausted but a fair number took the opportunity to say a few more moving words of their own. The party went well, well into the night, and then some of them had their own further wake round at Paddy and Christine's.

It was after three o'clock in the morning before Joyce found herself alone and able to talk to him about how it had gone. Like he had requested, she had taped the speeches, for whose benefit she knew not, since she knew she would never play them, didn't need to, they were there forever burnt into her head. To prove the point, and for his benefit, she ran over the best bits of them again. Danny had got it best, the essence of what Frank had been after. She was pleased that Danny had been brave enough to express his anger at Frank for his cowardice and stupidity, then go on to express his love for him. The anger had been a theme of the day. There was always sadness at a funeral, and often a degree of anger at the unfairness and waste of it all. But a suicide brought a different kind of anger and resentment, because of the avoidable nature of it and the conscious rejection. No-one had stood up and said that Frank Hunter was right to do what he had done, and those that did acknowledge that he had the right to do it, were clear in their view that he had been wrong to exercise that right.

Danny had talked of the two Franks, the combination of which made him such a complex man. There was the Frank he was angry with, the sad Frank. The Frank who seemed weighed down with a tremendous ever-present sadness that even the successful exercise of his considerable talents, abilities and personal qualities never seemed to mitigate. Danny had read them out the quote from Silone. "There is a sadness, a subtle sadness that's not to be mistaken for the more ordinary kind that is the result of remorse, disillusionment or suffering; there is an intimate sadness which comes to chosen souls simply from their consciousness of man's fate." Frank Hunter was one of the chosen souls. There was no doubt, he had said, that Frank Hunter had suffered from an overdose of that sadness and that it had affected much of his life

389

before it had finally swept him off to a place where at last he could find a peace freed from it. He had told them the story of how Frank had been quite amused at the distress Danny had felt recently following a classic Own Goal that he wouldn't go into any further. Frank had said something to him that was meant to console him and offer him some comfort. "Don't worry about it, Danny Boy, I've been scoring own goals all my life and I feel another, major one coming on." Danny had gone on to tell them all that he wished now that he had realised just how serious an own goal Frank had been talking about. Because that was what he had done, the stupid bastard, scored the own goal to end all own goals and put a stop to the game. He had been wrong to do that, and Danny would never forgive him. He should have stayed and fought, and helped his side win, rather than deliberately stick it in the other net and retire hurt.

But Danny had gone on to talk about the other Frank Hunter, the happy Frank, the one that had brought joy into all their lives. The footballer who had happily played all day and all night as a boy, the one who had once played King Kenny off the park; the political animal who would happily talk politics all day and then read all night. The Frank that had delighted in the company of his friends over a pint or four, the Frank that was always able to help his friends when they needed it. He had told them of two particularly happy Franks, both soldiers in the Tartan Army. One Frank, happy with the lads in Germany in 1974. He told them it was his favourite memory of Frank, litre jug of beer in hand, the night he had helped him to the greatest moment of Danny's football career, the real World Cup final of 1974 when Frank had held his hand on the park as their Scotland eleven had scrambled their way to an unforgettable 5-3 win over a German pub team, when they had all tearfully sworn loyalty to Frank's concept of political freedom for Scotland. They had all been so confident then, full of the promises of the future, but Frank had been more confident than any of them.

It was not just Frank's tragedy that his confidence in his football future had proved as misplaced as his confidence in the political one. Danny reckoned that was the greatest cause of the sadness within Frank, that he had never been able to find out just how good a player he could have been. It was Danny's view that despite that Frank had been probably even happier in a different way with Elaine in Spain in 1982. He could not resist reminding them of the sad Frank sandwiched in between, of Argentina 1978 and the effect that had had on Frank and his theory that that had cost them victory in the 1979 Devolution Referendum and irreversible moves to an Independence that would have offered some protection from that bloody woman. He had talked of what he and Frank had meant to each other, and how between them they had been best men to each other three times. He had pointed out with approval Frank's dedicated adherence to the philosophy he had adapted from Camus, with the motto that it was the lot of modern man to watch football, read the papers and fornicate.

He had concluded with the bit that had made cold Joyce cry out loud, despite her stupid promises to herself. He had reminded them all that Frank had been a virulent atheist, who denounced all religions as political contricks. He had admired the efficacy as an instrument of control, but had despaired of the effects, particularly on people persuaded to wait for the next life for the justice due to them. Frank had not believed in that form of after-life, but he had shared often with Danny his view that people do live on after death, but only in the hearts and memories of those who loved them. So, Danny had explained to them, in that sense Frank Hunter was not dead, and would not die while anyone in that hall that day was still alive. He told them to hold onto that, as he was going to do. He would do his part to keep Frank Hunter alive, and with him throughout his life. He knew he would never be able to see Celtic again without summonsing Frank to accompany him to the game. He would even take him with him to see a few Clyde games, penance for his sins. Also he would make sure the bastard would not escape his share of future Labour Party meetings. More importantly, Frank would go with him into the new future for Scotland, fight by his side in the struggle for Scotland to be free, to see attained the dream he had always had of a Scottish Parliament and a place of right in a Europe of Nation States. "He'll be with us when we celebrate that and prove wrong his fears that Scots are too weak and pathetic to have the courage to assert what should be their right, I promise you that Frank."

He sat down after charging them all to share that responsibility with him, to take Frank with them to every game they went to, to keep Frank Hunter and his warmth, his wisdom, his wit and his weaknesses, Frank the person, alive and well inside themselves. That way his actual death would become less important and he could continue to enrich their lives in the future in the way he had done in the past.

It had been a hard act to follow but both Paddy and Gerry had been sincere and relied on the integrity of their feelings rather than their well-developed political skills to make their desired impact. Paddy made generous acknowledgement of his political debts to Frank and expressed regret that he had never followed through on his political abilities. He too acknowledged Frank's role in converting him to a belief in the importance of Scotland being Scotland, and for the need for Scots to stop whinging, whining and complaining and assert themselves positively. He highlighted the irony that Frank had never really recovered from the double disaster of 1979 and that his heart had never really been in active politics since. Yet here we were, on the verge of the opportunity to assert ourselves again, the dawn of a new era for Scotland, and Frank chooses to walk away rather than fight for what he so passionately believed in. He expressed the hope that Frank's worst fears that once more the Labour Party would scupper those dreams would prove groundless, and that, from whatever resting place he had found, he could observe the turning of his dream into political reality. Paddy always found emotion difficult and kept it short less he perish. Gerry found emotion even more of a stranger. He had been moved by Danny's comments and knew they were truer than his own so he abandoned his prepared litany of Frank's Trade Union triumphs and talked instead, briefly, of his sadness at the loss of his good friend, who had understood better than anyone the true meaning of the sentiments about the brotherhood of man.

Des had spoken for the family, the Coyles that is. He had raised the bit that worried some, the nature and effect of the crime of suicide, the taking of a decision that should be God's alone. But Frank had never believed in God, never wavered from that view, so it could not be an act of blasphemy. And Des's God would forgive Frank his weakness because of his goodness. He was loved and would be missed, but they could only hope that he would find peace at last in some form of reunion with his mum and Gran whom he had loved and who had loved him so. Des knew they would now be together again and that would help Frank, and the survivors.

After that some others had got up. Jack Reilly had nearly destroyed them all. Jack, who got tearful, sentimental and distraught at end of season dances, had them all in tears nearly as copious as his own as he had paid his own eloquent tribute. Jack told them in his opinion Frank Hunter was talented enough to have become one of the greats, as all those who had seem him play could testify. He particularly regretted that Frank had never had the opportunity to demonstrate just how good a footballer he was and how that sadness of his loss must have scarred his soul. He had mentioned his video of Frank's goal against the Hibs and how he would ensure it was never forgotten. Joyce knew that for all Frank had loved Jack he could not have stomached the sentimental view of himself espoused that day, to hear Jack you would have thought Frank Hunter had been almost as perfect as Don Revie.

Father Andrew the politician not the priest, had said a few temporal words, as much about the mother and the family as the boy, but fair enough for that.

Neither Elaine nor Hazel spoke, and it was left to Joyce to overcome her family's strong conception that funerals were no place for ladies or even women, to take the role of talking about Frank the lover of women, a short but poignant speech. Overall she felt she had discharged her duty well and that he would have been pleased about the proceedings, and his own centrality to them. That was another one he owed her, she told him as she filled in the remaining details for him. She had fallen asleep crying again about her failure to have saved him, and at the pain and sadness of her own loss.

Several other things had been established at the Service. Danny had asked Des if Frank had managed to link up with them at the Cup Final and had been told that Frank had known they were all going to the Stand. Between them, Danny and Des worked out that he had been too embarrassed to admit that he was leaving before the end of the game to catch his boat. Peter McColl had found out that the gun with which Frank had shot himself was one of a kind he had heard of but never owned, and that Joyce had not the remotest idea of how Frank had obtained it. He had definitely not had a firearms certificate for it, but a policeman had told her that it was not too difficult in these days in Glasgow to get a gun like that if you had the money. Peter had nodded sagely at that remark.

The disposal of assets ceremony was conducted a few days after the memorial service. Paul Ross had gathered the principal interested parties in his office and explained what his instructions from Frank had been. There were no real surprises other than the £3,000 for Peter McColl, "to right an old injustice." Jack got all his football stuff, magazines and tapes. Joyce got the flat, with mortgage redeemed and a private note saying he knew she would not want to live in it because of the memories and could she let Hazel live there as long as she liked. In addition Joyce was left a considerable sum of money, as were Michael and wee Shona, to be added to Shona's trust arrangements, since it was her money anyway. Elaine had been present and was genuinely relieved he had left her nothing, but she did not object about what he had done to her son and daughter. Danny, Paddy and Gerry were given only his books and the costs of their forthcoming trip to Italy, with an injunction to drink some wine on their old friend. Hazel was left £10,000, which distressed her considerably. She politely refused Joyce's offer of the flat to live in, even when Frank's wishes were explained to her. Mary-Ann Ewing was to be given several sealed envelopes, a key and access to some files, her grandmother's letters, notes for two books and a moral injunction to complete one. The small residue was left to Paul to administer, with full power of attorney. It had been a surprise to many of them that the total estate disposed of was of the order of £100,000. They had not fully realised the extent of his mother's success, or his failure.

Certain other casual acquaintances of Frank Hunter were in mourning at this time although their grief was not aimed in that direction but was rather more self-centred. Many of the original collection rounded up in the immediate aftermath were released at the end of their six hours but a few were not so lucky. Once the link to Brownlie Street was made, Jim Morris's circumstances were fairly dire. The police did not believe in Santa Claus and Jim was soon exercising Civil Libertarians and legal experts as he was not released after his six hours but detained for a further period under the Prevention of Terrorism legislation, before eventually being charged with conspiracy to murder. At least he got his holiday as promised. Several other known southside Glasgow activists were also detained under that legislation and found they were being tied into the location of the crime in a way they found hard to understand, explain or deny, especially as their only alibi was each other and 50,000 others who could not swear they never moved. The integrity of the Glasgow police was upheld in retrospect by the absence of the slightest confession from any of those linked to the scene of the crime, but the circumstantial evidence alone was strong enough to have three others charged as well as Jim Morris. Also one visitor from Ireland was charged, and a warrant issued for another, both being also tied into the premises in question. No-one believed any of them were the one or ones who fired the gun or guns, although some of them did admit to knowing, and having seen that weekend, one or two more likely candidates from Ireland who were believed to have also come over for the game. But no statement or evidence tied them to No 37. They managed to disappear completely and no-one was ever charged with attempted murder.

The speedy arrests assuaged public concern to some extent, particularly as they appeared to rely on evidence other than unsubstantiated confessions. Trial was fixed for the end of August, just within the 110 days that Scots Law demanded. The police had been able to identify the kind of gun, a Parker Hale M85, that fired the bullet that hit the bag, and were also able to confirm from the crumpled bullet fragment that the cartridge cases found in No 37 were the exact same type and batch. They also confirmed a rest had been erected on the relevant window sill, and although there was private dispute as to the extent of evidence of actual shot, the cartridge cases undeniably had given evidence of having been fired. No trace of a second bullet was found, although with the soft and crumbling state of the wood at Hampden that was not thought surprising. The fact that it was not a make of gun normally associated with the IRA was not seen by many as a major problem. It was acknowledged as a fitting weapon for the purpose in mind. Police investigations continued with the expectation that identification and arrest of the actual gunmen would strengthen the rather weak and circumstantial case against the others, and that as the trial approached the unity of denial might crumble and a deal or two could be done. That Morris was for the high jump was the one certainty. His known but unproveable involvement in the McCabe death was confirmation that the evidence that was available this time was sound and justice would be done to him at last.

Charlie Spence did what he could, which was not a lot, especially as he could not afford to have too much public attention to the extent of his previous links with the man, but he offered comfort and money to Ann-Marie. Even though she was thoroughly pissed off with the stupidity of her husband she was careful to accept neither. Jim could not work out himself why he was in the mess he knew he was in, and why he hadn't just been asked direct. He felt a genuine insult that he had not been treated, by his side, with the dignity and trust that he deserved, but he took some consolation from his role as the major man charged. The poor bastard wasn't even sure if he was innocent or guilty, or which he wanted to be and which he wanted to be found. He knew either way if he ever got out his status would be enhanced, except in the one place that mattered. Ann-Marie believed him that he didn't know for whom he was setting it up or why, but that wasn't much of a consolation to her, or to his darling daughters, who experienced some of the pressures to which Frank Hunter had been glad he had no children to risk exposing.

The police also separately investigated the circumstances of Frank Hunter and got statements from his closest friends that he had been very depressed and despairing in the days before his disappearance. They also talked to wee Ewan Murray from Kamesthorn. He told them he would not have put Frank Hunter in the highest-risk category and that indeed in one sense there was nothing wrong with him at all, but he did confirm that his state of mind could well have lead to suicide. He had said in a wry but inaccurate remark, that if he had a £1 for every person he knew like Frank who had committed suicide he could afford to treat them properly. He told them that Frank Hunter was not mentally ill in any psychotic sense but that he had been suffering from a severe depression in 1989 brought on by a combination of events in his life, and that while he had made sufficient progress not to require hospital treatment he had remained on the depressed side of normal, whatever that might be. He had a naturally depressive personality, a similar trait apparently to his father, which had been exposed to considerable legitimate cause for depression. He had run through a brief catalogue for them, the loss of the job, the loss of the faith in the trade union and labour religions, the death of the mother, the never resolved grief from the failure of the marriage, the triggering of suppressed feelings from the Ibrox disaster by the Hillsborough pictures. Yes, any further cause for depression on top of that lot could induce a state where suicide was a realistic possibility.

The gun in the boat, which had been fired once, had no firearms certificate, but neither did it have a criminal history. The blood on the side of the boat corresponded to his blood type. The Sub-Aqua team report was negative but the Coastguard and Glasgow University expert evidence was that any body lost in that vicinity could take months if ever to appear. There was no evidence of the involvement of any other party. There was the farewell letter to his girlfriend and evidence that he had recently changed his will. The conclusion in the Police report to the Procurator-Fiscal was that there were strong grounds for a conclusion that he had killed himself, while suffering from depression, and that that conclusion was consistent with his behaviour in the few days before he was last seen alive. With no body, there could be no inquest or fatal accident inquiry and the case remained on the Fiscal's file, but no further inquiries were required and the matter was seen as effectively closed.

CHAPTER TWENTY-FIVE- SEA SCROLLS FROM THE DEAD

Detached from their master's body by an increasing volume of ocean water, Frank Hunter's last tentacles nevertheless contrived one final set of twitches, clamping their clammy pads on the necks and hearts of their chosen victims for one last emotional suck.

Frank Hunter had spent some considerable time worrying how he could arrange their delivery without awakening false hope by the recognition of the distinctive writing. His solution lay in the final instructions he gave his emissary, Paul Ross, that three letters were to be posted on a certain day in August after the World Cup, all to be sent inside larger legal firm envelopes with a note explaining that the enclosed letter was written and delivered to the lawyer before the Cup Final. The instructions, given to him after and separately from the will, also required him to hand over a fourth letter and a parcel, to Paddy McGuire at 9am on the morning after the other letters were posted. This second business was to be conducted in the presence of a Mary-Ann Ewing, who had also been given the authority to advance or alter the timescales, although she did not exercise that discretion.

The one that got Danny Campbell hurt, in a bittersweet way. The hurt came from the sense of not knowing who this author was. Not the passive creature eulogised in his farewell address but another more complex animal. He read it all the way through, then he read it again.

Dear Danny,

I am glad of one last opportunity to communicate with you. Although I realise that you will be reading this letter several months after I have written it, I hope that you will find it a fresh and more satisfying farewell communication than the one with which I left you in May.

I do not know, writing this, exactly which of my alternative plans will have been effective but what I can be sure of is that by the time you read this, Frank Hunter will be no more than a memory, and you will have had several months to adjust to that new reality.

I am writing this letter before the Cup Final when I will see you for the last time, and before the meal at Joyce's which I intend to be the last real opportunity to be with you.

I must apologise to you for the lack of candour I displayed in our last few meetings. All my life I have felt it very important to be truthful, particularly to my friends, of whom you are the closest and most important. But unfortunately in the last few weeks of my life I have had to depart from that standard and I was less than totally truthful with you. Indeed in the last few days I was deliberately dishonest and deceitful. The reason for this was that I felt it very important to me to create an atmosphere and understanding on the part of those closest and dearest to me, that I was exceedingly depressed and capable of committing suicide. I hope that in the light of what follows you can find it in yourself to forgive me that deception, or at least understand why I felt obliged to indulge in it. I know it will require you to reassess many of the things you have thought and said over the past few months, but I know you have always had a high regard for the truth and a preference for it over even comfortable misconceptions.

I know that Joyce will have organised my farewell service, whether funeral or remembrance, along the lines that I requested, and that you will therefore have performed the task that I allocated to you. It is one of my deep regrets that I will never know exactly what you said about me, but I do know that it will have been generous, honest and moving. I thank you now for that, and for a lifetime's close friendship. I have spent much time recently weighing up the elements of my life, a depressing process, but one of the most consistent measures of value has been the worth and weight of your friendship. I only regret that I did not acknowledge that more directly before I left. I know that it always disappointed you that neither I nor Paddy could deal openly with the strength of our feelings for our friends, and that we used to get uncomfortable at your efforts in that direction. I am sorry now, Danny, that I never said directly to you that I love you, but please believe that I leave knowing it both to be true and important.

The deceit was necessary to allow me to plan one kind of suicide while creating the impression of falling victim to another. I am going to ask you to understand the whole picture while keeping one part of the jigsaw to myself, one piece that even now I cannot share with you in full. I hope it does not tantalise you too much if I say that you and your football abilities had a small but crucial role to play in this. It would not be over-estimating matters to state that the game against St Anne's not only changed my life but effectively created the circumstances which carried the seeds of its end. I must assure you that you carry no blame or responsibility at all for those circumstances. Anyway, that game indirectly set in train a sequence of events that led me to realise the true nature and extent of my self-deception, and the poor motivation I had to continue with my life as the way it had been and inevitably would continue. The responsibilities I bore were too great to carry in the context I had created. I realise that I am talking in a code to which you do not have the key, but I am afraid that you will just have to take my word that I was able to come to a calm and measured realisation that I did not wish to continue that life any more.

You know more than anyone, except perhaps Paddy, that I have always had a strong sense of political destiny, of my being marked out for a major political role. As a callow youth I assumed that meant that I would become Prime Minister in Westminster. With the onset of maturity, sophistication and self-awareness I soon moderated that to becoming Prime Minister of a Scottish Parliament, a real one. I then realised that I was not temperamentally suited to exposing myself to the demands of the democratic process and all the lies and deceits that it inevitably detailed. But that still left open the prospect of power and influence within the Trade Union movement. I have talked to you before of some of the main reasons why I rejected that scenario too. But the feeling never really left me that my destiny still lay somewhere in political life, waiting to be discovered and enacted. Then almost simultaneously with my realisation that I no longer wished to continue with the empty and futile life I was living, came the realisation that there was one way left to me to exercise that destiny, a way that seemed more right and relevant the more I contemplated it.

Political assassination, the last meaningful and relevant act left to an individual not prepared to be part of the more conventional political processes, and one guaranteed moreover to ensure historical and political immortality. Ask yourself two questions, Danny boy. Who was the Secretary of State for Scotland in November 1963? And who got the credit for shooting President Kennedy? And you're politically very literate. Know what I mean. I know it was not your favourite pub game but you several times played with me, Paddy, Gerry and others, the one about if you had to die and were allowed to take someone along with you, who would it be and how and why. Well, we always only had one winner, didn't we, That Bloody Woman. It just suddenly seemed so obvious, I would go, and take her with me. We had always wondered, given that she was hated so much, why didn't some-one, anyone, just shoot her and do us all a favour. It wasn't long before that pleasant fantasy shared by almost all my countrymen of both sexes and all classes and parties, became for me a realistic plan of action. And the notion of doing it at Hampden just seemed irresistible, a fusing of the key elements of my life. The actual mechanics of organising it were far easier than I imagined. It is remarkably easy to kill someone, the harder bit is organising it in such a way as to get away with it, if that is what you want to do.

And do you know the funniest part of it all, Danny, the bit that I know will appeal to you. The more I read, the more I studied, the more I thought and discussed, the more I came to the conclusion that in effect I had been wrong, not in the idea of killing her, but in the conception that I really hated her. I was forced to the conclusion that I did not hate her. Dislike her intensely yes, but hate her no, not even despise her, rather a grudging form of admiration. As you know, I am not and never have been a pacifist. I can envisage situations in which I would feel it correct to kill someone, even assassinate an unarmed politician. But it did not take me long to realise that this was not one of them. It was neither morally correct to kill this woman, nor even politically sensible to do so. The time I took to work that out was one of the hardest and most confusing but in the end my conclusion was crystal clear. However, I am still determined to go ahead and demonstrate that I had the ability to implement my original plan, only that I disdained to do so.

So on Cup Final Day I will shoot at the Prime Minister but deliberately miss, but in such a way as to leave little doubt about the ability to have done more if desired. Reading this, you will have the advantage over me of knowing the outcome of my actions, and the way they were perceived. My main plan was to avoid the immediate recognition of my actions, and for the assumption to take root that it was the failure of the IRA clowns rather than the success of a Scottish humorist. To that end, I deliberately created grounds for confusion. Do not concern yourself about that, Danny. At the same time that you read this, I have arranged for Paddy to be given the evidence that will allow the confusion to be unravelled and the truer, clearer picture to emerge. I ask you only to grasp what I am saying to you and understand it. I know that you do not approve of acts of violence, and I suspect that you will feel that even a warning shot is excessive and immoral. Please understand that while I clearly came to a conclusion about my lack of right to kill her, despite my distaste for everything she has done to Scotland, it became very important for me to demonstrate my ability to implement that desire if I had chosen to do so. So many other things in my life I have failed to achieve despite the ability to achieve them. It is too late to reverse those processes, but I will leave with a successful political act of protest, a rejection of her and her values but also a rejection of the resort to violence and illogical indiscipline. In essence what I want to demonstrate is that Scotland's freedom is something for which it is worth protesting, even dying, but for which it is not necessary to kill.

My major worry has been that the political nature of my act will be diminished because of what will be called my history of mental instability and illness. You know Danny that I have never been mentally ill, and that I am as sane now, in the contemplation of this act, as I have ever been. Sad, yes, bad maybe, but mad no. I would be grateful if you could do whatever little you can to defend me and my memory against some of the wilder claims that will be made. I know that you will be angry with me for what you will see as abandonment and cowardice. I can only say that it is not a decision I have come to lightly but it is one about the appropriateness of which I have absolutely no doubt.

I can hear you telling me not only that shooting people is wrong, that killing myself is a crime and a sin, but that there are things worth staying alive for in Scotland, and that some of my dreams may be coming true at last. In a funny way, it is because that is true that I have to go. I do believe that slowly the Scottish people are maturing and realising that they have to take the full responsibility for themselves, and that after the next election, whatever the outcome an irreversible movement towards Independence will take place. I wish that more than anything else politically. But I would not be able to play an active part in that, those days are over for me. I could not face being a spectator if the game went wrong, but more, I could not be a spectator in victory. Scotland needs at this point people willing and able to make a commitment, not spectators, and if I cannot be a player, I will settle for flight rather than impotence, the choice made by generations of the brightest and second-best.

There is one strange irony you will appreciate Danny, that of all the reasons for killing her that I considered, the most compelling was one related to football rather than politics. There is a potential scenario that would induce me to commit murder to prevent, but fortunately there is no evidence that she is on the verge of pursuing it. I am always amazed that ardent defenders of the Union do not follow through on the implications of their arguments. Fortunately most of them have little interest in football and do not appreciate its importance in the life of this nation. Football has often been identified as the only real outlet for the national feelings of most Scots, although arguments have differed as to whether this is positive or negative diversion. The abolition of this outlet might lead to its displacement into other more political areas but it might also lead to its total dissolution. A unionist with nerve and bottle might feel tempted to test that hypothesis by insisting that the implication of the Union is that the United Kingdom should only be entitled to one Football Association, at least for international purposes. Scotland would no longer be entitled to enter the European Nations Championship, or the World Cup. The Olympic Movement is already a powerful precedent for this logic.

The argument that the Scots would support a British team in the 1994 World Cup could be a strong factor in defence of the Union and the commitment to it. I am aware of at least the ambivalence of the men in Scotland she would admire, the Murrays and the Mercers, who see their own and their clubs' future in a British and European context rather than a Scottish one. Rangers in Europe as a British representative would not need to count their English as foreigners and could afford then to sign up to three or four Europeans in addition. Likewise the major English teams would benefit by their Scots, Irish and Welsh not being foreigners. I can see the relish with which that bloody woman would approach a debate, and the diversions on the Scottish side that would weaken the resistance. If I thought that she would seek to do this before she goes, as go she will inevitably, then I would alter my aim as she is the only one with the tenacity and single-mindedness to see through such a course. Perhaps if it comes near that later, you can send her a letter saying Frank Hunter was not alone.

I have not mentioned this fear or motivation to Mary-Ann or to Paddy, as I do not want it made public. My one major fear is that she would learn of it and see the merit not only in implementing it for its own sake but as a form of punishment for me for my impudence. Now that would be what I would call an own goal.

I have given Mary-Ann Ewing full access to everything I have done and why, except for that last part. I have asked her to present my side and make sure that history knows what I did and did not do and why. I know that she and you seemed to like each other when you met. Please give her every co-operation and help. She is an excellent journalist and a smart politician who will tell my story well but she would benefit from your assistance, and your friendship. She has also perhaps come closest to my perception of the ideal woman for me. A combination of her and her grandmother would probably be that. I certainly love them both.

Another thing I ask of you is to help Joyce. I do love her and I know that it is very selfish of me to treat her so, but I can realistically expect that, as with Elaine, life without me will eventually offer her more rewarding experiences than continued contact would. Please help her free herself from my ghost, a much more formidable foe than a rejecting lover.

There is one thing I will offer you in return for those favours I am requesting, a piece of unsolicited advice, based on my lifetime's observation of you. I do not know if Sheila is the woman for you. I value her highly for her own sake, which was not the case with June and Jill and Senga, although I liked them all better than you did. But I know that you like Sheila and appreciate her as much as I do. But that was also the case with Heather, and that was not enough, or rather, it was too much for you. I know I have hardly earned the right to offer advice about other people's relationships, but I do wish that you would allow yourself to find happiness in a loving relationship based on mutual trust, respect and equal sharing. You have consistently denied yourself that opportunity, not as you kid yourself into believing, by a mistaken series of choices of partner but because of a failure to share your evaluation of yourself and your relationship with your partner with them. You need to learn to listen to and respect their views on both these matters. It is typical that the best Social Worker I know can assess everyone else acutely but is so inaccurate in his estimate of his own worth. Social Worker, assess yourself. It is sad that someone with the courage you display in telling Paddy and myself in a Glasgow pub how much you love us, cannot show a similar courage in relation to what should be your most important friendship. That is the favour I ask you for yourself, treat Sheila as if she were me, and call the first girl Frances.

One last favour, Danny boy, then I will leave you. Talk to me sometimes. I know you used to seem a little worried that I still talked to my mother, and my Gran, and old Mary, but believe me it helped me more than you can know, and I know it helped them too. It will mean a great deal to me to know that you will occasionally take me out, for the odd walk and talk, and quiet pint, and keep me up to date with the progress of your beloved Clyde and my heroes in green.

Take care, Danny pal, and thanks again for being my friend,
Love,
Frank

Danny read the letter several more times in a row. He cried when he read it, and he cried when he stopped reading it. He found it hard to realise he was not dreaming, and that his friend was serious in his claim that it was he who had shot the Prime Minister but had deliberately missed. But somehow he never doubted the truth of the claim. He wept for himself, and he wept again for his lost friend. He wept for the description of their friendship and how much it had meant to Frank. He cried for the loss to both of them of the inability of his friend to express these feelings in life and he cried for the pleasure and pride that even the posthumous recognition gave him. He vowed again to risk further social exile and abuse in the emotionally barren macholand of Glasgow males that he reluctantly inhabited, by expressing to the few others still alive the kind of feelings Frank was expressing and recognising lay between them. He knew Paddy would hate that, and resort instead to anger, aggression and denial, but at least these were feelings. Poor Eric was even worse, not even the diversion of anger, just suppression and repression. Still he would try again. He cried at the realisation he had concentrated on his friends and not his loves and cried again for Heather, and wondered if he could make it work with Sheila. He sighed for Joyce but guessed that this would actually help her. It should reduce her guilt. But most of all he wept for the stupid waste and tried to make what sense he could out of the strange and twisted tale his strange and twisted friend had told.

It didn't make much sense to him, although he was glad Frank had opted not to kill her. That's what Danny would have called an own goal. He didn't find Frank's little joke with the IRA funny. He knew the local four of those arrested, hadn't seen them as terrorist types. He realised why Frank had gone for Jim Morris, a bit over the top really but Frank always had had a vicious streak in him for traitors of his causes or friends, but the other three and their families must have been through hell. Frank had always hated the IRA and had a special vituperation for those who colluded in its activities. They make the murders possible and respectable, and give a political credibility to thugs and idiots had been his line. Both he and Frank actually quite liked Jim, or at least used to. He wondered if Paddy would realise why, and whether he would be glad. It would be ironic, another better part of Frank's joke, maybe he was getting it after all, that Paddy would be the man's saviour and get his release.

Overall, through the crying, the letter made Danny happier than he felt it ought. It was better to do that than just to end on a note of despair. He still did not think his friend was right to do what he had done, but at least he had done something, and would be remembered for it. He felt a peculiar sense of pride, that man was my friend. He preferred him to the more pathetic one he had not buried but praised. I never thought you were mental Frank, son, just silly sometimes.

Gerry's letter, which he too kept to himself and never showed anyone, was along similar lines but had a slightly different effect. His letter also apologised for the deception and hoped he would understand both the deception and the action. It explained to Gerry why he had decided he had had enough, and why he had resolved to do what he had done. It acknowledged that Gerry would think both parts wrong but hoped he would accept Frank's right to come to those conclusions and follow them through. The letter explained to Gerry the process of logic Frank had gone through, of his need to go, of his desire to do something significant with his going. His initial assumption that that would involve killing the Prime Minister, the dawning realisation of not only the moral wrongness of such a course but also the political weakness, the determination to prove that it were possible anyway and that Frank Hunter could do whatever he set his mind to do. It explained the fear of being dismissed as mentally unstable and the role of the IRA joke. It told him not to bother about that as other arrangements had been made to resolve that matter. It also explained the role he had given to Mary-Ann and asked Gerry to help her in any way she required. It also told Gerry how much Frank had come to love him, and how he despaired for him, and what he wished he would do and stop doing.

Gerry found his letter irritating, amongst other emotions, which were not his strongest suit. How could you know someone so well, and feel they were so important to you, and then be so wrong about something as important as their death and their destiny? With wondrous advantage of hindsight it seemed so clear to him. The bastard had even had him up to three o'clock several mornings debating his view of the Prime Minister and the political implications of her assassination by the IRA, or even by a Scotsman. Gerry had a sudden vivid memory of the dismissive tone he had adopted to that hypothesis, while reiterating about what a wonder it was no-one had done so, seeing how hated she was. Ya stupid bastard. Gerry had not taken the more common line of Paddy and others that she was a liability to her party and an asset to his. He had felt that she could easily win another election and would appeal more to the English than any of her potential replacements. Perhaps if Frank had believed him he would have followed it through all the way. But he was glad he hadn't, glad his friend had stopped short of that. Although he had a lingering doubt about how confident he could have been about his ability to control a miss. Frank hadn't been an expert shot like Peter. Okay he had won a coconut or two at the Shows, but that wasn't a strong enough base for such certainty. And where the hell had he got the guns, although Gerry knew well enough that you can buy anything for the right money. Gerry also dragged out a forgotten fragment of a conversation, both well-oiled, where Frank had claimed with unlikely pride that the one thing his father and grandfather had had in common was skill as a sniper.

Gerry was by nature a paranoid conspirasist, a civil libertarian without civility and with no faith in liberty, and his mind was soon full of several permutations. He had always believed Frank was dead, and had meant to kill himself, but that gun in the boat had always bothered him. Frank wouldn't do it that way. So these new facts helped offer alternative possibilities. He developed two early favourites; the IRA worked out Frank's involvement and killed him to prevent him claiming credit, or Special Branch had done the same for similar reasons. Both explained why the gun had been left in the boat, to keep the suicide option open in case the body turned up with gunshot holes. Neither party would know that the smart Frank had made his arrangements for posterity. Things could start getting interesting now. He wondered if Paddy would want his help in handling it, it could get a bit risky. It would certainly get messy and all his friends would get caught up in the publicity.

The third letter had the most beneficial effect. Joyce had felt a strong sense of unfinished business since her previous letter. She had always felt that was not what her Frank would say to her, that it had not been a farewell to match their relationship. That had disturbed her and caused her to ask if she had mis-assessed its worth, or his or hers. Although she had always had a feeling that more had to come, that somehow he would find a way. She had been disappointed there was no message for her in the disposal of assets although she had intuitively felt Paul Ross was willing her to keep the faith when she had pressed him. She had occasionally woken in the quiet of the night, to find herself thinking of another hiding place where he might have left her a note, always to be depressed by its emptiness. The most promising had been when she remembered the book Frank had always gently mocked her for relying on for regular relief. She consumed it every six months, like a prescription, and felt revitalised and refreshed every time. Frank had claimed to despise Jane Austen but she knew it was no coincidence his favourite town coffee place was Darcy's. He had had his favourite books but none of such medicinal nature, which made him slightly jealous. The night she woke thinking about that she would have sworn she had a sudden sharp returning memory of him pausing amongst her books on his way out for the final time. He would have known it was a further three months before the next intake was due. That had been the greatest disappointment, and for once the prose that was there did not help. Once, before the letter arrived, she had had a strong sense that her flat had been entered. Nothing appeared to have been taken, but she had feared in her secret soul that someone had stolen her hidden letter. But she still had kept the faith that it would be somewhere, the further fuller version, so her response to the handwriting had been less surprise or shock or hope, but relief and a feeling of justification.

It had been a pathetic note the first one, but she now realised that it was meant to be, that it had been the last lie of several, the last departure from his promise to be nothing but openly honest to her. He used those actual words in the second letter, one of many passages she soon committed to memory and carried with her everywhere. He had also asked for her understanding and forgiveness, which she gladly gave on the basis of the better message, as he had hoped she would.

The letter referred to the McGoldrick saga in code, a code which reinforced as it was meant to, the earlier promise that he had extracted from her in another code never to reveal to anyone in any circumstances the nature of his responsibility for his foe's exit. She now realised that he meant even when far more serious responsibilities become public knowledge. In this new communication he reiterated to her how heavy that responsibility for McGoldrick's death weighed upon him, and how interwoven it was with his own sense of pointlessness and despair. She found surprising how much comfort she derived from the realisation of the calm weight of his decision to abandon the fight rather than the flustered flight she had previously imagined.

He knew she would be less interested in his political considerations than in the personal ones so he laboured less on the taking someone with me, fulfilling destiny angles to concentrate more on what she had meant to him and how his decision to leave did not undermine the worth and importance of that to him. He took a while to get to her, travelling through his mother, his grandmother, Mary Ewing, some strange odyssey of woman I have loved. Although the rational part of her knew he could and should not have left Elaine out of it, it still hurt her more than she wanted that he could not downplay her importance in his scheme of things. He mentioned Mary-Ann and advised Joyce not only to co-operate fully with her in her enterprise but to seek and take her advice about how to protect herself and her and their privacy from the others that would follow. He mentioned Hazel and asked Joyce to try to be her friend, or at least help her, for his sake.

But at last he had come to her. She learnt from the first reading to quote that section from memory.

"Joyce, I can truly say that my love for you was the most honest and true of my life, the most equal commitment I ever made. Although I did not prove able to keep in full the promise I made to you to be totally honest in all my dealings with you and hold nothing back, I came far closer to that ideal than I ever did with anyone else. You saw the innermost of me that I denied to everyone else, glimpses only perhaps, but more sections than I had ever hoped to be able to show. Without your love, and the sense of equality you enabled me to create with you, I would never have had the courage and ability to claw my way back up that tunnel chimney of despair down which I had far fallen before you came into my inner life. I know you well, Joyce my darling self-abusing fool. Why are the best Social Workers those with the lowest self-regard? My major fear about going was my knowledge that you will have spent the last few months tormenting yourself about your dual failure to prevent me. I know you will have blamed yourself for failing to have helped me avoid the black despair, and I also know that you will have felt responsible because you and the everything that you so generously offered and gave me were not a sufficient inducement to stay.

My darling, lovely girl, I am sorry for leaving you with those weights so long but please please cast them away and release yourself from their effects. If you had not had the courage and the ability to love me in the way that you did, I would never even have been able to complete my painful journey up that chimney and poke my head over the side. I would have perished then, from the fate you have assumed I suffered these last few months. But you gave me so much, so much that I had feared I would never experience and enjoy in my life, that I was able to make that ascent and enjoy again for a brief period a spell as a happy functioning achieving human. You helped me exercise my broken wings until I felt brave enough to attempt to fly again. The fact that the final flight took me over tundra, crash-landing back through the ice to the frozen depths below was not a defect of yours but a fault inherent in my design. But I do know that it was better to have flown and belly-flopped than never to have loved and left the ground.

Our continuing love then helped me re-gird the machine for the one last flight of which I was capable. I apologise to you again for the deceit about the destination, or at least the route, but it was important for me to make that flight. You and my love for you sustained me and allowed me to depart on that journey and secure my sense of achievement that I had feared had been lost for good. So do not judge yourself harshly. I have nothing but gratitude and affection for the value of what you so selflessly gave me. Do not spend too long looking back but go forward into the future secure in the knowledge that you are capable of giving and receiving love of the highest quality. I will give you one more sign of the value of what you have done for me, which you should regard as the final release from any obligation. I know, and am proud, that part of me will live on with you forever but I do not wish it or me to disable you, rather to sustain and support you in the achieving of your full potential as a loving, giving person."

There was more but that section was the essential core. She felt better about Elaine after that. Elaine was still large in his heart but Frank had still given her more of him than he had given Elaine, and more of himself than Brian Kirk had ever given her. And a little bit of Frank was worth more than all of him. So most importantly, she felt better about Joyce after the letter. She found

410

the readiness with which she accepted the truth of his role as the Prime Minister's assailant slightly frightening. She had lived with this man, lain with him, without the slightest conception that he was capable of that. She remembered he had been obsessed with her in the weeks before he left, had talked and read of little else. She was glad her Frank was not a killer, but then she had never thought he could have been. She knew the gentleness that lay behind even the sometimes harsh words.

She was grateful for her letter, glad of the role it restored to her, glad of the absolution it gave her from her own charges. For a period it increased her grief about the Frank she had lost rather than the one she had been mourning, but it was a healthier feeling, and she slowly recovered.

There was no letter for Hazel, and no Hazel there for a letter. Frank Hunter had found out that he was correct in his initial instinct that no letter for her would be possible. The attempt proved to him that he was too much of a smart-arse for other people's good. For all his rationalisation that everyone has to be responsible for themselves alone, the attempt proved to him that he had let her down. Every formulation was patronising, or worse. He could not overcome the inherent logical defect that any attempt to incite her to assert herself and be positive, foundered on the rock of his own action proving the greater attraction of the opposite course. Could he keep her alive by keeping Frank Hunter alive, was a question that haunted him to his watery grave and beyond. Nothing is certain and the choice had to be hers, just as his had to be his alone. But all the same, you rotten bastard. When Joyce went round to talk to her, about her letter, there was no trace, no forwarding address. She had thought of checking at Kamesthorn, which she eventually did but she wasn't there, hadn't been back. They remembered Joyce's interest though, and when the word of the body eventually reached them, they let her know. She was buried in Motherwell, united at last with her family, which ensured someone would visit her occasionally. Joyce made one visit to the stone, and placed some flowers from Frank and shed his tears on the grass. She heard later from Paul Ross that Hazel had not touched his money but had put it in trust for the children of a Mr and Mrs Lyons. So she sold the Shawlands flat, and got a few thousand extra for the voyeuristic factor.

Peter McColl didn't get a letter, but he got a message all right, and the seed of doubt that had been flourishing in the darker recesses of his midnight mind, worrying him sick since the news of the kind of gun used to shoot the Prime Minister, sprouted a further few inches in the direction subconsciously sent but denied since Frank Hunter's disposal of assets ceremony. The further growth almost scrambled his brains with fear. It would ruin him, if the unspoken were to be declared the real. It took several conversations with Paddy, who fortunately wasn't good with names and had a higher opinion of his pal Frank than Peter now or ever did, to reassure Peter. Even Mary-Ann didn't know exactly where Frank had obtained both guns, although she knew why he had felt he needed two. She had been told by him of a route involving certain named Glasgow pubs, significant sums of his own money although no receipts, and certain named names Peter was familiar with from his work rather than his leisure. But no suggestion of a Baillieston break-in, or a lawyer taking stupid risks with unregistered guns. So Peter was less scathing about Frank Hunter's actions than he otherwise would have been and felt maybe the sheet was more even than it could have been. He did not use Frank's money to buy himself a new Parker-Hale but did replace the three guns with two new ones that did not make him as happy as they once would have done. It was a long time before he learned to relax again, and always a blacker shadow than before hovered over his inner fears threatening something other than the self-destruction he had always anticipated. Although if that particular cloud broke and drowned him then it would be down to that anyway, with only an assist from a friend.

Paddy used the agenda for action inherent in his message, letter and parcel to avoid the full force of an emotional response, although he included in his normal angry ranting the possibility that Frank Hunter had indeed flipped his lid, but rejected that, as a recent development anyway. He did feel a strange sense of distance from the close stranger who had actually done the thing he, Paddy McGuire, had often threatened, - shoot the bitch. He repressed most of his other personal reactions to concentrate on the agenda he had been set. It was all there; the detail of the fabrication of evidence: dates, time and places for the acquisition of every glass and tankard, every item of clothing, every personal possession, the technique behind every false appearance of presence, plus a map showing the placement of each article in the rooms at Brownlie Street; copies of the letters to Jim Morris; details of the guns and bullet cases, rests and results of tests. Even Paddy smiled at the poster of Graeme Souness with the wonderful grouping round his heart, and the solitary hole in each elbow. The details of the

412

dummy run, and the false plates, and the hired car, and the assurance of garaging, were all there. Frank had given instructions as to what to do with all this but they were unnecessary, Paddy knew exactly what to do and why. The role given to Mary-Ann irked him slightly but he could see the sense in getting it well-documented and published before the forces of secrecy, discretion and the interests of the state security took over.

He wondered initially if his best friend were bequeathing him a form of poisoned chalice, a hand from beneath the sea reaching out and offering him a sword with which he would have no option but to cut his own throat. But for one last time, Frank Hunter's political instincts proved shrewder and sounder than Paddy McGuire's. The calm skill, dignity and discretion with which he implemented his remit of unravelling the confusions and securing the release of the Govanhill Five, the Brownlie Street Boys, without alienating the establishment or undermining public confidence in the Scottish legal system enhanced his official position and public reputation as a politician and lawyer of stature as well as weight. More importantly for the conception of his future held by Frank Hunter, his role in securing the release of the innocent men repaired the considerable political damage that had been done to him in the eyes of the Glasgow Irish Catholic Labour community by the Deeley business, and made him once more a feasible candidate for further political honour and advancement. Even Charlie Spence shook his hand. Only Christine ever saw even a glimpse of the down side, the cost to him in personal terms of the rehabilitation of his career at the expense of his friend's life. He resisted all attempts by Danny Campbell to talk about that or anything important and a little bit of him died with the re-death of his friend. Although he re-appointed Frank as his closest political adviser and ever afterwards ran every major and minor political choice and decision he had to take past him for his viewpoint and advice.

Mary-Ann Ewing was also seen to handle her responsibilities with dignity and professionalism. She wrote many articles, and the definitive book, and added to her stock of prizes, on both sides of the Atlantic. The fact that she had known the principal man personally, some sceptics even hinted intimately, did not discredit her work. There was at one point some talk in certain circles of charging her with withholding evidence or obstructing justice or perverting the course of justice, but there was insufficient evidence that she knew the exact nature of Hunter's plans before the August release, and she had co-operated fully from then, so it came to nothing.

Events took on a momentum of their own after Paddy McGuire's press conference and handing over to the police all the evidence of Frank Hunter's guilt and the Brownlie Street Group's innocence. There was a general perception leaked that they all except Morris would probably have been released before trial anyway. Public faith in the different Scottish system was not damaged, indeed favourable comparisons were made with the Guildford and Birmingham scenarios. The absence of supporting confessions was seen as a vindication of the integrity of the Strathclyde Police, and the Procurators-Fiscal could not be blamed for the creation and location of realistic artificial circumstantial evidence. The inquiries into the circumstances of Frank Hunter's disappearance were reopened but the new evidence did not lead to any different conclusions and the continued non-appearance of the body meant that the file continued to remain an open one.

Police records confirmed that a white Maestro car with the registration claimed had been identified on Stanmore Road the night before the Cup Final and further enquiries confirmed that the car with that number had been parked in Troon all weekend. The helly-telly film confirmed its presence on the corner at some points and its absence at others although its move downhill was missed. The police constable who had been in trouble for missing 6, 7 or 8 people slipping out of number 37 by the back close if not the front door, was vindicated, at least to himself.

There was a degree of bitterness on the part of the Brownlie Street Boys that they had been fitted up, but their best legal advice was that there were no grounds for a claim for wrongful arrest or compensation, and that the only course open to them was to sue the estate of Frank Hunter under civil law, for recompense, a pointless course as its assets were known to be negligible. Jim Morris felt the bitterness personally, he had really liked Frank and the bastard had done that to him. He knew why, of course, and thought it ironic that he had made his peace with the fat man and was now in his debt. Still, he had the considerable compensation that they all were heroes now, especially Jim, and in the long run his holiday did him far more good than harm. Charlie Spence helped make sure he was properly set-up in the leisure travel business and demand for the cachet of going on his trips boomed. Just a pity the Celtic weren't good enough to give him many opportunities to benefit, but that wasn't Frank Hunter's fault, but a cause of equal pain to him.

Frank Hunter also did his bit towards industrial regeneration in Scotland. In no time at all a thriving branch of the political assassination conspiracy theory business was alive and flourishing. Several leading newspapers devoted much space to the output and among the more credible theories that soon emerged were that Special Branch had known all along about the involvement of Frank Hunter in the shooting. Surveillance files provided evidence that he had been seen several times in the company of IRA activist leaders in the weeks before his death. He was regularly described as a Glasgow Irish Catholic, although one paper made great play of the paradox of his intense Orange background. The possibility seemed real that he had not been acting totally alone and that his "evidence" was an attempt to muddy waters, after its exposure rather than before.

One quality paper, on a different tack, quoted Special Branch sources as claiming that in fact the IRA killed him as soon as they had worked out his role, following him to Arran and ensuring the competence of his efforts to kill himself, in order to guarantee that he would not divert credit from them for the event. They had not known about his sleeper letters. There was an alternative theory that they had not realised that the evidence had been manufactured by Hunter rather than the Establishment desperate for quick arrests. The IRA through its usual routes made a quick response that it was well-known in the appropriate circles that in fact it had been the Special Branch that had terminated Hunter, to ensure that the IRA took full responsibility, not realising about his sleepers.

Several other wilder theories appeared over time including "proof" that there were two gunmen, one in the car and one in the flat. One version had the two acting separately, another in conjunction. There was a "confession" from a known marksman that he had fired the bullet, in an attempt to kill the Prime Minister. This was backed by proof that he had been in Glasgow at the time. Several books appeared over time offering new insights and theories and new evidence. One book proved that Frank had been a secret member of a fanatical group of Scottish terrorists, another that he had committed four previous murders for the IRA including the McCabe one.

Mary-Ann Ewing had intended to turn down the offer for the film-rights of her book, which remained widely regarded as the most respected and credible account of the whole affair, but when she realised it would be done anyway she took the money in exchange for a promise of some influence over the script. Overall she felt confident that she had discharged her obligation to Frank, to ensure his place in history with a proper understanding of his motivation and objectives. She knew Frank would have been amused at some of the alternative theories advanced, and horrified at others, but felt he would have been happy enough at the official consensus and the version that entered Scottish political mythology. His second worst fear, that his deed would be dismissed as the act of a madman, proved to have some foundation but not enough to destroy his achievement. A fair percentage of at least the local jury felt any madness lay in the decision to miss, others were convinced that the successful pulling-off of the IRA trick could not be the work of a fool.

So Frank Hunter got his wish and became a small footnote in British political history, and more importantly to him, a larger one in a growing separate Scottish history. He was generally accepted as the man who could have killed the Prime Minister but chose, as an act of political protest, to shoot instead her symbol of refusal to listen to the voice of the Scottish people. And he was credited with fooling the system and deliberately getting the IRA the blame before confessing the Scottish connection. His greatest fear came to nought. The Prime Minister never learned of his concern that she might kill his national team and his greatest dream and thus never thought to exact poetic justice by doing just that. Furthermore, she was not given enough time to work it out for herself before she fell foul of assassins more politically astute and ruthless than a sad and humane Scotsman.

One final curious fact about Frank Hunter escaped most of the book-writers and historical assessments. Since no-one ever had any vested interest in making an application to the Court of Session under the Presumption of Death (Scotland) Act, and no-one ever did, to this very day Frank Hunter is still technically alive. Since Glasgow never puts up statues to live people, no matter how eminent, or how great their contribution to the nation, Willie might have to wait some time before his pal is allowed to join him for another chat, and compare notes for eternity on the strength of the new nation they each played a small part in freeing. And the chance for a more Scottish name for George Square has not yet been taken.

THE END.

POSTCARDSCRIPT

Fluttered was the word Joyce always used to describe to herself the movement of that card from her letterbox to the floor, almost as if it had flown itself directly from Rio, and the two foot drop was the last part of its total flight. She regarded it as a gift from a previously less than kind fate that she was in her hall at that precise moment on that Saturday morning in September. She knew immediately that it was a message from him, the one he had already promised her.

She looked at the picture first, a large circular bowl of a football stadium, and knew it was a sight she had seen before, several times. She turned it over slowly and knew she was correct, it was his hand-writing right enough, no-one could imitate that scrawl.

Despite herself she checked the postmark before she read it. It was Rio de Janeiro, a date in late August. She delayed deliciously by reading the description 350-250-RIO DE JANEIRO -RJ -Vista Aerea do Estadio Mario Filho (Maracana). Then she read the message,

Dear Joyce,
The best part of me has found peace and happiness here. I am free at last from my burden of sadness. My spirit can roam in this temple of life, rejoicing in the atmosphere. My essence can be blown round as the wind and attend every game. Now I am free, do me a final favour and you be free too, and happy. Go with my blessing and love, and know I will be with you always, but not obtrusively,
Your ever-loving friend,

Frank, XXXX.

She knew she knew what it meant. He was free, and so now was she. She did not think, as others might have and would, that the Postcard was a cruel trick, or a crueller one. She knew it was a trick right enough, but a magic one, to entertain and educate not torture, and she thought it clever.

417

She had known since her second letter what her Frank was, and where. He was still alive and in her head. She had known she would carry him around there with her for the rest of her life, and he would be available to help her if and when she needed it. But she had been uncertain about the exact relationship. She now understood, as he had known she would. This piece of magic was just a message to ensure she kept him in his place, and in the right perspective. It was a farewell gift from her lovely friend, the key word, obtrusively, being a private code they had discussed long before. She kissed the signature, said for the last time, thank you Frank, and walked away, tall, freed to start the task of getting on with the rest of her life.

If you want to know more about Frank Hunter's family background, and the experiences that led to him being the person he was in February 1990

read

"A Subtle Sadness"

by Sandy Jamieson

Published by Ringwood Publishing 1997

Copies can be ordered from
Ringwood Publishing
258 Kingsacre Road
Glasgow G73 2EW
0141-632-9002